I0760891

# Blade *of the* Moon

Legends of the Clanblades: Book 2

BY R.K. THORNE

IRON ANTLER
BOOKS

Copyright © 2023 by R.K. Thorne. First edition.

All rights reserved. No part of this book may be reproduced in any form or by electronic or mechanical means, including information storage and retrieval systems, without written permission from the author, except for the use of brief quotations in a book review and educational, noncommercial uses.

Edited by Holloway House
Cover design by Damonza, damonza.com
Interior Design by R.K. Thorne
Map by Terrance Mayes
Version 1.0

This is a work of fiction. Names, characters, places, and incidents are a product of the author's imagination. Any resemblance to actual people, living or dead, or to businesses, companies, events, institutions, or locales is completely coincidental.

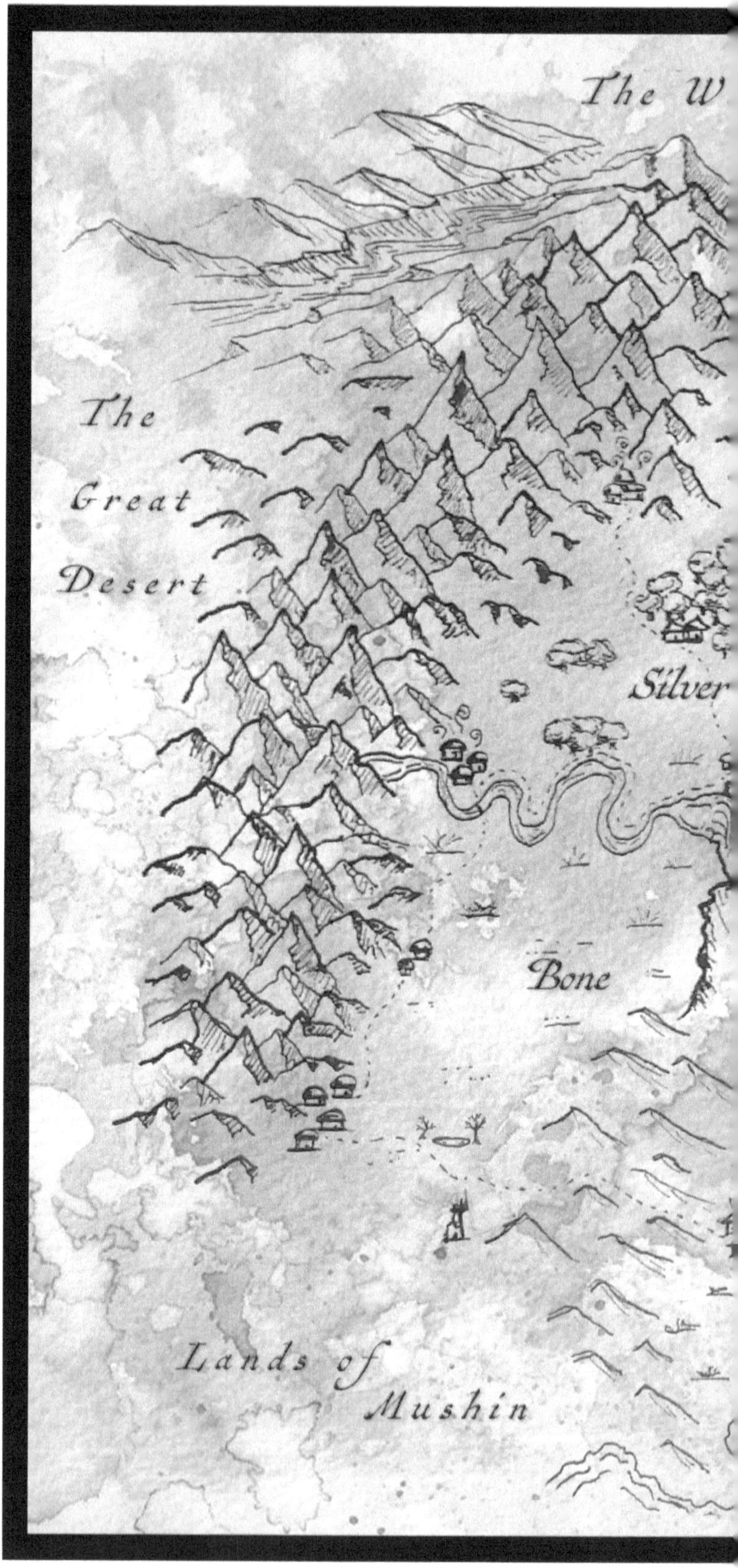

*An approximation of the lands surrounding the Empire of the Six Clans, shortly after the Unification period, prior to the Second Break*

*Artist Unknown*

The Empire
— of the
Six Clans

Obsidian

Lapis

Salt City

Pearl

Lands of
Mushin

# Contents

# Blade *of the* Moon

*Chapter 1*

# Fresh Meat

Lara squatted down, squinting at the fresh boot prints in the dirt. A breeze blew short strands of blonde hair into her eyes, and she absently brushed them aside. She'd been hiking for over an hour without seeing a soul, not even a trace of a suspicious "hunting party" in the distance.

These boot prints appeared out of nowhere and led toward the waterfall and into Yeska's cavernous den—her and Nyalin's temporary home after fleeing the Contests a few weeks back. That event had been either disastrous or momentous, depending on your perspective. Lara leaned toward the former, Yeska the latter. Perhaps it was a little of both.

She double-checked in the fading light, but it was true. Not far back, the mud and grass were undisturbed, and then suddenly, the boot tracks began.

And they led straight toward Nyalin.

She took off at a run. He was alone in there. The rushing of the waterfall drowned out all other sound. Since they'd left the city, there'd been a strange distance between them that she'd been unable to find a way across. If she lost him now...

A scent caught her nose over the waterfall's ever-present mist as she reached the rocky path that led behind the curtain of water. Fresh bread? What the... No, it couldn't be.

Her stomach growled, though, disagreeing with her.

Her boots slipped more than once, but she didn't slow down, keeping one hand on the smooth, reassuring stone beside her, the other on her blade, her clan's Dagger of Bone.

Two voices, both familiar, reached her ears as she cleared the turn and the harshest roar of the water. She stopped, listening and sizing up the situation.

A robed form was silhouetted by their small fire. Nyalin sat on a log facing the newcomer, frowning. The long, wavy mane of their visitor would have been a dead giveaway, even without the majestic sword, Shadow Wing, hanging at its usual graceful angle on his hip, the raw chips of obsidian glimmering. At the sword's forging, the obsidian had fractured into a shape reminiscent of a dragon wing, hence its name, but ironically it was not bound to the Dark Dragon. Dozens of charms of every color glittered from their loop on the sword's hilt.

Emperor Pavan.

Her pulse quickened. Was someone in trouble? Or was the emperor himself the trouble? It'd been a few weeks, but perhaps he hadn't approved of their little stunt at the Bone Clan Contests.

The men's voices were hushed. Nyalin's expression was... wary. Cold. Was that anger in his gaze? His glare reminded her of that day she'd accompanied him to the Obsidian mansion to get his things, the day she'd learned how little love was lost between him and his stepfather, Clan Leader Elix. The day he'd joined her clan, everything had changed.

Why was Nyalin glaring so hard at Pavan? She thought back to when Nyalin had last seen the emperor. He told her they'd spoken about the lock on Nyalin's magic. Emperor Pavan had admitted to placing the lock there at Nyalin's birth, with the help of Linali, Nyalin's now-dead mother, and Elix, clan leader of the Obsidian Clan. Linali had never shared who the baby's father was, so upon her death, Elix, though a callous man, had taken him in and raised him as his stepson—or at least tolerated Nyalin's presence in the Obsidian mansion. Lara couldn't understand Elix's neglect of Nyalin; as the clan's leader, she had expected better of him. Elix's refusal to teach Nyalin was the reason the young mage had shown up at Lara's door. At the time, she'd been angry at Elix for refusing to see magic she *knew* Nyalin had. But to realize he'd helped to lock Nyalin's magic away? That he'd deliberately tried to deprive Nyalin of his powers? Why? What could possibly have motivated them?

In Nyalin's last talk with Pavan, the emperor had refused to remove the lock so Nyalin could access his magic and compete legitimately in the Contests. Given no other options, she and Nyalin had decided to cheat. In hindsight, even if Nyalin had had access to his magic, there had been so much cheating on Andius's side in the final round of the Contests that they probably would have had to cheat anyway to survive. But why had they even put the lock there in the first place?

Yes, now that she was thinking about it, Nyalin's pissed-off expression made perfect sense.

His voice rose a little. "You could have told me..." he was saying. "You could have..." The words were lost to the waterfall again.

Twisting her lips, she tightened her grip on the handle of the Dagger and slipped closer. She stuck to the shadows, rolling her feet from heel to toe delicately, deliberately, to stay silent. Just a little closer—and a little further from the rush of water.

At the right moment, she sprang like a cat at its prey, her blade drawn, landing with soft feet just behind him.

The emperor jumped just a little as the tip of the blade poked between his shoulder blades. Then he went still.

Pavan was too tall for her to wrap an arm around his neck and press the blade to his throat, but she could very effectively apply it to his back. Kidneys would have worked as well, but this seemed more dignified, fitting for an emperor and all. She fought a smile sneaking into the corner of her mouth.

"Emperor Pavan," she said, voice smooth but still a little amused. "Great luck to you."

Pavan glanced over his shoulder at her. "With that kind of welcome, Lara, I'll need it. Honor to you, this fine day."

"What brings us the honor of your presence?" She kept her voice as cold as Nyalin's expression.

Pavan cleared his throat. "Is this your standard greeting these days, Clan Leader?"

"Yes." She arched an eyebrow at his choice of title. Was he accepting that she'd stolen the blade—and clan leadership—then? "At least to those who appear in my home uninvited."

"I approve. And I see the weight of the clanblade has not changed your usual, uh, forthright style. Might I have your permission to turn around?"

Her cheeks heated. If he turned, she'd lose her advantage. She pressed the blade ever so slightly. "Answer my question first. Why are you here?"

He raised his right arm—his sword arm—indicating a burlap sack. The scent of fresh bread hit her more strongly now. "A diplomatic offering of peace."

She narrowed her eyes. Why would the emperor bring anyone a peace offering, let alone her or Nyalin? She exchanged a concerned glance with Nyalin.

But if he *did* mean them harm, he could just as easily have held his sack in his other hand, his non-sword hand. She had a feeling the choice was deliberate. Not that the slight delay would have truly prevented him from dispatching them with Shadow Wing. She and Nyalin were good fighters, but Pavan was a war veteran with twenty years of practice on them. She didn't like their odds.

*You're forgetting. I would not let him.* Yeska murmured in her mind. *And he knows that.*

*So you'd kill him after he killed us? What good would that do the empire?*

*Perhaps they can make some use of a charred monarch?*

*Yeska!*

*I would speculate he agrees with you that would be quite a waste, which is why he's holding bread and not a sword.*

*But he's hardly been straightforward with Nyalin. I'm not sure we can trust him.*

*I don't disagree, but if he had wanted to kill either of you, he could have done it already while you were separated.*

*Good point.*

Swallowing, she took a step back but kept her weapon raised and ready in her hand. By Dala's light, let her be right in trusting him. "Fine. Turn around, if you like."

The emperor turned his face to look over his shoulder at her, revealing half a smile. He had that way about him, always seeming amused and in control. "Perhaps we could all sit down around the fire and have a friendly chat. I won't draw my blade, if you'll sheathe yours."

"And I should just trust you on that?"

"Well, *I'm* trusting that your ambitions end with your clan, and you're not eager to usurp the entire empire."

She narrowed her eyes.

"You *do* have ambitions with your clan, don't you?"

"I never had ambitions. But I don't fancy being abused property either."

"I imagine such a desire is universal. But not everyone acts as bravely as you, nor goes to such lengths for their freedom." His smile was gentle. "Perhaps Nyalin could inspect my offering and tell us both if it's adequate to let us break bread together in peace." Without waiting for an answer, he tossed the sack over the fire toward Nyalin.

Her shoulders tensed, grip tightening. Nyalin caught the bag, now glaring at it instead of the emperor. Yanking open the neck of the sack, Nyalin dug inside and withdrew an oblong object wrapped in linen. "Bread. Fitting." But rather than looking pleased, his expression turned even more sour.

She understood the bitterness about the lock, but her instincts flared that something more was going on here. Who gets mad about fresh bread?

The emperor waved at him. "There's more. Go on, look."

Grudgingly, Nyalin put the wrapped loaf on his pack near his feet—Yeska didn't exactly have tables—and peered inside again. He looked up sharply and gasped. And a moment later, she saw why—he pulled out a kebab. And it was *steaming*.

Her mouth immediately watered.

"Well? Satisfactory?"

Nyalin met the emperor's gaze, still cold. "Your generosity is appreciated, Emperor. I think we can justify a few minutes to talk with him. And eat these kebabs. Lara?"

"As long as you promise to explain why you're here. And how you got here. And how you found us. Promptly."

"Of course," the emperor replied. "The short answer? I bring news, and I flew."

"I did not think the dragons served you with favors," she said. Reluctantly, she lowered her blade. "Or rides."

"They do not." Emperor Pavan turned toward the fire and took a seat on a log, casual and confident as ever, his red crossover under his dark robe falling elegantly, with effortless grace.

She wasn't quite sure how he'd flown then, but as he offered no other details, she let it drop for now. The why was much more important than the how. She sheathed the clanblade but laid its scabbard across her lap as she found a seat beside Nyalin. They'd made a small camp here. Unfortunately, a dragon's home wasn't terribly comfortable for two humans, so they'd had to build a fire pit and rough places to sit and to sleep. Basic accommodations at this point, but, with time, they could improve it. Or they'd find somewhere else.

She accepted a kebab from Nyalin. "I apologize if my greeting was a bit hostile, Emperor. It's just I am not quite sure who I can trust these days."

"No apology is necessary," he replied. "In fact, I am glad to see that you understand just how much danger you are in."

"Suspicious folk have been tracking in these hills," Nyalin said, "and we are fairly certain they're looking for us."

"These aren't exactly prime hunting lands," Pavan agreed. "Especially not with a dragon to compete with for wild game."

She took a bite—a massive one—and used that as an excuse to let the silence linger, to hope he'd say more. Nyalin, too, was chewing.

"As to your conditions of my tentative welcome here. As I said, to your first question, I flew." He must have read the slight deepening of the crease in her eyebrows—because she certainly didn't say anything more than a grunt. "As myself. As a bat, in particular."

"A bat?" Nyalin swallowed as he raised an eyebrow. "Interesting choice."

"I practice different animal forms as often as I can."

"What about human ones?" Nyalin cut in, an edge to his voice.

The emperor coughed. "Well. Can't get rusty. Transformation has always been a specialty of mine, but practice is required to keep the skills sharp. But you know that. You wouldn't have done so well in the Contests without a great deal of practice."

"Practice is right," Lara murmured. "Practice at cheating."

Nyalin raised an eyebrow. "Hey, we did also practice the spells."

"What? I don't care if he knows. In fact, he ought to know. Andius cheated too." She was done hiding. She and Nyalin had cooked up quite the scheme to keep Andius from becoming clan leader by working together—something that was strictly not allowed. She'd fed Nyalin pure magical energy, but he'd still been the one to cast the spells. It'd been the only way to get around the magical lock, a desperate attempt to keep Lara from having to marry Andius. From that perspective, so far it had been a success, but things hadn't gone as they'd hoped. Andius—and the dark forces helping him—had cheated so hard that they'd nearly killed Nyalin. Instead of winning the Contests, Nyalin and Lara had chosen to flee.

Guilt still nagged at her over the things she'd done and the rules she'd broken, but the unfairness of the game itself made it a little easier to live with herself.

"It's okay." Nyalin waved a hand at the emperor. "He knows. He knew about our plan before the Contests started, in fact. He put the lock there, remember? He knew I couldn't do any of that alone."

Pavan frowned. "Now it wasn't *just* me—"

"Oh, right. Elix knew too. That makes it better." Nyalin's eyes were hard and black in the firelight. Lara couldn't blame him; she'd seen precious little kindness directed at Nyalin from his stepfather. Perhaps there was more to the story, since Elix had gifted Nyalin the sword of Nyalin's mother just before the Contests, making their ploy more plausible. But considering the history between them, she had to wonder what Elix's true motives were.

She chewed thoughtfully for a moment. "Wait, didn't Elix show up and give you that sword just before the Contests began?"

"Yes, he did have that bright idea." Pavan's flat tone said he hadn't approved of the choice.

"He was actually helping you and me cheat," Nyalin said. "If you can believe that. The sword was an excuse—a reason I could say why I suddenly had power."

She looked from Pavan to Nyalin and back again. "What I don't understand is why neither of you tried to stop us."

Pavan sighed and spread his hands, then rested a palm on each knee. "Why did you compete, if you already had the clanblade?"

She shrugged. "Because winning would have made everything simpler." Nyalin could have become the clan leader, and she could have given him the Dagger of Bone, and they could have ruled together as a team, no one else ever needing to know the truth of it all. An idealistic plan, but it had been their best shot.

"Same reason we didn't interfere."

"If Elix had really wanted to help Nyalin, he could have just removed the lock and taught him himself." She licked a finger, delighting in the lack of decorum.

"Unfortunately, things are not quite that simple." Pavan leaned back and folded his arms. "Tell me, Lara. Do you think I *want* a ruthless, ambitious man like Andius as leader of the Bone Clan? Do you think he'd make my life easier or harder?"

"Harder." She ripped off another bite with her teeth, smaller this time but a little more viciously. Was it possible to spend too much time with a dragon? The warmth of the food—probably orchestrated by a careful combination of spells—should be civilizing, but she hadn't realized she was so hungry.

"Correct. Harder. I know the type. Ambitious without limits. And while I have an ability to influence clan affairs, who becomes clan leader is a bit ... outside my purview."

"He is indeed ambitious," she mused. "I never thought of that ambition reaching *beyond* the clan, but I think you're right. Why wouldn't he aim high? If his underhanded tactics work once, why not try again? If you can steal one throne, why not another? And since you as emperor don't have an heir, who exactly is standing in his way? It's even easier now. Myandrin is gone, and if I'm out of the way, who knows *what* Andius would do for power?"

At those words, Nyalin went very still, his gaze darting off to the side. Lara frowned, her attention flicking to the emperor, who was frowning darkly into the fire. Both sported similar abrupt scowls.

That wasn't the reaction she'd expected.

Did they know something she didn't? Nyalin had alluded to other secrets; there hadn't exactly been time to discuss the conversation he'd had with the emperor in detail.

Or was it something else? Had Andius already done something especially heinous? Her heart suddenly pounded faster in her chest, acid pumping into her veins. The emperor had said the purpose for his visit was to bring news. At first, she'd been eager to hear, but now that thought chilled her veins.

"Is my father all right?" she whispered into the silence.

~

The terrace looked out over the estate, the moon painting the many buildings with a soft white glow. Zama stood at Unira's side, waiting while she gazed up at the only lunar body of this world. She might admire it, but he didn't. This moon seemed to glare down at him, as if it knew the truth. He didn't belong here; he belonged in his own plane. But Unira had summoned him here, to this plane where they called otherworldly creatures like him *demons* and harvested magic from the dead.

He still could not get used to this place, this uncooperative realm, and, even now, he could not shake the feeling that this moon knew he did not belong. He did not think it approved of his presence.

"Have you had any luck locating Linali's son?" Unira asked softly. Her skin was lit by the moon, but the black crossover of her Obsidian Clan made her all but disappear into the night and the dark stones of the terrace.

This late in the year and at this late hour, there was only the cold mountain wind's whisper to compete with her words. The fields and forests and small huts were quiet, smoke curling from chimneys. An accomplished necromancer, Unira had long hunted the son of her nemesis, the legendary mage Linali, but her many, *many* attempts had been thwarted. At first, he'd assumed she simply hadn't been cut out for murder. But as he watched his own attempts go sideways, he was starting to see there was quite a bit more complexity to this picture... to this boy, Nyalin moLinali. He should have guessed that a necromancer powerful enough to summon him from another realm would be capable enough to kill a mortal human. And she was.

But this boy—a mortal human, he was not.

He tried to look stoic, reserved. "We only just arrived here at the estate. We've been busy."

"So, no then?"

"No," he said, trying to conceal the regret in his voice. If only the spirits in this realm would cooperate, he could have killed the boy long ago. But he couldn't even *find* the rat half the time.

"We must find a way to locate him." She brushed her black hair over her shoulder. "And soon. I don't like him teaming up with that girl."

"I agree. I have... a few other methods I can try, now that we've arrived." He lifted his chin a little. "I will find him."

"Something has occurred to me. If we do track him down—"

"When," he cut in.

"When we do track him down, he will have the sword. Linali's sword. Do you suppose he can use it, bond with it like a swordmage?"

"Doubtful. From my reading about the ways of magic in this world, most swords have a single owner. And you have that sword's owner locked away downstairs unless something has changed."

"Nothing has changed. Some clanblades bond with more than one clan leader, though. There are exceptions."

"Yes, but that is because the sword is the conduit to a living dragon, who forges the bond."

"Hmm. That is what they say, but we can hardly verify it for ourselves, can we? I just... Linali's son is growing in power."

"Only power lent to him by the Bone Clan girl. If we can find one, we'll find the other. Cut her out, and he'll be powerless once again."

"And we can find her dragon."

Zama shrugged, hiding his concern. Every world had powerful creatures that radiated magic, but in each world, they seemed to be different. These dragons were not like mages; they seemed somehow connected to the land. "There are ways of dealing with dragons," he said, but it was a bluff. He assumed there were because there had to be. Every creature had a weakness.

Just because he didn't know of any didn't mean they didn't exist.

"I had trouble killing that boy when he was a defenseless child. How will we accomplish it now that he has Linali's sword, the girl, and the dragon?"

"Well, you didn't have a demon on your side then." He smiled. She returned his smile, but half-heartedly, turning to gaze at the moon once again. The dark skeletons of trees reached black fingers up toward the sky, as if they wished to escape this realm as badly as Zama did. "I heard whispers in the crowd that it was Elix who gave the boy the sword," he added. He'd been saving that tidbit to share for when her confidence in him ebbed;

unfortunately, this seemed to be the time.

"What?" Her head snapped to face him, eyebrow raised. "When?"

"Shortly before the first round." He smoothed the dark lapels of his robe.

"I made it very clear that he shouldn't interfere." She tightened her grip on the railing. "This is a transgression we cannot ignore. It demands a response. He's broken the deal I made with him."

"A deal you forced him into, just like you forced him to keep Linali's spawn from being taught." He didn't say it out loud, but the boy had competed in the Contests and had obviously circumvented what she'd planned. He couldn't help but wonder if Elix had helped the boy or simply conveniently neglected to intervene. "You've already hamstrung Elix's heir apparent with the deals you struck with the sword smiths. None of them will ever agree to make the young Grel a sword. Isn't that enough of a punishment for one man?"

She snorted. "Never forget and forgive, Zama. It only gets you stabbed in the back."

"Much better to get stabbed in the chest."

"Obviously. I know what we need to do."

"Does it involve stabbing someone?"

She laughed. "As if I could—or would—attack anyone myself."

"Don't limit yourself, darling."

She shook her head. "Elix wanted his daughter off limits. It was the only thing he bargained for in the exchange. He wanted Sutamae to be left alone."

"How precious." A slow smile spread across Zama's face. "Sounds like the situation has changed."

Unira nodded absently. "She'll be brought into the fold—or pay double the price for his disobedience and her own. And I know just how to do it."

"How?"

"Idak." Her eyes were fiery when they met his. "I need to speak to Idak immediately."

"By all means, don't let me hold you back."

She was gone in a whirl before he could even turn away from the balustrade.

He slipped away himself then. In truth, he chafed to be so at her command. It tormented him even more that he struggled to even achieve this one simple goal: finding and snuffing out the boy. If Unira could hear his thoughts, though, she would insist it was not so simple, and he was finally starting to admit that perhaps she was right.

Zama slumped down in his comfortable armchair in the rooms she'd provided for him. The estate was expansive, well-appointed, decadent. It had everything from luxurious beds and baths to locked cells to house her enemies. Plenty for one woman to live an entertaining life. It even had the silk-production facilities to create even more wealth with very little involvement on her part. He understood her vindictive longing—for revenge, for... significance. But there were many beings across many worlds who would have been glad for this arrangement.

He'd set up his own scrying area here. For a while, he'd worked in her studio, but as their efforts wore on, he'd requested one of his own. Now, he could fail in private.

He took a deep breath and centered himself to begin. Alone at last. Let her torment Idak for a while. Perhaps he could make a breakthrough while she did.

On a low, ornate wooden table sat a mirror trimmed in wood painted silver. Originally, it'd been covered with gold, but he'd ordered them to paint it in his preference. One needed things to be just so, when powerful magic was at play. It was still a little too ornate for him, but it would do.

He pulled his chair up to the table and lit several candles with flicks of his fingers, then leaned forward over the mirror. The gleaming surface reflected his own image, for now, as well as the pale ceiling overhead, and Zama stared at the human form he'd assumed for this world. He was liking it less and less as the days went by.

As a demon summoned from another realm, he was supposed to be immensely, awe-inspiringly, pants-wettingly powerful. Mighty as lightning and thunder, full of omnipotent wrath.

Usually, he was. He hadn't conquered and ruled three afterworlds without at least a little talent and skill.

But ordinarily, when he traveled to a new plane, he was able to harness the aimless spirits caught between worlds and use their souls' energy to power his magic and satisfy his whims. In his second world, it'd taken but a few hours to enslave thousands, and mere days to conquer continents.

But here, he could never be quite sure if the spirits would go along. Most of the time, they didn't, in fact. He'd barely amassed a few hundred thralls, paltry really compared to what he was usually capable of. What was it with this place? If he'd reminded himself how dreadful this plane was, he never would have answered Unira's call.

But enough musing. He suspected that his problem and Unira's were one and the same. Because the most unusual thing about this plane was the boy—Linali's son.

He was an anomaly. A half-spirit, or as Unira would insist, merely a quarter spirit. He'd often pointed out that any amount of spirit was enough to be a problem.

Zama placed his hand on the edge of the mirror to activate it. His own image shifted, shot through with black and green until only a misty whirlpool remained, the reflection gone.

Every single time.

Every time he tried to marshal the spirits to follow the anomaly, to aid his search, they resisted. They slipped away.

He hated to admit it, but it appeared the spirits of this plane and its nearest mirror world were on the boy's side. If this quarter spirit was truly part of the spirit world, then perhaps that made sense. The spirits were protecting their own.

This, of course, wasn't helping him with Unira in the slightest. She thought herself in control. Sweet, really. Supposed partners.

But if he could not get the spirits of this world to help him, the next strongest source of magic easily available to him would be Unira herself—and her slaves.

Trapped in their little magical prisons underground, comatose yet still breathing, they offered her more magical power than anyone could need, especially with Linali in the mix.

Who needed dead spirits to help you when you could use living beings? It was brilliant, really. He had to hand it to her. Most of those he'd considered his nemeses he'd killed as promptly as he could, but *she'd* gotten creative.

He'd refrain from trying to enslave Unira's magic for as long as possible, because then she could keep hunting down mages and adding them to her collection. And it would give him more time to ensure he would succeed in his attack. But right now, she had her own agendas, her own unpredictable demands, and he sensed she could easily be as fickle as the spirits, if his opinion and hers ever differed too greatly.

If that happened, he knew what he would have to do. He might not yet be strong enough to do it, but... it was close. If too many spirits deserted him, she might still be able to banish him back to his home plane.

Soon he would eclipse her, but for now, it was not yet clear.

He drew out one of her long, black hairs that he'd gathered in the carriage and carefully added it to the jar of crystals below the mirror. He was preparing the rose oil. Soon, he would be ready to take things to the next logical step.

In the meantime, he had another plan to work on these anomalies.

From his bag, he drew the jar of sand he'd harvested from the Contest grounds. Where the boy, this Nyalin had last fought before he and the girl had fled.

He considered pouring the sand over the mirror, but he wasn't quite that desperate yet. That would contaminate the sand with dust from this room and gradually diminish any power it had to locate Zama's prey.

The spirits might not want to help, but with the boy's blood and sweat, he might not need their help. He set the jar carefully on top of the mirror and began to work.

The image in the mirror shifted from the swirling mist to the land. His mind's eye flew across the hills, across sandy, craggy, awful hills and valleys. Desolate. No wonder this was the poorest clan.

As he neared the large waterfall and trees began to take over, a bony wing slashed past his mind's eye.

That was the only warning he had before the dragon's roar split his skull, deafening and powerful.

He collapsed back, dropping the spell, reeling away. The dragon screeched again as he recoiled. The mirror reflected only the ceiling again.

There was a slight crack in the jar. Not leaking yet, but not entirely intact. How had the dragon managed it?

He sat panting for several minutes, disgusted.

This plane was truly awful. Could he accomplish nothing here? Wouldn't a single spell work the way it should? Why did a dragon have to interfere.

And yet...

He must have been getting close for the dragon to notice. It didn't intervene right away. So while he hadn't found the precise spot of the anomaly, perhaps he had a starting point.

The waterfall. Yes. That was something they could work with, a place they could start. There could only be so many waterfalls in the desolate lands of the Bone Clan.

He stood and started toward the stables. They could send word via raven or a messenger on horseback to have their spies in the Bone Clan send men looking for them.

But before he even reached the hall, he stopped short. Knowing the boy's location had never been enough to kill him. Unira had tried so many times. Would a few lackeys truly be the ones to finish the job? Even the boy's own stepbrother Raelt had failed to kill him when he and Unira had gone out of their way to give him a powerful weapon and a perfect opportunity.

He needed something else, something new, innovative—*creative*. He paced back and forth in the hall, not caring if a servant or two passed him and stared.

There were places where the veil was thin, where crossing between worlds was easy. These places had helped him many times. Perhaps he needed more than Bone Clan lackeys and Obsidian fools.

Creatures from his *own* realm would be far more loyal and determined. Crossing planes might weaken them, but if he could find a thin spot, it just might do the trick. At least he'd be able to say he'd tried something new that Unira hadn't.

Those places of power could also be broken, warped, destroyed. The boy seemed to have some kind of innate bridge to the afterworld. Could he, too, be broken?

Or if the boy couldn't be broken, perhaps he could be enslaved. Perhaps he could talk Unira into that, if she'd managed to do the same to Linali.

With the two of them, Zama would have all the power he could need or want. He could rend the land and flood the rivers and rip apart this despicable, disgusting plane. And then he could go back to a far more pleasant one.

A thin smiled curved Zama's lips as he strode back toward his rooms, considering what monster in his several realms would be best.

---

The old man guarding the cemetery locked eyes with Sutamae, braziers lighting the stone wall behind him. His gray eyes squinted at her, puckering scars over his forehead and left eye. He'd probably been lucky not to lose it. Both of them knew the way of the blade, and he seemed to sense a fellow warrior. He gave her a slight nod instead, which she returned with an odd feeling of kinship.

Perhaps he knew his job was to look out for other, darker creatures of the night. Perhaps he could recognize another being who was scarred. Not all scars showed up on the outside.

If he knew the whole truth, though, perhaps he'd count her among the dark ones.

And perhaps he was just an old man who nodded at everyone.

Her cloak wasn't adequate against the frigid wind that ruffled it as she passed him, but she wouldn't be out in the cold long. She was halfway there.

A rare torch's light flickered across her and the dark cobblestones. The sky was peaceful and reassuring, blue like the deepest ocean and studded with diamonds.

She passed bustling inns and taverns, all of them too wholesome for her current purposes. Each closed shop and hushed home might as well have been another world, one that belonged to people who had a family, a calling, a purpose. People who could be happy. Content to just live their lives.

She drew her cloak's hood up over her ears.

Her usual tavern was a cave of shadows. Figures clustered in corners, hunched over heavy earthenware mugs, grumbling and swearing. Some silent and sullen.

She slid into an empty corner table lit by a cluster of small black candles of three different heights. A shroud of plants and incense burners hung from the wood-paneled ceiling, creating a measure of privacy.

The innkeeper frowned at her from behind the bar. She gave him a cold smile back, barely more than a baring of teeth. It didn't matter if he approved of her or not.

He was concerned about his business, not the welfare of his patrons, so she ignored him. There were innkeepers with soft eyes, caring hearts, that shepherded the flock they attracted. Sutamae didn't choose those inns as her hunting grounds.

The innkeeper sat an ale on the bar and motioned for a serving boy to carry it over. She accepted it and dropped two coins in return. One for the barkeep, the other for the boy, if he thought to pocket it.

She would need at least the span of one ale to find her target—a young swordmage named Chosko. She knew he frequented this place.

The first step in the quest the Bladed Women had given her was finding him. She already had two successful quests under her belt.

This third one was something she'd done before—steal a blade from a man who didn't deserve it.

It was a dangerous proposition. She had to admit she liked it. It wasn't the first time she'd done it, and it wouldn't be the last, but it was the first time she was risking more than her father's and her clan's disapproval. For the first time, she had others rooting her on.

It wasn't quite the challenge she'd thought it would be, though. Before she was halfway through her ale, Chosko slid into the seat across from her.

And he didn't even ask if it was taken.

A cold, predatory smile curled her lips. "Well, hello."

"A lovely creature like you shouldn't be drinking alone." His smile was just short of a leer, his eyes the pale watery blue she'd seen when Bladed Woman Baelinin had pointed him out to her in the square, hair the shade of many Obsidians: black as coal.

"Shouldn't I?" she said. She kept her tone sweet and dropped her gaze to her drink as she took a delicate sip. "How should lovely creatures drink?"

"In wealth and good company."

"Hmm."

"Do you mind some company?"

"Probably easier to find here than wealth. I wouldn't want to watch a good seat going to waste. Can you guarantee the company will be good?"

"I can guarantee I'll buy you a second ale."

"I suppose that will have to do, for both wealth and company." She smiled slyly as she took another sip.

And just like that, the dance had begun.

It took only a question or two from her to get him talking. And talking. And on he talked. This earning of trust would have been more exhausting had she actually had to say anything, but as it was, she simply had to not fall asleep from boredom. She nodded, smiled, sipped, and nodded some more.

He didn't ask her name, so she didn't ask his. He clearly didn't know hers, though. Her reputation often preceded her.

Or perhaps he did know, and he, too, liked to live dangerously. Doubtful, but perhaps.

They got progressively drunker. She let the beer blur her edges, let her smile turn relaxed, although, in truth, the effect was mild. She'd been sipping wine at dinner for years, and this was water by comparison.

He leaned forward over the table. "We're having fun. Come home with me. We'll have more fun there."

She could almost pinpoint the moment when he'd decided he had nothing to lose. She raised an eyebrow and lowered the beer. "Home? Why? We're perfectly fine here."

"Because you like me." The words oozed out of him.

"Do I?" A corner of her mouth quirked.

"Yes. I can tell."

"Hmm." He'd think differently if he knew what she was planning.

"C'mon." He gave her his most charming smile, which wasn't terrible. She just wasn't capable of being charmed by anyone anymore.

"Hmm. I don't know. I'm quite comfortable here."

"This ale might as well be river water. Let's go get the good stuff. I have

Lapis Clan wine, straight from the caravan. And brandy from beyond Mushin."

Now she raised both eyebrows. "If I drink much more, I might fall asleep." She had no doubt he already knew that, perhaps hoped for it.

His knowing smile, tinged with a wicked gleam, didn't redeem. "I'll hold you if you fall asleep, beautiful."

"Are you sure it's good wine?" She needed the words to cover the revulsion she was feeling at the moment.

"I couldn't say. Haven't tried it yet. Why don't we go taste some fruit of the vine and find out?" His smile broadened.

She forced a smile in return. "All right. Let's go. But if it's not good, you owe me a bottle of brandy."

"You drive a hard bargain."

"Good brandy."

"Deal." He stood straight up. And then swayed slightly.

"Aren't we going to finish this beer?"

"Who needs to? The night slips away from us. Come." He was already reaching for her arm.

She shrugged and rose, letting him usher her out with an arm around her shoulder. She winked at the bartender, who only stared back bleakly in return.

Let him think what he would. If he knew the truth, he might think differently.

The walk was a slow and meandering one. They zigzagged across the streets, his arm around her and not just romantically. If he hadn't been leaning on her, he'd fall straight down.

As they neared his home, she realized with a sick weight in her stomach that it was barely a dozen houses from her own. All the wealthiest Obsidians lived in the same district. Perhaps that was half the joke, though—that if he'd just bothered to pay attention to the women in his clan or his neighborhood or simply ask her her name, he might not face the consequences he was about to face—if she had her way.

Because it was widely frowned upon to steal a night of comfort between two who hardly knew each other, who were unwed. And although Su didn't exactly agree with that notion, she knew that it was very frowned upon by the clan leader in particular to take the clan leader's daughter home to bed.

And when it came to frowning, her father Elix was quite the master. Tomorrow, he'd get to display his mastery once again, directed at her and her deeds tonight. If she was successful.

Now, was Chosko the type to sneak her in the servants' entrance or parade her through the main door? He'd been fairly brazen in the bar, but in the moonlight, she guessed he'd be a servants' entrance kind of man. Especially if he drew women back to his home—his father's home?—without even asking their names.

And, indeed, he slipped her through a back entrance and up a side set up stairs. He stumbled into the door frame as he tried to unlatch the door.

She did smile now as she reached around to help him. The timing couldn't have been more perfect.

Three doors down on the right, he pulled her inside and shut the door hard behind them. She held her breath, wincing as he locked the door and slipped the key into his pocket.

That complicated things.

Coming in here alone was enough to tarnish her honor if she were seen, but, apparently, he didn't care. Well, she didn't care either. What had honor ever done for her? No amount of purity was ever enough. Why even bother?

Instead, the fool lazily unlatched his sword belt and let the sword in its scabbard and the leather clatter to the floor where he stood.

She slipped her fingers into her pocket to find the cold metal there as he drew her into an embrace, pulled her toward the bed, and made no mention of any wine, Lapis or otherwise. She kept the shackle in one hand, still tucked in her pocket, while with the other, she sought out the key.

He was a pawer, but not a kisser, thankfully—she made a point to never kiss them if she could help it. It also made it all the easier to slip her fingers into his pocket, fish out the key...

"Oh, well then—" he started, misinterpreting her gesture.

Unfortunately, the moonlight caught on the key at just the wrong moment.

"Hey, what are you—" He grabbed for the key.

She tossed it behind her on the floor and grabbed his wrist instead. He fought her, spinning her around to slam her body against the nearby bedpost, pinning her against it with his weight.

None of that stopped her from slipping the shackle around his wrist, though, and snapping the lock in place.

The clicking sound made him falter, squinting to try to figure out what she was doing in the darkness. Quickly, she snapped the other end around the nearby bedpost over her head. Luckily, the post stretched all the way to near the ceiling with a curtain to boot.

He jerked his wrist. "What is the meaning of—" He clawed at her, but he caught only a bit of her hair as she slipped out of reach. She stifled a yelp, determined not to let him know he'd hurt her, even a little.

Enough men in her life had done that, she didn't want to gratify a single one if she could avoid it.

"I find the night has slipped by all too quickly, dearest Chosko." She was already striding away, heavy boots punctuating her exit.

"How do you know my— Hey!" Even now, his slurred words were hushed. Were there folks nearby to overhear? Good.

She hurried to find the key, hoping he couldn't see her searching gracelessly on her knees. He babbled further questions at her, and it was apparent it was too dark for him to see her when she found the key. Or when she bent to pick up his sword at the door. But unless he was so deep into his cups that he'd passed out, he'd soon realize what she'd done as his blade got farther and farther away.

And if he was a strong enough mage, and not as drunk as she thought he was, he'd find a way to free himself and pursue her. And who knew what revenge he might seek.

Since everything else this night had gone fairly easily, it would hardly surprise her if her luck ran out now. She needed to hurry.

"What are you doing—don't—"

She tucked the sword amid the black folds of the skirt of her extra-long crossover, straightened her hair, and opened the door. "May you find better drinking companions next time. And may you ask their names."

"Wait!"

*Chapter 2*

# Well Meant

Lara's breath had frozen in her chest as she waited for the emperor to answer.

His expression was grim. "I am not sure how well Cerivil is, Lara. He's secluded himself. Refusing visitors. Even me. I asked to see him, but they'd only send a note on. I got no response."

The kebab bites were forming a lump in her gut. "Refusing *you*? Then who's relaying your request to see him? Who's carrying the messages?"

He said the words languidly, one by one. "Who do you think?"

"Andius." She gritted her teeth.

*Your father is alive,* Yeska put in. *Even if he has given up the Dagger of Bone, I will always have a vague sense of him.*

"I didn't expect this, to be honest," said Pavan. "An attack on your father is terribly obvious and not popular. Andius might be well-liked, but Cerivil is loved. I didn't think he'd risk it."

Lara scowled. "Tell that to my brother's ghost."

Pavan blinked at that. Nyalin placed a comforting hand on her knee.

She didn't drop her eyes from Pavan's. "Andius is dangerous. Dark forces are helping him. I'm not underestimating him again." She touched her now-short hair, a reminder of the day he'd grabbed her by her once-long blonde tresses and threatened that, no matter what she did, she wouldn't be able to escape her marriage to him. That was the day she cut it off, and it served as an ever-present reminder of how dangerous he was. In truth, the memory of that day still woke her up in a cold sweat at night.

"As you shouldn't." Pavan was nodding.

"Yeska says my father is alive."

Relief flooded the emperor's face. "Well. That is good to be certain, at least. But this... I don't know if he's truly ill or if Andius is somehow keeping him prisoner."

"The council should demand to see him."

"As should I," the emperor agreed. "But I need to know the lay of the land before I do."

"What do you mean, the lay of the land?"

"I need to know your ambitious... Or if no ambitions exist, at the very least, your intentions." His expression turned earnest now. "And I figured you would need some supplies. Another reason I came. To check on your well-being."

"Why did you need to—" she started, then she stopped as it hit her. "Oh. If Andius had already found us and killed us, that would... change your demand a bit."

"Yes. I don't think he'd defeat you in a fair fight, but we've all seen how fair the fights have been in this empire recently. Also, if he'd murdered you both, then he'd have already obtained the clanblade, and I'm sure he'd have been quick to show that off. But... well, it is always better to know more before acting if you can."

"That's rich, coming from you," Nyalin grumbled.

By the Twins, what other secrets did Nyalin suspect the emperor held? She could understand his bitterness about the lock on his magic, but she sensed there was something more. Nyalin just looked away, not offering any clues, which stung her a little.

The emperor for his part gazed uncomfortably at the fire.

"Yes, knowing more does help," she said. "What do we need to do to help him? What do you need to know?"

He blew out another breath. "I need to know what you plan to do next. How we'll settle this situation for your clan."

"I wish I knew that."

"Well, now is the time to decide. Surely, you've given it some thought, the possible avenues you could pursue..."

"Half my heart would like to leave," she replied. "Run off and leave these fools behind. See the places I've always wanted to see. Someplace where I'm not a clan leader's daughter, and he doesn't have to be Linali's son."

He nodded, with more sympathy than she'd expected. "Neither of you has been dealt an easy hand in this game."

"The other half of me knows my clan deserves better than Andius. I know they need me as clan leader. But turning that into reality... I know there must be a way, there's got to be, but I can't see it just yet." She shook her head. In truth, she had seen it, but she had yet to come up with any plans or strategies she deemed plausible. "Can you tell me what has been going on while we've been here? Maybe that will help clarify what can be done."

"Of course." The emperor took a deep breath. "Bone Clan has rescheduled the Contests to run again a month from now. I'm not sure they'll actually have them, though, or if it was just a way to buy time. Now they have a month to ponder all the questions we all have. Like, what the hell are they going to do? Will they support you as clan leader?"

*Yes.* Yeska's tone was impatient.

Pavan winced, so even he had heard it. He cleared his throat. "Not all agree. Many argue Andius has worked for years to be in line for the blade, and that they should denounce you and forcibly take the blade back. Others support you as the hereditary heir. Some support the tradition of the clanblade itself—who holds the blade wields the power. Others complain you circumvented tradition, didn't win the right to lead fairly, as Andius sought to do—"

"Nonsense. He cheated worse than we did," Nyalin said. "The whole crowd saw."

"That has not been forgotten, I assure you, though some are certainly pretending they didn't see what everyone else saw."

"I may have stolen the clanblade and broken tradition. I may have done it for selfish reasons," Lara said quietly, "but I am also certain Andius should not lead our clan. If I had to break some antiquated rules for the good of the clan, so be it."

*Glad you're coming around to my point of view,* Yeska cut in.

Pavan smiled, to her surprise. "Here's the secret the elders won't tell you. *Many* people cheat when they can get away with it. In the Contests and in life. That's just a part of the game."

Nyalin jerked back. "You can't be serious. We would have *never* tried if we'd had any other choice—"

"Ah, but not everyone is as moral as you, my—" he faltered, cutting himself off from some word he was about to say with a glance at her. "A good person is the one who makes the moral choice when no one is looking. Unfortunately, good people are rarer than you might think. And do you know what is not rare?"

"What?" Nyalin demanded.

"Desperation. You didn't have another choice, did you? You think you're alone? Or that everyone is so principled?"

Nyalin pressed his lips together but said nothing.

"And not everyone is desperate; there are those who will simply try to see what they can get away with. To find where the edge of morality and possibility is. It happens all too often. You think the clan leaders aren't breaking my own rules behind my back? If I have proof, and it's important, I act on it. I don't always have proof, and it's often unimportant. But I know plenty."

Lara blinked. What could her father possibly have been doing that Pavan wouldn't approve of? He probably only meant *other* clans. As clan leader, her father had never been one to defy rules of any kind.

Or was she just that naive?

"There are other debates floating about, calls for Nyalin to be clan leader as Linali's son—"

"Of course there are," he grumbled.

"Well, you did nearly win, and likely would have if it weren't for the most egregious cheating even the crowd could see. Andius is acting like he won the Contests, end of story, but there is not widespread agreement on that. And there is another interesting group growing that has devoted itself to the dragon."

"The dragon?" Lara arched an eyebrow.

"Yes. Her mighty appearance after so long moved more than a few. Other clans, such as the Obsidians, regularly interact with their dragons. Yeska's appearance to offer you aide and support moved many."

*As it should,* growled Yeska.

The emperor winced again. "I am the least clear on the opinions of this group, as they are almost all commoners, but I can try to find out more. I can't tell if they support you because of her support or if they've simply decided to worship the dragon."

"Worship her?" Nyalin asked. "I mean, certainly Yeska deserves it, but..."

Lara chuckled softly.

"They have made a shrine to the Bone Dragon outside the Bone mansion. Or maybe they reinvigorated an old one? There are constantly people there, making offerings, writing poetry in her honor, singing."

Lara smiled. "Sounds like you need to visit your acolytes soon, Yeska. But, uh, did my father weigh in before... before he secluded himself?"

"No. It happened quickly." Pavan took a deep breath.

She frowned. She needed to think this through. Get a second to clear her thoughts, guess at the next steps of their enemies. Like... would Andius hurt her father? Or was Cerivil firmly under his control, in which case, he might switch to hunting her down instead, to take the clanblade for himself?

*Over my dead body,* Yeska put in.

*That's not funny.*

*I meant it literally.*

*Good thing those fools can't kill you.*

*Nothing is impossible.*

*Not helping.* Those words knotted her stomach.

*This visitor united an impossible group of age-old rivals.* Yeska gave her the mental equivalent of a shrug. *Perhaps he has some advice?*

"You want to know what I aim to do," she said slowly. "To tell you the truth, I'm not sure. I've never been in this situation before."

"Few clans have. Few people have." Pavan smiled. "You took all the symbols of power and literally flew away. Without stating your intentions. It's mild chaos right now."

She coughed. "Mild?"

"Well, it's better than before Unification."

She snorted. "At least there's that, I suppose." She met his eyes for a long moment, sobering. "What would you have me do?"

His eyebrows raised. "Truly? You may not like my advice."

"Yes, truly. Nyalin is a brilliant advisor to this clan leader, but I am certain two excellent sources of advice won't overwhelm me."

Nyalin snorted, a smile creeping into a corner of his mouth for the first time.

The emperor narrowed his eyes, seeming to measure her more thoroughly. "Let's start with this. Do you mean to keep the blade?"

"Yes," she said without hesitation. She knew too well she had no real choice about it now. "Giving it up isn't an option."

*Glad we came to an agreement.*

Lara was lucky not to roll her eyes in the emperor's face.

Oblivious to her internal dialog, Pavan gave a small nod. "Then you must lead the clan, so you must maneuver yourself into that position—"

She opened her mouth, but he kept talking. She shut it again.

"—and as your clan's sovereign, first, I would have you pledge your allegiance to the empire. Then I would suggest you make your demands to those who should serve you."

"My… demands?"

"Tell them your terms. What you demand of them as their leader, and what you will do if they don't comply. What you will provide if they agree to your terms. You need to win support. Prove worth. You might play to some of these groups more likely to support you—the dragon worshipers, for example. You need to take control, or you're no clan leader at all, clanblade or no. Do you want to be?"

Their eyes locked, and something quavered inside her—fear, maybe? Insecurity? She thrust it aside. "Not really. But I want Andius to be clan leader even less. My people deserve better."

"I think you can work with that."

"I can make demands. I'm not sure of what, though."

"For starters, demand the council and your father sign scrolls pledging their loyalty to you. This might also serve to highlight how strange it is that Cerivil is not even seeing you. Maybe require Andius to sign one too."

"Andius most of all," Nyalin put in.

"You could demand he be exiled instead. Imprisoned. Or banned from a council seat. Refused a sword. Or awarded stewardship of a herd that is far outside of the city and out of your hair. How will you punish him? Or bring him back into the fold? Or both. Lots of options."

"He can't be brought back into the fold. I don't think it's possible. Lots of options, but which are the right ones?"

"That's always the difficult question, isn't it?" He smiled, something warmer in his eyes now.

"Respectfully, Emperor," Nyalin said slowly, "was that what you did?"

The emperor arched an eyebrow. "What I did?"

"When you were working toward Unification. Did you unite the clans by making demands? Force them into an alliance? Truly, we weren't there, so we don't know."

He looked thoughtful. "Well, no. I pointed out their common needs and goals. How they had much more in common than different. But there's nothing like an external enemy to unite people against it. Too bad you don't have that."

"Don't we?" Lara asked. "Andius has attacked my father. Dark forces are helping Obsidians hunt down and curse members of our clan." She almost said "my clan" at the last moment. Interesting.

"Yes, and in truth, the Mushin threat is rising. They will return. But I fear, by then, it will be too late to unite the Bone Clan around you in their shadow. In the meantime, you could certainly benefit by calling attention to these external threats faced by the Bone Clan. You are, indeed, under a quiet siege; a fact, I expect, will not remain quiet forever. But you will still need a reason why they should choose you. Unless you have hard proof of Andius's treachery, which I cannot yet provide. We shall see what I can discover."

"I have a lot to think about." She bit her lip.

"The tactic is up to you. Just don't ignore the problem. My primary interest is peace among the clans and inside them. The Bone Clan is far from peaceful right now. We're lucky we've had as little bloodshed as we have, but it won't continue like this. They must have a leader, and it must be you, or you must give it up to someone else *specific*, and somehow make everyone comfortable with that."

"Is that really an option? Yeska has made it clear she won't let me give up the Dagger of Bone."

"Perhaps the right person could convince her to change her mind, but I doubt it." Pavan hesitated. "If someone else assumed the position of clan leader, and that person did not wield the Dagger, then the Bone Clan would be turning its back on the dragons, the magic, and the clanblades. Abandoning this legacy of magic would be a sore loss for the empire indeed, but we will do it if we must. When the Mushin return—"

"You mean, *if* they return."

He shook his head. "Your father should have kept you more apprised. They're building an army. *When* the Mushin return, we must have every clanblade we possess in the hands of a skilled magic user leading an army. Anything less will risk our destruction."

She heaved a deep breath. Leading an army? "I'm no general or soldier, Emperor."

His lips twisted, a sudden warmth shining in his eyes. "You think Linali was?"

"I—" she faltered.

"You are exactly what you need to be," he said quietly.

"The dragon chose well," she replied, "or so she keeps telling me."

"So. You asked. As your emperor, that is what I'd have you do. Take that clan by the reins and lead them."

As your emperor. Had he ever used that phrasing before? Why was he doing it now? Because he was speaking more as a leader? Or as someone who could give her direct commands if he wished? He'd always been that, but... Something was different now.

Was it... that she was more truly his equal? Was this something akin to respect?

"Thank you, Emperor," she said. "I will take it under advisement. And of course, the Bone Clan swears its allegiance to you. As it always has."

He grinned. "Always is not as long as you think. You don't quite speak for the Bone Clan yet. I want to know of *your* allegiance, Clan Leader."

Did he really question her allegiance? "My crossover may be smudged with dirt, but I will always be Bone Clan, Emperor. I still wear the stud in my ear." She tucked her hair back so he could see the small gemstone stud that he had given to her as child. The gems came from a strange tree that grew in the heart of the emperor's palace.

"I'm glad to hear it," he said sternly, "but I was really concerned with your allegiance to me. Would you be willing to swear it? We must be certain of each other."

She froze for a second, eyes wide. Then she stood, bowed, and remained low. To her surprise, the emperor rose as well. "I swear my personal loyalty and allegiance to you, Emperor Pavan, to serve in times of war and peace, and all who serve under me, however few or many that may be." She straightened. "Was that right?"

"It was perfect. What it lacked in pomp and circumstance, it made up for in sincerity." His hand rested on her shoulder for a moment, then fell to his side. "You honor me."

They both sank back to a seat.

"What do we do about Cerivil?" Nyalin asked softly. "Can you use those transformation powers and at least check on him, Emperor?"

Pavan nodded. "Yes, now that I know where the two of you stand, I can sneak my way in. Let me go and attempt it and return tomorrow with what news I can find."

"Speaking of that, how did you find us here?"

"The lock," said Nyalin, before the emperor could answer. "You can sense its magic, can't you? Since you cast the spell."

"Why did you lock his powers in the first place?" she asked.

Pavan held up both palms defensively. "Yes, I can sense the magic. But I'm not oblivious to knowing where the Bone Dragon resides. As to the locking spell, well—it's complicated. There is a great and dangerous power inside you, Nyalin. One that can be distorted and hijacked, if you are not fully trained. One that can destroy you, if you let it."

Nyalin scowled. "And so it's up to you to decide? I don't see you choosing the path of powerlessness."

"I don't see you choosing it either," Pavan shot back, waving a hand at Lara.

"What do you mean, hijacked?" she asked.

Pavan sighed, as if he'd hoped she wouldn't pick up on that word. 'There are those who have learned to harness the magic of others to power their spells, in place of swords."

"I know what necromancy is," she replied.

"No." His hand cut through the air. "Necromancers borrow the essences of the dead, thinning the veil and reaching out to them in the afterworld and powering magic through spiritual, consensual communion. It's collaboration."

She frowned. "I know. Talk like that, and the sword smiths will almost think you approve of the necromancers among us."

"I have no qualms with them. They do no harm. And there are plenty worse to worry about."

"What do you mean?" Nyalin asked. "You said harness the magic of others. Not the dead?"

Pavan's face had gone cold and bleak as a stone statue. "They harness the magic of the living."

"How?" She caught her breath. "How can they do that?"

"I don't know the precise method. I don't want the temptation. I'd prefer the knowledge died and was long forgotten. But it isn't. And to those who would harness the essence and power of the living—they know quite well how to accomplish their goals. Were Nyalin to fall into their hands, his power without the lock would be..."

The silence grew pregnant. "Would be what?" Lara demanded.

"Well, it could be limitless."

They all sat in silent dread for a moment.

"Who?" Nyalin demanded. "Who does this? Who are you so afraid of?"

Pavan's eyes narrowed, but he sighed again. "I suppose it is long overdue for you to find out. I had hoped you would never need to know. It is the woman who killed your mother."

Nyalin's face paled. "What are you talking about? *I* killed my mother. In childbirth—" He faltered, then swallowed hard. "Another lie?"

"Another untruth, designed to protect you." Sadness had taken over Pavan's face, more powerfully than she'd ever seen.

"You let me live my whole life thinking I was to blame?"

"I didn't realize you thought that." His voice was almost... tender and definitely alarmed. "Even if it had been childbirth that killed her, it wouldn't have been your fault. It was never your fault, Nyalin. It would have been no one's fault; a baby is innocent—"

"Who? Who killed her?" Lara demanded. They needed to know every last detail.

"Her name is Unira, of the house of Giran. Runs a great estate in the north, the silk farms. She was a student of magic among Obsidians in my youth. But she never earned her sword."

"Why not?" she asked.

"She was married, and her husband would not allow it, nor would her father."

"The Twins deliver me from such a fate," she muttered.

"I believe you have delivered yourself from it," the emperor replied. "Quite literally."

"Why did Unira kill my mother?" Nyalin asked. "And how?"

"How? We're unsure. Her remains were not recovered. We tried, but..." Pavan's jaw was hard as he shook his head. "Why? Jealousy? Hatred? Linali was a prodigy. Her talent poured out of her, even before she earned her sword. She emerged from the wild lands like a dragon herself, strange and fierce and powerful. With the Mushin bearing down on us, smiths competed to make her a sword."

"This sword?" Nyalin held up the one Elix had given to him.

He flinched. "The very one. That was the one she selected."

"Who made it?"

"The smith is long dead."

"Under mysterious circumstances?" Lara asked.

Pavan frowned. "I'm... not sure. I didn't think to ask. Most sword smiths are quite old. I will inquire."

"Why do you ask that?" Nyalin said to her.

Lara shrugged. "You said this Unira was jealous of Linali. Jealous enough to try to kill her. Jealous of her power. If she's still bitter now, years later, then killing the person who created the sword that focused that power doesn't seem like a big leap. Assuming her family barred her from getting the smith to make her a sword of her own."

"That... seems all too likely, now that you mention it. But Unira wasn't just jealous of Linali's power. She coveted... other parts of her life as well. It was... obsessive." He looked uneasy. "Ultimately, I think Linali was more of a symbol of what Unira believed she deserved but never got. Linali could have been kind or cruel, arrogant or humble, ambitious or afraid, and Unira would still have hated her."

"Was she kind?" Nyalin asked, voice soft.

"Kind, yes, very. But not humble." Pavan smiled, a warm memory lighting his eyes. "Not humble at all. And almost never afraid. That probably didn't help matters."

Nyalin shook his head. "If Unira had the power to harness the magic of living people, why wouldn't she do that to my mother? Why just kill her?"

Pavan frowned, looking sincerely thoughtful. "We only found evidence of her imprisonments a few years ago. I doubt she had that much power back then."

"What evidence?" Lara asked.

"Villages in Obsidian territory, far out, were being raided, but no valuables were stolen—only people. We tracked some of the people to a farm where we found them suspended, touched with death. Their power was being siphoned. We freed them, but I am certain there are more."

"That's terrible."

"Indeed. So there is that risk. But she wasn't the only reason for the lock. The powers being out of control can drive even the sanest adult to near insanity. It's not fair to make a child live in such chaos. Nor can anyone ensure a child's safety if he's constantly flicking between this world and other planes."

"I get the kid thing. Fine. That doesn't sound like it would have made life in Elix's house more fun or stable. But why not take it off now? This is all to protect me from this Unira woman, whom I've never met or seen or interacted with or—"

"Haven't you?" Pavan leaned back.

"What do you mean?"

"Do you really think that ordinary people have as many 'accidents' as you have? We have had to intervene... so many times."

Nyalin's face paled further. "Wait, what do you mean, we?"

The emperor's expression faltered, as if he hadn't meant to say that and even more hadn't wanted Nyalin to notice. "Elix and I."

It sounded like a lie, but she sensed that pushing an emperor to admit to a lie he didn't choose to himself wouldn't be very fruitful. "The magic helping Andius at the Contests—was that Unira?" Lara asked.

"Yes. She and her minions. Her hate flows strong even now, transferred from your mother to you. Ironic, really."

Nyalin tapped his chin. "I did see this woman glaring at me from the seats, now that you mention it. She stood up at one point and focused on my mother's sword. I wonder... But I haven't done *anything* to her. I'd never even seen her before."

"True, but hate is not always rational. The world gave Linali everything she wanted, before she even asked, to Unira's deep resentment. Ironically, you've gotten none of that, and Unira still hates you. You have more in common with Unira than you have with Linali, oddly enough, in terms of the way life has treated you."

Nyalin's frown deepened into a scowl. "*You* made it that way."

"Hoping it would protect you—"

"You could have asked. You could have let me know."

"When would we have asked? When you were an infant, a toddler? On the day you were born? Would knowing a woman stalked your every footstep, trying to kill you every chance she could, for your entire life truly have helped? We have given up a great deal to protect you, Nyalin. More than you know."

"So tell me. Enough secrets. And who is 'we'"?

"It's not all my story to tell. But you know more now than you did an hour ago."

"I see how it is." Nyalin's jaw clenched, anger throbbing at his jaw.

Lara fidgeted. This was going downhill fast. They didn't have many allies; they couldn't afford to lose this one. She needed to get them back to working together. "So she helped Andius in the Contests. Did Andius know she was helping him?"

Pavan looked relieved to turn toward her. "Yes, he's accepted support from Unira, both in spells and in silver. Or more likely gold."

"He's... he's a traitor to another clan?" Her eyes widened. "Even I did not suspect him of that."

"He's covered his tracks well. And there are many who would benefit from Obsidians having greater control over the less powerful clans. But he is not the only one corrupted by Unira. We believe the Pearl Clan has been tainted as well. In fact, we believe Unira kidnapped one of the clan's betrothed and is holding her hostage somewhere as leverage. Another disaster I need to address. Somehow."

"By the Twins," Lara breathed. "Is the Pearl Clan the only one?"

"No certain information yet. Whatever Unira is up to, it's ambitious and far-reaching. But I have no leads on where the kidnapped person might be. Your father, however, is purportedly at home. So I'm starting there. And the hour is getting late. I should really head back soon."

Nyalin's expression was hard as he spoke. "It's important to know if

Cerivil is okay. Lara and I will try to figure out what to do next, how to help him, while you're gone."

"Thank you for coming to tell us," she said, rising. The men followed her lead. "Nyalin's right. You should hurry to the city, so you can get back to us with word about him."

"I'll take my leave then. Be well, and stay warm, Nyalin, Clan Leader."

She opened her mouth automatically to correct him but faltered and didn't get another chance. He winked, already transforming into a tiny bat again, flapping up into the dark of the cavern above them.

She sank back to her seat, head spinning with all the information he'd told them. Beside her, Nyalin was scowling at a hunk of meat in his hand, chewing hard.

She doubted the meat was the problem.

"There you are. I finally found you." Unira closed the door to her son Idak's bedroom suite.

The fire was crackling away, merrily as always. She'd been searching for him for a good twenty-four hours, and now, here he was, in the most obvious place. Reading.

"If you've come to drag me to dinner, I'm not coming." He did not look up from his book.

"Dinner was over an hour ago."

The warmth from the hearth's blaze should have been welcome after the cold night air. But something inside her seethed, something that demanded action and made her skin burn hot enough already. She sank into an armchair across from him.

He glanced up now. "What do you want then?"

She frowned. "Can't I simply want to enjoy your company?"

"No. You cannot."

Her lips pressed together. Well, this was going so well already. She needed to be calm, steady, and persuasive right now. Not sniping back and forth at each other. But all the time looking for him had rattled her nerves. He hadn't been anywhere on the premises. "I looked for you earlier. I didn't want to interrupt your reading."

He sighed. "I was in the forest."

"Hunting?"

"No."

She stifled an urge to investigate that further. It was possible he had just been hiking around. His enjoyment of the outdoors was a boon, because it was one of several things that kept him from noticing the power that could be his if he wished it. He would swear up and down he wanted a simple life, and out of her plans, but she didn't believe it for a minute. Boys who cared little for power could sometimes grow up to be men who strove for it. Pavan was a perfect example. Idak could be next, and he wouldn't have to do much to get power, other than take it from her. It could be easier for him than picking up a cup of tea from the table, if only he desired it.

She had to find a way to ensnare him, to dig her claws into his share of the power for good. And soon, before it was too late.

He reclined in an armchair by the fire, too, feet propped up on the leather ottoman. He took a sip from the mug beside him. She stifled another powerful urge to demand to know what was in it. It didn't matter, and she needed to spend her questions on more important things.

When she said nothing for a long while, he finally spoke. "All right, we've established I missed dinner and you don't enjoy my company or seek it out for leisure purposes. So what purposes could you possibly have, Mother? What brought you here?"

"Your grandfather asked me to come," she lied.

"What's he want now?" He went back to scanning his book.

"He said it's been too long since you've been to the city. That you have potential. You need to go—meet people, make connections."

He snorted. "Impress the sniveling fools and their clockwork machinations? Really, Mother? Why didn't you just tell him to shut up?"

"I did, but he's been quite persistent."

Idak rolled his eyes as he turned a page. "Old men have big dreams. Sometimes, silly dreams. I'm quite content here."

"Are you going to tell him that?"

"No. But I'm surprised you haven't. Who cares what he thinks? No one in the Salt City is listening."

She smiled. "I see some flaws in what he says, too, but I do think there could come a time when you wish for more than just reading and long walks in the forest."

Idak snorted. "I didn't realize you took any of his drunken nonsense ramblings seriously, Mother. Next, you'll be saying I should replace Grel as clan leader. Or why not Elix, while we're at it?"

"Well, why not?"

His eyes widened. "I'm trying to read."

She pursed her lips, letting the silence grow as she considered how to proceed. "Grel is never going to get a sword, you know."

His brow creased, and he looked up from the book for the first time. "What do you mean? Why are you saying that?"

"The sword smiths will never give him a sword. No one has been turned down so many times, let alone a clan leader's son."

"He's had a few troubles, but I'm sure eventually—" He stopped short, his eyes sharpening. "Don't tell me you're behind that."

"I'm not behind the delays. Your grandfather is." That was more than half an untruth, because the old man would have never thought of the plan if she hadn't suggested it. But she had claimed often that she'd only carried out their—conveniently bedridden—patriarch's orders.

Idak groaned and dropped his book onto his lap.

"But I think your grandfather is thinking bigger than that," she said quietly. She kept her eyes on the fire as she folded her hands in her lap.

Understanding dawned in his eyes. "You can't be serious. Talk like that will get you killed. End of discussion. Sweet Seluvae. Does Jylan know about this sword nonsense?"

"She might." Her daughter was far more practical than her son, so she absolutely did, but she didn't want to emphasize how much more she kept confidence with Jylan than with him.

"She has no issues with you ruining the future of her beau?"

"Jylan sees the bigger picture. Can you?"

He cut a hand through the air. "Whatever you've done to Grel, you need to undo it."

"Some would call that a little ungrateful, if you ask me."

He swore. "Call me ungrateful if you want. I say it's foolhardy. What will Elix do if he finds out what you've done? You can't possibly have perfectly succeeded in bribing all of them."

"Oh, but I have."

"Every single sword smith?"

"Every one."

His frown was more curious now than angry. "How did you possibly manage that? Especially without Elix finding out."

"Oh, I suspect he knows. Everyone can be manipulated, Idak, if you understand what levers to pull. And I would pull all sorts of levers to give you the position—and the future—that you deserve. The position in our empire." She eyed him to see if he bought it. She'd never been great at faking intense maternal devotion, but at the moment, the pretense of it was critical. Certainly, he had to expect her motives were self-serving, but admitting it now would only drive him away.

Hmm, perhaps she shouldn't have let him get a sword either, but it was too late for that. He could have simply learned her dark arts from her books anyway and worked around any lack of a weapon. Grel, however, was too noble and idealistic to take such measures, and he couldn't lead the clan without a sword, no matter where his magic came from.

Nothing in Idak's expression said he bought her enthusiasm, but he didn't fly into a rage either. "So you're actually helping the old man. In his crazy schemes."

"I'm trying to help you. For him, they are crazy schemes. For me, I'd say it's more of a high-risk gamble. But what do you think?"

"I think you're both mad." He set the book aside, though. "Tell me exactly what you did. It sounds like all that would take quite a bit of time."

"Let's just say that it depends on the smith. Some smiths were eager for a chance to take Elix down a peg. He's hardly been properly respectful to them. Others required a bit of coin. Still others required more... direct and elaborate means of persuasion."

He winced, his eyes haunted. "More kidnappings? I thought you said we were done."

She waved a hand. They would never be done, but she told him what she must to keep him at bay. "A few children locked in stasis, nothing more."

"Children? Until when?" he demanded.

"Until you ascend."

He shook his head. "That's awful, Mother. Don't do that on my behalf ever again."

Internally, she flinched. She was pushing him too close to a line she didn't want him to realize was there. "Of course, Idak. I was only looking out for you. For the good of the clan. For the good of the empire."

The lines in his face eased. Good. He believed that much of her lies. "Why do you even want control of the clan anyway?" he asked.

"I told you, I don't want control of just the clan."

"That's treason. You're going to get us all killed."

"Pavan has no heir! Why shouldn't we try?" She folded her arms. "If he cared so much, he could at least bear a child or two. Or marry. And who's going to tell on us? Are you? The one we want to lift up?" Of course, if Pavan did marry or spawn offspring, there'd be no one in this land she'd work harder to kill.

If he wouldn't have her, he wasn't going to have anyone. But she wouldn't tell Idak that.

"Tell me why you want this so much." His voice was hard.

She scowled. Perhaps he didn't believe her maternal devotion excuse as much as she'd hoped. Why did he even want a reason? Why couldn't he be power-mad and selfish like a normal twenty-year-old man? "The empire deserves a solid future, a solid succession path. A clear and strong future leader. A leader like you."

"Emperor Pavan is a good emperor."

"I'm not saying you should depose him. I'm saying befriend him, win him over, become his heir. Someone has to be. How do you know he wouldn't approve of a fine young man like you offering his service?"

He shook his head. "Offering my service. Ridiculous. Like he wouldn't see your power grab for what it is."

She gritted her teeth. "It doesn't have to be that. Your motivations can be whatever you wish them to be. All leaders need good men at their sides, who incidentally benefit through growing power."

"My motivation is to read my book, but that's clearly harder than it looks. Mother, he is our emperor for a reason. He's the one person who was able to line up the targets on his back so that his enemies were pointing more arrows at each other than at him. I'm not that man. We're not that family." He stood up, as if to leave.

She stood up, too, grabbing his arm to stop him as he started toward the door. "We should be," she whispered. "We deserve it."

"Why?" he demanded. There was that haunted look in his eyes again. He had seen too much, knew too much about the ones locked in stasis in the catacombs—her source of power. Indeed, he'd harvested all too many of them. Clearly, he hadn't forgotten the experience.

She squeezed his arm tighter, marshaling every drop of persuasion left in her dark soul. It wasn't much. "My son. I've sought to raise you to have a healthy dose of skepticism. I wanted you to see what I saw—the truth of the people around you. To be able to sort the facts from the lies. The sycophants from the truly loyal. The honest from those who would bend the image of the world to their will. But I fear now I failed you."

"How? Of course you haven't failed me, Mother." He turned back toward her now, and she released her grip on his arm.

"While I was so concerned about truth, I fear I've failed to give you a sense of vision. It's critical to see the world for what it is. But the people who change things, who do great things in the world—sometimes, those people must see more than truth. More than just what's there. They must see potential. What could be."

His eyes sharpened. "I'm listening."

"Do you think that when Pavan was a boy in an orphanage he went around telling everyone he'd be emperor someday?"

"I doubt it even occurred to him."

"He's spoken about how he saw the wasteful warring between clans and how it kept us ripe targets for our enemies. So many lives lost fighting each other, and then more lost when the Mushin would come, exploiting fresh weaknesses." She took a slow, bracing breath. The words hurt. It hurt to even remember how much she'd admired him then. Still admired that version of him, in truth. He was a brilliant man in so many ways, and yet brilliantly stupid in others. If only he'd seen how she could have been a part of those lofty visions. "He saw the problems, that they needed to be fixed. And he set about fixing them, and people were grateful. Do you see problems, my son?"

"Well... maybe."

"Such as?"

He sighed, almost in defeat. "There's no plan as to what would hold us all together if the emperor should die. He has no wife, no heirs, no clan leader designated as someone who could succeed him. If he dies, everything he built will crumble. That alone would encourage foreign adversaries to try to make that happen, compared to if we had a solid ruling succession plan."

"Yes, if he were to be assassinated, that could be a grave situation indeed."

"The empire would crumble quickly too. The relations between clans are tense, not amicable. Bonds have not truly been forged. How unified are we really? We'd be at war again with all the other clans, if not right away, then soon enough. And ripe for the picking from foreign enemies."

"Do you think he truly can't find a suitable wife, if not in the empire, then in the entirety of the world?"

He shook his head. "I know Grandfather says he should have married you..."

She toyed with the idea of revealing more of the past to him, that there was more to that idea than incoherent grumblings. She'd also hoped Pavan would choose her. But how could she really capture the truth of how life had been in those days? Pavan's refusal to choose her—or any wife at all, for that matter—had planted a seed of frustration. When other Obsidians had heaped her with scorn and rejection, that frustration had grown into a choking vine of hate that simply longed to tear the whole system to the ground.

Was this system good? Was it just? The fact that it barely kept them all from killing each other did not make it good. How many magical souls went without discovering the beauty of magic because of how they were born? How much power was the empire squandering by leaving these souls to languish—or turn to necromancy and the mantle of shame and rejection that came with it? Could her son, born with every advantage, understand the condescension she'd endured by simply being born a woman?

No, she wasn't quite ready to explain all that.

She forced a casual laugh, a flip of her hand. "That's nonsense. And that is beside the point. As you said, old man, silly dreams. And yet... Emperor Pavan remaining a bachelor when there are many eligible women like me is a good example of his willful defiance of his duty to provide stability after his death."

His gaze hardened now. She'd lost him some in that phrasing. "Let us hope his reign is long then."

"Should we?" She smiled. "Or should we hope his reign comes to an end soon?" From the widening of his eyes, she had a feeling that a little too much menace was seeping into her expression, so she sobered. "Regardless, someone should be ready to pick up the pieces were such a terrible event to occur. Someone the other clans were already willing to support. Anticipating, even."

"That someone is not me. Elix?"

She barked out a laugh. "That someone is you. Elix is feared but hated. They wouldn't trust him to lead."

"The other clan leaders don't even know me."

"Exactly what makes you a better choice. And they can get to know you. You could win their support for when the time comes."

He sighed. "I'm not sure about this."

"You don't have to be," she assured him, "but what if you took a trip into the city? Simply talked to some folks. Made some friends. Made yourself more... known. Offer help, perhaps. See if you don't see problems that need fixing... a vision for a better world..."

Idak's lips were pressed into a thin line, but the anger, the resistance had gone from his expression. "Well, I have been a bit bored around here. I've walked every inch of those woods."

Maybe he had been telling the truth about that after all. "Excellent. My carriage is still ready from my trip. You could leave in the morning."

He waved a hand in defeat. "Fine. Fine. You'll have the servants pack for me?"

"Of course. And I'd like to point out one more thing you could... look for... on your trip."

"What?" He sank back down into the chair, picking his book back up. She was running out of time to make her requests.

"A wife."

"By the goddesses, Mother—"

She held up a palm. "She needn't be yours immediately. But there are very few women here in our estate, and even fewer that would make an appropriate mate. If you were to show yourself as a powerful figure to every clan, to be trusted by the emperor, and you were already married..." Then he'd be a more suitable emperor than Pavan for sure.

"I know, I know. Why not make it a pregnant wife while we're wishing on waterfalls?"

She frowned at his sarcasm, but said, "Well, that would be even better."

"All right. Fine. I'll look for a broodmare for you."

"Idak!" she snapped.

"Would you prefer I find a bitch then? Does species matter? I hear some lovely black puppies were born to the stable master's daughter—"

"Idak." She viciously forced down the urge to stride over to him and slap him across the face. This wasn't the moment to push him toward realizing she no longer had any right to do such things. He could control this household and all their holdings and everyone in them if he only bothered to lift a finger to do so. "You will find a woman. A human woman. Of high breeding."

"Any other specifications?"

"Preferably of our own clan. And I do have a suggestion, if you're up for it."

"A suggestion, eh?" He raised an eyebrow. "I'm listening."

"Elix has a daughter. Older than Raelt. She'd have been next in line after Grel if she'd been born a boy."

"So as her husband, I'd be... not at the top of the unsaid hierarchy, but quite near it." He shook his head. "You're craftier than you look."

She decided to ignore that comment. "A clan leader's daughter from another clan wouldn't be a bad choice either. But why marry below yourself if there's a reasonable option available?"

"Reasonable. Always what I longed for in a woman."

"I didn't say she was reasonable, only that the match would be. In fact, I've heard she's rather the opposite."

He arched an eyebrow. "I'm listening."

"Oh, do you have a longing for more the rebellious sort?" She rolled her eyes. So impractical.

Both eyebrows quirked up with his smile now. "I do, as a matter of fact."

"Then perhaps she'll be 'reasonable' enough for you."

"What's her name? I can tame her."

She shook her head. Her son was grown but still very naive to the ways of the world, wasn't he? Or at least the ways of women. "Her name is Sutamae naElix mo—"

"Yes, yes. Sutamae. Got it." He opened the book. "Have the servants tell me when the carriage is ready to leave. Tonight."

She paused, brow furrowed at his somewhat rude dismissal. But she'd gotten what she wanted, hadn't she? She needed to let this go. "So soon?"

"Why wait? This place is boring anyway. I can sleep while they drive."

"Your initiative is admirable. Strength to you, my son," she said, quietly pleased, and made her way out.

The lonely side street was empty but for a dim lantern casting golden halos around cobblestones.

Sutamae had left Chosko's residence, but she hadn't headed home. Instead, her tasks for the night carried her down to the Pearl District, where the bustle of the Feast of the Tides was frothing in nearly every street and market square. A few blocks ago, she'd finally found her destination, thank the Twins. Her black Obsidian's robe stood out sharply in the white-robed Pearl District. How did they ever hope to keep them clean?

She wondered at the choice of time and location. Had one of the Bladed Women chosen it intentionally, or was it a simple coincidence? She did not yet know their inner workings, how meetings were scheduled. She knew only that she'd been invited to this one—and its place and time.

The Feast of Tides officially celebrated the seasonal fish harvest, but it also carried other meanings, especially among the most dedicated Pearls. The tides also were cyclical, like women, like the moon, like fertility. She'd hurried past too many tavern windows that revealed much wilder revelry than simple eating and drinking.

The rumble of the feast was a quiet hum in the background now. Although the gong had not yet struck for midnight, she'd hear it soon. Before that sound could come, she heard what she'd been waiting for. Leather armor creaked. The stocky figure turned the corner and lumbered toward her, sword following the motion like a dog wagging its tail.

"Blade Baelinin," she said, her voice warm.

The Bladed Woman eased to a stop and removed her helmet. Brown locks tumbled free, lovely in spite of their obvious lack of care or style. The goddesses must truly hate their gender. The women who wanted glorious coifs were always gifted with exactly what they would prefer *not* to have—and the ones who didn't care at all always got the best of it.

It was good for Baelinin's hair that it required no effort, really, because that was all the effort it was ever going to get. "Done so soon?" said the woman with a smile.

"Luck." Su inclined her head.

"Were you waiting long?"

"Not long."

"Come, let's go. They'll be waiting." They started down the street. Baelinin was her escort toward the secret meeting—she'd only been told the approximate location. "Did you get some of that luck from your Bone Clan brother?"

She smiled. "Perhaps I did. He certainly seems to have plenty." Nyalin's performance at the Contests and his and Lara's escape were nothing short of miraculous in her mind. It'd been exhilarating to watch, and not just because she had a horse in the game.

Bael grinned and was quiet for a moment. "Your father hasn't decided to marry you off like prized cattle yet?"

"Not yet. I think my nocturnal exploits discourage him."

"Indeed, I hope they do. Do you think he just doesn't want to bother?"

"Or has he tried, and no one is agreeable?" She gave her a crooked smile. "I hope it's a bit of *both*."

Baelinin smirked. "Are you still letting them think you are—when you, you know—"

"Shh! Honorable women must not speak of such things."

A chuckle was her only reply.

"I let them think whatever they want to believe. They don't actually ask. If they want to make assumptions, then they deserve to be wrong. But it doesn't matter. Their opinions don't matter to me. No one's does."

"Now don't lie to yourself. *My* opinion matters to you."

"Hah. Well, yes, I suppose it does. All right, but the circle is small. And it's filled *entirely* with women. If I could, I'd live in a world without men." She swung her arm wide at that flight of fancy.

That wasn't being fair to her brothers, though. Sure, she could deal without Raelt, but Grel and Nyalin were kind.

But also rare specimens. And Nyalin had vanished into the literal wind, and Grel was always off studying, politicking for his own damn sword, practicing. That man never took a break. Of course, with the number of times they'd denied him his sword, how could he ever relax? He couldn't afford to look like he was doing anything but trying his damnedest to be the best possible future clan leader there ever could be.

She had no doubt he *would* be a truly great clan leader. If they ever just gave him the stupid sword. It was the one thing that sometimes eased her bitterness over her own pursuit just a little.

If they didn't take one look at Grel and realize he was worthy, the sword smiths were stupid indeed.

"Speaking of a world without men." Baelinin stopped and held an arm wide, indicating the unmarked door beyond. The secret location of the meeting—they'd arrived. "Shall we?"

Swallowing, Su steeled herself and pushed her way inside.

Stairs led down into the darkness, and she had to feel her way along the wooden rail. She was as careful with it as she could be, but it wobbled and shook just the same.

The scents hit her before she caught sight of the cellar itself—spice and geranium, oak and nutmeg. There was magic here. Excited feminine voices murmured, some brash, some sweet, rising and falling in waves punctuated by the occasional peal of laughter. Every one of them wore some piece of armor, though rarely a full set. Just as many—if not more—wore visible scars.

Low, thick white candles were peppered around, on ledges and benches and stools. No fire or torches were present, so the faces were all tickled by the glimmer and shadow of the dim candlelight.

Varene sat near the center of the room on a low stool, her sword drawn, tip in the dirt. Her hands rested on its pommel. It twisted a little in her hands, gnawing into the rough floor. Her smile was calm, relaxed. Sutamae couldn't remember a time when Varene hadn't looked at ease and in control of everything around her. She had a thin, lithe frame, eyes of glittering black, and a crown of short, cropped, almost silver hair. Beside her sat Tyro, red-headed and dark-eyed. Tyro was of course the first to notice Su's arrival, her eyes hardening in wariness. Most of them had been welcoming to her, but for some reason, not Tyro.

As Su entered and slowed, Baelinin behind her, Varene turned and met her gaze with a slight inclination of her head. Su gave a slight curtsy—Varene was not a fan of overt displays of subservience, but especially as only an aspirant, Su couldn't repress the urge to show she knew her place. That she respected Varene.

Respect was so rarely deserved. It was a privilege to be able to show respect honestly and sincerely for someone. For once.

Varene cleared her throat and rose. Had they been waiting for her to arrive? "Bladed Women—I call you to order. Most of us are here, so let us begin. Aspirant Sutamae."

She raised her head. "Yes, Blade Varene?"

"Do you have the sword? Have you achieved your mission?"

"Yes, Blade."

"Bring it forward."

She drew the sword from the folds of the skirt where she'd concealed it. Then she slowly waded forward, minding the low candles and the swaying black fabric as well as the other Bladed Women and aspirants. She stopped before Varene and held the sword flat across both hands at the height of her chest. "The sword of Chosko naFaweh moSelul."

A hum went through the group. Varene, for her part, smiled sweetly. "Good work. You've passed several of our tests now. Are you ready for the final—and the most difficult?"

"I'm ready."

"You know we live by a code. Honoring certain virtues. Why do we do this?"

"To uphold our goodness and truth even if others won't acknowledge it. To prove our worth to ourselves even if others don't know it."

"Yes. We have found a way to a gift of magic that most of our kind do not find. And we must protect that by ensuring that all those who become Bladed Women know their worth and have earned that title."

Varene paused, and Sutamae had to fight the urge to sink to one knee. Or both.

"All have sworn to help those who aspire to that gift to earn it. The granting of this gift demands that we use it wisely. Justly. Virtuously. Tell me. What are the virtues we live by?"

She cleared her throat. "Bravery. Justice. Gratitude. And honesty."

"There is no doubt you've shown an abundance of bravery. Your courage in the pursuit of justice won you much favor and your consideration here."

A soft "Thank you" was all she could force out.

"You have shown gratitude for your inclusion here, and you've also taught gratitude to one young man unlucky enough to come to our attention tonight. Or you will soon."

Chuckles rippled through the group. Sutamae smiled but lowered her eyes. She had continued to hold the sword high, but Varene finally took it now, seizing it and holding it high for them all to see, then examining the scabbard.

"He will learn gratitude *especially* when he finally gets this sword back." She gently placed the blade back in Sutamae's waiting hands. "But there remains one virtue that may prove... more of a challenge."

The room grew quiet, and Su forced her shoulders back and her chin up, lest the tension in the air make her scrunch her shoulders to her ears.

"You will give your father this sword. That, you've done before. A genius move." The corner of her mouth quirked up as she spoke. "But our test requires something further, to push yourself. When you give your father this sword, you will tell him of your true desires and request a sword of your own."

Her heart stopped in her chest. "W-what?"

"Tell him what you've told us, Sutamae."

"But I don't want to learn from him. I want to learn from you." Her voice couldn't have cracked on those words. It was barely a falter.

"You will, if you can do this." Varene's smile was soft, sympathetic. "Tell me. What is the final virtue?"

She swallowed. "Honesty."

"Yes, honesty."

"I've *never* lied to my father."

"Ah, but you haven't been truthful with him either."

She bit her lip. They were right, of course. A certain part of her could appreciate that it was a fairly brilliant test, requiring of her all their virtues. And all at once. Most of her, though, was groping for an excuse, for some way out of it. "Why can't we handle this without him? Just women—on our own, our own way."

"The goddesses made us this way, every being intertwined with every other. We Bladed Women understand that even better than most."

"But—"

Tyro shot to her feet. "It is not about what is convenient for you or what is pleasant. It is about what is honest and what is true. This is our way. You will live by it, or you won't."

Su's breath was shaky, but she fought to hide it, to keep up the facade. If she could trick a half dozen men well enough to steal their swords, she could pretend to these women that she wasn't crumbling inside. She looked imploringly to Varene, not that she expected anything to change from the look. She wasn't sure what she expected, but her dreams were crumbling here amid the candlelight.

"It takes even more bravery to be honest with the ones we love than those we despise." Varene's eyes were soft, her voice as gentle as a summer breeze, and yet, somehow, the words were cutting.

"He'll just turn me down."

"Then so it is," said Varene. "Let him. Come back and tell us his response."

She looked from Varene to Baelinin to Tyro and back again—all of them glorious and powerful, each so different from one another. And yet they were all images of what she *wanted* to become. Was it foolish to wish to be a little of all three? Strong, powerful, deserving? Women who wore their power openly, rather than twisting it like a knife in the kidney in a back alley somewhere?

That covert sort of power was all Su had yet been able to manage. If she wanted to grow, to become more, to embody the strength and power and integrity they had, she shouldn't expect it to be easy.

And yet. By the Twins.

Her father.

## *Chapter 3*

# Well Matched

The sound of the river burbling passed usually relaxed Lara. But that was before she contemplated washing herself—or her crossover—in it. How cold could it be?

She shifted from foot to foot at the river's edge. With hunting parties roaming the steppes, that limited her options... As did the temperature. The simplest option to get cleaner would be to plunge in fully dressed and then dry herself in the sun.

Unfortunately, a layer of white clouds hid the sun at the moment, even as it grew dimmer with winter. That sounded like a good way to freeze herself to death.

Accepting the fact that there were no good options, she stripped off the crossover as quickly as she could and threw herself into the water.

Dala's light, that was cold. Perhaps the countryside wasn't *all* delights.

*Laundry will have to wait. Aren't clan leaders supposed to have people for this sort of thing?* She forced a smile as she scrubbed at the dirt on her skin and scratched at her scalp.

*Make your demands and you shall have them.*

*You are an eternal optimist.*

*No, I'm just older and have seen more than you, even for a young dragon. Including what a dragon can do.*

She twisted her lips and considered that as she pondered her laundry. She didn't really know exactly what a dragon could do. If her clan knew, they hadn't bothered to tell her. *Don't you think you catch more flies with honey than vinegar?*

*Flies are stupid, people are complex.*

*I agree. I think that means I need something to offer them. I need to show what I'm worth. What else justifies me having the clanblade? My birth? My theft? That's not going to make them very loyal to me.*

*Your vision is better. Your morals are better. Andius will only abuse the clan for his own gain.*

*I agree. But how do we convince the people of that? The clan council?*

*Dragons are not much for convincing people. The truth should be obvious.* Lara almost thought Yeska was dismissing her question, until the dragon's tone shifted to almost remorse. *So, unfortunately, I will have to leave that mystery up to you.*

Emerging from the river, she shivered as she tried to shake off the water like a common street dog, then bundled herself in her crossover and ran for the warmth of their fire, glad she hadn't spotted any other humans during her errand.

Her thoughts returned to Nyalin. Could she find a way to touch on the strange distance between them? The emperor's visit seemed to have aggravated it somehow. They needed to talk about what they could do to look for her father, but by the Twins, she wasn't really sure they could do anything. She had no idea where to look or how to look—and being a bit of an undesirable in the city didn't exactly help. Was that what she was? It probably depended on who she might run into. She'd exiled herself at the very least.

Yet she was also clan leader, so they had to do *something*.

And she *had* to understand what was bothering Nyalin. She steeled herself. If she could jump into that freezing river, she could bring up these things with him, hard as they were.

But when she crept inside, she could hear twin snores—Yeska's and Nyalin's. He was already asleep.

She sighed. She shouldn't be surprised. With Yeska here anyway... who wanted to express their love in front of an audience? Especially a giant snarky one that called you "daughter."

A snort made her jump, though. Both snores abruptly cut off.

*I heard that. I was just dozing.*

She shrugged, even if Yeska wasn't looking. The dragon could feel her gestures. *What? It's the truth. Go back to sleep.*

*No, I'm done sleeping. I can take a hint. I'm going for a flight.*

*Wait—no—*

*Goodbye, Daughter. I'll stay out till morning.*

Nyalin was propped up on his elbows and blinking blearily into the dark mouth of the cave as she made her way in, the wind from Yeska's sharp wingbeats ruffling her hair back. His sleep cleared a little from his eyes, and they met hers. He smiled.

Something in her chest eased. Sleepy Nyalin still saw her and smiled. Things would be okay. She knew what she had to do.

"Where's she going in such a hurry?" He waved at the dragon's escape route.

"Night flight," Lara murmured as she came to sit near his feet. "I hear it's the thing fashionable dragons do these days."

He sat up fully and rubbed his eyes. "Really. I didn't know that dragons had fashions. There's what, six of them?"

*More. But I'm not here, so that's the last thing I'm telling you.*

She kept her laughter inside her mind and just shrugged. "Who knows? They don't line up for me to take attendance."

He grinned, propping elbows up on his knees. "You look... well."

"I look clean. For once." She smiled. She might have flushed; it was hard to say since the cave was already so much warmer than outside. "I finally braved the ice baths—I mean, the river."

Her eyes got lost in the fire for a moment before they drifted back to meet his again. They had that open, dreamy look she remembered, from before everything had happened. She wasn't sure what exactly it meant, but damn it felt good.

"Sorry my return woke you up," she added.

"I didn't mean to fall asleep anyway. Book was just a little dry." He glanced pointedly over his shoulder, and, sure enough, there was a brown-leather tome abandoned just beside his furs.

"You didn't mean to?"

"Well, you weren't back yet. Yeska said not to worry, but..."

"You were worried about me?" She flushed more as she said it. She was being silly.

"Please." His brow furrowed, though his smile didn't waver. "Isn't that obvious?"

She ducked her head. What was this sudden shyness, this uncertainty? It wasn't her style. And if Yeska was giving up the warm and cozy cave for the night, she needed to make the most of what time she had. She wanted to bring back the way she'd felt that night at Pyaris's—bold, a bit reckless.

During the Contests, her best friend had lent her home to them to use as their hideout, while Andius had been looking for them in his attempts to end their bid to win in a not-so-peaceful manner. Pyaris had even been so kind as to go visit a fellow necromancer friend of hers, leaving the two of them alone for the night.

She'd still had to reach down deep and be brave enough to tell him her truth. That he was so much more to her than a simple partner in their ploy to free her from Andius. That night, she'd told herself she had nothing to lose, so she might as well be honest.

It had been true at the time, but now things felt so different, even though she had even less. Or did she have more? They'd shared a night. A partnership in cheating the Contests. A kiss or two. An escape from Andius's clutches and a wild flight away on Yeska's back. Nyalin had risked a lot for her, but he also hadn't had many choices or better options... But what did all that add up to?

Holding tight to her courage, she met his gaze, then shifted herself up the furs till her back leaned against his knees. "It's hard to get time alone in here, huh? Who would have thought fleeing to the wilderness would give us *less* privacy than before."

His grin returned. "We're alone now."

That was enough of an invitation for her. She let her own knees twist toward him as she swiveled to press her lips to his. It wasn't a fast motion, and he certainly saw her coming, so there was a thread of relief when his mouth pressed back, a reassurance to be found in the warm, gentle pressure and the now familiar zing of strange energy from skin to skin.

Her lips parted, politely demanding more, and he met her demands stroke for stroke, all the worry she'd balled up quietly unraveling into a warm pool of gooey joy. She ran a thumb over the stubble at his jaw, down his neck, resting her hand on his collar bone, tiny pinpricks of magic sizzling every now and again.

She hadn't realized how much she'd missed his kiss.

Except after a moment, he faltered, went still. Then pulled away. And she could see a crease in his brow. She was right. Something was wrong.

"What is it?" she whispered, hardly audible over the crackling fire.

"We promised to always be honest with each other." His hand moved to wrap around the wrist of her hand as it rested against his shoulder. She tensed, thinking he was about to remove it, but his fingers tightened instead, a weird little embrace.

As if he wanted to keep her close to him. As if he didn't want her to run away once he said whatever he was about to say. The worry that lashed wildly within her eased, and she swallowed. "We did. We will."

"That's not always easy, though." He took a deep breath.

"Neither were the Contests. But we survived."

"Low bar, that." He grinned. She'd told him those words not so long ago.

Her smile was lit by his, and she shrugged. "A smart young man I know taught me to live simply."

"Should I be worried?" He tilted his head to the side, eyes twinkling. "What's his name? Is it Faytou?"

The rest of her worry evaporated.

She tightened her fingers against his neck in a quick squeeze. "You should worry only about my inability to launder my own clothes and live in the wilderness. Never about my loyalty to you."

He pulled her closer, so their foreheads touched. His mouth opened, but then closed again.

"Just tell me," she whispered. "It will be okay."

He bit his lip, then met her eyes. "I never got to tell you what the emperor and I talked about, that morning of the Contests, although we touched on some of it while he was here."

She lifted her eyebrows in question, raising her head to see him more clearly. "And...?"

"And... Well, I discovered he's my father."

"No, he—he couldn't—but—" Blinking, her knee-jerk reaction was to deny it. But no. No, it made a certain sense. Especially in the way they'd *both* gotten so uncomfortable at her mention of the emperor not yet having an heir and how Andius might act as a result.

How had she missed it? She'd been so focused on what might happen in the Bone Clan, and there was the truth staring her in the face. Emperor Pavan *did* have an heir.

She started back slightly. His hand tightened around hers. Fear had crept into the corners of his eyes now. He made no effort to hide it—hide anything from her at the moment.

Heir.

"You're... You're his heir? The heir to the six clans, to all the empire. The whole damn empire! Of salt and rivers and dragons."

"To six clans that are always a hair's breadth from stabbing each other in the back?" He shook his head. "Clearly, we haven't talked about it yet. I don't know if he considers me his heir or not. If he wanted me to be his heir, why not raise me himself? Why hide it? Or if he wanted to hide it, why not hide me more completely, and not let anyone know who my mother was either? Raise me as a commoner. Raise me in a foreign land. Why in Elix's house, of all the damn places?"

She let her forehead fall back against his. "It doesn't make any sense."

"I know. And he doesn't *seem* like a man who doesn't make any sense, does he?"

She nodded her agreement, moving both their heads in response.

He smiled at that. "I need to figure out why. Without biting his head off."

"That would be ideal. Although your anger seems very reasonable."

"Anyway, I am hoping I'm not his heir. I suppose I could refuse. I'm not sure what his thinking is on the matter. But I thought you should know before you—"

She cut off the words with a hard kiss. "I thought you had had second thoughts. I was worried you were angry with me. This is the best news ever."

"That now we have a dozen extra reasons that we might never really be able to be together?"

"We're together right now, aren't we?" Her eyes twinkled as she grinned. "Haven't you learned, Nyalin? My determination can fix *anything*. If you don't want to be emperor, we'll find Pavan someone who does. I don't think anyone should have to be anything they don't want to be."

"I don't know what I want," he said simply. "And not everyone who wants that job would be fit for it."

And that... That did raise a question in her chest. A hundred questions, actually, and not ones she could yet ask aloud. It was far too soon. But the implication was there.

If he did want to be emperor—would she want to be his empress? Was that even an option? The Obsidians would lose their minds if two Bones took over leadership of the whole empire.

And yet. Emperor Pavan had no one else. That they knew of, at least. If he'd hidden one son, who was to say he couldn't have hidden another?

She frowned as she remembered the way the emperor had carefully asked her questions that day at the palace. *If he wins, will you regret asking for honor and justice of me today?* Do you know what you're signing up for?

She hadn't. But Pavan had known, hadn't he? He'd known more than she had, anyway.

But she still would have said the same thing.

"Well, I know what I want," she replied, smiling. "And I don't care if I have no idea how I'm going to get it." She pulled him closer for another kiss.

"Determination isn't magic, you know. It can't fix everything."

"That's what Da keeps telling me, but it's never stopped me from trying. And look where it's gotten us." At the mention of her father, a pain streaked through her chest, but she tried to suppress it. There wasn't much they could do until they knew more.

He kissed her, almost as if he were testing out the ease of this, the certainty. Then he gestured around them. "A dank cave with no beds or doors or wells or even a library?"

Stifling a laugh, she put on a haughty air. "A library is the most lacking attribute of these accommodations, I think. Just a bunch of books strewn into a canvas pack. I'm surprised it's even waterproof. Who designed this place? Hardly fit for nobles."

Somewhere distant, Yeska muttered, *I heard that.*

Lara barely contained her mirth. "We do need somewhere else to go."

He bit his lip. "I have a thought."

"Really? What is it?"

He seemed loathe to move away from her, but he twisted slightly and reached for his sword. "Look at this."

He turned the blade so that the fire's light slid across the hilt and the pommel. There... on the smooth flat pommel, there was something inscribed. Drawn or *carved*, maybe. Etched? The decoration went up the hilt all the way to the crossguard too.

"What is it?" she whispered.

"Stragg's Shadow, I think. The volcano. Where all the obsidian comes from."

Fiery plumes curled up the handle from the top of the mountain cut into the blackness. She ran her finger along the cool metal. And there, at the base of the volcano... what was that? It almost looked like a building. Or smaller? A house? There was a roof, four round windows—no eight. The carving was intricately detailed. What the hell could it be? And why would his mother—or whoever had made this sword—have engraved this here? For what purpose? Just for fun? Out of beauty? To remember something?

"Elix said this was my mother's sword."

"Yes. And the emperor didn't seem overjoyed that he'd given it to you."

"I noticed. When he was here, he said that she'd come from the Obsidian wilds but not exactly where. At the time, I figured he just didn't know exactly. But what if he did and he didn't want me to know?"

She frowned. "Why would he.... Never mind. If he didn't want you to know he was your father, then what *wouldn't* he hide? It's weird, though. He always seemed so honest and open."

"I know. He still seems that way to me. He said he has more he needs to tell me, so maybe more will become clear. Anyway, there are plenty of wild lands sparsely populated around the empire. But the valley of Stragg's Shadow is the stuff of legend. People talk about the ghosts."

She raised her eyebrows. "Ghosts. Like you've seen?"

"And like my mother saw."

"We need to go there, then, don't we?" She pointed at the tiny building. "You think maybe this was a drawing of a home?"

"What do I know? I've never had a home. But I think if a certain sweet dragon would fly us over, it couldn't hurt to check. Maybe this place even has doors."

Her cheeks flushed. She'd worried about that comment, but now she realized who he really wanted privacy from, and it wasn't her.

*You are lucky I'm a generous all-mighty beast.*

"Tomorrow then? Once the emperor has returned with news of my father?"

He winced. "May he be speedy, for all our sakes, but especially Cerivil's. He may bring news we need to act on, which might delay this trip."

"I'll think of what we can do to help him. We said we can look for the place Andius held us captive. We can see if we could enlist Pyaris for help."

"And Grel," he added.

"If you insist."

"I do."

"Any other ideas?"

His shoulders slumped. "Maybe Faytou? We don't really know who we can trust."

"Yes, we should ask Faytou. He supported us even when his neck was on the line. I'm tempted to ask those who worked most closely with my father, his advisors and aides. But then I'd have to go to the mansion. And if I go, I'll have to be prepared to... make my demands or what have you."

He winced. "Yes. We need to think about that too."

"I wonder if there is something in that house that could help us?" Lara pointed at the sword again.

"That'd be nice. We could use a stroke or two of luck."

She nodded. "As soon as it's prudent and Yeska is willing, we should head there. At least there, we won't be hunted at every turn."

*A flight toward the lands of black rock? Picturesque. I sense you haven't seen it. You will see. It will be quite the journey. The Dark Dragon will want to speak with us.*

She didn't tell him any of that. No sense in ruining the moment by mentioning the Obsidian Dragon that had slighted Nyalin when he sought teaching. She simply nodded her agreement.

"We should practice some of this transformation magic." He pointed a finger at the book he'd dozed off reading. "Then we can hide a lot more easily—right in plain sight."

"I like it. Never my favorite spell, but we don't have much choice now, do we?"

"We'll figure this out. Don't worry." He ran a hand over her hair. "Where were we before I interrupted with all that nonsense about beds and libraries and practical concerns?"

"And don't forget doors. And baths. That'd be nice. Ah, I think I was expressing my affection and loyalty to an emperor's son."

He grimaced. "I'm just a simple scribe."

"You know that's not true," she said quietly. "You're a powerful sword-mage, no matter who your parents were."

"Only with your generosity, though." His smile was crooked. They had yet to understand or figure out how to unlock his own magic, but accessing hers had worked well enough.

"With my *collaboration*. We'll find a way that doesn't require my assistance. We'll find some answers. Maybe there are even answers there." She pointed at the sword over his shoulder.

"I hope you're right." His face was growing more worried again.

"Haven't you been listening? We don't need to be right. We just need sheer force of will." She chuckled, and he didn't look convinced.

But optimism was catching hold, and the laughter—and enthusiasm—in her kisses soon smoothed his worried expression away.

---

The meeting continued into the night, but Sutamae excused herself to go face her fate. Also known as her father. She found herself back in the Pearl District markets. Perhaps an hour had passed, but the Feast of Tides showed no signs of dying down. If anything, the energy was building.

The finest gowns and crossovers swirled in lively dances; others crowded around high tables with delicate glasses of golden liquid, the wine glittering like sunshine swinging from hand to hand. Pearls studded ears and hair and necks and wrists. Lanterns flickered above the revelers in the blue-gray and blue-green of the sea. Steam and smoke from roasting fish skewers filled the cold air with the scent of pepper and lemon.

At feasts like these, individual fortunes were on blatant display. She spotted more than one glittering aquamarine hung around a throat or dipping dangerously into a crossover's neckline. No clan could match the wealth of the Obsidians, but the Pearls did their damnedest to try.

They didn't ignore her, either, which made her skin crawl. Of course, the black robe was clearly out of place, but this kind of wealth meant the powerful families of the Pearl Clan would be here. People who might even recognize her from the emperor's gatherings.

People who might delight in mentioning to her father that they'd spotted her here.

Inwardly, she groaned at the idea. Oh, let him know the games she played with Chosko and the supposed young wolf pups of the Obsidian Clan. Too many of them were coddled calves, not dragons at all. If anyone was a dragon, it was she.

Or Grel. But would they give *him* a sword? No.

But her exploits were all within her own clan. She didn't want her father to know about her presence here—or about the Bladed Women. And even if she could muster the courage to confront him, as their quest demanded of her—they'd only required requesting the sword. There was no need to mention the Bladed Women themselves yet. Not at all.

Her nascent relationship with them was too precious to her. She couldn't let him or anyone else know, lest they destroy what little hope she had left. She wasn't sure she'd survive.

There were too many eyes here. She needed to get out of sight.

She ducked into a side street, then turned down the next, looking for a less festive street to take back to the Obsidian Clan compound. And then she'd have to face her father. She wasn't entirely sure she could, though. At least not yet.

What if she asked for a sword, to be tested, and he said yes? What then? Did she even want that anymore?

A pebble clattered to her left, cutting through her thoughts.

She sharpened her ears as she walked. One foot after the other, keeping her boots quiet on the cobblestones. Don't let on you've heard anything.

There were no forms in the shadows, no movements. The mouth of the alley was a bare ten paces away. Maybe she could make it.

Abruptly, a long-faced man with a torch emerged from a side door ahead of her. Steel hissed against steel—a blade leaving a sheath. But *this* sound was behind her.

She stopped, slowing her breath, the rush of blood speeding up through her veins.

"What's an Obsidian doing in this district on such a cold night?" said the man with the torch, his face perfectly impassive.

"Cold?" She quirked an eyebrow. "I'm hardly chilled."

"Maybe it's her gold that keeps her warm," growled a deeper voice from behind her. She didn't turn her head.

"I'm simply passing through," she said.

"Passing through the Pearl District. In the middle of the night." The torch bearer pursed his lips, even as another man appeared behind him.

Three. Great.

"Pay the toll," growled the knifed man behind her. "Or pay the price."

"As if I carry any gold on me." She scoffed. It suggested a careless confidence she didn't feel. But let them underestimate her.

"With a dress that fine, you expect us to believe that?" The knifed voice came closer, enough for her to feel his breath on her neck and smell the stench of beer and desperation. His laugh rolled like thunder, low and cruel.

"Believe what you like," she replied. "I have nothing to give you." Other than perhaps her stolen sword, and she wasn't parting with that. It was a coincidence really, that it was the truth, but if she'd had gold, she wouldn't have given it to them either.

"Pay with the dress then," he growled.

Her gaze flicked to the mouth of the alley, where another man had appeared. Watching the show? A fourth helper?

At least she thought it was a man. The silhouette of a hood and cloak was all she could really make out in the moonlight that reached the street. Oddly, the moonlight seemed to brighten for a moment, before fading back. Strange. Must be a trick of the eye.

She scowled at them. Boldly, she took a step forward, away from the knife. "There's nothing you can take from me that someone else already hasn't."

That was true, though it wasn't, of course. There was always more to take.

He tracked behind her, stepping forward, too, dropping back his hood to reveal a face that was a depressing combination of extremely ordinary and bland. Then he tossed his blade, spinning in the air, and caught it again. "Final warning, Obsidian. Your gold—my hand."

Her hand slipped into her sleeve and flipped aside the thong that held her dagger in place. She might not have gold, but she wasn't unprepared. "I'm warning you. The price you'll pay for attacking me is steeper than any gold I could possibly carry." Her hand tightened on the still-hidden hilt as she rotated away, no longer letting him hover behind her. "I won't hesitate to kill you."

Their laughter went up around her, heating her cheeks in spite of herself.

The fourth man at the mouth of the alley didn't laugh, though. Or move.

"Does that sound reasonable to you?" her knifed assailant asked the stone-faced man with the torch and his partner.

The two of them silently shook their heads.

"Let's take our fee in silk then." His grin widened, and he raised the knife and lunged.

Keeping stock still, her eyes followed the hand, the glint of faint light on steel, tracking it closer until—

She jerked aside, catching the man's wrist with her free hand and twisting.

He screamed. The dagger clattered against the cobblestones. She tried not to smile at his enraged gurgle. She was far from done here.

She kept twisting, using his momentum to pull him toward the wall. Cheap wood planking groaned as their weight collided with it. The other two behind her surged forward, but she had to deal with this first. End this now. Before it got any further.

She whipped his forearm up instead of the downward twist she'd had him in before. He was too surprised at the choice to even resist.

She slammed his hand against the wood and drove her blade straight into his palm. The blade bit into wood behind with a dull thud, punctuated only by his gasp.

The men behind her should have been on her now. Her target screamed and clawed at her with his free hand.

She twisted the blade in response, keeping a tight grip on the impaling blade.

He groped toward his belt—

She fought him for whatever was there, each of them with one hand. She barely triumphed at getting his backup knife before he did.

Damn. That could have ended her days right there. Luck, this was all damn luck. His fingers were slick with blood, and he'd fumbled. She hadn't.

Still, she didn't hesitate to hold his own knife to his throat. The alley was silent.

Why weren't they helping him? His eyes burned with rage, flicked over her shoulder. But he didn't look toward the torch bearer, he looked toward the alley.

She glanced back too. The hooded stranger was in the same place. Hadn't even turned. But he'd raised one arm to shoulder-level, holding a sword.

Its tip held the other two men at bay.

"What are you doing?" She wanted to trust this man—he was the closest thing she had to an ally at this point—but how could she?

"Evening the odds," the stranger said into the silence. His voice had a tinge of a foreign accent, one of high breeding.

"Why?" she demanded.

"It seemed only fair." His voice was flat, maybe even sarcastic.

"What are you waiting for? Kill them!" her captive grunted.

"Won't she kill you then?" the torch bearer's companion pointed out, speaking for the first time.

"She doesn't have the guts." He spat at her, but missed her face. "Come on!"

She narrowed her eyes at them all. "I don't *need* to kill him. I could just start with an eye. Or an ear. Which do you think he likes better?"

"Whatever you give comes back threefold, woman." The torch bearer drew his blade.

She smiled, pouring every drop of her viciousness into the expression. "I only have two eyes."

"Perhaps we'll have to change that." He lunged, the torchlight careening wildly, sending shadows flying.

She spun to the side, leaving her hostage pinned. The torch bearer was quick, though. His blade caught the fabric of her dress and tore. She didn't *feel* any pain, but that could be just the rush of battle. She swung an elbow at him. Her strike didn't reach the target she'd planned—his throat—but she heard a nice satisfying crunch as her elbow collided with his jaw.

He staggered back, taking the torch with him. Her original attacker, though, had yanked the knife from the wood to free his impaled hand and lunged forward anew. She caught the movement just a moment too late in the shifting darkness.

She danced back, raised her dagger to catch his, but—

Before his thrust could reach her, it drooped. Fell short. Short of everything, actually.

The sickening sound of a sword leaving flesh sliced the air. The stranger stood over a fresh dead body, face first on the ground. The torch bearer had dropped his torch, and it lay burning on the cobblestones, casting a long shadow from the still form.

The torch light also illuminated the stranger's face under the hood—but she saw no human features, no eyes or nose, just a dark blank slate like a round, smooth river stone.

What the... What *was* he? Some god or apparition? He'd had a human voice, a man's voice.

Blood glistened on his long, beautiful blade. The wide, silver hilt of it held a molten white stone the size of her eye. Its glow played across his cloak and crossover underneath.

She'd rarely seen any sword so beautiful, even among clanblades, although she certainly hadn't seen many of those.

"Who are you?" she whispered.

He spoke, but he didn't answer her. He'd turned to the timid third man—who hadn't yet attacked anyone. "You can continue this foolishness." He looked to the former torch bearer, now clutching his jaw. As he turned, she could see his face more clearly, or rather—his mask. *That* was why she couldn't see his features.

He raised the sword, and she tightened her grip on both her daggers and crouched a little lower, readying herself for the next move.

But he pointed it at the two men standing. "Or you can leave."

His voice was rough, almost raw, and carried the threatening edge of his tone to every corner of the alley.

Slowly, the two men eased toward the street, backed around the corner, and took off at a run.

She listened to their footsteps, but the stranger's eyes had turned to her. Had she been rescued—or had her problems only just begun?

"Your lucky night," he drawled, shifting his weight slightly to one side.

That voice... A warmth stirred deep within, one she'd forgotten. His tone was hard to read. Was that sincerity or sarcasm?

Her blade was still bloody, but she tucked her hands back in her sleeves, the hilt still in her grip and ready. She forced a smirk. "I could have handled them."

"Perhaps," he said. "Likely, even."

"At least you'll give me that." Not many would.

"Is it wise to take to dark streets during drunken, debauched feasts?"

"You must have come from a better part of the feast than I did. All *I* saw were fish kebabs."

"A better part, or a worse one? Fish kebabs sound delightful just about now."

Silence settled for a moment. She narrowed her eyes at him. "Your cross-over is black." She could see it more clearly now, under the cloak. "You don't belong here anymore than I do."

"Neither of us is wise, then," he said, and she had the strangest feeling he was glaring at the dead man at their feet.

"I never claimed to be wise," she muttered. "I was looking for my brother." The lie rolled off her lips so readily. So easily. She regretted it, a little, but aspiring openly to be a Bladed Woman would only get her in more trouble.

"You might want to get a little wiser, if you want to live to find him."

"I'm not afraid of death." Her eyes ran over the body at their feet coldly. "I am afraid of being so determined to be wise that I don't live. Then I'd discover myself a fool."

"All too common a phenomenon." Was that a smile in his voice? "You're lucky I am fast then. And that I showed up." He waved across the alleyway. His hands were gloved in dark leather. "Do you claim to be lucky?"

Her face fell. "No. Definitely not."

"I am... sorry to hear that."

For a moment, only the clanging of a distant gong and the faint murmur of revelers filled the air. She waited, taking note of his cloak, his boots, his height. The mask hiding his face was a masterwork of intricate white scrolls across slate gray. He didn't move.

Pursing her lips, she cocked her head at him. "You're not going to hurt me. Are you."

"No."

"Then I am lucky tonight at least."

"You are. I should be going." He didn't.

"Thank you for the assistance, sir."

"You're welcome." He paused again, but still didn't turn. He hadn't even cleaned or sheathed his blade, but he did so now, on the corner of his own cloak.

She frowned as she withdrew the hand that held the dagger and bent to wipe off the blood on the attacker's cloak. She hadn't been sure he'd been dead, but now up close, it was clear. A little regret gnawed at her stomach.

But *he* wouldn't be feeling the same had their positions been reversed.

The masked man lingered. They both regarded each other in silence for a long moment, as if a strange thread had sprung to life connecting them, and neither was ready to break it.

Finally, he spoke. "Let me walk you away from here. In case they're waiting around the corner."

Walking with him could be its own trap, but he'd already had his chance to hurt her, hadn't he? He'd chosen to defend her instead. That was rare—rare, indeed.

A man who sought to even the odds. And even crazier, succeeded at it.

Of course, she'd learned not to trust her sense of who was trustworthy and who wasn't. She'd made her mistakes there, and she tried not to think of them. Even alone in her bed at night. Definitely not now. She kept that box locked tight.

Still. Foolish as it might be, she trusted him. "All right. We should leave before we're seen here. Not that that'll be an issue for you." She gestured at his mask.

"You'd be surprised," he grumbled.

They stepped over the body and eased to the edge of the street. She returned her dagger to its sheath. The street appeared just as empty as it had before. But it hadn't been then, so was it really empty now?

She crossed the street, scanning the shadows. He trailed her.

They walked silently through the damp streets, keeping away from the revelers and the crowds. It felt natural. It felt right. More natural than it ought to feel to walk next to a man wearing a mask.

But when they reached the border to the Obsidian District, he slowed. "I suppose this is where I'll take my leave of you. You should be safe here."

He was right, she should be. But she had a vague sense that something else was stopping him, holding him back at the edge of her clan's district. Why would that be so, if it was his clan too?

It wasn't, was it? The black of his cloak wasn't an Obsidian black. She'd just assumed it was. He was from somewhere much farther away. She stopped, easing to the side of the street and into the shadows. She was a little too pleased that he'd followed her. Perhaps it was just that kindness was so rare. She didn't want this brush with it to end so quickly.

"Who is this brother of yours? I will be traveling far. I might encounter him." He kept his voice quiet. The stones could make words carry.

She frowned but couldn't summon the necessary distrust to resist the request. She really did want to know if Nyalin was okay. "His name is Nyalin moLinali."

"All right. Unique enough. I suppose I can remember that. And yours?"

She blinked. No Obsidian or Pearl or anyone in the *entire* empire would fail to react to that name. But he seemed far more interested in her own. "You're not from around here, are you?"

He said nothing.

"Not from within the empire, I mean."

"I can't tell you, so don't ask. But if you give me your name..."

"Why?"

"How else will I send word if I see your brother? Or tell him who is looking for him?"

Her lips twisted. "I'm Sutamae naElix moVanae."

He jerked slightly. Flinched? Without meaning to, she sensed. When he recovered, he leaned further way from her. She frowned and stepped closer in his direction out of spite. He said nothing.

"Please don't judge me by them," she murmured. "We don't choose our families."

"Indeed." He paused, one long great breath. "Indeed, we do not. Your brother—his mother is different from yours? Do I understand your naming conventions correctly?"

"Ah, yes. He's like a stepbrother. An orphan. My parents raised him... so to speak."

"So to speak?"

"They mostly ignored him. But we grew up together. He's my brother in my heart, if not in my blood."

"I see. Well, I will keep my ears open then. You live at the Obsidian mansion, I take it?"

"Yes." Not a total foreigner apparently.

"All right, if I see this Nyalin moLinati I will—"

"Lina*li*. Linali."

"Right. Linali."

She snickered. He must be the only man in the empire right now who didn't know that name. They stood in silence for a few moments longer, the wind tickling her crossover's skirts and his cloak. "I suppose I should be on my way. Are you sure you'll be all right?"

"Right as roses, I swear it."

He straightened slowly, clearly reluctant. "If I see your brother, I will tell him you are looking for him."

"Thank you, that would be most appreciated." She hesitated. She wasn't ready for him to leave either.

"Good night... Sutamae." He almost seemed afraid to say her name, but it also sounded natural in that rolling voice. "Stay safe."

"Wait—I don't know your name." She stepped closer.

She couldn't see a hint of a mouth or nose, but there was the faintest crinkle in the corners of the eyes behind the mask. "People tend to don masks for anonymity, you know."

A laugh escaped her, echoing off the walls. She eased closer to him. Some of the smile in his eyes faded, but he didn't move away. "Is there somewhere I could see you again? Keep your mask, if you must, but at the very least, I owe you a drink. A tavern? A dark and muddy alleyway this time next week, perhaps?"

"No."

She glanced down sharply. "Ah. I see."

"I wish there was," he added hastily.

She was close enough now she could lay a hand on his chest if she wanted to. And she *did* want to. "I won't bite. Or betray you."

"How can you say that? You don't know who I am, so you don't know. Maybe I'm your direst enemy."

Her lips twisted in laughter this time. "Are you a Mushin under there, planning your next invasion? I don't see any fur."

He laughed softly. "No, that I am not."

"I only mean harm to one kind of person, and that kind isn't likely to rescue people in alleyways." The person who had hurt her was nothing like him, and she too had her own score to settle, her own odds to even.

"I thought you had all that"—he cleared his throat—"under control."

Her smile was wide, and far more honest than she usually let it be. "I might have gotten free, but not without a lot more injuries. Now tell me—some way I can see this mysterious mask one more time." She dared to reach up and run one fingertip across the cheek of the mask. It left a thin streak of blood on the metal.

She winced. Apparently, she'd missed a spot or two cleaning up.

His eyes were dark, though, and not because of the blood. "Unfortunately, you caught me leaving the city."

"Ah." She ducked her head and hastily rubbed the remaining blood off on her crossover. "Well, when are you coming back?"

"I'm not."

"Oh." Her chest shouldn't feel so hollow over that news. He was a stranger—a magnetic, mysterious one, but still. She tilted her head as an idea hit her. "Someone's after you. Is that it?"

He nodded slightly. "She's smart as well as capable."

"Where are you headed? You go without a horse?"

"For now. I'll walk into the foothills. The mountains maybe, if I need to." He breathed deep, almost a sigh. He didn't want to be telling her even this much.

"Is the person you are running from associated with my father? Or is it my father? I won't tell him."

He said nothing but the mask and neck moved as though he swallowed.

"Really leaving then." She ducked her head a second time. "That is sad news."

"Not as sad as if you'd lost an eye to those men back there."

"*Three* eyes, remember?"

"How could I forget?"

"I owe you. A drink at least. I want to see you again."

"Technically, you've never seen me at all."

She chuckled now. "He's funny. Skilled and honorable. It's tragic, really."

"Tragic, indeed." His tone seemed sincerely pained.

Her stomach dropped. This really was goodbye, wasn't it.

"Thank you for the compliment, Sutamae naElix moVanae." He bowed with a wide flourish that she hadn't seen before. Someone of lucky birth in some foreign land, he had to be. Who? How strange.

He would go now. He had to. This was her last chance to know anything more about this enigma. A strange idea climbed into her head. She refused to kiss dishonorable men like Chosko. But what would it be like to kiss an honorable one?

And whenever would she meet another man she could be sure was truly honorable?

She stepped right up against him now. "Call me Su, please. Not all that nonsense." She could smell leather and sweat. Boldly, she skimmed a hand up his chest. She could sense his uneasiness, but he didn't shift away. She'd been wrong, there was no crossover underneath this cloak, actually, which fit her theories; it was leather and laces smooth under her palm. Carefully, she reached for the bottom edge of the mask.

Strong, rough fingers caught her hand. The touch of his skin sent strange streaks of fire dancing across her skin, up her arm, making her wince, but she didn't let go. A spell?

"Let me see you. Not all—just a little," she whispered. "If I can't repay you with a drink..."

His hand still on hers, she eased the mask up until she revealed his mouth. Tanned skin, an angular jaw, and thin, precise lips.

Life was too short to not take risks. She lifted her face, parting her lips. Lifting up on her tips of her toes, she closed her eyes and waited.

If she'd still had faith in Seluvae, she would have prayed. But the dark goddess had never answered her prayers.

To her surprise, the risk paid off. His lips met hers.

They both inhaled sharply, as if trying to breathe each other in. The strange flick of pain, like another streak of fire, danced across her lips, too, before fading—how odd. It was just like in the stories, that brilliant flash... But no, it couldn't be, could it?

She dropped her hand from the mask, and so did he. His arm slid around her waist, pulling her against him hard.

Surprise, surprise. The tightness of that grip told her he wanted more, wanted to deepen the kiss, wanted to explore her. After a long moment, he broke away.

"Just saying thanks didn't seem like enough," she murmured.

"You don't owe me anything." He was breathing harder than he should be. "And a kiss is not a payment."

She bit her lip. "You seem clever enough. Stay here. Come hide with me in the Obsidian mansion and kiss me again."

He shook his head. "I can't."

"Just for one night?"

"I can't."

"Why?" She didn't really expect an answer, so she was surprised when she got one.

"You are at best a vulnerability."

"And at worst?"

"A carefully planned deception."

Eyebrows raised, she groped for words, but nothing came forth but her own hurt. Who would plan a deception via *her*? Her father? Impossible. He'd have to actually pay attention to her first. But if there was anything she'd hate, it would be putting this kind stranger in danger's path.

"But—I wish I could stay anyway." He kissed her again to her surprise, firm and warm, kindling the strange, sharp heat. The first kiss had been a leap of faith, a jump into the abyss, but this second was a pact, sealing something between them, even if all it could ever be was a wish for more.

He lingered for one more long moment. And then he vanished into the night, as smoothly as he'd first appeared.

*

Andius stopped and stood in the doorway of his family home and sighed. It was a shame it had all come to this.

Stupid woman. Even more stupid men. He'd put so much on the line to ensure his ascension to clan leader, and still they'd meddled. Messed things up. Resisted the only possible outcome.

In the back bedrooms, his brother cried out, but the sharp sound was quickly cut off.

Andius pursed his lips. Really. He'd given careful instructions to be sure his brother Faytou was taken silently. Clearly, his adversaries weren't the only ones messing up. Thank the Twins his parents were dead and couldn't interfere with this little plan of his, but if members of the council heard of these tactics, he doubted they would approve.

But those same hypocrites wanted peace, stability, tradition, and all that went with those comforts. They wanted this nasty little situation with Lara absconding with a fancy shard of metal and bone to be swept under the rug so that things could go back to normal—simple, predictable, uncontroversial.

Andius wanted that, too, but it would be his way. Cerivil had had his reign, but it was time for someone new. It was time for Andius, and that *was* one thing he was going to change.

Cerivil wouldn't openly resist him, but Andius wasn't going to feign mercy or leniency for those who were ultimately in his way. If only the old man hadn't released the Dagger of Bone so soon. If he hadn't, then it wouldn't have been lying around for Lara to steal it.

A niggling suspicion crept into his brain. Could Cerivil have plotted with Lara for this little coup? No, he'd given up the Dagger in preparation for his son Myandrin to become clan leader. Besides, Andius didn't think Cerivil was capable of such machinations. He was too honest. Too bad his daughter hadn't inherited his scrupulousness.

Lara and her nonsense wouldn't stop him; nobody would. Andius had sacrificed far too much for it to fall apart now.

He narrowed his eyes at the men that carried the squirming, grunting black bag out of the house toward the wagon. *Hardly* what he'd instructed.

His sacrifices had cost him his dignity at times, as well as a seemingly endless amount of gold. But the most surprising thing had been the people he'd had to sacrifice along the way.

That Obsidian woman had warned him of this. Unira. He hadn't hesitated to make foreign alliances. Wasn't that what rulers did all the time? He shook his head as he walked to the wagon and signaled them to move out as he silently closed the gate.

It was purple twilight, so he walked along beside them, hood raised, face hidden.

He hadn't realized the true cost of his alliance with the Obsidians. Though it wasn't with the ruling family, but rather another upstart like himself. He'd thought that'd been good, that they'd had that in common.

But at times, he couldn't decide if Unira truly wanted conquest or destruction. He shuddered. There was something about the look in her eyes, something dark and smoldering, that frightened him even if he'd never admit that to anyone. He'd never admit *anyone* frightened him, but certainly not some rural, scheming matriarch.

But most rural, scheming matriarchs were out for better marriage prospects for their children or perhaps a better price on grain.

Unira wanted souls.

She'd never quite said it so explicitly, but he was sure that was what she was after. Her requests for people as part of the payment for their alliance had at first seemed bizarre, and he'd assumed she kept them as slaves. It grated his every nerve—his clan did not deserve to be slaves to hers just because of the status of their birth.

So he'd kidnapped members of other clans. Unaffiliated folks his people could track down. He'd made it work.

But after his fourth or fifth payment to ensure her support, she had complained that none of the people in his deliveries had been mages, and he'd started to wonder. He'd begun to ask questions, to research. And he'd started to form a guess at what she might be doing with those he was kidnapping and shuffling off into her service.

There were ways... ways that were frowned upon, but still, there were ways to use people's souls to augment one's own power.

Andius smiled to himself as they slowed in front of the Bone Clan mansion where he'd taken up residence. The wagon headed toward one of the clan warehouses nearby, which he'd been magically insulating and locking for weeks now, thinking about this plan.

Lara would have been an excellent person to do his first experiment on, especially because she most deserved the possible side effect of death if he failed, but he was gathering an array of others to start his very own collection.

If Unira could do it, so could he. Oh, it would be convenient to kill them, and he always had that option. But how was he going to crush the Obsidian Clan and all the others—and lead the Bone Clan to the dominance and greatness it deserved—if Unira had a pool of magic exponentially larger than any one man could have?

If he had any hope of challenging the Obsidians—or, in truth, defending himself against Unira should they come to blows—he needed the magic of the best and brightest of the Bone Clan. The Contests did have it right that murdering all the others at the top squandered clan resources. He couldn't have them competing with him or interfering either, though.

So he would harness their power. Like Unira had done. Oh, and she *did* have magic, much as she played coy about it. Her son Idak could be an actor in this play as well, but Andius was certain it was only Unira pulling the strings. Hell, she was the one directing the stage.

For now.

The men dragged Faytou from the wagon. The little shit had gotten one hand through the hole and almost untied it all, but, fortunately, they'd made it in time.

The boy yelled out. One of the men clubbed at him to quiet him.

Andius swept his fingers in a circle, then closed them with a snap, casting an envelope of silence around the boy. Yes, these new fellows would not do. He'd send them as his "special emissaries" to Unira in the next shipment.

He unlocked the door, and his men dragged the bag in, tossing it into one of the cells he'd had constructed here. The whole place was the result of months of work, both magical and manual labor.

His brother, the ever persistent, stubborn little twit, squirmed the bag open again and spat at him. "I knew you were behind this. I can't even have a different opinion from yours?"

His smile was cold, grim. He'd never been under the illusion his brother would be an ally to him—they'd been naturally too different from the beginning—but he certainly hadn't anticipated this. "If your opinion is that a traitor is our rightful clan leader, then you are correct. You may not."

Faytou had gotten one shoulder out of the bag. "Where am I? What is this—" He stopped short as he saw the cell next to him. And the next. When he spoke again, his voice was weaker. "Clan Leader? Is that you?"

"It is I, child, yes," replied Cerivil. "And there's no point in arguing here. The magic is thick around us. Can you feel it?"

His brother didn't appear to try, just scowled at Andius, one eye apparently blackened from the excessive violence. Really unnecessary, if they'd have just followed his instructions. "You cesspool snake. You're worth even less than I thought you were."

"Such friendly words from a political prisoner," he mused.

Both shoulders had emerged from the sack now, with much effort and a few winces. "I can only assume that there is nothing I can say that will change your plans."

"You are right about that, you pesky little dung-eating ant." He smiled, more genuinely now, and turned away to head for the door.

"You're leaving? Just leaving me here?"

"For now. The sun will be up soon. There will be questions to answer, concern to fake." He waved a hand in the air.

"You're a coward. Rounding up everyone who disagrees with you? Shutting us up in cages? It's pathetic. You're supposed to win people over!"

"Oh, I did that too. I put a lot of effort into that. And where did it get me?"

"You didn't try to win Lara over."

"Why should I? She had a duty. If you ask me what's pathetic, it's dodging your responsibilities, especially if they've come upon you fairly." Of course, they hadn't. But people didn't know how far his elimination of political opponents went back, and ideally, they were never going to.

"Women are people, too, you know, Andius."

He laughed. "I might not be as quick as you, little brother, but I'm not blind."

Shaking his head, he left, ignoring the shouts at his back. His brother did have a way of getting under his skin, despite being barely more than a child, so it was best not to dally. He'd slip, and Faytou would sense his victory.

Even now, he hated to concede the boy had a point. He hadn't wasted time on Lara not because she was a woman, but because she'd always suspected the truth—that he'd been involved in killing her brother Myandrin. He wasn't an evil man. He just knew what he wanted, what was truly best for the clan, and he was going to get it whether anyone else liked it or not. And he had carefully invested his time along the way.

Considering the way things had gone, though, perhaps he *had* underestimated what she would do. If he'd just killed them *both* in one go, he'd be clan leader already.

Anger at himself welled up inside, but he tried to find calm as he made his way to the communal hall for breakfast, waving, smiling, and asking after each person's family. His usual friendly façade—but behind it, he was still steaming. Yes, he should have just killed them both and been done with it. He'd thought marriage to Lara would provide him with even more legitimacy, and one more death was one more way to be caught, but he had the benefit of hindsight now. How could he have known Lara would steal the Dagger of Bone? He'd expected she would resist marriage a little, sure, but that? No one could have guessed.

The situation was a shame, yes, but perhaps this was a good realization—that he had some share in the blame. If he'd been more ruthless, more decisive, the matter could be settled already. And with less bloodshed. And he'd be one step closer to being free of Unira's yoke. Yes, he should have murdered Lara along with her brother when he had the easy chance. He should have been more merciless, more cutthroat.

Well, it was never too late to learn his lesson and apply it to his work.

*Chapter 4*

# Missing

The dirt road out of the city was empty. Which was good, because Daridian had had enough of people for one day. Maybe for one lifetime.

If he didn't have a duty to his sister and his father here in this horrible land, he'd be tempted to go find a cave to hide away from humanity for a while. But alas—he did have a quest. Two quests, now. Father's orders would be obeyed, stupid as they were. They always were.

He'd passed the city walls a few minutes back. As the night wrapped around him like a cloak, his certainty grew that no one was following. Maybe they didn't know yet that he was gone. He'd vanish, like a wisp of steam in the wind.

A few more miles, and he'd be certain.

The Salt City was now at his back, thank the Great Spear. Each step took him farther away from these liars. Father would rue the day he'd ordered Daridian and his sister Sha'lien to this awful place.

At least he hoped. He kept waiting for the day Father regretted his foolhardy, impulsive orders, but it hadn't arrived yet.

And it should probably remain in the distant future. Because if Sha'lien died here, he would make sure Father regretted ordering him on this mission.

He gritted his teeth as he walked. The truth was that he could only do so much. One knight couldn't steer a foolish king, and one knight was not an adequate bodyguard, truly scant protection in a foreign land. Even if he was a skilled warrior and Sha'lien's brother, being her protector hadn't granted him access to her every minute of the day or to her wedding chamber. As they all could have known. Oh, he was going to do what he could to keep her alive, but he wasn't blaming himself. Or kidding himself.

She could already be dead. And he could already feel himself beginning to hate this place forever.

Regret stirred as he passed the dense homes of the city's hinterlands. He should have left the city to follow Sha'lien's kidnappers straight away. Dallying with the girl couldn't have made a tremendous difference since he wasn't hot on their trail, but... it'd been foolhardy. Impulsive.

Perhaps he was more like Father than he wanted to believe.

Houses faded into empty fields, long ago harvested. He kept his hood up, his eyes locked straight ahead, and his ears perked. As far as he could tell, no one followed.

Not even the girl. He was vaguely disappointed, and then angry at himself for being disappointed. Did he need yet another person to evade? He had plenty. He was much safer and better off this way. Nothing to regret.

That was a lie, of course. He could lie to himself, but kisses didn't lie. Not ones like that anyway. The Spark couldn't be faked.

He had heard the stories. Few people were lucky enough to find the flint to their steel, their soul's complement, and here, he'd brushed up against his. One of his. The stories always claimed there were a handful of perfect matches out there in the world. The chance that he'd ever meet one, though, let alone meet one of them here, was very, very slim.

And he'd walked away.

He gritted his teeth harder. Sha'lien needed him. He had orders. He had achieved his primary objective—obtaining the sword—but he'd also been ordered to see his sister safe and settled. And she'd gone and gotten herself kidnapped.

But he would find her. Bring her back to the city. Get on the nearest, fastest ship, and get out of this place. Get home. Home was where he wanted to be, where he belonged. He'd deliver the sword to Father, and the man would finally respect his youngest son.

Lies.

He hated lies, especially lies he told to himself. Finding her would not be easy, and his journey home would not be soon, most likely. He had never belonged anywhere, least of all at home.

And, well, respect was hard to come by everywhere, wasn't it?

His jaw was beginning to ache, so he forced himself to relax it and ran a finger along the hilt of the sword hanging at his hip, absently checking that it was still there. Steel spiraled from the white jewel at the hilt to its plain, round pommel, a twisting silver cage guarding the wielder's hand.

It was a clanblade, something truly special, they said. Rare. They said the magic of dragons was imbued in this blade. That was what had sent Father initially off on this line of thinking.

That perhaps if they had the magic of the dragons as their own, they'd rule the seas like no other. They said the clanblades were stuff of legend.

Of course, people also said they could cure the pox with silver coins on the eyes and curse one's enemies with a throw of bones and innards.

People were liars.

One universal truth about humans—all liars. Did dragons lie too? Maybe he'd find out in this cold, desolate land. He hated liars, any species, any land.

He'd met many such people at every port. The promises changed with the locale, but the falsity didn't.

He hadn't felt anything strange—or magical—when he'd resorted to drawing the sword against those ruffians in the street. Of course, peddlers of lies would probably say he simply wasn't gifted with the very special magic that allowed them to feel its power.

Perhaps true. But awfully convenient.

Magical or no, he'd stolen the sword anyway. Even if he hadn't had orders from Father to do so, he'd have done it anyway. If they'd wanted to keep their fancy sword, they shouldn't have crossed the Annikyre. They shouldn't have crossed Annikyre royalty.

And they definitely shouldn't have crossed him.

He had planned to wait until he was about to leave for home, with Sha'lien safely settled, before he'd made his move to take it. Of course, he'd warned Father a few dozen times that they could punish her for the theft, if they left her behind.

But Father had just scowled those heavy dark brows at him and thundered him out of the hall with his shouting. He wanted the dragon magic. He wanted a diplomatic union. He would have them both. From the same clan. Only a dolt would tell him that both at the same time were impossible, whether it was the truth or no.

Daridian had heard he was a dolt enough times that it had lost meaning. He never even got around to pointing out that a diplomatic union with a clan you'd just hamstringed by stealing their heirloom sword might not be the most advantageous match.

He'd warned Sha'lien, too, but she hadn't listened either, too caught up in the idea of escaping Annikyre for a foreign land. Or maybe she hated her life so much that she didn't care.

A woman's boisterous laugh drifted across the fields from a farmhouse, a dim candlelight flickering in one window. The girl had laughed, too, when it was all said and done. Dark and sweet and musical. He'd hear that laugh in his dreams.

His family had always been more annoyed with his quips than amused by them. So it was a shame to have such a short acquaintance with someone who actually got them. Clever, she'd called him.

Clever.

Not clever enough, or he wouldn't have lost Sha'lien in the first place. And not even to Pearls. What did these black-clad Obsidians want with her anyway?

If he were truly clever, he'd have figured out a way to keep her safe, a way to steal a sacred sword without getting her in trouble. And he had been planning to look for a way. Once the wedding was over, by the summer, he'd thought maybe he could hire someone to do the deed and perhaps he could have gotten out of it without suspicion.

But that wasn't how it had happened. Sha'lien was gone, dragged from the courtyard by Obsidians into their dark carriage and driven away. And he was fleeing to the woods with his tail between his legs, relying on his mask and a stolen sword for protection.

Which reminded him—it was high time he removed the mask. Its magic had protected him enough.

Wearing it, people thought he couldn't see much if anything, but in truth, it gave him a supernatural vision, wider and more detailed than his eyes alone ever had. His sense of movement sharpened, and he could see—or maybe feel—the air move about him, even behind him.

It wasn't the only magic the mask granted, but it alone would have been enough. The masks were a great gift to all the great knights of the Annikyre. It was perhaps his greatest honor to have earned one, even if six of his brothers and two sisters also had. None of them were here now, to judge him, but he knew what they'd say.

He was alone now, thank the Spear. Fields were starting to turn into meadows, marshland, and forest. Scrubby grass and sad, emaciated trees lined the road on both sides.

By the time he reached his destination—the foothills—the woods would have taken over. That'd be better both to hide and to survive. But he was far enough now that small clusters of trees were appearing. A particularly large grouping by the side of the road caught his eye.

Reaching it, he ducked into the stand of trees and went still—listening for anyone he might have missed out there in the fields. Wind rustled the leaves on the trees, and the only sounds of humans were faint and carried to him over the distance.

He removed the mask, cloak, and sash, tucking them into his pack as he withdrew a plain black garment he'd regrettably had to steal on his way out of the city. Crossovers, they called them. The Annikyre wore no such garment, but here it had been the most common, among both the wealthy and the poor. All that differed was color and fabric, and often enough the color was boringly the same among every member inside a clan.

He tied the black belt at his waist and stepped out of the trees. Just like that—a common man of the Empire of Six Clans.

Well, except for the sword. He'd have to find some way to disguise the thing. Or hide it. It would draw attention, and the white jewel would stand out. Especially since he had traded a sea of white-robed fishmonger Pearls for a throng of dark-robed miner Obsidians. Or something like that.

He'd read up on the Pearl Clan, not these Obsidians who'd interfered. Not that they'd had adequate time to prepare for this whim of a mission. Father had gotten the idea in his head to ferret out all their secrets through Sha'lien's seduction, to use her information to dominate trade at every port in the Great Eyrie Seas. And why not steal something while we were at it?

It was a stupid plan. Sha'lien had only basic training as a spy. If she survived the theft of the clanblade—or this kidnapping—sharing Pearl Clan secrets with her family would likely cost her her life. Father was a fool, and this was a fool's errand. He had a feeling, though, that Sha'lien either didn't care, or perhaps was planning on simply not sharing the secrets, so as to survive once the marriage pact was sealed and she was out of Father's clutches.

He sighed as the sand and rocks crunched under his feet again. Behind him, the Salt City receded further into the distance. He'd reached the edge of the massive river basin that the city called home. Maybe he could make the hills tonight if he kept going.

If he had to hide in a wilderness, it would have been nice if it could have been the wilderness of home. The jungle might be more dangerous, but he knew it better than this. He knew its sounds, its moods, its hisses and sways. It wouldn't betray him.

This land might. Or it might surprise him.

Either way, he wasn't going home anytime soon. Not without justice or Sha'lien safely married—or blood on his sword to avenge whatever they might have done to his naïve little sister.

But it was a different woman his mind kept drifting back to as he trudged on.

The oddly empty feeling carried her all the way home, from the edge of the Pearl District where she'd had her meeting to her father's mansion in the Obsidian District. She should have been more concerned about the blood she'd failed to fully clean up, but she could hide her hands in her sleeves, and it all faded to black in the end anyway.

Once home in the Obsidian mansion, she slipped in a side entrance, cleansing her hands in a fountain outside first. Then she took a lesser-used staircase toward her room. She quickly changed from her slightly bloodied, ripped dress, to a simple black crossover, as all in her clan wore in one fashion or another, then quickly washed her as much blood as she could from her dress, dumping the pink water out into the gardens. She might still get questions from Uli or others, but the fewer obvious reasons to ask questions, the better.

Next, she headed to her father's study.

The latch of the door was quiet. The dusty scent of old paper, leather, and ink crowded the tiny room. It should have been utterly dark, so she'd picked up a candle from the hall, but strong beams of moonlight fell across her father's desk. Neat and empty as usual.

She set down the candle on the desk and withdrew Chosko's sword from her skirts, untying the pommel from the loops designed to conceal long blades.

She examined it one last time. The scabbard resting across her palms was dull and black. The Obsidian Clan had six sword smiths. Chosko's sword had been crafted by the worst of them. Not a terrible blade, but not the finest craftsmanship.

In the moonlight, the sword didn't look magical. A fair, slightly curved blade. A chip of obsidian in the handle—for show. It didn't add dragon magic like the glittering dragon scales in the clanblades.

The sword did have some magic. It had to. But she felt nothing.

Where did the swords get their power? How? That was a closely guarded secret of the sword smiths.

She let another second slip by, two. Waiting, hoping she'd feel some twinge. She drew the blade a finger's length from its scabbard. The steel glinted, perhaps a scowl, perhaps a wink. But again—nothing.

No tingle of magic in herself.

That stolen kiss had been more magical than this sword as far as she was concerned. She didn't know how magic should feel. And she probably never would.

Sure, it was amusing to torture them—both her father and the fools. But every time she'd held these pilfered swords, she'd waited, longed to feel the zing of magic. A throb of power in her veins, a flash of blinding energy, something.

Maybe a tickle. She'd settle for a nauseated gag.

But it could have been a walking stick or a cooking spoon for all the shivers it gave her. Perhaps she had no magic.

But she also couldn't bring herself to stop trying, if she didn't know for sure. So she'd tried six times, found the Bladed Women, passed their tests...

She'd keep trying. There was no definitive answer, so no reason to stop.

Yes. She would confront Father, but not over the test like the Bladed Women wanted. She'd confront him over this.

Because asking out of turn could cost more than any reasonable person might expect. She'd paid a steep price in the past for her questions. And that was not something she could explain to any of them.

Would the masked man understand if she told him about the secrets of her past? Probably not, but it didn't matter because she wouldn't see him again anyway. Sad, though. It'd be nice to know if he'd understand. Until she heard his words of rejection, there was always that off chance that he might not reject her, that he might understand.

As dark as she could be, deep down, she was an awful optimist. Painfully so. That same part of her was dreaming, wondering, thinking about jolts of heat and old fairy tales... speculating if she'd see him again, despite what he'd said.

Sometimes, fate had other plans. Or perhaps it was the Twins that might be weaving the strings.

The moonlight out the window seemed to flare brighter for a moment. But by the time she'd glanced up, it was normal again.

She sighed. Well, she'd given this blade its chance. Just like the others. Why she'd ever thought up this idea was beyond her. If she was ever to smell or touch the truth of magic, it wouldn't be with this weapon.

That was only fair. She had stolen it after all. Perhaps all of the stolen blades knew, and they just didn't want to play with her. They were supposed to bond with their owners, so she wasn't surprised.

Only deeply jealous.

She never kept them, of course. Any of them. She lowered Chosko's sword onto her father's desk with a wretched smile.

Then she turned without a word and headed for the solarium to wait.

Bitterness mixed with a strange satisfaction that could be achieved no other way. They wouldn't give her her own blade. Hadn't even thought to try.

So of course, she had no choice but to take them herself.

Solariums were supposed to be about the sun. Cold and dark weren't the atmosphere they usually boasted about offering, but as she sank onto a lounge near a lovely view of the sky, she felt some of her tension ease. She wasn't going to be sleeping right now, so she might as well be here. Try to relax, until her father found her. Thoughts of the sword dead in her hands, the lively kiss, the brush with death swept through her mind. The impossible challenge demanded of her by the Blade Women... The intensity of these experiences wasn't going to fade easily.

She had her candle. And a book. With time, she'd have the sunrise too. This darkness often felt more familiar than the light anyway.

As she flipped to her page, the smell of the plants and soil filled every deep breath, and more of her tension slipped away. The room was utterly quiet, so every page turn seemed melodramatically loud.

She must have been more tired than she thought, because she was drifting to sleep, and as the book fell to her lap, she could have sworn she saw a glimmer of light in the sky. Again, like a flash from the moon. But that made no sense. Maybe a falling star? At the moment, the night sky looked a bit purple as it crawled toward dawn, but nothing actually moved.

A wave of exhaustion washed over her, her eyelids heavy, and she plunged into sleep.

When she opened her eyes, she still lay on the lounge, but the air was warm and smoky now, the solarium gone. Above her was only the starry night sky, except the stars were brighter than she remembered them. No moon.

Dreaming? Odd. She never dreamed, unless they were nightmares.

A flash of light streaked overhead. She rushed to sit up, then gaped at the scene around her.

Perched on a rugged mountainside, she was fenced in by craggy black boulders. A primitive road snaked through a pass. Stragg's Beard rose high in the distance—but much closer than she'd ever been. By Seluvae, where was she?

The flash of light streaked by again, and all thoughts of the volcano slipped away. By the Twins—that was no flash of moonlight. Or even a falling star.

It was a dragon. A tiny one, shining white like the moon itself. It couldn't be bigger than a cat, but it cast a halo of light in a pool around it where it perched on the black rock just before her.

"Who—" she started.

The sound startled it—or maybe it had been waiting for her to speak. Because it darted away again, between two boulders and down toward the road.

She jumped to her feet and started after it. The rocks were treacherous, though, and she'd barely made it a few steps before a different figure appeared on the road below. She froze and ducked down. If this was a dream, it could hardly matter if she was seen, but she had the vague sense she wasn't supposed to be here. Wasn't supposed to see this.

The man was tall, unusually so, and power radiated off him in crushing waves. The heavy hood of his cloak obscured many of his features, and the rest were hidden behind a mask.

She caught her breath, then covered her mouth with her hand. Was she trying to hide or not?

Him. It was the masked man from the alley. The charcoal gray oval covered his entire face except for the eyes, where she could see dark orbs that glinted, bronzed skin around the edges. Him.

The bright, snowy dragon flitted from behind the rocks now, over the man's shoulder. It flew straight for her, so close she had to dive out of its way and—

She woke abruptly as she tumbled off the lounge.

From the hard stone of the solarium, she groaned. Of all the things she could worry over or dream about, her brain had generated a volcano, a tiny Pearl dragon—for what else could it be?—and the masked man. What was that even supposed to mean? A glowing white dragon? Did she hate being an Obsidian so? What would the Dark Dragon think of such nonsense?

How sad her life was, that one little kiss embedded a man in her mind so.

Grumbling, she jerked up, righting herself by degrees and curse words. Good thing she hadn't damaged the book. Carefully smoothing its pages, she extended a hand to set it on the lounge and stopped cold.

The same tiny shining dragon from her dream was perched on the lounge now. It was no bigger than a large dog, and this one had whiskers that twitched, as if judging her. Behind it, sweet, cold air blew in from an open solarium window.

She twisted her lips. Who had opened the window was pretty clear. The question was more like... why? What was this little creature doing here? Was she so tired she just thought she'd woken up, but she was still dreaming?

One way to find out. She dropped the book and lunged toward the creature. If she could feel it, touch it, that would prove something, right?

But it was too fast. It was back out the window, little more than a streak, a burned bright memory on her eyes flashing yellow in the darkness. She ran to the window and searched the sky, but didn't spot it. The stars seemed dim and far away.

Sighing, she sat on the lounge for a few minutes, head in her hands. She was just exhausted. This would all make sense once she'd dealt with Father and relaxed enough to have a good sleep.

But she made no such move. She set aside the book, however, and pulled a sketchbook from under the lounge. First, she tried to draw the dragon, but how could she best draw a thing that shined in darkness? She didn't have the right tools to do it justice, and she wasn't a great artist by any means. After two or three attempts, she turned to trying to capture her stranger's face. Or his mask, rather. Her eyes kept drifting toward the sky. Looking for the dragon or trying to decide if it had been real—she wasn't sure.

She didn't close the window though.

Eventually, she set the unsatisfactory drawing aside and took up the book again, but she just stared at the words, then checked the sky again.

The sun rose. Color filled the glass overhead with bright ribbons of purple, orange, yellow, and blue. No streaks of light or glowing dragons caught her eyes, and with time, she drifted toward sleep.

*

It must have been sometime around mid-morning when her father found the sword on his desk, because Sutamae awoke with a start to the sound of the solarium door crashing, iron shrieking against iron, glass shaking in its panes. The air was warmer now under the sunlight, yet a cold sweat broke out on her forehead. She sat up at the sound, rubbing her eyes as the book tumbled to the floor.

"Why? Why do you do this, Sutamae?" His voice was a dragon's growl. His hulking form wore his usual black crossover, Chosko's sword in his hand and his own swinging at his belt. Her eyes caught on the sword for a moment. Elix's Obsidian blade was dark, the jagged dragon scale embedded violently in the crossguard, the scabbard a dark grey with holy symbols faintly painted in black along its length. A thing of beauty. It only made her more jealous.

She blinked at him and rubbed her eyes, struggling to wake up. He waved the sword at her, the belt still attached and swinging wildly. His eyes were bloodshot, and a vein throbbed in his temple.

"Don't you dare ask what. You know very well what."

She paused. When she finally spoke, her words were as cool and collected as a frozen mountain lake. "I thought you might care to know who in your service is a fool."

"By testing out each and every one yourself?" He made a noise of disgust, tossing the sword onto the lounge beside him as if it made his skin crawl. Maybe it did.

She shrugged, not looking at it. "You should be grateful."

"Grateful? *Grateful*? Sutamae—" He seemed about to say something deeper but stopped. "You're just like your mother."

She'd thought he'd long ago lost the ability to hurt her, but at that, her head jerked back like he'd slapped her. "No, I'm not."

"You're egotistical, vain, manipulative— Stop me if you disagree."

She only frowned harder.

"Oh, and a liar." He let out a huff of breath. "Why do you keep hurting yourself this way?"

"I'm not hurting myself. I'm hurting them."

"Not anywhere near as much as I see it hurting in your eyes."

Silence fell across them for a moment, as pleasant as a blanket woven of needles. She held her words till she could take it no longer, but finally the only thing she could think of burst forth.

"I'm not vain."

He rolled his eyes. "Foolish girl. I'll never understand you. You should be finding a *husband,* not wasting yourself over nothing." He turned to go.

"I drank some ale and chained him in his room so I could steal his sword." She bit out the words, staring daggers at his back.

He froze mid-step.

"And that's *all*. I'm not a fool." She was a lot of things, but she wasn't her mother. A fool? Well, maybe. She wasn't a fool in the way he thought, though. "And I don't waste my time."

She'd let him believe the lie long enough. Perhaps the Bladed Women were right. She might not be ready to ask what Varene wanted her to ask, but she could be honest about this much. More honest than she'd been before.

The moment was utterly still, but she thought she could feel the venom drain from the room. He sighed, but she didn't miss the tension releasing from his shoulders.

"You should teach your swordmages to not get their swords stolen so easily," she said.

"You should find yourself a better hobby." He started walking again.

"You forgot the—"

The door slammed shut. The sword glinted malevolently at her.

She stood up. "Well, *I* don't want it."

The door stared back at her, completely apathetic.

"Father!"

~

Grel *had* been humming to himself before this morning went awry.

All right, a lot of things were going awry lately, but he was determined to be positive. Make the best of things. Wallowing in misery didn't get anybody anywhere, did it? And it had been a good morning so far. He'd woken with Smoke cuddled against his shoulder, and the tea had been especially good, even if his mother had stopped by to hassle him—again—about the overgrown length of his hair.

He'd been on the verge of whistling, even, as he headed from his rooms to the library to work.

But his father's grim look and gruff order to go to the solarium and "deal with her" was enough to kill that mood and drop him into a mood of weary caution.

"Her" was usually one of two people in this house, unless someone new had arrived. Oh, and how he hoped someone new would arrive. Without Nyalin, the days had grown even duller than they'd been already. But his mother had taken an extended shopping trip in the countryside around the time Raelt had vanished so he didn't even have their annoyances to break up the monotony.

So that meant that "her" had to be Sutamae.

He eased the solarium door open quietly, trying to get the lay of the battlefield before he went in. Sutamae sat slumped on a lounge with her head in her hands, the morning sunshine outlining her in gold but leaving most of her in shadow. A rush of relief hit him, until his eyes caught on the sword that sat beside her on the lounge, its dark scabbard like a wound, vibrating in the silence.

The door opening further finally squeaked a little and revealed his presence. When she met his eyes, hers were red. From crying? Just tired?

He ran a hand to brush his much-too-long hair out of his face as he shut the door behind him. "Good morning, sister." Even all this didn't fully drain the cheeriness in his voice. In truth, that was a hard thing to do.

"Good morning, brother," she replied.

"Father sent me to deal with..." He hesitated. He couldn't very well just say "you." "The situation," he settled on instead. As he strode closer, she rose and stepped over to the window. Not exactly running from him, but not looking him in the eye either. He stopped just short of the offensive blade and ran a hand over his features, unable to hold back a sigh. "Oh, Su."

"I suppose he thinks this is funny." Her voice was tight from where she looked out, over the rooftops, over the Obsidian District.

He pursed his lips. "I doubt that."

"Then why else would he send you here?"

"To be hurtful? That seems more his style. To see if this stops you from this... pursuit of yours."

She was silent for a moment. "Perhaps he is beginning to hand down his responsibilities to you. He should hand down more. You're beyond ready. Maybe then the sword smiths will—"

"I don't want to hear it." He grimaced. She even turned to glance over her shoulder at the uncharacteristic sharpness in the words.

The sword smiths hated him. They should have begun making a new clanblade for the Obsidian Clan's heir apparent—him—ages ago. Grel was beyond old enough. He had no idea what their problem was, nor how to fix it, so he just kept on being the best son and heir he knew how to be.

It hadn't changed anything so far.

"Fine, fine," he muttered, picking up the damn stolen sword. "I get your point. Neither of us is perfect."

"That was not my point." She turned fully and took a step toward him. She held a book in her hands, but he didn't think she'd been reading it. "I'm not like Mother, giving compliments that are secretly designed to cut."

He shook his head. His sword—or lack thereof—was a sore spot for him. It was hard to see or think of anything clearly when the matter came up. How it could be anything beyond a source of hurt, he had no idea, but, clearly, he hadn't quite understood her.

She tossed the book to a nearby chair and folded her arms. "I don't know why you and Father are so determined to think ill of me."

"Ill of you? What should I think?" He waved vaguely at the sword. "Is this supposed to speak of virtue?"

Her features darkened, eyes closing off. Whatever he'd said, it had hit home. It had hurt. Good. Much as he didn't like the feeling, maybe then she would stop. "Fine. Think whatever you like."

"Go on, tell me then. Where did you get this one?" He drew the blade slightly from the scabbard, but the particular, somewhat sub-par design didn't ring any bells to him. The magic in the sword hummed under the surface, not especially strong, but there all the same. Who was he to judge the workmanship? Whoever she'd stolen this from had a sword, and he was one who didn't. He ought to wish for this much of a sword.

He didn't, though. A clan leader needed a clanblade, and a clanblade needed to demand respect. And this blade... did not.

"I got it at the tavern." She waved a hand vaguely in the air.

He rolled his eyes. "I meant from whom?"

"I know what you meant." She lifted one shoulder, then let it fall.

"I can't return this if you don't tell me who you got it from."

"Father always figures out who on his own. You don't think a complaint will reach him in an hour or two? Or does it take a few days?"

"Is that part of your fun?"

Her arms flew to her sides, hands balled into fists, and she stepped right up to him now. "It's not about fun."

"What is it about then?"

"It's about justice."

His eyes searched her face, brow furrowed.

"I don't expect you to understand." Scowling, she gathered up her skirts and headed for the door. "You've made it clear that you don't want to."

"Sutamae—" he started, regret stirring in him. He shouldn't push her if he didn't really understand. He'd need the wisdom of Seluvae to understand her, and he didn't have it, but he ought to at least try.

She opened the door and silenced him with a glare. She opened her mouth as if to say something, then stopped and seemed to rethink it. "Any word from Nyalin?"

His shoulders slumped further. "No."

"I was out looking for him. Last night. Before..." She waved at the sword.

"Any sign of him?" He swallowed, a dubious hope kindling in his chest.

"No."

And he let the flame die. They stood in silence for a moment. Wherever Nyalin was, if he had the help of a dragon, it ought to be okay. He ought to be okay.

But Grel sure would like to have known for certain.

"The sword belongs to Chosko," she said quietly. "You can give him the same advice I did, if you dare."

He raised an eyebrow, not hiding his surprise. "And what advice was that?"

"That it is wise to ask a lady's name upon first acquaintance."

Grel snorted in spite of himself. "The idiot."

"Exactly what I told Father. He should be grateful, really."

"I doubt he'll ever be that."

"I'm testing the ranks of your mages, Grel. Their judgment leaves much to be desired."

His expression hardened. "I'm sure when the Mushin infiltrate the empire, seducing us all into idiocy via high-born daughters of clan leaders, we'll be highly trained to resist, thanks to you."

She pursed her lips. "Female spies have swayed wars since there were wars. You should perhaps consider that threat a little more fully."

Some of the venom drained out of him. Perhaps the proper way to deal with the Sutamae "situation" wasn't just to return the sword. Maybe that was just what his father was hoping, that he'd go a step further and find a way to stop Su's exploits completely. Someone ought to, and his father wasn't trying.

He took a deep breath. "All right. True enough. I'd still rather you come up with a way to test them that didn't involve... well, you know."

"What?" She tilted her head, in mocking innocence.

"Don't play dumb with me. We're nothing if not honest with each other."

Her head jerked back, as if he'd struck her, and he stared for a moment. Weren't they? Everything in her expression said things were perhaps not as simple as he thought.

He opened his mouth, searching for a way to ask, to understand it all, but before he could find the words, she turned and slipped out the door of the solarium. Clearly, he was mistaken about something. Very mistaken. The question was—about what?

He glared at the sword in his grip. He knew there must be consequences for this—for the impropriety, for a swordmage to allow himself to be so easily disarmed. For the stupidity, frankly. There had to be. But that didn't mean he was going to enjoy it.

Shaking his head, all chance of whistling or humming quite gone for the day, he stalked out. "Might as well get this over with."

The next night when the emperor returned, it was with a similar abrupt appearance, an eagle screeching down via the opening in the top of Yeska's cavern. The golden and brown bird swooped to land just by the fire, rapidly transforming into the man Nyalin both knew and didn't know at all.

He did no better this time at hiding the simmering anger that erupted at the sight of… his father. Supposedly. Weren't fathers supposed to be there? Not lie to you? He had some vague notion, but what did he know about what a father was supposed to do, between Elix, Dalas, and Pavan.

"I am afraid the news isn't good," said Pavan in a huff. He was panting, as if he'd flown as hard as he could to get here. "I can't stay long."

Lara stood. "Is he all right?"

His eyes darted between her and Nyalin. "I can't confirm. You say the dragon says he is alive?"

"Yes." She took a step forward. "But you were there—why are you asking me?"

"Because I got inside. Tiny as a mouse." He made a creeping gesture with his fingers. "They hadn't even bothered to ward the place. They say he's in his rooms, but there is no one there. Empty. Wherever he is, it's not in the Bone Clan mansion."

Lara's jaw tightened. "Andius is going to pay for this."

"Indeed. As I said, I must return. I want to check a few other places in the city. But I must add, another has gone missing, a Bone Clan swordmage named Faytou. Andius's brother."

Nyalin swore. "Faytou is our friend."

"And supporter?" Pavan asked.

Lara winced. "Yes. Unfortunately. We should have brought him along."

"There was no time," Nyalin pointed out. Faytou had vocally supported him and helped him during the final round of the Contests, but that didn't mean he'd wanted to join them in exile. He looked to the emperor. "Did you see any signs of who might have been involved? Could this Unira woman you mentioned have done this instead of Andius?"

"Or perhaps on his behalf?" Lara asked. "It seems a crazy risk on his part. What is he thinking?"

"I don't know what he could be thinking." Pavan shook his head. "I found no clues, so I can't say for sure who might have been involved. I will look for more. As to Unira…" Raising his eyebrows, Pavan hesitated before continuing. "Unira's family is quite powerful among Obsidians. The silk farm estates to the north generate a great deal of wealth for them. This isn't the only way she's been vying for power."

"Wait—the silk farms? Isn't that Jylan's family?" Nyalin asked.

"Yes. Her courting of Grel is not unrelated to their quest for power. But it's one of the more appropriate, legitimate ways to do so."

Nyalin swore. "I knew there was something I didn't like about her."

"It gets worse than that. I also believe they are interfering with Grel's acquisition of his sword."

"What? How?"

"The sword smiths have power all their own," Pavan replied. "They answer to no one."

"Does Elix know about this?" Nyalin demanded.

"Elix's hands are tied. He took a risk by giving you that sword, even. Who knows what the price will be for that?"

"You're the damned emperor," Nyalin snapped, still standing. "And he's the leader of our most powerful clan, and you're getting your arms twisted by this unheard-of woman?"

"Yes, as a matter of fact, we are." Pavan's voice remained calm, but he seemed to be struggling to keep it.

"You're supposed to be in charge." Nyalin jabbed a finger at his chest.

"So am I," Lara said mildly.

He gritted his teeth. "That's different, and you know it."

"I... am sorry for not giving you the details of the threat sooner," Pavan said, a little grudgingly. "And I am sorry the situation is not better."

"Why are they bothering to meddle with the Bone Clan if they are powerful enough to cause you and Elix problems?" Lara asked. "Are they worried Nyalin could be tapped as an Obsidian heir if Grel is disqualified?"

"Disqualified? He won't be disqualified," Nyalin growled. "He can't be."

She bit her lip. "If Andius is in their pocket, maybe there's some way he can help them. Or do they simply see him as the weaker candidate, to keep our clan weak? Which also helps them."

Pavan nodded gravely. "I think you will make a fine leader of the Bone Clan, Lara. Might I suggest it could be all of those things at once?"

She winced. "This is... worse than I thought."

"I'm sorry to be abrupt," Pavan said, "but I'd like to return and continue the search. I brought you a few more... things that might be useful." He held out a leather pack stuffed with supplies, and Nyalin reluctantly took it. "As much as I'd like you to come back as soon as you can... I don't know what will be realistic. I was an orphan on my own, once, you know... Life in the wilderness is not always easy." He seemed to want to say more but stopped himself.

"Is there anything we can do right now?" Lara asked. "To help my father?"

"I don't know specifically. Contact the council. Make a move for power. That would be my recommendation. Let Andius know he is not unopposed."

"Couldn't that also encourage him to hurt Cerivil?" Nyalin's voice was weak, but he had to say it.

Now even Pavan gritted his teeth. "If he does, Lara won't be the only one who will make him pay."

"But that won't help us if Cerivil is harmed." Or dead, he thought to himself.

"True," Pavan admitted.

"I will think about what to do," Lara said. "Thank you for... for everything."

"It is..." He glanced at Nyalin. "It is the least I could do."

Nyalin pursed his lips and said nothing.

"I will be in touch when I can," Pavan said, and, in a blink he changed. Off again, wings flapping as he disappeared, high into the darkness of the cavern.

In the awful silence that followed, he met Lara's eyes. "What the hell are we going to do?"

"Tomorrow, we'll head to the Obsidian lands to see if we can find that house. We need all the help we can get. Maybe there will be something there that can help us. And I can think about our options during the flight..."

But she was rubbing her chin as she sat down on the log by the fire, frowning, and he knew she was going to be thinking about it every moment until then as well.

By the Twins... Cerivil. Faytou. He closed his eyes and, in a rare moment, muttered a prayer. Dala, protect them.

He, too, sank into a seat and only then remembered the bag Pavan had brought them. Mildly angry at having to think about Pavan for one more minute, he flipped the leather flap and yanked open the drawstring neck of the pack. This one was much higher quality than the one from yesterday, something they could use on the road.

Steaming right out the top was that familiar smell. He couldn't help but take a deep breath of the bread, the gorgeous aroma that seemed almost like it was from another lifetime, or two lifetimes ago.

"Ooooh," Lara murmured, eyes going wide.

He broke off a piece and handed her the loaf. "Feast, my lady. Let's see what else is in here."

The pack also contained a blank book, a bottle of ink carefully wrapped in silk, a quill, and a sturdier pen. Even more than the bread, this made his throat tighten a little. It was a strange and confusing reminder that—although he had thought he hadn't had a father, and indeed, in many ways, that was the truth—Pavan *had* been there. He *did* know him. He *did* care. There he'd been in plain sight, but in his disguise as the baker Dalas, a frequent fixture in the Obsidian mansion's kitchens. To stop thinking of them as separate people was going to be hard.

He set aside the writing implements and found some more practical supplies, hard yellow cheese and fresh apples, and two books. One was titled *Transformation Magic Fundamentals* and another *A History of the Mushin*. Studying them a second longer, he wondered if these weren't directly from the emperor's—his father's—collection. They seemed to his interests, and the bindings were far finer than he suspected most shops would bother to carry. Nor were magical treatises commonly sold. Further down, two transformation charms glimmered, their colors ever-shifting in a pouch, the fabric so thin he could see the colors through it.

Was this a message? An implication—learn about these for when you follow in my footsteps? Or simply a father grabbing some books for his son who clearly loved them?

As he bit into the sharp cheese, he paged through the one about transformation. His ability to teleport had helped them evade Andius once. Maybe he could do it again, but if not, transformation could be a less dangerous back-up option.

"The place where Andius kept us before the Contests," he said quietly. "The one we escaped. Do you remember quite where it was?"

She gazed at the ceiling, thinking. "Do you think Da could be there? It would be a place to start. I'm not sure I remember."

"I'm not sure, either, but I bet we could walk around and see what we could recognize."

"That's a long shot though. And even if we find it, what do we do? Storm in, swords drawn, and slaughter everyone?"

"Um... yes?"

"Maybe... But captives can die first in that sort of situation."

He held up the transformation book. "Perhaps there's a stealthier approach. But even if that's the plan, Andius could suspect we might try that. There ought to be wards. Mages guarding Cerivil. We'll need multiple back-up plans."

"And help. We're going to need help. Could Pavan come with us?"

“I’m... I’m not sure I trust him enough yet for that. He never seems to be telling us the whole story. Always keeps some of his secrets tucked in his crossover.” He rubbed his chin as she frowned. “Maybe after our trip to the ghost lands, we can stop and see Grel? He could help.”

“We shouldn’t get him involved. It’s not fair to him. He’s struggling enough as it is.”

He hated the implication of that. That Grel, heir apparent to the powerful Obsidian Clan, was too weak to help. “We are going to need all the allies we can get. And like it or not, if what the emperor said about this Unira is true, he already *is* involved.”

She paused to think, chewing. “True. We could contact Pyaris too.”

“Four of us would be better than two.”

“Dammit, Andius. Why did you have to do this?” She stared into the fire.

“We’ll figure it out, Lara. Like you said, we’re determined. There *has* to be a way, right?” He smiled at her crookedly.

She snorted. “You’ve been hanging around me too much.”

“On the contrary, dear Clan Leader. Never enough.”

*Chapter 5*

# Breaking Point

Dawn was just breaking when Nyalin heard the beating of wings. He sat up in the still quiet. The patch of sky visible from inside Yeska's den was a light purple, hardly full-on morning yet.

He'd been around the rushing water long enough that he could tune it out, push it to the background. But something was strange about the sound.

He reached over and squeezed Lara's shoulder, then shook it.

She cracked open one eye, scowling. "Hmm?"

"You hear that?" he whispered.

Beside them, Yeska raised her head, her brows furrowing.

Instincts flaring, he scrambled to his feet, to a fighting stance. He'd woken up far too many times to... inconvenient accidents. Ones that his father would have him believe weren't exactly accidents. He wasn't sure what he thought about that—and there was no time to think about it now.

"What are you doing?" Lara whispered. "Preparing to flying kick a flock of geese?" But she stood up to, drowsily mimicking his stance.

Because even if he didn't know what the hell he was doing, or he'd possibly had a bad dream, she was ready to fight beside him.

He couldn't help but smile at her sleepy, blinking eyes. "Geese? Out here?"

*It is not geese.* Yeska's voice was riddled with alarm, which cleared more of the sleep out of Lara's eyes. *In fact, I do not know what they are. At least six flying creatures approaching. I do not recognize them as creatures of this world.*

He bent and grabbed for his mother's sword. Lara cocked her head. The beating of wings had grown quieter and moved away from the lightening sky of the cavern opening.

*They are by the water. Can you not sense them, Lara's mate?*

"I'm not sure I want to," he murmured, blushing at her turn of phrase. Every instinct said hiding would be better than fighting right now.

Lara drew her blade and moved toward Yeska's side. "Look—the silver."

He eased to her side, looking where she pointed. There was a bit of a tunnel between the waterfall itself and the larger area of the cavern, but even in the dim dawn light, he could make out black figures emerging from the water, landing on the stone. Two—no, three. Where were the others, then? At least three more were somewhere else...

In each of them, two silver points of light glowed, like eyes made from the stars stolen from the sky and imprisoned in darkness.

"I don't like this," he whispered.

"They're approaching our wards..."

One seemed to slash claws right at the spot Lara had cast the ward. Blue light flared, and she winced. The cedar scent of her magic cut into the air. "This is not good. That should have stopped or at least slowed them."

Nyalin glanced over his shoulder and his eyes widened. Three dark forms now perched on the lip of where the cavern opened to the sky. Blocking their exits?

Yeska raised her head, bellowing at the creatures in the tunnel. *Be gone. This is my domain. You are not welcome here.*

Hissing was all they got in reply. And the sudden swishing of air. He had time to grab Lara and pull her down. Years of honed reflexes got him something at least, besides paranoia and excessively light sleeping.

Yeska, however, could not move so quickly. Arrows swished over their heads, several clicking off her bony plates, but at least one made it through. The dragon staggered back a step, immediately rising to her feet and her fullest form, wings spreading. It was all Lara and Nyalin could do to get out of the way.

And then she roared. To his shock, the tunnel was swallowed in fire, the flames white and wild in the darkness. It was not fire like in his hearth or his campfire, no, it felt caustic and dry, almost like he could feel the moisture being sucked out of him from even being near it. Power as white hot as the sun roiled through the tunnel, and it was so bright, he had to look away.

The creatures in the tunnel screamed.

*They are injured, but not dead. These arrows are not mere projectiles. They carry poison. It should be minor to me, but to you? I cannot say. We should flee.*

"Flee your home?" Lara stammered, even as she moved toward the dragon's leg and started to climb.

*Unless you fashioned yourselves shields, armor, or some other defense against poison arrows?*

"There must be some spell..." he started. But the image of the creature clawing through Lara's wards flashed through his mind. He climbed up behind her.

"See if you can distract the ones up there with light while we fly by," Lara said. "Or maybe fire? I'll try to close the tunnel off to keep them away from our stuff. Once we're out, I can try to close the top too."

*Nyalin, can you sense if they are part spirit?*

Again, his instincts recoiled at the idea. "Once we're in the air." Maybe...

He focused instead on drawing the magic from Lara, centering it in himself. He held out his hand, light flashing around the mouth of the cave as Yeska leapt into flight.

The arrows rained down around them anyway. He gasped as something sharp pierced his left thigh.

Then they were in the clean morning air, gaining altitude. He tried to hold on, but his hands slipped for a second, his head spun. He usually hung on with his legs, too, but the searing pain in his left leg worsened when he tried.

*Nyalin is hit.*

Lara let out a stream of expletives. And then a stream of magic back in the direction of the creatures. "How many left?" she yelled.

He tightened his arms around one of the smooth spikes on Yeska's back and closed his eyes. Yeska did not recognize them, and she had been alive for a few centuries, even if she was younger than some other dragons. Could they truly be creatures of spirit?

The sky was blessedly empty of energies, aside from the two of them and the dragon blazing into the deep blue. But behind him, he could feel the tinge about them—silver, yes, but also a watery reddish glow, not at all like the afterworld he was familiar with.

And yet. And yet—unmistakably not of this world. He could tell that much.

Only three creatures followed, and in his mind's eye, they did not have wings. They just floated up after him effortlessly, or like they were swimming. Like they were used to being underwater. Strange. There was no sign of the other three creatures from the tunnel.

The pain in his leg flared, and he hoped Lara had collapsed the whole cavern on them.

Another swish brought him out of his spirit's eye and back to the world. By the Twins—these creatures had arrows too.

"They are from another plane," he shouted over the wind. "And they're not done firing arrows."

"Faster, Yeska!" Lara shouted.

A dragon could only pick up speed so quickly, however, and these things didn't need to catch up to keep firing. Glancing over his shoulder, he could see they had arms as well as wings, but even in the growing dawn light, they seemed to be made of pure blackness. No other features showed, except those creepy soulless eyes.

He turned back, trying to think of how they could best fight them. Just the simple act of turning made his head spin more. He instinctively tried to grab on with all four limbs and grunted hard at the resulting pain.

"Nyalin—hang on. We'll outpace them soon," Lara said.

"I—" he started.

But he would never finish whatever he had been about to say. Because just at that moment, an arrow sank into his right shoulder, between the shoulder blade and the spine.

His limbs weren't his own. The pain was like a fire igniting his body. Even the wind felt excruciating across his skin.

He had a vague sense that he was sliding, falling, before the pain became too much. Everything became too much, and he fell into oblivion.

"Nyalin! No!" Lara's words exploded out of her as she saw him slide from Yeska's back out of the corner of her eye.

Yeska was already diving, but he was falling fast.

"Can you catch him?"

*I can't turn that fast. But I'll try.*

The creatures were still behind them. The wind hurt like hell, so Lara sheltered behind a bony plate, trying to peek out and see what was happening, but the wind made her eyes ache and water.

Looking down was a little easier, but also more painful.

Her stomach felt like it had left her body, falling with him as he plummeted. They weren't catching up. She groped for a spell to help, but everything she could think of was useless.

The river swallowed him, his form vanishing in a blink. By the Twins. Maybe the water had softened the fall?

Or would it drown him, or carry his body to where they couldn't find it?

The rage that exploded inside her seemed to move outward, to hijack Yeska from her dive. This was their fault. Those cursed, horrifying, evil creatures.

As one, almost without thought, the two of them rounded on the creatures together. Magic and fire intertwined, like a flash flood or a forest fire, consuming the three creatures almost in one moment.

Only ash fell to the ground.

Exhaustion overwhelmed her. Her eyelids drooped, and Yeska had to adjust her flight to keep her unsteady body from falling.

But no—she had to find Nyalin. "What if we lost him, Yeska?" her voice was raw, like she'd been screaming. Had she been?

*We couldn't have followed without dealing with them first. We could allow you to be poisoned as well.*

*Can you sense him?*

*I... No.*

*What?* She clung tighter now, Yeska responding to her unspoken need to go faster. To dive. *There—in the water.* She pointed.

A pale brown form floated in a large swell in the river. Yeska scooped up Nyalin in her claws and deposited him on the shore.

Lara was already sliding off her back. She stumbled in the pebbles of the riverbank, more rocks than sand here. But she didn't care. She hit her knees at his side.

His lips were blue.

Thank all Dala's dreams she'd learned those healing spells. She splayed her hands across his chest.

*He's dead, Lara.*

*He can't be. He can't die.*

*No, he—*

She pressed her ear to his heart. Silence. No—it couldn't end like this. She worked the spells anyway, siphoning power into him hungrily. Desperately.

After a second, his form flickered.

*More, Yeska. I need more.*

*I'm going to need a nap.* The dragon sighed as she lay down heavily on the riverbank.

Another flicker. Light glimmered at the edges of his eyelids.

What was she doing? She had no idea what she was doing. Her instincts refused to stop to think.

She pulsed him with power again. "Come back to me, Nyalin moLinali!"

A moment later, his entire form vanished, leaving only an imprint of his body in the pebbles of the shore.

She gasped, caught somewhere between irrational glee and terror.

*Is that a good sign?* Yeska asked.

*I don't know. It seems like a good sign.*

*That your dead mate has now entirely disappeared?*

*If he can activate his mother's powers, then he's not dead, right?*

*He's not alive, though. Certainly not in this world. I can't smell him. Or sense him.*

*I'm trying not to fall apart here.* She sat back on her heels, chewing on a fingernail. Dala's light, her whole body hurt. Where was he? Would he ever come back to her? If he stayed in the afterworld too long, could he get stuck or lost there?

Did being a quarter spirit-demon-whatever make you easier to kill—or harder?

He flickered back into existence again.

"Nyalin!" She dove at him but hit the rocks instead. Gone again. She swore. Panting, she realized the air was filled with the scent of her magic and his—cedar and blackberry.

*Daughter, the lock. The lock spell—it is gone.*

*By the Twins.*

*Perhaps his death made the spell lose hold—but his anchoring to this world is unusual and you used his connection to you to bring him back.*

*Do you sense any other enemies around us?* They were terribly vulnerable right now. She wracked her brain to try to remember what Pavan had said the danger was. But it was all a blur.

*His powers are fully unlocked now,* Yeska put in. *But if he is too weak to harness them, to gain control... I fear for what it will mean.*

She needed some way to truly anchor him here. Her voice hadn't worked. She'd barely had a moment. What did she know about these strange powers? He could move between this world and the next. At first, it was only a mental crossing over, but the second stage allowed for a complete physical crossing over and changing location in both realms.

Fortunately, he had seemed too exhausted from the attack to move around. So at least he was staying in one place. Somewhere. That simplified things. She'd healed him quite a bit, yet he still seemed so weak.

Golden goddess, how could she have been so stupid. *Yeska, do you think there was a curse in the arrow? Like they tried at the Contests, and when Raelt attacked him?*

*If he flickers back, we must check.*

There wouldn't be enough time—unless she found some way to hold him here. Yeska had mentioned their unique connection. They'd felt it before they'd even known each other. The shock of energy when they touched wasn't quite so frequent now, and it surprised her less, but it hadn't gone away entirely.

Could that be the key?

She positioned her hand near where his had been the last time he'd appeared. And waited.

In truth, it could have been hours or days. It was probably only a few minutes until he finally reappeared again. She seized his hand like an eagle plucking a fish from the ocean.

The power of the shock this time made her arm spasm, an involuntary yelp escaping her lips. That got his eyes open. She almost let go automatically but stopped herself just in time.

"Lara," he whispered. "Are you..."

"I'm fine," she said too quickly, bubbling over in relief at hearing any words out of him at all.

*Looking for a curse...* said Yeska.

"That one really stung," he muttered.

"Yes." She fidgeted. Holding this iron grip on his hand was odd. "Nyalin... Yeska says the lock is broken."

His eyes finally focused a little. "Is that why I keep ending up somewhere else?"

"I think so. I don't know what to think, but I have a feeling that's not good for you. I think you need to stay here with me."

"I'd also prefer that." A smile ticked up the corner of his mouth.

"Let's keep a grip on each other until you're a little stronger."

Found it—in the shoulder.

"Yeska says there's a bit more healing we need to do. It might be a bit hard for me. Can you hold my hand and whatever I do, don't let go?"

"That, I can do." He shut his eyes, but his grip around her fingers was tight.

"I don't know if that will be enough to keep you here, but..."

"Got any other ideas?"

"No."

"Me neither. It's okay. I'll hold on like a badger. Go for it."

She nodded and closed her eyes. The curse this time was weaker than the others, although some dark part of her wondered if it had had less time to take hold because he'd died. Had he really died? And come back to life?

*Yes. Death means something different for creatures like him.*

*He's not a creature; he's a person.*

*You know what I meant.*

She felt like she was groping around in a dark, muddy basin, looking for the cork to pull to drain it all out... This didn't feel like the last curse. It felt less evil, less caustic. And the spell was so small, she kept losing it. Just a little farther, push just a little more and then—

"There, broken." She let out a happy sigh. "We should be able to actually heal you now..."

When the healing spells were complete, he sat up, eyes clearer now. "Thank you, Lara. I thought I was dead for sure for a minute there."

You were, Yeska insisted.

"Semantics," Lara grumbled. She let go of his hand without thinking as she started to stand up. "Yeska, did you say you'd need a nap—"

But he was gone again. She swore. A moment later, he reappeared—and dove for her hand himself.

*I am quite tired. But I think I know who can help us,* Yeska put in. *I think we need to get there sooner than later, then I can rest. Climb on.*

⁓

The morning was growing late when there was a knock on Sutamae's bedroom door. Yawning, she considered not answering it. But when it came again, softly and with that certain cadence that identified it was her brother knocking, she jumped to her feet.

Grel had a bit of a rueful smile on his face as she flung open the door. "I thought you were in there."

"Sorry. What is it?" Although her heart lifted at him stopping by, she also had to wonder if this was yet more about Chosko's sword. The stirring dread made her words brusque.

He held out a folded piece of parchment. Inside, in delicate ink, a fine hand requested the pleasure of her presence at a celebration of the Feast of Coal. A minor holiday that nobody cared much about, and many didn't even celebrate outside of their clan. At least half of that had to be due to the fact that coal was a powerful but hardly festive substance. But among Obsidians, it was quite a source of wealth.

And also, apparently, an excuse to throw a party. The letter was signed by Jylan. She raised an eyebrow. While she had attended feasts before, Jylan had never invited Su directly, even though she had been courting Grel for quite some time. Did that mean things were getting more serious? "Is this...?" She glanced quickly for the details. "Is this for this afternoon?"

"It's right now, basically," he said, nodding sheepishly. "Want to come?"

Her eyes widened. Normally, she avoided these things. But... something concerned her about the invitation. And if she snubbed Jylan's only invitation, she might not receive another one, which would limit her opportunities to observe the woman courting her brother. Su wanted the best of everything for Grel, even if they didn't always get along or understand each other. And she was not at all sure if Jylan was sincere in her pursuit or if there was some pretense at work. "I need a different dress."

"I can give you thirty minutes."

"Done. I'll be ready."

She was already dashing to the wardrobes as he walked away. No amount of extra effort would be enough to impress Jylan and her fashionable ways. And anyway, Su's clothes were about function. But there had to be something suitable here. She'd been to more than one such feast.

Not that fashion and function couldn't be combined, but more often than not, it was a major undertaking to acquire a garment she found acceptable, and then another major task to alter it to her specifications—whether via seamstresses or doing it herself. Most skirts didn't come with loops strong enough to conceal swords, for instance. Some clans like Nyalin's Bone Clan even wore such short crossovers that they simply wore pants with them. But longer crossovers with skirts afforded more opportunities to hide things, and her modifications were more about adding secret pockets than stunning visual details to impress other women. Besides, she found herself drawn to the simple, the traditional, the classic...

Jylan, on the other hand, pulled off bold brush strokes of dramatic new dresses every time Su saw her. Admittedly, that wasn't very often, and, until now, it had only been at major feasts celebrated in the emperor's palace itself. But Su would never measure up to her.

Su shook her head and began to change from her casual crossover she often wore around the house.

Grel was waiting when she made it downstairs. With a few servants in tow, they headed out into the street. She sensed irritation —a rarity, coming from Grel. Was it directed at her? Perhaps it was best to dunk the proverbial dragon and address the obvious. "Have any trouble with Father's errand?

I'm... uh, sorry about that."

He didn't flinch, although his eye twitched slightly. "No. I think he was rather expecting it by the time I got there, although he wasn't suspecting me."

"I'm sorry that fell to you."

"Don't make me have to do it ever again, and I'll forgive you." He gave her a tight smile.

"No promises," she said. If she was practicing being more honest...

He sighed. "If you're just doing this to get on Father's nerves, I can give you plenty of other options."

"On Nyalin's behalf?" She snickered. "You seem to have a whole range."

He smiled, laughter in his eyes. "We stirred up a bit of trouble, didn't we? More than I expected."

"Our family is good at that, I think."

He raised an eyebrow as he slanted a confused glance at her, but before he could ask more, they'd arrived. The residences of the largest families of the clan were not far from each other.

Jylan's family's mansion was different from Su's own. Most people would probably deem this mansion more beautiful, more fashionable, and newer, with slate and slick walls shining cheerfully in the sunlight.

Su preferred her home with its cracks, its character, its history. The Obsidian Clan mansion towered a massive four stories, topped on the corners with grumpy, craggy old spires. It had served as an old fortress, existing since the Salt City was just a small trading post.

Another fortress had once existed where this mansion now stood, but it had been a simpler wooden structure. Had it burned down, or was that just a fanciful tale that children had told at the time? She'd have to ask Grel later.

Wide, pale stone steps managed to look inviting and pretentious at the same time, surrounded with an array of ornamental trees, delicate lanterns, and statues of the Dark Dragon. Did dragons require statues? If so, someone should tell her father. The Obsidian mansion was notably absent of such ornaments.

She and Grel were quickly admitted. The air inside was breezy from the street and filled with musical bells tinkling in a distant room.

The hallway led to a pair of carefully carved oaken doors that depicted the woods and mountains of the Obsidian hinterlands. Servants swung the doors wide, and they were thrust into a bustling hall packed with three times as many people as Su had expected.

Grel pulled her to the right, leading her by the elbow.

"Where are we going?"

"To the food, obviously."

She snorted. "I figured it was to your beloved."

"She'll find us eventually."

"There are so many people here. Don't we need to make some introductions?"

"We do. But all this fighting between you and Father has me famished. I don't know how you do it." He gave her a wink.

She glared back, but she deserved the comment, so it was playful too.

Long tables of ordinary oak held heaps of food. Translucent silk hung from the edges of the tables in red, gold, black, orange, and white. Mostly Obsidian colors, although the red was crossing the line a little. She knew it was silk—what else would Giran's family have? Of course, Giran their patriarch was long dead, and people said his wife kept the family afloat, but Su didn't know her name specifically. She'd never seen the woman at any of the emperor's feasts.

She and Grel scoured the tables. He'd devoured two roasted pork skewers before she finally selected a small pile of some dried apricots, figs, and exotic spiced almonds. At her nod, he headed for Jylan and didn't wait to see if she'd follow.

Of course, what else was she going to do? Talk to random strangers? She laughed to herself. That was what got trouble started. Greeting Jylan first was necessary either way, so she followed.

The object of Grel's affection was gorgeous as always. Jylan stood near a potted tree, gazing into a glass of wine she swirled in her hand. A man stood next to her, but his back was turned, and he was speaking to what looked like a servant. Black silk wrapping a nearby pillar highlighted Jylan's unique features—skin like moonlight and eyes that sparkled like black diamonds, if Su was being charitable—and like coal if she wasn't. It was the Feast of Coal after all.

Admittedly, Su had never seen Jylan in her own element like this, as host. Their encounters were primarily at the emperor's large feasts, the most important ones where the clans united to celebrate. And most of those had occurred when they were both much younger. Su had avoided those—and the people sure to show up at them—for years now.

No one had ever asked why. Time would tell if Su would regret making an exception this time.

True to form, Jylan's dress enslaved the eye, with novel lines that were both lovely and surprising, sheer fabrics combined with solid ones of different shades to create an unusual, shifting effect. Woven between the ebony and charcoal tones were ribbons of amber. And also crimson.

She raised an eyebrow at the red. Could a dress be an act of rebellion—or treason? Few people sought to flout the societal traditions of exclusively wearing the clan's colors, and this was such a subtle way and referencing the coal fires that the Feast centered on. But it felt like a transgression nonetheless. Only the emperor wore red, not any of the clans.

Su also knew Grel wouldn't chastise the girl for the minor rebellion. Jylan knew that too. That bothered Sutamae all the more.

"Grel!" Jylan exclaimed as the two of them approached. The man beside her still hadn't turned to face any of them, occupied with the servant. "You're a sight for sore eyes."

"Not anything compared to you," he murmured with a smile. Grel turned toward Su quickly. "Jylan, may I present my sister, Sutamae."

"Strength to you," Su hurried to say, ducking her head with a curtsy.

"Sutamae," Jylan said. Her smile reached her eyes and made them twinkle a little. "It's so good to see you. I wasn't sure if you'd make it."

Hearing Sutamae's name, Jylan's companion turned, finally joining them.

"Neither was I," she said. The statement begged explanation, but Su just smiled wider. A sudden awkward silence descended on them, a kind Su was partial to causing and not partial to easing. And perhaps she was a bit too distracted to formulate what to say as her eyes drank in the man at Jylan's side.

Green eyes glinted beneath sharp black brows and raven hair. He stood like a marble statue, which made the liveliness in his eyes all the more impressive. And on his hip—a sword. He couldn't have been much older than Grel, and the presence of that blade both stung and impressed her a little. She must have stared just a little too long, because his growing smile indicated he'd read her reaction.

"Forgive my sister," said Jylan's companion smoothly, bowing. "She's too much in love to think clearly and introduce me."

Jylan cleared her throat. "My brother," she said, voice polished and hard as glass. "Idak naGiran moUnira."

She tried to think of what she knew of him, what misdeeds she had on record. Nothing. She cleared her throat now, to buy herself time to formulate a response. "Jylan, how can you have such a handsome brother, and yet I swear I've heard nothing of him?"

Jylan's lips twisted. "Perhaps that's his good fortune."

"It's certainly not my good fortune," she replied, expression serious.

Idak's eyebrows raised. "Jylan, why invite this lovely young woman only to snipe at her?"

Jylan narrowed her eyes at her brother, but then slipped an arm into Grel's and forced a smile. "I apologize, brother. It's just I'm so used to having Mother to swipe at." She looked at Su, although her eyes looked more loathing than imploring. "Do forgive me."

"Forgotten, of course." She bowed her head. "Where is your mother? I should like to greet her too." That was a complete lie—but also the proper social protocol.

"She stays back to manage our estate in the north," said Jylan, her tone unmistakably cool. Both men's brows frowned just a touch at her words.

"I see the elaborateness of this Feast has stressed my usually sweet sister," Idak said.

"Hardly, I'm fine—" Jylan started.

But Idak ignored her, to Su's surprise, his attention suddenly fixed on Su alone. "Let's leave it to her intended to soothe her, shall we?" Idak held out an arm.

She glanced uneasily from Grel back to Idak. Grel had drawn to Jylan's side, naturally, but was looking like he was regretting it.

"I'll show you around." Idak stepped toward her. Grel opened his mouth as if to stop them, but Idak was already looping his arm through hers and steering her away. "And you can point out for me whom to avoid," he murmured in her ear as they moved away.

"How do you know that I'll know who to avoid?" she said, eyes laughing. He was right, she supposed, but it still seemed presumptuous.

"You look like the right sort." His eyes locked with hers, and her breath caught in her throat.

"What sort is that?" she breathed.

"Elite. And the sort who does not tolerate nonsense from anyone."

Well. Right on one count at least. Thankfully, he didn't require a response. And just like that, he was leading her around like his oldest friend, giving out formal introductions to all sorts of folks. More than a few eyebrows raised, and Grel's eyes bored into her back, but she couldn't help smiling. Perhaps it was just a bit of harmless fun to torment Grel so. People liked to talk, and if she was honest with herself, it amused her to make them talk. This was just one more thing to say about her. Was there something going on between the misbehaving daughter of the clan leader and this young man from the country? Was that what they thought he was?

In truth, she didn't know who they thought he was—or who he actually was. She should really be more careful. At least she'd gotten his name first. The thought made a corner of her mouth quirk up.

The bell rang to signal the beginning of the meal, and he didn't release her arm. "Grel will be sitting up here with my sister. I'm not sure what she had planned for you, but... would you care to join me? I'm sure they won't mind."

"And if they do, can they really argue with you?" She smiled. "Aren't you the ranking male of your family?"

He shrugged. "Yes, I suppose you're right. I don't take many liberties with the power though. I respect my mother too much for that. Besides, I have better things to do. Responsibility is boring."

"Like what?"

"If you sit with me, I'll tell you. If you leave me for your brother, though, I'll be too busy being heartbroken to explain much, I fear."

She snorted, but her cheeks flushed. Fool, she thought, make him work for it. But hadn't she had enough manipulation and subterfuge for one lifetime? Couldn't she be straight for once? She found herself nodding. "Lead the way."

He grinned and pulled her along. At the head table—disturbingly near the center of it, to the side of Grel and Jylan—he pulled out a chair. Damn. This man... It was far too soon to consider these things, but did she want this sort of seat at a table? A very important table?

Sitting there once could lead to her sitting there for the rest of her life, if she wasn't careful.

"Tell me the truth now," she insisted, turning to him. Time to stop being generous and starry eyed and find that horrible underbelly he was hiding somewhere deep down. If she had any special talent, it was finding such dark corners of people's souls. "How can I have never heard your name before? Don't you ever come to the city?"

He smiled, his eyes twinkling. "Why, Sutamae, I'm deeply offended. Do they keep you locked in that Obsidian mansion?"

She laughed. "Me? Not exactly."

"Well, I prefer my family's estate to the north."

"I didn't realize there was a man of your age in your family. Though you find responsibility boring, I'm surprised they've let you dodge it for this long. My father has been shoveling work onto Grel for years now—even having yet to receive his a sword."

He looked thoughtful. “Well, on top of my mother’s wise oversight of our family’s holdings, my grandfather is still quite engaged with the estate’s affairs, even though he’s an invalid. But I don’t have much interest in estate management.”

“Neither do I.” Two glasses of wine were set before them, and she quickly took a long draught. She sighed and leaned back in her chair. “Where do your interests lie then?”

He frowned into the distance. “I’m a swordmage, as you might have guessed, but I’ve studied mostly on my own. I’m fond of the outdoors. And books. Beyond that... it’s a little hard to describe. A family industry, you might say.”

She quirked an eyebrow at him. “I thought your family’s industry was silk?”

“Among other things.” He flicked his fingers in the air, dismissing the question.

“Ambiguity piques the curiosity, Idak. Not the other way around.”

Laughing eyes swung to meet hers. “That is... a good point.”

“So be specific.”

“No.” His grin was veiled, mischievous. “So, do you take studies?” he asked deliberately.

“Changing the subject, are we?” She took another sip of wine, scanning the crowd to dodge those laughing eyes for a moment.

“Indeed. I like you, Sutamae, but there are some pieces of knowledge about me you’ll have to earn.”

She raised an eyebrow. She wanted to hate him for that, and for the way he leaned on one elbow, green eyes sparkling at her, a laughing smile on his lips. But she didn’t hate him. Far from it.

Dammit.

“Perhaps I could say the same thing,” she murmured.

They were both silent for a long moment, her looking out into the crowd, his laughing eyes studying her profile.

“So...?” he said.

“Yes?”

“What about you? What lights up your soul, Sutamae?”

“Oh. I’m not interesting.” Another lie. She winced inwardly. But let others reveal her reputation as they would. “Magical studies, no.”

“What about non-magical ones?”

“What difference does it make? It’s all meaningless anyway.” She waved it off.

"Young men like me all study the same things, but daughters of clan leaders are another matter. Humor me?"

She pressed her lips together before admitting defeat. "Well, I refused any more lessons in estate management a few years ago. Not only is it boring, but I already knew it well. How many times can you be instructed on the proper time to order chickens for the Feast of Souls before you remember? I can tell you the proper stores of grain for a variety of populations and seasons and time periods. Would you like to know how many cushions a woman needs to embroider before she can create one to a satisfactory level of quality?"

He snorted. "Yes, I would."

"Exactly zero. I am satisfied with not being able to do it at all."

He chuckled. "What else?"

"I like history. I'm reasonable with a harp. Philosophy." And there was the sword, but she always kept that bit to herself. It had come at too great a cost to speak casually about it. "Plants as well, at times." She groped for a way to be authentic with him. "And... annoying my family from time to time."

"A time-honored pastime." He smiled. "Your brother over there looks quite annoyed. Or is he just depressed?"

It was true. "I'd say he looks irritated, with a touch of annoyance and a dash of depression." Shouldn't one be more uplifted by the presence of their intended? Not that that status was official, but it was all but assumed within her family. Perhaps Sutamae shouldn't take it for granted.

Although, no couple got along all the time, did they? If her parents were any guide, no couple got along for any percentage of the time. Her mother's extended shopping trip had had quite a peaceful effect on the household.

"Do you think he's happy?" Idak mused.

"Happy?" She snorted. "Who is? No one is happy."

"If anyone is, shouldn't he be? Leader of the greatest clan, a beautiful, intelligent woman at his side."

"I suppose." She didn't point out the problem with the sword. If Idak didn't realize it, she didn't need to point it out to him yet.

"You're not happy?" His eyes bored into her.

"No, I'm not."

"I'm very sorry to hear that."

Her eyes flicked to his, surprised at his heartfelt tone. His gaze was trained on her, thoughtful. It showed no sign of wandering. She shrugged and looked away, dodging the intensity. "Here we sit. Pensive, meet unhappy."

He smiled crookedly at her. "I don't plan to stay pensive forever. I, unlike you, want to be happy someday."

It was hard not to smile back at such bald-faced honesty. And possibly naïveté. "I'm glad. But sadly, there's nothing to be done to change my sorry state."

"There's where you're wrong."

She raised an eyebrow.

"What makes you miserable, my dear? I'll remedy it."

"You can't."

"Is it a man? I'll talk to him."

"This isn't a man you can talk to."

"The emperor himself?"

"Worse. My father."

"Ah, well. Pensive and unhappy, meet stubborn."

"Yes."

"You're right, he doesn't much like me. Though it's been years since we last spoke."

"He doesn't like me much either, I'm afraid."

"I doubt that's true."

"You didn't grow up with him."

"Sometimes, the people who love us the most struggle to show us how they really feel."

"Is that so?" She frowned. Was there any truth to that? She had always assumed her father was as in control of his words and emotions as he was everything else in his life. A more complex reality had never occurred to her.

"My mother is still terrible at it, if she even loves me at all. My father could be warm and distant all within the span of a few minutes. I never knew what he really thought, but it seemed a struggle. And he died a few years ago, so we had fewer chances than most to get clear on things."

"I'm truly sorry to hear that too." Her own sincerity surprised her almost as much as his did.

He shrugged. "What does Clan Leader Elix do to make his daughter so unhappy?"

She sighed heavily. "It's a long story."

"We have time."

"Not enough."

"This banquet could go till morning."

"I won't be here that long."

"Got a late-night engagement?" He raised an eyebrow.

She rolled her eyes and shifted her knees away. So perhaps he knew more about her than he was letting on. "And just when I thought we were getting along," she said coldly.

"Did I say I have an objection?"

"No. But—"

"I care much less about that than about whatever it is that hurts your heart. Unless of course said nocturnal adventures are what hurts the heart."

"No." She shook her head. "They're not."

"Then forget I mentioned it. What does Elix do to sadden you? I—"

"It's private," she murmured. And who knew what he would think of her? She threw caution to the wind often enough, but even she didn't go around proclaiming her longing for magic to people she'd only just met.

He took a long swig of wine. "Let me guess, then. But you have to promise to tell me if I guess correctly."

She sighed. "All right."

"He wants to marry you to an old curmudgeon from another clan for riches."

She snorted with laughter. "As if a clan other than ours has enough riches to entice him."

He chuckled. "She's not afraid to tell it like it is. I like it."

"As if any curmudgeon would be willing to pay to put up with me."

He took another drink, eyes still crinkled with laughter. "All right, let me see... He wants you to cut this glorious black hair because you're competing with your mother's beauty, and she's jealous." He took a strand and curled it around his finger before dropping it again.

"That was just an excuse to touch my hair. Admit it."

"Guilty, it is as you say. She has an insightful wit. I like that too." He propped an ankle on his opposite knee and leaned back, assessing her. "He's afraid of the darkness in you, the power, and so he tries to keep you shut up in that little mansion of his, away from the world, from playing on the big stage, because he isn't quite sure what you'll do. And you can't forgive him for that."

She blinked, then hid her surprise behind a sip of her own wine. "Are you speaking of me or yourself?"

"Perhaps I know what I see because I see it in myself. I'm right. Admit it."

Chewing on her lip wouldn't delay the inevitable. "He tries. But he mostly fails at containing me."

"My mother does the same."

She frowned. "And yet you're here."

"She sent me."

"Ah, I see. On what mission?"

He grinned and took a sip. "Wouldn't you like to know? I'm not telling."

"Maybe I'll play a guessing game of my own."

"We might have to raise the stakes." His eyes glittered with laughter and a hint of suggestion.

"But our first game isn't finished. You still haven't guessed the ultimate cause of my unhappiness. Is this you giving up?"

He pretended to clutch at an arrow to his heart. "She skewers me with her words. But, somehow, I like that too. I never give up, my dear. And resolving any areas of your unhappiness is the one thing I am growing sure I'll never give up on."

Her breath caught in her throat. She was usually a good judge of character. Though they'd only just met, it seemed like he actually meant those words. Idak was definitely someone to be wary of if he could so easily win her over with laughing eyes and pretty lies.

And yet... when he leaned closer and drew her toward him with a crook of his finger, she drifted closer like a moth drawn to the flicker of fire. He leaned closer, his scent mingling with hers, until his lips brushed against the soft hairs on the lobe of her ear.

"Here's my real guess." His breath tickled, and she shivered. Her cheek brushed his. "You have magic, but your father denies it. And you rightfully hate him for that."

She reared back, staring. Then she managed to shake her head. It took every drop of her strength not to slap him, and she had no idea why.

His face fell. "I was sure I had it that time."

"I mean—no." No, it wasn't fair. He'd been more straightforward than almost anyone she knew, except perhaps Grel. She owed him what truthfulness she could pump from her dry well. "No, you guessed right."

His eyes lit. "Truly?"

"Please—don't speak of it here."

"I won't."

"But I just don't know for sure. That's what he denies."

"You mean, he refuses to check?"

She nodded, lowering her eyes.

Idak sighed.

"You win. Happy?"

"No. How could I be happy in the presence of your unhappiness?"

This man was too much. She turned away from him, pulling her chair back into the table and looking out at the crowd. Too many eyes were flicking their way. They weren't guarding their actions closely enough. Although... she supposed there was nothing truly to hide. A young man from a noble family flirting with another noble woman at a banquet was expected behavior, wasn't it? She hardly knew what people expected and what they disdained anymore. Probably because she'd never cared to learn very well.

He mirrored her, pulling close to her side as he faced out on the tables of people feasting. "I could check, you know."

She shook her head minutely. "If it's there, it needs awakened. A friend already checked, but the awakening...."

"Carries risks. And he isn't a teacher, this friend?"

"She. And no."

He quirked an eyebrow. "A woman? Did this woman have a... blade?"

She hesitated. Should she deny it? But weren't the Bladed Women the ones that wanted her to be more candid? Or did that only apply to her father?

He seemed to gather the truth from her silence. "Ah, she has brave, bold friends who like to break the rules. I find more and more to admire about you with each passing minute, Sutamae naElix moVanae."

Even though she shouldn't, she turned sharply to stare at him. "Admire? Don't toy with me, Idak."

"I'm not." He casually sipped as he gazed at the crowd, not turning. And it was true, his face was utterly serious now, even the hint of a flirtatious smile gone.

"You'd be friends with me? You'd... 'admire' me? For fraternizing with... well, you know. For... For—I'll admit it—wanting to become one of them."

His eyes flicked to hers, then back out at the crowd. "She longs for honesty, but grants it grudgingly. Are you trying to make me fall for you, or are you doing it unintentionally?" His perplexed frown seemed deeply sincere.

"What? I—"

"Unintentionally, then. I see." He put down his cup and turned to look her squarely in the eyes. "I am not toying with you. I'm the one with the blade in this conversation. I carry its power. Would I joke about that?"

She sat back in her seat at his sudden intensity. "Thanks for the reminder. What does that have to do with anything?"

"Only an idiot wouldn't want such power, if she could have it."

She whipped her face back to the crowd, struggling for composure, jaw tight.

"I don't want an idiot. For a friend or a lover or a wife."

Her jaw clenched harder, and ice sliced through her veins, her heart leaping higher in her chest. What in Seluvae's name was happening? How had she admitted so much to someone she knew so little? The air felt thin and hard to breathe. And Seluvae was the right choice to invoke, goddess of love and of darkness too.

And fear.

"Excuse me, Idak. I think I need some fresh air."

He leaned back, body casual but eyes no less intense. "I wouldn't deny you anything, my dear."

"I don't think you know me well enough to make promises to me," she said, her tone gentle and cutting at the same time.

"I don't think you know me well enough to know whether I can keep my promises."

"Right again."

"I do keep my promises, though. But go on. Get a breath and some sunshine. I'll be here, should you want to continue this conversation."

She held his eyes a moment longer, then strode briskly toward the grand archway.

*Chapter 6*

# Dark as Obsidian

The wind whipped through Nyalin's hair as Yeska lurched into the sky, sending droplets of river water flying. The dizzying wobble was not one of the better parts of flying. He clung to the bony spike in front of him, leaning against the one at his back, and hoped the cold sweat on his brow wasn't too noticeable. Considering he was soaking wet, it probably wasn't.

Lara clung to his hand, her arm reaching back, refusing to let go. He still felt woozy from... by Dala, whatever had just happened. Had he really fallen that far? Lucky the river had been there, or he wouldn't have lived.

*You didn't,* Yeska put in. *That's the problem. That's why the lock is broken. That's why you can't stay on this plane.*

No, it couldn't be just that. Yes, he was exhausted. But if he could rccover a little more, he should be able to control it, shouldn't he? He had been able to, at least a little, during the fight with Raelt and when they escaped from Andius's imprisonment.

*I figured it out then,* he replied. *I'll figure it out now.*

*Don't push it. You were just dead after all.*

*Well, perhaps I'll take a nap first.* He was still not quite used to Yeska's ability to easily read his thoughts, probably through his close relationship with Lara, but it was becoming a convenient way to chat in the air.

*On which plane?*

*Hmm. Concerning point.* Could he stay on this plane while he slept? Where would he wake up?

Lara's crossover flapped in the wind, pale and golden in the early morning sunlight. The world flickered again. For a moment, Lara and the dragon were gone and nothing but green sky surrounded him. The sting of her skin against his brought him back.

The air was cold up this high and stung at his eyes, so he kept his head ducked and was glad he didn't really need to see where they were going. But they weren't over Bone Clan lands anymore. Trees raced beneath them at an alarming rate. The forests grew hillier and taller, and finally the great volcano of Mount Stragg and his "beard" of vast lava fields came into view.

Stragg's Beard was a huge plain of black lava rock that flowed out and around the mountain. No one lived here.

No one currently alive, anyway. But he was starting to realize that the state of being "alive" might not be quite as straightforward as he'd have liked to believe.

*We are almost there. She waits to greet us.*

"Who?" Nyalin asked, swallowing.

*Nerutoa. The Obsidian Dragon.*

His stomach sank, even though he'd known she'd be here. He hadn't realized the Dark Dragon had a name. He swallowed, hard. The last time he had seen her was when Grel had made a last-ditch effort to get Nyalin properly taught and demanded he be seen by the dragon.

Elix had met the request, even if he'd scowled the whole time.

But it hadn't helped. The dragon hadn't confirmed his magic. But nor had she denied it. She'd simply... turned away. The effect had been the same as a denial, however. Everyone had interpreted it as evidence that he was empty of magic, a dud.

Well, that hadn't been entirely wrong. But it hadn't been entirely right either. In hindsight, the dragon's strange reaction made more sense than he could have imagined.

*We will land here, on the beard, and greet the matriarch.*

"The matriarch?" He frowned, his stomach outright rebelling now as Yeska dove into her landing descent. His exhaustion might have been multiplying things.

*She is far older and wiser than I. And she asks that we meet properly. I'm inclined to agree.*

"Of course," he muttered. Although, did he truly feel entirely cordial? He'd held at least some ill will for the dragon. She should have been able to see the truth, or so he'd always thought, and so she should have been able to help. But the truth had turned out to be more complicated than he'd realized.

And perhaps *helping* himself had been the only option, in truth.

His head spun a little as they met the ground, Yeska settling to let them slide down her smooth left side. Yeska's scales were so beautiful up close. Sometimes, he forgot to appreciate it, but the stark lava rock underneath her made for quite the contrast. She wasn't white, but she almost looked so here.

Lara held close to him, hand still gripping his like a vice. The last thing he needed was to blip out of existence now, so he was grateful for her determination to hold on.

The black earth was lumpy and uneven, and he steadied himself against Yeska's side. A wave of wind from just ahead alerted him of what was coming.

No, who.

Both he and Lara staggered as the ground shuddered beneath them, and he fell back against Yeska. The posture was a relief. He was too tired for this. He needed to sleep for a hundred years. If only he could be confident which plane he'd wake up on. Or if he'd wake up at all. What if he stayed on another plane so long that he just moved on to yet another one after that, like the truly dead would?

Lara had steadied herself beside him. Dust and wind battered his face, and he raised his hands to block it as the shadow before him grew. The world went still, and he cautiously lowered his arm, squinting up.

The Dark Dragon herself loomed over them, massive in height as she sat on her haunches.

In spite of himself, he went down on one knee, still holding tightly to Lara's hand. Lara remained standing but bowed her head. A strange feeling of gratitude was stirring in him.

Now that he knew about his father, the lock, all of it... None of the Obsidian teaching would ever have worked. In a certain way, Elix had been right; he *couldn't* have taught him, not without undoing the damn lock.

Only by leaving—and all that had followed—had Nyalin found a way through to his magic. So, the Dark Dragon's pseudo-rejection had helped him, in her own way. This life was also *far* superior to a life with magic and lessons and a bunch of Obsidians who hated him.

By the Twins. He hadn't felt lucky at the time, but perhaps he had been.

The immense dragon puffed once, and he realized he'd begun staring at the lava rock in shock. He looked up sharply at her.

Sunlight beamed out from behind her, around her neck, and glistened off the craggy obsidian scales and ridges that were slick and shiny, even with all the dust. Her face was too obscured by the sunlight, but she abruptly lowered her snout to his level, hot air blasting across and around the two of them.

*Welcome to Stragg's Beard,* said a gravelly voice in his mind. *The three of you are welcome here.*

"We thank you," Lara said, her voice as calm as if she were talking to a shopkeeper about the weather. "I thought dragons were territorial."

Nerutoa's great head swiveled slightly to look at Lara. *Her guardianship of the Bone Lands doesn't impinge on my guardianship here. We work together.*

Nyalin said nothing, just ducked his head.

*Boy. Why are you surprised at my welcome?*

He raised his eyebrows at the same time as he raised his head to meet her gaze. "I'm surprised you're welcoming me, not her. I thought... well, you didn't like me."

The dragon let out an amused puff. Or was that his imagination? *I just knew there was a time and place for you. This is it. That was not.*

"Well, I never thought I'd say it, but... thank you."

*No need. I defend the land, and we are going to need all the help we can get.*

He frowned. "Against whom?"

*Against the Mushin. They strengthen their numbers. They work to return. They poison the lands. Their own are nearly ruined. They will come to try to despoil this land again soon.*

"Why don't the clan leaders do something about this? The emperor?" Lara asked.

*They know. They just do not want to tell the people yet. But the people will need to be prepared. The Mushin have learned things. It will not be the same war it was twenty years ago.*

"War is coming?"

*Oh, yes. And it festers within too. You have felt the dark demon among you, have you not? At your Bone Clan Contests?*

He rose to his feet now. "Yes. Is there anything else you can tell us about it?"

*Not much. I feel the demon at a distance, poisoning my lands, like a thorn wedged in my scales.* Nerutoa raised her head and looked toward the horizon, a low growl rumbling in her chest. *The demon is a little afraid of the dragons. As it should be. It lives in the great estate central in my territory. The one known for its silk farms. The one we hate.*

"Who is we?" Nyalin frowned.

*Elix and me.*

He'd never thought of Elix actually communing with the dragon the way Lara did. But of course, he must. That didn't matter, though, he needed to find out more about the demon and these people. "Why do you hate it?"

*The woman manipulates, destroys, vies for power. But most of all, she seeks to destroy. She blocks Grel's sword. She summoned the demon.*

*That is the darkness I felt,* Yeska put in. *It is a demon.*

Nyalin looked sideways to Lara. "Isn't Unira the one with the silk estate? Could she be so powerful?"

"Could be." Lara looked worried. "If she could even block Grel's sword? I would have thought that impossible too. Why hasn't Elix confronted her or done something about it?"

*She manipulates. As I said. Elix is sworn not to tell, to protect those he loves.*

"Then why are you telling us?" Nyalin said carefully.

The dragon puffed up her chest, head rising. *No one can bind me. Not even Elix. I am the Dark Dragon.*

Nyalin couldn't help but smile at that. He opened his mouth, but there were too many questions to even figure out where to start.

*They have not told you the truth about many things. They are afraid of your true power.*

"Maybe they should be," Lara said quietly.

*I do not agree. I will tell.*

"The lock is broken, Dark Dragon. We're afraid." Lara's hand squeezed his a little tighter.

*This, too, will help us defend against the Mushin. You will see. The young Nyalin is freed.* The dragon let out a triumphant bellow. *We grow strong.*

"I don't feel strong," he murmured. What could the Dark Dragon know? How would he even know what to ask?

*Death will do that to you,* put in Yeska.

*Your gifts have allowed you to survive that which most cannot. But you are not indestructible. Your powers must be mastered, and as soon as possible, for all our sakes. I see you have Linali's sword, so at least there is that. Have they told you about the house?*

"No." He raised the blade, pointing. "The house on the hilt?"

*Yes. You've come looking for it, haven't you?*

"We'd planned to," Lara agreed. "Although the attack made us undertake our voyage... a little earlier than expected. Can you show us?"

*I can. You will need it; it will give you the time you need to master your power. Climb upon Yeska, and follow me.*

Su stopped as soon as she hit the sunshine of the expansive balcony, gulping in big deep breaths like she'd been suffocating in there at Idak's side. The scent of late-fall flowers perfumed the air, painstakingly gathered and put in tall vases along the balustrade as well as adorning the gardens.

Grel caught her arm, making her jump. "Sutamae—you can't."

"Where, by the Twins, did you come from?" She shook off the surprise. She'd already had enough acid in her veins; she hadn't needed to be surprised too. "I can't what? Stand here on the balcony?"

His frown deepened as he guided her further away from the main room. He lowered his voice. There was no one else in their immediate vicinity on the balcony, but it was certainly hard to know who could be just around the corner or below or above you. "You can't play your games with this one. Not him. He's dangerous."

She pulled her elbow away. "Leave me alone, Grel."

"Chosko is one thing, but Idak is too powerful."

"I'm not playing a game."

"Call it a test, call it whatever you want. But if there's a sword of his on my desk tomorrow, I can't just waltz in, judge him, and give it back. Father loves to ruin the lives of your conquests, but Idak is not someone he can touch. No one can."

"It's not like that." She stepped away from him, toward the rail. "I actually like him. He's been... surprisingly sweet. Gallant, even."

Grel blinked. "Sweet? Are we talking about the same person?"

"Well, I wouldn't expect him to be sweet to you. What do you know about him?"

"Not much. His mother has kept him locked up on their estate much of his life. Supposedly managing their silk farms. But he's got a dangerous glint in his eye."

She knew the glint he meant. She liked it. She said nothing, letting the silence linger.

Grel hesitated. "And I've... heard rumors."

"What kinds of rumors?"

"I can't be sure if they're true." His voice was barely audible, and he stepped closer. "But there's talk of... of harassment of villages near their estate. Some claim it's bandits, but others say it's Idak and his men."

"What kind of harassment? What could they possibly want to steal?"

Her stomach dropped. Unless it wasn't monetary valuables they were after...

"Selective kidnapping... But no one is sure why, in the rumors. It's very mysterious. People disappear. A few villages have burned."

She frowned. "Why would they—"

"I certainly have no idea. Villages are good for trade. Burned husks aren't good for much. Maybe they want the land? I suppose the captives could be forced into labor, but why not take all the villagers, then, and not just some?"

She scowled. "How do we even know this is true?"

"We don't. But he knows how to use that sword, and you can tell he's been in battle by the way he sits, the way he carries himself. Who's he fighting at that farm estate of his? They're far from the Mushin. You need to stay away from him."

"Really. Based on rumors? Conjecture?"

"Look, I'm just trying to help, and you don't always seem to be the best judge of a man's character."

She stiffened. The words stung, and she pursed her lips. "Maybe you're just jealous that he has a sword, and you don't."

As soon as the words left her lips, she regretted them, but her regret doubled when she saw the fissure of hurt in his expression. He opened his mouth, but no words came out.

"I'm sorry," she said quickly, trying to shove her own hurt down, even though it didn't feel fair. His own comment hadn't been kind, and where was her apology? Still, that had been too low a blow. "That was cruel and unfair. You deserve a sword more than any man I know."

But the darkness didn't clear. The damage was already done. Damn it. He shut his mouth, opened it again, closed it, and then sighed.

"Look, I'm not playing games," she said quickly. "I swear it."

"I just have a very bad feeling about this, Su. Something is wrong here. His family is one of the most powerful in our clan. He shows up from the country, never in town, and he immediately starts wooing you? After his sister has been latched onto me for years now? Don't you think that seems a little, I don't know, deliberate?"

She bit her lip. "Maybe. What are you getting at? I don't see you throwing off Jylan."

"I'm afraid it's a bit late for that."

"Speaking of judging one's character..."

He shook his head. "Sorry. That was... unkind of me. Sorry."

"I'll forgive you if you forgive me."

A corner of his mouth quirked up. "Deal, little sis. Look, just please be wary. And careful. Make sure he's not just saying whatever you want to hear."

"I could offer you the same advice, big brother. What would he even want from me anyway?"

"Your status."

"I have no status."

"Yes, dammit, you do. You would be an extremely advantageous match to someone like him. You are the absolute best choice available to him. And to a lot of others too."

"With my reputation?" She rolled her eyes.

Grel's face darkened further. "Tell me. If something were to happen to Father, and to me, and with Raelt missing... who do you think would come next?"

Her jaw tightened. "I don't know. Someone from the council."

"Or a very eligible young man married to the clan leader's daughter. I just want to make sure you understand what he has the potential to gain here."

She folded her arms across her chest.

"A wealthy young man," he added. "Who was granted a sword at fifteen."

She winced. That was early. If Idak was precocious, it wouldn't surprise her, but Grel was sharp as a knife too. And a strong mage. How were these sword smiths making their decisions? Damn them. Something was amiss here, there had to be.

"Idak may be sincere," Grel relented, sighing. "He is also the best match available to *you*, so I'm going to stop telling you to stay away. But please, Su. Be careful."

"I understand, Grel." She nodded, biting her lip. "I'm sorry for what I said. Thank you for looking out for me."

"I try as much as you let me."

"Can't say that's very much, is it?" She grinned.

He shrugged. "Just be careful. More than your usual level of not-careful-at-all."

She laughed. "I'm more careful than you know, dear brother."

"I wish I could believe that. All right. I better go back. Jylan has been scowling for at least three minutes now."

"Good luck." Her lips twisted as he walked away. If only she had justifications to warn him against Jylan the way he was warning her. There didn't seem to be much love between them that Su could detect.

Alone on the balcony, she gazed out over the gardens and took a long, deep breath in, calmer now. She smiled at the sunshine, the flowers. Grel was absolutely right, but it was hard to deny the halo of warmth that had gathered around her with Idak's words...

He had truly seen her, seen through the facades that her father and even Grel were thrown off by. Facades they were so used to that they didn't even know they were fake.

Most of all, Idak had understood her longing for a sword. Which might mean, as unlikely as it was, that she might get one if she chose to marry him.

Of course, promises could turn to lies after marriage rites. Grel was right; it was what she wanted to hear. But it might be possible to extract the truth, perhaps even guarantee the sword as part of the matrimonial deal.

Most bizarre, though, she didn't think Idak was lying. He'd justified his approval of her longing for magic. The logic was sound—and not at all complex. Who wouldn't want power if they could have it?

And in his eyes was the same rebellious spirit that kindled in her own heart.

It would take a rebellious spirit to arm his wife... But there had to be at least a few men out there brave enough and smart enough to do so, didn't there? They *had* to exist. Was it an unrealistic dream to hope to find one? The great Linali had had a sword—and a man who loved her. Su wasn't powerful like Linali, but...

She had to believe there were such men in the world. Because if there weren't... that was a reality too dark to consider. She'd never be a legend like Linali, but she could be happy with much less.

She glanced back over her shoulder, as briefly as she could. Idak didn't catch her glance. He was sitting alone, sipping his wine and looking as self-assured and at ease as before. As always. Almost as though he were waiting for her.

Returning to his side implied much more than agreeing to another conversation, even if no one said it aloud. The hints were there, the proposal implied if not explicit. *Are you trying to make me fall for you?*

She swallowed. She hadn't been, of course. And she wouldn't be now.

As if she knew how to truly make a man fall in love. No, this time she'd try to do just the opposite. Instead of lies that seduced, she'd hit him with the truth. It was what the Bladed Women had asked of her, after all. Idak wasn't her father, but... perhaps it was a start.

If his affection survived the truth, well... that would be rare indeed.

The lava plains were mostly black rock, with sparse vegetation here and there. Stragg had erupted recently enough that some large areas were fresh, and Lara could still see red lava frothing at the top of the mountain's mouth.

Yeska flew low over several miles of this bleak place before they reached a forest that started up into the hills. Nyalin's hand was still intertwined with hers. She hoped wherever they were going had some answers. It was nice to touch him, but, sooner or later, one of them was going to have to pee.

Nerutoa—the Obsidian Dragon—landed with another earth-shaking thunder at the forest's edge. Her great head turned to face them, and another thrill of fear went through her.

The Dark Dragon was at least three times Yeska's size. The great creature's eyes smoldered scarlet and amber, even in the bright daylight. Lara shook off the feeling and forced herself to climb down as if she felt brave.

The sky and sun were as bright as ever as Nyalin slid down by her side. "Does something about this place give you the creeps?" she asked. Maybe it wasn't just the Dark Dragon. It was eerily quiet. Like a graveyard, although the ones in the city weren't even this quiet. Where were the birds, the people?

There were trees here. Why wasn't there a village close by? It might have been the least populated place she had ever been. Well, she had wanted to explore.

He nodded. "Yeah, the air feels... charged."

"Charged? I was just thinking it's so empty."

"Yes, it is. I don't hear any birds. But... it feels charged to me. My skin itches. It feels like the royal graveyard, where my mother's buried."

"Huh. It reminded me of that too." Her brother was buried in the royal graveyard, too. She'd been visiting his grave the day she'd first met Nyalin. Strange to think that if nothing had ever happened to Myandrin, she might not have met Nyalin in the first place. Or perhaps they would have met, either way. And yet there, the air was always filled with holy chimes and the sounds of the city. Here, the silence was deafening. "You don't think any of those stories of ghosts are actually true, do you?"

He opened his mouth, faltered, and then his eyes caught on something.

*They are true.* Yeska was following behind them. *The spirits are thicker here.*

She shivered. She wasn't sure she wanted to know.

Nyalin pointed. "The Dark Dragon calls. Let's go."

"Of course." She was in motion before she finished the words.

The Dark Dragon—Nerutoa—flew over them, creating a sinister shadow. Yeska managed to maneuver underneath the tall pines and oaks with them as they ran, hand in hand, following the Nerutoa's lead.

Lara wasn't sure how far they went into the forest, but it wasn't the long hike she'd braced herself for. Abruptly, as they neared a tall cliffside, the trees suddenly cleared again to reveal a squat house nestled against the cliff.

"How lovely," she breathed. It had a dark slate roof with curved corners and eight round windows. A square iron door stood in the center of the home, a ring beckoning them to pull it open and enter. Gardens lined the home's perimeter with thick lavender bushes and spiky plants she didn't recognize. Neat stone walkways circled outside the gardens, leaning downhill toward a hole near the base of the cliff.

"Is that a stream?" Nyalin pointed.

"I think so, yes. Maybe a spring?" She pulled Nyalin with her around the house to the side. Big-headed red flowers bloomed there, nearly as tall as she was. He pulled her toward the stream, and at the edge of the water, she dipped her fingers in—ice cold. Yes, it had to be a spring coming down from the mountain. "This is beautiful. Finally—people! Dark Dragon, who lives here?"

*No one, now.* Nerutoa perched on a cliff ledge above the home and curled her tail around her forelegs.

They walked briskly back toward the entrance, stopping just short. "No one? Then why... How will this place help us?"

"It's the place on my mother's sword," Nyalin said.

"Her home?"

He nodded, and she was glad they'd stopped. She waved for him to go first.

*Yes. Linali was born here. Lived here for most of her childhood.*

Nyalin frowned as he took hold of the ring that hung on the door but didn't try to open it yet. "They said she grew up in the wilds. This place doesn't look very wild. I figured she was raised by wolves or something."

"Maybe they were wolves with excellent gardening and carpentry skills?" Lara smiled.

"Who built this out here? Why out here?"

*Because here in Stragg's Shadow, the space between worlds is thin. And there are no people to fear those who are different. As to who? Your grandparents.*

Stragg's Shadow? Was it really a real place? She swallowed hard as he heaved on the door. It groaned a little, then a lot, then gave up its resistance and swung open.

"Why do you think this place can help me, Dark Dragon?" Nyalin asked, not stepping inside, just staring into the dusty darkness.

*You will need time to master the new powers. This is where Linali mastered them. These ghosts are friendly.*

Lara bit her lip, a little too hard.

*And you will need shelter while you practice. And food and water. Spells keep this cabin cared for and nearly self-sustaining.*

His Adam's apple bobbed as he swallowed and stepped inside. She followed, clutching his arm now.

"Can you see anything?" she whispered. It was pitch black as far as she could tell.

"No, I, uh—" He faltered, and Lara felt why before she could see it.

Something wrapped around her ankle, climbing and twisting around her shockingly fast. She caught her breath. Something stabbed into her calf, even as whatever it was had already reached her hips. "What the—" she started. Or tried to.

Beside her, Nyalin swore. She clutched his hand harder.

Then abruptly, the vines released.

"What by the Twins was that?" Nyalin demanded, staggering back out of the doorway to glare and the Obsidian Dragon.

*The house has verified you are related to Linali. You didn't think it would let just anyone in, did you?*

"What would it have done to me without him here?" Lara said. "Can I even go in?"

*It will let you in with him. Go on. It should be all clear now.*

Nyalin held up the forearm of his other arm. "I'm bleeding."

*Nothing time won't heal.*

He shook his head and sighed. "That wasn't exactly encouraging. And now it's dark as that dragon's hide in here."

"Maybe there are shudders we can open?" she replied. "There are windows."

It took some feeling around and painfully bumping into furniture, but once they got one set of shudders open, the rest came more easily.

But as light flooded inside, Lara caught her breath. The walls were a vibrant blue, hung with framed drawings of all manner of flora and fauna, but especially flowers and, indeed, wolves.

The place was surprisingly clean. A large fireplace was carved into the cliffside, and beside it was a doorframe painted with green grasses at the bottom and a symbol like a moon or something near eye level. She pointed. "Do you think there are more rooms inside the mountain?"

As he studied the fireplace, she grasped the knob and opened the door.

Beside her, Nyalin caught his breath. A shock went between their palms, sharper than usual. But she was only frowning because the door didn't reveal any rooms.

It was just rock.

"Who makes a door to a solid wall of rock?" She shook her head. "Doesn't make any sense."

Only then did she catch Nyalin's shocked expression.

"What is it?" she asked. "What do you see?"

"Into the afterlife," he whispered. "There are... some wolf spirits. And a few people, but in the distance. They're... headed this way."

She hurried to shut the door. "It's a ghost door?"

*Yes.* The Dark Dragon's voice was heavy in her mind. *It allows creatures from our afterlife to enter our world, if it is opened from this side and especially if they are summoned. They are not fully of this world, but they can take on a body. For a time.*

"Myandrin," she whispered. She immediately regretted the thought, but how could she think anything else? She should leave well enough alone, leave spirits to move on to new and better lives. Leave her brother on his course.

But if there was a way, without a terrible cost, could she get her brother back? Even if just for a little while?

She shook her head. My, that was tempting. She couldn't do it. But it was sorely tempting.

Nyalin seemed to shake off the shocked trance. "Amazing. But let's... keep that closed for now."

"Why isn't this place guarded?" Lara asked. "This seems like a powerful artifact."

*It is guarded,* said the Dark Dragon. *By me.*

They explored the rest of the home. Cozy shelves in the main room were lined with books. A bedroom held a large bed and a smaller child's one. Another room held a wash basin and a worktable, shelves heavy with all manner of herbs. For healing? Tea?

Necromancy?

She and Nyalin finally settled for a moment on the large, padded couch in the main room, not far from the still-empty hearth. "What do we do now?" she said, still looking at her surroundings like they couldn't be real.

"You know," he said, "you'd think my mother would come back here to haunt this place. If she enjoyed herself here as a child. I guess it's possible she didn't. But you'd think this would be an ideal place to haunt if you were dead."

"You'll have to ask Myandrin," she said, only a little bitterly. "What makes for an ideal afterlife stomping ground?"

His features softened with sympathy. "Especially if she knew about the door—maybe she could even come back to life... I wonder, could Myandrin?"

She held up her free hand. "Already thought about it. Let's not go there, shall we? Not now. Tempting but... I don't want to mess with the order of things. I don't understand the implications here either."

"Maybe it's in some of those books." He pointed at the shelves.

"I sure hope there's something here. How is any of this going to help us with your lock? Or my father?"

*The spirits here remember Linali. They cared for her. They will help protect Nyalin as he gains control and power.*

"Protect him from what?"

*The other spirits.*

"That's reassuring." She squeezed his hand.

"We can't do this forever," he said softly, looking at their hands. "She's right, gotta try sooner or later."

"You need more rest. Sleep first."

"What if we let go of each other while we sleep?"

"I won't sleep. You will. I'll... um, read a book."

A corner of his mouth twitched up. "Because books are so your favorite."

"Just because I like to be read to doesn't mean I can't read it. C'mon. You need more rest."

"I think you're right; I'm just teasing. That's a good idea. If I have more rest, from the fall and all that... um, difficulty with the river, then I can be more conscious in movement between planes. I've done it intentionally before."

His voice sounded uneasy, though. "How many times?" she demanded.

"Maybe... twice. No, four times. When Andius had captured us—and in the catacombs challenge in the Contests. That wasn't too bad."

"That was with the lock still in place though."

"Yes. But I have no choice but to try. It's broken now. And I do not want Elix and Pavan to put it back on."

*I would agree,* put in the Dark Dragon.

*As would I,* added Yeska.

"Besides," he added, "we need to get back to the city to look for Cerivil."

She grimaced. He was right, but as she had literally no clue where to start looking for him, and hours of thought hadn't placed her any closer, it hurt to think of it. "All right," she said. "Let's find me something to read, and then you shall take a nap."

Maybe if she couldn't read, she could just pray to Dala for inspiration, for a clue, for something. For her father to be safe from Andius. For everything to work out all right in the end.

She didn't see how such a thing could be remotely possible. But this house with its doorway into another world was pretty strange.

Who knew what the future could hold?

~

"All right, let's try this," Lara was saying.

Nyalin nodded, as determined as he'd ever been. The two of them stood now before the hearth, palms pressed together, facing each other. Bracing themselves.

He felt better, more like himself. He had no idea how long he'd slept, but the sun had dipped low on the horizon. Lara had dutifully perused a book they'd found on the shelves, but the tome on the history of the Obsidian Clan was excessively old and not particularly helpful.

"Ready?" she asked. Her brow was creased, and her expression said she was anything but ready.

"Yep." Still, he didn't move his hand. He groped for words to reassure her, to try to comfort her that with all they'd gotten through, they should be able to deal with *this*. Here, there was no Andius, no Elix or Raelt, no dark forces sabotaging their efforts. It was just them and the dragons.

And thousands of spirits on the other side.

And he actually had no idea if he could do this. So, he just swallowed hard and tried to look confident.

"On three." He squared his shoulders. "One, two..." He swallowed again. "Three."

Both pulled their hands away, leaving their palms barely a finger's width apart. For a moment, nothing changed.

And then her face vanished entirely.

There wasn't even any flickering this time, no world tilting or nausea. The afterworld engulfed him like a black ocean, pulling him down, swallowing him whole. It was like the place was hungry for him, like it was eager, like it'd been denied too long.

He tried to blink away the pitch black in his eyes, and color started to come slowly into the world around him. But not much of it, just touches of the greenish hue here and there. There were no grassy fields, nothing waving in a strange wind like there had been closer to the city.

The lava had touched this plane too and left behind its indelible mark, it seemed.

The white, ghostly outline of a wolf crept closer, its posture weary and stalking. Not at all friendly. Did the Dark Dragon really know anything about the ghosts and spirits here? She couldn't cross the planes herself to find out, could she?

But the Dark Dragon could be wrong.

A new wariness settled around his shoulders as he turned, looking in all directions. A brilliant golden outline stood where he believed the enchanted doorway should have been. That would be the doorway back, right? The rest of the terrain held very few distinct features, except a slow gradual rise toward a black mountain that seemed to be where Mount Stragg would be.

To what he guessed was west, something strange caught his eye, a black mark on the horizon. Around it, he felt the strangest sense of the energy being forcibly pulled out of the world. What in Dala's dreams was that?

Thank the Twins he was this far away. It pulsed, growing and shrinking. Terrifying.

Well, as lovely as this place was, he preferred the mortal plane. He reached for it, the way he had back in the Salt City, like reaching toward home.

Nothing happened. There was nothing to reach for. He didn't feel anything like home, another realm or plane or any of what he'd felt before. Evidently, the nap hadn't been enough in the end.

His heartbeat got louder in his ears. Apparently, he still had a heartbeat here. Interesting. But did he have a way to get home? He glanced at the outline of the magical doorway. He had been transported with his body intact. If it allowed a spirit to go through to the mortal plane and take flesh, what would happen if he went back through? He already had a body that seemed to be here on this plane with him. Would this body die if he went through the door? He wouldn't try it until he was absolutely desperate to return.

But the worry pumping through him was getting more intense. He fidgeted, from foot to foot, scanning the horizon again. There was nowhere to move to, everything was flat. Nowhere to hide from this wolf or anything else for that matter. Did he need shelter? Were there storms? Weather? If he were stuck here, indefinitely, he didn't know the first thing about this plane—what was safe, what wasn't, what the rules were.

Did spirits eat?

He'd have given anything for a book to guide him right now. He should've done more research on this while he could have. The wolf was coming closer. In the distance, he could see others. No people around though.

Raised by wolves, indeed.

"Something wrong?" the creature growled.

He hesitated, his breath quick. "I don't think I belong here," he said slowly, not sure how else to explain, or what the creature would know already or understand.

"Oh, I think you do." It sat, staring at him as its comrades broke into a trot, picking up their pace.

He tried again, reached—nothing. Maybe he needed the power from Lara still, only she wasn't here. Maybe the lock wasn't really broken, or hadn't broken the right way, or maybe his father had been right, and this had been a really bad idea and they should have left well enough alone—

Not that he'd had much choice about nearly drowning in the river.

Maybe he belonged here more than he knew.

"I..." He cleared his throat. "I didn't die. This is where the dead go, right? To wait to take on their next form in the next world?"

"That's a simple way to look at it," said the wolf.

"What's the not-simple way then?" he demanded.

"A spirit is a cross-planar thing, a being that will have many experiences, based on many aspects of their current instantiation, and their current plane of existence is both important—and relatively minor—because they are all so similar."

He took a step back. "You're not just a wolf. Are you." It wasn't really a question.

The wolf tilted his head. "What tipped you off? My vocabulary, my espousing on interdimensional existence, or the fact that I appear to be an animal that can talk?"

"A little of each, I think," Nyalin said. "If you know so much, then do you know how I can get back?"

"I do," said the wolf.

"Okay, so tell me."

"Oh, I don't think so." The other wolves had finally joined them and were coming to sit at their leader's side. "I have some... requests... to discuss with you first."

*Chapter 7*

# Among Wolves

Unira crushed the clay in her fingers, kneading it back and forth. She didn't really have a plan to sculpt anything today, but sequestered away in her studio, busying her hands helped her think. Something needed to happen. Something needed to be done. But she always seemed to be slogging through honey.

All her plans seemed to roll along in slow motion. She preferred to work indirectly. That meant she couldn't get caught. And when plans failed, she could simply start over with another minion, another strategy. This had worked for her in the past. But was it working now? With Zama in his own studio now, she couldn't keep an eye on him as she once had. What was he doing in there? Was it truly what she'd asked of him?

Zama had been busy at work all day again, as he had been for what seemed like days and days now. Absently, she formed the dough into the shape of a human. But how could she give it silver eyes? Indicate that somehow it represented something... more than human. Or if not more, different.

Abruptly, in the door to her studio burst open, the demon she'd been thinking of rushing through as if summoned by her thoughts. He was breathless. "I've done it! I've finally done it!"

"Done what?" She adjusted the angle of a limb, not moving from her seat.

"I, my dear, have done the impossible." He grinned wide, extended his arms out broadly, and then bowed. "I have killed Linali's son."

"No." Now she did move, starting to her feet. Abandoning her creation, she took a step closer. "How?"

"When creatures from this realm wouldn't do, I simply imported a few from another realm. A nastier kind. Come, come with me and see."

She followed him down the hall to his studio, fighting the urge to jog. The gilded mirror he used for scrying was still hard at work on the low table by his armchair.

He indicated it with a flourish. "See? The mirror can't find him. No trace of him in this world. It's been searching for hours. And it will keep doing so, because it can't find him. Because he's gone!" He danced back as she leaned closer.

Indeed, the mirror was flying across the landscape. But could the mirror really get a true lock on someone as slippery as Nyalin moLinali? "How did you trace him?"

"Blood and sand from the Contest grounds."

That did give her pause. "Clever." She knew of no such spells, but she didn't doubt that he might.

"Whenever there's blood, I always try to get a drop or two. Much power in that."

She was suddenly grateful she'd never been injured around him. Another benefit of having others do your dirty work. The mirror continued to fly across the landscape. "I... it is hard to believe after all this time. Could it really be true?" She rubbed her chin, then slid into the armchair. She'd tried and failed too many times to believe so easily. She needed more proof. "Show me the body."

"I saw him fall down into the river myself. He was swept away, out to sea."

"Human bodies tend to wash up, not just disappear into the sea. The fat in them makes them float—"

He stopped his dancing. "I do not want to know how you know that."

"Well?"

"Alas, I have not found the body. But how can he live? There is no trace of him on this plane." They both leaned toward the mirror, the silence growing tense.

A chime echoed down the hall. From her scrying mirror. Lucky they hadn't missed it with their bickering. They left Zama's mirror searching and hurried down the hall to the other, where a young man in a white crossover looked nervously out at them.

She rang the chime again to answer him and listened to his report.

"What do you mean, they lost their clanblade?" Unira narrowed her eyes. She should calm down and ask more pointed, clearer questions. This wasn't her usual poise. But seriously, was she surrounded by morons?

The spy she'd planted in the Pearl Clan looked uneasy in the scrying mirror. "They… lost it. The Pearl Clan leadership is quite distressed. The servants could not avoid hearing their concern."

"You're sure? That's a mighty convenient lie."

"Yes. But I believe it's the truth. They seem to have lost it before your deal was even completed."

"Treacherous fools." She blew out a disgusted breath. "Deal" was a generous term for her extortion. She'd kidnapped the foreign dignitary brought to marry their bachelor clan leader, and then she'd demanded their clanblade if they wanted the woman back. And now, they were claiming this?

So far, the clan leader of the Pearl Clan had quickly capitulated to her demands for obedience and her "requests" of financial support. That might have had something to do with her having possession of the man's betrothed.

After all the nonsense with the Bone Clan girl, Unira had demanded their clanblade as proof. And now? A whole new wealth of nonsense in its place.

"What is it with these people? How many clanblades can possibly be stolen at one time? Does Elix even wear a true Obsidian clanblade? Or perhaps it's just a toy sword and they've hidden the real one, because goddess knows someone's going to try to steal it. Perhaps we should test him on it."

Zama took a bite of an apple as he leaned back in his chair. "These poor clans do not know how to care for their riches; that's why they are poor."

"Did I ask for your opinion on clan economic and social structures?" She narrowed her eyes. Why was she being testy with him? Was it because, maybe, just maybe, he'd succeeded where she'd failed for so long?

The spy cleared his throat. "I was told to assure you they are crafting another one."

She sighed. "Of course they would say that. How do we know if they're lying? Buying time?"

"The Obsidians do it all the time," Zama put in. "With every generation, or so I've read."

"And are the Pearls of that stock?" she said. "I didn't think they were able. Have they usually created new clanblades for their heirs?"

"No." Her spy straightened his pale white crossover, as if the color chafed him. He'd of course been born an Obsidian like most of her better spies, but some she simply acquired with gold. "But they are willing to do it now. For you. And to keep the clan leader's betrothed safe."

She cackled. Safe. Right. At the wide eyes of the spy, she sobered. "She's quite safe. Don't look at me like that." She shook off the mirth. Her control wasn't as tight as normal today. She needed to get it together. Clearly, no one else had it together, so somebody had to get a grip.

Well. At least the Pearls were trying to make amends. "What do they say happened to their clanblade, though? And we need a plan for if they fail to create a new blade. Or even if they succeed—we can't have this rival blade out there."

Zama shrugged. "It will sow more chaos that way. It might even work in your favor."

She did like that element of it, but the spy didn't need to know of her dueling plans. "It's an insult. It's like they stole it from me."

A smile quirked at the demon's mouth. "Even though you never had it?"

"Details. Now, you—tell me. Do they have any guesses as to how this happened?"

The spy pursed his lips. "Apparently, the woman has a brother. A bodyguard. They believe he stole it around the time we brought the woman here for her stay."

Unira snorted. Such polite words for a kidnapping. What was more rude, to kidnap someone or to only speak in euphemisms about your crime? "Well, where is he?"

"They have been looking since then, my lady. They have found nothing. They do not know."

She turned to Zama. "Could you find this man?"

The demon nodded. "With the right information. Not on this pathetic description alone."

"Could we get what we need from the woman?"

His lips twitched ever so slightly. "Not... right now."

Unira sighed. She had been the one to put the woman in stasis. It kept her out of trouble, out of her hair, and from absorbing any information they didn't want her to have. And it also put her to some use. No reason to let a soul lie around doing nothing as a prisoner if that prisoner could also be feeding her magic. Even untalented, unbladed women had a life force enough to be tapped by the right sorceress of the dead, if one knew how.

But stasis froze the mind. She would have to be brought out if they wanted information from her—and that was not without cost. It took large amounts of energy and very careful spell crafting to create the stasis in the first place. Few mages, even if they knew how, could pull off both the spell and the enormous resources required. Fortunately, she had built her collection of souls slowly and used the reserves to build it further. And now she had Zama too. Still, to bring a woman out just to ask her a question she certainly wouldn't want to answer, and then put her back in? That would be costly indeed.

Also, they'd managed to keep her fairly in the dark about the nefarious nature of this "stay" she was having. She'd mostly believed their lies that this was a trip sponsored by her betrothed, right up until the point they'd knocked her out from behind.

"Get me more information on this brother of hers," she ordered the spy. "Where he came from, his appearance, his manner of travel. Find out where he stayed with the Pearls and see if he left anything behind. Use whatever resources you deem necessary. I will have Jylan send you more gold. Go."

He bowed deeply. She waved a hand, and the image in the mirror was gone.

Beside her, Zama cleared his throat, and she turned. "Dinner?"

"Didn't you just eat?" Her eyes flicked to a core of a pear beside him.

"But we must celebrate my victory. There are some things in this world I can't get enough of," he said, smiling. "And you are just one of them."

She rolled her eyes.

"The other is bread."

"Your charms are truly overwhelming. I suppose a bit of wine is in order. Even if Pearl isn't complying as I'd like, they're still a terrible mess, thanks to me."

"So there. We both have our tortures—I mean, victories—to celebrate."

"I'll be right there."

As he strode toward the balcony and called for a servant, she hurried back to her studio and grabbed the sad little unfinished figure she'd sculpted. Did she keep it, dry it, put it away? She glanced over her shoulder in his direction. Victories. He'd had precious few of those. And now, she was supposed to believe this outlandish claim? That Nyalin was truly dead? With no proof?

She wanted to. But she was no fool.

She crushed the little figure back into a ball of clay and put it back in the bin. Wiping off her hands as she went, she rejoined Zama. Servants were already at his command, bringing a wide array of delights. He might be an expensive guest, but at least he had good taste.

"And wine for us both."

"All right, where were we?" she asked as she folded her legs and sat. Although she knew perfectly well what they'd been discussing. The setting sun cast a dramatic light across the elegant table and his always alluring features, but she steeled herself. Now was not the time to relax and admire, it was the time to think.

"We were celebrating my tremendous victory."

"I am not so certain—"

"Listen, this conquest has given me a brilliant idea."

She sighed. "What is it?"

"If a few otherworldly creatures could be this effective, what could dozens do?"

She raised an eyebrow. "I'm listening."

"What about hundreds?"

"They could do a lot, under the right controlling hand." She twisted her lips and took a sip of the wine.

"It's time to make your decision, Unira. Hedging your bets is fine and all. But if you install your son as clan leader or emperor and then destroy said empire—don't you think he'd be at least a little pissed off? You need to narrow your operations. Which will it be?"

She chewed on her lip. "Idak is not close to being clan leader, emperor, or even a well-married, well-placed candidate. But he has just taken his first step on that path. He's had very little chance, although that's his own fault for ignoring my other nudges. On one hand, we should give him more time. On the other..."

"Yes?"

"On the other, people have... frequently let me down. I'm tired of it. Any path that doesn't lie entirely within my own two hands makes me nervous. But..."

"But what?"

"But I can't burn down an empire alone, with just my two hands." She shrugged one shoulder.

"No, but you are very capable with your magic. Don't underestimate your abilities."

"I want to give Idak more time."

"How much? The boy isn't exactly driven. He could court the girl for years and still not seal the deal."

"Two weeks. See what he can do with this girl."

"My plan is better. Who can get married in two weeks?"

"You know, we could try to expedite the process." She sipped a spoonful of soup.

"I'm listening."

"Well, if this attack of yours on Linali's son was so successful, why not spring the same thing on Elix's son as well?"

He grinned. "I like it."

"I do enjoy torturing the boy as he fails time and again to get a sword, unaware that no one will ever agree to give him one... But perhaps we should put him out of his misery. Do you think that could be arranged?"

"I'll move it to the top of my list."

"Then we shall see if Idak can step up—or if he'll walk away. And in the meantime, you can prepare your... alternative. Tell me more about these hundreds of creatures."

"I propose we open a portal, straight into the middle of the Salt City. We fill the city with monsters under our control. It might take a day or two of channeling to bring over enough, but then you could have whatever end you wanted. Pure mayhem? Utter destruction? Complete capitulation to your rule?"

Her eyes were wide. "What do we need to construct such a portal? Cast such a spell?"

"It won't be easy... I'll need some time. And basic materials to construct a simple frame for the spell. Workers to assist me in constructing something like... a large door or gateway structure. And we'd need a location inside the city."

"Well, that sounds like two weeks' worth of work."

"Yes, but the day will come—"

"Oh, I know. I'm sure one of you will let me down. Possibly more than one. We shall just see who is the first. Our mansion in the city could provide a location for your portal. And we have souls a plenty. The materials should be available readily at our mansion if not otherwise in the city."

"Shall I head there straight away? Now or in the morning?"

"You're in quite a hurry." The plan by itself made her a little uncomfortable, but his haste made her even more so.

He leaned back and gave her a crooked grin, lifting his glass. "We have both been delayed in embracing the true power we deserve for long enough. Let us wreak havoc on this world or die trying."

She paused for a second, a smile tugging at the corners of her mouth. "All right. Let me write you the necessary letters to get what you need from my people. But you mustn't open the portal without me—and my signal that I have made my choice." She lifted her glass to his.

"Of course," he said. "I would never."

She reached for a piece of paper. If only she could believe that.

"Walk with me. The pack has something to show you." The wolf moved toward Mount Stragg.

There wasn't much else to do but follow. Nyalin wouldn't gain much from resisting. Slowly he trudged after the wolf as it trotted. His limbs felt heavy. Where had all his energy gone?

"You actually do belong here, you know. I can sense this sort of thing. You have the right sort of scent. You are one of the proper denizens here, although you have another home too."

"I'd like to go back."

"In time."

"What do I need to do?"

"First, you need to listen. You need to understand that you belong."

"I don't understand why—"

"Yes, that is precisely the problem."

He frowned. "All right, I'm listening."

"Not only do I sense the power of the spirit in you, but you have the aroma of recent death around you. But not yet rebirth. You exude the unique scent of someone who fought it off and gripped onto life at the last minute."

"I was drowning. Someone saved me."

"Ah, I see. So I was right."

"Yes," he admitted grudgingly.

"And yet what do you know about life on this plane?"

"Less than I'd like," he admitted.

"A shame, a real shame."

"Well, it's not my choice. I didn't even know I could come here until a few months ago."

"Yes, a shame they kept you away."

He went still. "They. You know... them."

"I do."

"Who are you?"

"Who are *you*? You haven't even told me your name."

"I apologize." He bowed. "I am not used to employing proper manners with animals. I am Nyalin moLinali... of the Bone Clan." He hesitated. Nyalin *naPavan* moLinali was the truth, the truth he'd finally discovered. But could he trust this wolf spirit with such a secret? The emperor hadn't sworn him to secrecy in any way, but he must have had his reasons for not openly acknowledging him as his son. He'd told Lara, though. He'd planned to tell Grel as soon as humanly possible—which at this rate, might be never. No, it was too soon to know if he could trust this wolf. For all he knew, the wolf could be a complete enemy. He seemed to know about the lock and those who'd put it there, but that didn't prove trustworthiness. "I'm a scribe. And a swordmage, a bit, a little."

"Pleasure to meet you, Nyalin of the Bone Clan. I am Batu."

"Are you really a wolf?"

"No. I took a familiar form from your mind. My true form cannot be observed by you."

Nyalin went very still. What could that even mean? Was he some even more powerful creature, one that could easily traverse many planes? Or something else entirely? It seemed rude, however, to simply blurt out "What are you?" so he held his tongue.

"Wolves are predators in my home plane," he said slowly. "Packs of them have been known to eat humans."

"Worry not." The wolf's lip curled. Was that a gesture of amusement or disgust? "I do not eat."

"I wish I could say that's reassuring." He yawned. "I don't understand why I'm so tired here. I just slept."

"You consumed energy making the jump. And because you are not used to having to defend your reserves, it is leaching out of you."

"Defend my reserves? What?"

"Yes. This you must learn before you may leave."

"Who made you the arbiter of if I can leave?"

"No one. You simply won't have the energy to make the jump if you don't learn from me."

"Oh." He blushed a little. "Sorry. I didn't realize you were trying to help me."

"Forgiven. I suppose I could have been clearer about that. I thought perhaps appearing in the same form as we appeared to your mother would help, but perhaps I am being a bit...subtle. I apologize as well. I am trying to help you."

His mother. Nyalin tried to digest what Batu had said, but maybe it was the fatigue that left him feeling nothing but a bit stunned. Almost numb.

As they talked, they crossed a strange amount of distance, an amount that didn't seem to match up with how long they'd been walking. He had to wonder if time and space worked differently here, or if the wolf had some sort of magic it was working, speeding their transport.

They were about halfway up the side of the mountain when the wolf turned to look out over the land. Here, Nyalin caught his breath.

The landscape before him was strange, shifting. He could see pieces of land above others, floating, or holes in the land, as if somehow pieces had been dislodged from their original spots in the real world, but the laws of nature, of physics, with which he was familiar hadn't applied. The land that appeared to be in the most chaos was near where the Salt City *should* have been. A shimmering glow emitted from the area, brighter than anywhere else. Other points of faint light dotted the landscape—souls hovering around the villages, trading posts, but most of all the city.

His eyes drifted to the pulsing black smudge. The wolf's eyes were already there.

"What is that?" he asked, pointing.

"An abomination. A necromancer who takes more than her fill. One of the reasons you must learn to protect yourself."

The woman Pavan had mentioned, what was her name? "Unira?" he asked.

"That is the one. What do you think of this plane?"

"Strange, but beautiful. A bit dark." He looked up at the sky more, but the strange green glow made no sense. The clouds seemed more like a dream of clouds than real clouds, and if he looked out toward the ocean, he couldn't see anything that looked like waves or ships.

Batu's lip curled again. "Dark it is, unless there are spirits around. There should be more of them."

Impulsively, Nyalin reached for home again, wondering if time or this new location would have changed anything. It hadn't. Nothing, again.

"These spirits, I protect. I would like your help protecting them too. They must remain here to travel on. If they are pulled back to from whence you came... even if only temporarily..."

He frowned. "How could I possibly help?"

"Once you have learned more skills, it will be clearer. But most of all, you could help by putting an end to that." Batu pointed his snout at the black vortex in the distance.

"If I knew how..."

"There are two wrongs that must be righted."

"I'm listening."

"First, there are prisoners being kept. Free them, and the vortex will be broken. Second, there are the swords."

Nyalin almost choked. "The swords?"

"Yes, the swords. Where do you think the magic in them comes from?"

"The smiths always said it was from the sword itself."

"The smiths lie to you. It is not from the metal."

"Then what is it from?"

"It is from souls. Spirits. Spirits like these"—he swept his hand toward the chaos—"Bound forever in the swords. Never moving on."

"So the sword smiths are... are... no better than necromancers?"

"No better? They *are* necromancers, but less ethical. Necromancers ask permission of those spirits they involve in their magic. The sword smiths don't even tell you of the spirits they've imprisoned in the swords—never able to move on. Spirits that you mages will keep enslaved for many lifetimes."

"That..." He was breathing harder than he should have been. "That can't be."

"You know it is true. Think about it."

"Yes, but—but—"

"And have you seen your mother's sword?"

His breathing steadied. "Yes. It doesn't have magic inside it like the others."

"Because she would never. Because there was and is no need. She was able to link her own power to the sword as a focus and a conduit. And you can do the same."

His shoulders slumped. "How can I learn to do that? That knowledge is all gone. Because she's dead."

"Oh, she is not dead."

Nyalin's head snapped up. "Excuse me?"

"She is not dead. Do you see her here?"

He felt like he might fall down. There was nothing to grab onto to steady himself, so he sank to a seat on the hard rock. "I—uh—they told me. They told me she was... I've been to the royal graveyard and seen her grave."

They'd told him other lies. But Pavan had truly seemed sad, truly seemed to believe it. He thought back, trying to remember.

"They do not know." Batu's ghostly eyes seemed to contain a hint of empathy. "They cannot sense her. But do you see that vortex?"

He raised his head, looking at the malevolent wound on the horizon.

"Her power makes it possible. Her connection to this world—Unira is abusing it to siphon the power from more souls than just Linali's."

"Then I'll stop her," he said quickly.

"You will need to be cautious," Batu said slowly. "You hold the same potential as your mother. If you were to be lost... the vortex would grow, you a part of it."

"I'll tell my friends. So even if I can't defeat her, they can try to rescue us. People need to know my mother is—" His voice faltered. "My mother is still alive."

"And the swords?"

"I'll give you my promise to work on that. But the prisoners, the vortex—that must come first. If my mother knows another way to harness magic, harness the blades, without imprisoning souls, she could teach me. Then we could let everyone know the truth and teach them how to harness their own power. Right now, nobody's going to listen to me. But with her immense reputation on my side, sharing her knowledge, I'm sure we could succeed."

"I agree, the vortex must be addressed first. But do not underestimate yourself. You, too, can make a sword that will show them their old ways are not needed."

He caught his breath. "What about Grel?"

"Grel?"

"My... brother. Stepbrother. The sword smiths won't give him a sword. Could I make him one and teach him how to infuse it with his own power?"

"It will be difficult. I can show you some of the skills you will need. But you will still need the forge."

"The forge?"

"There is a forge. The Obsidian Dragon will show you. Ask her, and tell her I said that you are ready."

He bit his lip. The idea of confronting the whole system of swords and swordmages and turning it on its ear was terrifying. But... by Dala, would he want his own soul to be trapped that way after death? Lara's? Myandrin's? Cerivil's or Faytou's? Gosh, he hoped they were all okay.

He paused, realizing he'd called on Dala in that moment. Hmm. Some things did change, even when you weren't looking.

"I'll do it. But first, the vortex. And this Unira."

Batu nodded his head. "Excellent. Now, meditate with me here, at the heart of things." After a moment, the wolf's form shifted into Faytou's. Nyalin swallowed hard again. Was Batu trying to say he was a friend? By the Twins, he hadn't realized how much he'd missed him. How worried he was.

"All right," he choked out. Folding his legs, he closed his eyes and took one deep breath.

"I will give to you some of the knowledge you need, in ways that only I can. But please, you must remain calm. Meditate."

"All right. When do we start?"

"Now. We start now."

—

"Let me walk you back," Idak said as he helped her into a borrowed cloak. He'd insisted it'd grown too cold to depart the way she'd arrived. "It's late."

"Not that late." Sutamae hesitated on the steps of Idak's home. Night had fallen, a fragrant incense from the party spicing the air. The street outside was quiet, empty.

"Details." He waved a hand. "It's dark. You shouldn't go alone."

She shrugged. "I've gone alone often enough."

"Our streets aren't *that* safe." He smiled crookedly.

Of course, her misadventures the night before had proven that well enough. That was hardly typical, though. "All right, I'll admit it. They're not safe. But I'm also not afraid of danger. Nor do I need an armed guard or protection."

"I believe it. Don't you see, I'm not actually asking to protect you?"

She frowned. "Yes, you are."

"I'm just looking for an excuse for a few more minutes at your side."

She went still. In her focus on her ego, she *had* missed that nuance. "Oh. Well. Give me a second to think about it."

He leaned against a stone column, watching the crowd back in the large party room and smiling, like he already knew what she would say.

She bit her lip, thinking. Grel was back at Jylan's side, and his attention to his supposed betrothed—and the food—had allowed him to lose sight of her, which was probably a mistake on his part.

There were those who would talk if Idak walked her home from such an occasion. But they were already out of sight of many. And when had she ever cared what people thought? Except maybe to use them as an audience, as tools to embarrass fools.

She would not be playing her games tonight, though, and given her history, the rumors might spread anyway, people assuming that games would be played. Did she want that for Idak? Even if they just said goodbye at the door, though, some might form that impression.

Did either of them care? She ought to ask Grel to take her back. Not Idak. That would be the proper thing to do.

A wicked smile crept to her lips. Oh, the hell with proper. What had it ever done for her anyway? "All right. Let's go."

Even though they'd already been in the darkness near the door, a few sets of eyes followed them as they stepped out into the night. She didn't notice one particular set of eyes until it was too late—a set she would have preferred to avoid.

They were barely down the steps when Chosko's voice rang out after them. "Idak, wait!"

Her stomach clenched as Idak slowed beside her and turned toward the call. Chosko's feet pounded on the pavement. How hard had he run to catch up with them? By Seluvae.

"Don't do this," Chosko blurted. "She'll ruin your reputation."

Idak straightened, his chest rising. "What nonsense is this?" It wasn't clear whether he was talking to her or Chosko.

"She's not what you think she is," Chosko said between heaving breaths. "That wine might look lovely, but it's been sampled."

"Not by *you*," she said dryly. "Although not for lack of trying."

"Does either of you wish to clarify the situation?"

"She might look well-bred, but she's a common alley cat, Idak. She'll ruin you. Tried to ruin me and embarrass me in front of Elix, the Council, Grel—everyone."

She smirked at him, even though some survival instinct was flaring. Goading him could be dangerous, lighting a match in a dry forest. But she couldn't resist. "I didn't try, I *succeeded*. At least, in embarrassing you. Ruination, I can't say just yet."

"By the Twins." Idak raised both his eyebrows. "These are some tall claims on both sides. And how could this... pre-sampled wine... manage such a thing as ruining your life?"

Chosko blustered but couldn't seem to form words.

Her smirk shifted to a grin. "I seduced him in an inn. He never asked for my name. Then I shackled his hands to the bed before the deed could be done and stole his sword. And then I gave it to my father."

Idak burst out in laughter. "Before the deed, eh? Oh, that is too rich."

"Don't go telling people that, you gutter filth—" Chosko started.

"Watch your language." Just like that, Idak's voice had gone ice cold.

Chosko looked ready to snarl at them both. "Like you haven't done enough damage already. At least let them think I bedded you."

"I let them think whatever they wish," she said, glaring, "but call me one more name, and they'll be calling you a gelding."

He held up his upturned palm, looking imploringly to Idak. "You see?

She'll ruin your reputation."

"As if I have a reputation to ruin." Idak looked more amused than anything else as he let his arms fall back to his sides. "Why, Sutamae, would you do such a terrible, amusing thing?"

"Amusing!" Chosko sputtered.

"Because our clan should not suffer such fools," she replied.

Idak's chuckle was low and quiet now. "I find myself in agreement, yet again. Not that I'm surprised."

"Excuse me?" Chosko gaped. "How dare you."

Idak's eyes flashed, the night making them black and menacing. "You let an opponent steal your sword. You let your guard down. No one is responsible for your mistake but you."

"It's not like I left it on the table! She set *out* to steal it." He jabbed a finger at Su. "Four times she's done it now!"

"Seven," she corrected. "Some people are more effective at keeping it quiet than others."

Idak smiled now, dismissively. "You are out of your element here, Chosko. Do scurry along. If she ruins my dismal to nonexistent reputation, I really couldn't care less." He shooed the younger man back toward the mansion.

Chosko scowled at that, but he didn't move.

"Go on. Go hang out with those who care what people think. I see it's working out so well for you." He turned back toward the direction they'd been heading, taking her arm and drawing her with him.

For once, she didn't resist.

"You haven't heard the last of this," Chosko called. He walked back into the mansion, muttering to himself and probably calling her names again, worse things. But he wasn't worth following up on her own threat. Not at the moment, at least.

They walked in silence for a while. A small thrill was coursing through her, each step waiting for the bubble of illusion to burst. He hadn't been shocked. Or affronted. He hadn't rejected her at the news.

He'd been amused. He'd seemed to approve of her... little pranks.

But what did he mean, he had no reputation to ruin? Because he hadn't been in the city much? Certainly, there were many who knew him, there must be. He'd just been unfamiliar to her because she'd avoided gatherings like this. Until now.

But Grel had tried to warn her of something... Something vague. And, apparently, nothing important enough to keep him away from Jylan? She didn't see how if he was allowed to court someone in the family, she shouldn't be allowed to do the same.

Was there some way to broach the subject with Idak, though? He hinted at things, and when she dug deeper, he'd explained, but information was rarely offered on its own. Sometimes, she'd hit a complete stone wall. But if she was going to find out anything, she'd have to pursue it directly. But how?

"You don't mind all that?" she ventured.

"As I think I've already explained, I find people who break rules and think for themselves much preferable to those who fall in line."

And what if it was *his* line she wouldn't fall into? How would he feel then? But that wasn't what she wanted to explore. "I'm *clearly* tainted. Chosko's not the only one, you know. It's a bit of a hobby of mine."

He chuckled again. "You are so full of surprises. I'm not worried."

"It could rub off on you."

"What could, clever stunts like that? Count me in." His eyes twinkled as he glanced at her, but he mostly kept his eyes on the street. He chuckled.

"I just mean..." She needed to turn this conversation the same direction it'd gone before. "Even if I don't care about reputations, that's to some degree because I am limited in how far I could go with a good one. If I have an excellent reputation as a virtuous, obedient woman, perhaps I'll earn a good husband. And if I'm wild and disobedient, I'll..."

"Still earn a good husband because your father is clan leader?"

"Precisely. So, I really can't influence my fate either way."

"Oh, but I think you have."

She frowned. This wasn't working out the way she hoped, but it was still interesting. "I'm just trying to say, I won't think less of you if you choose to prioritize your reputation. One must be practical at times. You might better yourself more than I can by having a good one. My father, for example, might not be the most enthusiastic about this walk we are taking."

The lack of reaction in his eyes made her realize that he knew this quite well, that Idak was quite sure Elix would be irritated by this. Could that even be the reason he'd offered? It wouldn't be the first time she'd been a pawn in someone's game.

"Sutamae, your concern only further convinces me of your virtue. But let these worries slide. There's nothing good left in me to taint. And as such, any hope to salvage my reputation is long gone."

"Oh, I'm sure that's not true."

"You'd be surprised."

They'd reached her home, but she wasn't ready for this conversation to end. At the main gate, she drew him to the side, between two high fir trees, where there was a stone bench for passersby on the street to rest in a small quiet haven during the day. During the night... it was a pocket of darkness and, tonight, a bit of moonlight.

"So tell me then. What has earned you such a dark, foreboding supposed reputation?" And why did the idea of it make her even *more* interested, rather than less?

He shrugged. "It's complicated."

"I'm smart. And ready to listen."

He barked a laugh out into the night sky. "Indeed, you are."

For the first time, he was truly dodging her questions. "I can stand here all night. It would take an exceptional man to have a reputation so terrible that it had failed to reach the knowledge of an average city noble like myself."

"I *am* an exceptional man. And you are far from average." His chuckle was even deeper now. And the grin on his face so sincere... She was too busy admiring his grin to take note when he leaned forward, lifting his hand unexpectedly to brush her cheek, then curl around her neck.

She stopped breathing. Stopped thinking. Stopped everything. The gentleness of his lips seemed almost ironic. The kiss was firm and certain, reassuring and gentle.

But there was no flash, no strange flicker of energy.

The electric shock that had hit her the last time she'd kissed the stranger in the mask came back to mind. Hell. This kiss was fine, but it had been nothing like that.

Idak withdrew quickly, then reached into his pocket.

She watched him, still as a statue. Had that really just happened?

He held out his open palm. A small roll of black fabric was coiled there.

She reached for it automatically, then hesitated. Why this? Why now? Her eyes were hard when she met his. "What is this?"

"A gift."

She narrowed her eyes at him.

"Is that so hard to believe? I like you, Sutamae. Perhaps you noticed." Ignoring her hand still poised in midair, he unrolled the thin strip of fabric knotted in the center and reached toward her neck. "May I?"

She was nodding before she'd really thought about it, if only because it brought him closer. As he leaned in, she could smell leather and wood and smoke. The fabric was silk—breathtakingly smooth and a little cool against her skin. She bit her lip at the sensation, and a corner of his mouth quirked up. He tied the choker gently at the nape of her neck. The brush of ribbon and his fingers there sent goosebumps down her arms, up her neck. She hadn't assumed him to be the gentle type.

Or perhaps he just knew something about taming wild creatures like herself.

"To protect you." His breath whispered across her skin and left her wishing he hadn't drawn back.

"I don't need your protection. I thought we covered this already."

He smirked at her biting tone. "Oh, but you do. You just don't know it yet."

"From whom?"

"My mother."

She raised her eyebrows. "Well, that's foreboding. Is it magical?" Her fingers played across the smooth ribbon. At the center, over the dip in her collar bone, sat an intricate knot. No, knots. Several in a little grouping. What did it mean?

"Sorry to disappoint you, but no. It's perfectly ordinary. Only a sign of my affection."

"That's not a disappointment." Her smile was smaller and more genuine than many of her smiles in a great many years. She had a feeling affection wasn't the only thing it was a sign of. Ownership felt more likely. Whatever else it might mean, she needed to know if the promise of that kiss would amount to anything.

"Come to my mother's estate with me," he said suddenly.

She sat back in her chair. "What? And besides, isn't it your estate?"

"As you like it—come to my estate. With me. Come see the farms and the mansion. The orchards. The forest. The trees are beautiful, even in the snow."

She tilted her head to the side, then cleared her throat and swallowed. Could this be some kind of trick? Someone more methodical than Chosko could plot revenge or retribution. With him, she'd be outside of her father's protection, at least to some degree. And outside Grel's as well. And Jylan had never invited Grel along, so... that was complicated.

But his eyes... his chuckle. She found herself clenching her hands, forced herself to stop. "Don't you think it's a little soon for that?"

"It is. But I'm a man who *acts* when he sees the proper course ahead of him."

"And what is this proper course you see?"

"Having you. As my own."

She raised her eyebrows. This probably wasn't the proper time to smack him across the face for equating her to a thing that could be owned. Especially since he was the first man she'd ever met who might be *worthy* of being owned by.

Or... no. Perhaps he was the second.

But mysterious strangers in alleyways shouldn't count on the same level as true potential suitors, should they? Still, the mask flashed past her mind's eye again. The keen gleam in his eye when he'd laughed at her jokes. The flare of energy dazzling her nerves.

Ridiculous. Here she was thinking of a phantom who left her, when a real man was right in front of her, trying to talk about the future. Fated souls, hearts well-matched... that was probably just a silly old myth anyway.

Idak didn't seem to have noticed her inward spiral, or maybe he thought extensive thought was appropriate. "These things must go in steps," he added, as if to further convince her, "and even a man of action can't skip all of them. One of those steps is my mother. And another is for you to see my estate. And all that would be ours, if you were to have me."

Ours.

Her heart pounded in her chest. She ought to push him away. He hardly knew her. Not to mention that *she* hardly knew *him*. She should at least make him work harder for this. She ought to argue; he assumed too much.

But on the other hand, he didn't.

She measured him a moment longer, pushed thoughts of her phantom further down, and then took a deep breath.

"All right," she murmured. "When do we leave?"

~

What if he never came back?

Lara had done everything she could think of to keep herself busy. Cleaning the home was over quickly, as she wasn't an ardent cleaner and the place cleaned itself anyway. She foraged more berries than she could possibly eat. She sketched until she'd nearly exhausted the house's art supplies, leaving some in case they were needed. She dunked herself and her clothes in the frigid spring and regretted it less than the first time, since she could warm up inside while they dried—unfortunately alone. She pulled a weed that had snuck into the flower bed. She read a dozen books or more... or, at least, skimmed them before nodding off. Many of them were old, archaic, or highly technical.

But as the minutes slipped by, and the hours—all right, the seconds—her question seemed to press harder behind her eyes.

What if he never came back? What if he never came back?

And how long should she wait to find out? How long *could* she wait? If he never returned... No, he'd come back. He had to. But if he were gone too long, at some point she would have to leave. Her father needed her. Maybe he even needed her right now.

Maybe Andius was—

She shut off that line of thinking. Unless she was going to leap onto Yeska's back and fly into the city now, there was no point in thinking of it. And maybe not even then.

*There is no way to know how long he will be in the afterworld. We don't even know if time works the same way there.*

*I know...*

*Perhaps you should go and look for Cerivil. His energy grows... weaker.*

She swallowed hard. *What if... what if Da dies while I'm just sitting here, twiddling my thumbs?*

*If you would like to go look for him, the Dark Dragon can tell us if Nyalin returns.*

*But what if he needs help when he returns?* It'd still take time to get back from the city. And that would be if nothing dangerous happened and she wasn't caught up in the middle of saving her father—which is kind of the point.

*It is a difficult decision. Only you can make it.*

The unknowns nagged at her, ate at her insides, and turned her stomach to acid. As she washed berries, as she searched the shelves, as she carried up water from the spring. Every dull sound of the wind or the forest would make her jump, hoping it was Nyalin returning.

What if my father is in trouble and needs my help? What if I go to him, but Nyalin does come back, and I'm not here? What could Andius be doing to my clan while I'm out here in the Obsidian wilds? On and on the questions circled. What if Andius destroys the clan such that there's nothing left for Nyalin to come back to?

That last bit of it sealed the decision, finally, after so much suffering over it. Nyalin wouldn't be happy, either, if she was frozen in time, waiting for him while Andius did whatever he pleased.

She found a piece of charcoal in a drawing box and a sheet of parchment and wrote him a rather inelegant but effective note. The parchment had to be two or three decades old at least, but it was still in good condition.

So he would know where she'd gone, that it'd been a hard decision, that she hadn't run off lightly. Her heart ached a little as she stood up and stretched. Would anyone actually come back to read this note?

Or had he really died falling in the river, or when the lock had broken, and he was really gone for good?

She physically shook herself as she gathered her meager things. They'd left everything at Yeska's cavern. She needed to retrieve what they'd left. And she had to do something, anything, to look for her father.

*So, we are going then?* Yeska asked as Lara strode out into the sunlight, squinting. *Now?*

"The sun is high now, but it'll set soon. Let's get our things from your cave, then we'll head into the city."

*And if the cave is not empty?*

"Then perhaps we'll head into the city first. Let's go and see, shall we?" She started climbing along Yeska's spine, pulling her way forward spike by spike.

*I can try to determine Cerivil's location once we are in the Salt City. I should be able to sense him better when we are closer.*

*I'm eager to try as well. But I fear "should" may be the most meaningful word, there.*

*What else shall we do? Even if we can locate him, it's unlikely he's unguarded. Will you challenge Andius alone?*

*If I must. But not just yet. I do have one idea. It might even help Nyalin too.*

*What's that?*

*A visit to Pyaris. I have questions, and she may have answers. She hears rumors. And...*

*And?*

*And she may be the only friend left I can trust in the entire city.*

*Chapter 8*

# Near and Far

It wasn't until later, as the carriage bounced along the road going north, that Sutamae truly had time to think.

Idak was charming, intelligent, and best of all, he was frank. He said what he was thinking, and if he didn't want to tell her, he simply said so. It was a combination of traits that were turning out to be almost irresistible.

Except... he had never really answered her question. It hadn't been that long since she'd started her sword-stealing antics, but the turnaround in how people treated her had been swift and predictable. They mostly wanted nothing to do with her.

Why was he the exception to that rule? What gave him such a supposedly foreboding reputation that any taint from hers couldn't damage him. She'd asked, and he'd kissed her instead. It'd surprised her.

That had probably been his plan.

Something about it knotted her stomach. Maybe she should have tried harder to get information from Grel and her father. She'd left without the slightest word to either of them.

Because they would have stopped her.

They would also have stopped her from meeting with the Bladed Women or torturing young scions by charming them and then stealing their swords instead of closing the deal. And they would have been wrong about those things. They were some of the only times she felt alive.

Would they have been wrong about this? She wanted to be sure, but as the carriage creaked and groaned over the ruts and bumps in the road, and the leafless trees skimmed past like soldier after soldier held at attention, she wasn't sure at all.

Many thought her father's influence protected her wherever she went in the Salt City, but she knew all too well there were holes in that protection. She had the scars to prove it, even if she never spoke of them to anyone.

She'd survived. So far.

A cold wind cut into the carriage, seemingly determined to remind her that she wasn't in the city any longer. She pulled her cloak closer.

Well, her father and Grel could have told her already about who Idak was, about Idak's family, about so many things about the world, and they hadn't. They needed to start understanding that she was no longer a child. She was a player in this game, not a pawn. Players needed to know the rules, and if they wanted her on their side, they ought to act like it.

She couldn't avoid being a pawn at times; no one could. But she was going to make her own moves on the board. Whether they liked it or not.

---

Grel stood in the door to Sutamae's rooms, shaking his head, his hand still on the doorknob. Where had his sister gone?

She had had many late nights, some strange mornings. But she didn't usually fail to return at all. Something about it bothered him.

First, Raelt had gone missing. Then, his mother's shopping trip up north, from which she hadn't yet returned. It had been a few weeks, there weren't that many places to shop outside the city. What was she really up to? Not that he'd missed her meddling or her harassment or her constant negative remarks.

Were their disappearances all related?

At least when Nyalin had fled the city, he'd clearly had a good reason. Not that Grel knew where *he* was either. What in the world was going on?

He stopped by his father's offices but found them empty. He sighed. He might just have to take this into his own hands this time.

He got his cloak and his boots, then grabbed his usual bags of rice and oats, a few loaves of bread, and headed out, waving goodbye to Uli the maid on his way out the back. The city was calm today, peaceful, the weather drab and cold.

He stopped by to see two or three friends, dropping off the extra much-needed provisions. Sutamae wasn't the only one who could rebel. They definitely had different styles, though. He didn't think his father would approve of his charity, especially not the frequency with which he did it.

He didn't especially care.

Galil, who ran the orphanage, hadn't seen Sutamae, not that that surprised Grel. Porfin at the temple hadn't seen her either. Finally, he tried the boys who ran a bit wild near the emperor's gardens near the city center. He wasn't even really sure they were Obsidians, though some of them definitely had black crossovers. Maybe they were just that dirty. They should probably be under Galil's care. But he wasn't pressuring them. What did he know about their lives?

The one thing that he knew was that they always looked hungry. The bread was for them.

There was the greatest chance that they might have seen his sister, since they frequently roamed many parts of the city and saw a lot of things. Kids like this went unnoticed by most people, so they saw even more than most would realize. But they hadn't spotted his sister.

"Sorry. Isn't that your cat?" one asked. "Looks like she's following you."

He turned and, sure enough, there was Smoke standing at the edge of the alleyway. Huh. "Yes. I suppose it is."

When Nyalin had headed off to the Bone Clan, Smoke had gone with him, but after he'd fled on the dragon with Lara into the wilderness, his cat been found back in his old room, sleeping on the pillows on the window seat more often than not. Grel couldn't recall having seen her this morning, though. She was quite independent and went where she wanted when she wanted, but he still worried about her when he saw her wandering the city, fearful that she might get kicked or mistreated or stolen. But then, she'd show up back in his room, so he had come to accept her nomadic spirit.

Even so, he couldn't recall her ever following him around. And wouldn't have noticed today if the boy hadn't pointed her out.

"What's her name? Can we pet her?"

"Her name is Smoke, and only if you're gentle and she's okay with it."

As the boys approached, Smoke sniffed at them but seemed to decide they were not a threat.

Grel shook his head at himself as he watched the children coo over the cat and scratch between her ears. If he hadn't noticed his own cat, what else might he have missed?

And where did he really need to start asking about Sutamae?

Scooping up Smoke, he waved goodbye to the boys and headed for the taverns. He had more than a few he'd have to stop at, but they were the logical places to try.

His gut twisted at the idea that something could have happened. The last he'd seen her was with Idak at the feast. He'd never expected to keep track of her, and, in truth, he'd lost her pretty quickly. It hadn't worried him at the time.

What if his warning about messing with Idak had been too prescient? What if she had tried her sword prank with him? He shuddered, hardly wanting to think about it. Even if it hadn't been Idak, what she was doing was dangerous, and as word spread, her marks would be less easily fooled.

Had her luck finally run out?

He stroked Smoke's back, trying to calm down. He had no idea for sure that something had happened. She could have been out with a friend. Not that she had many... or that he knew any of them or where to check if that was the case.

The fourth tavern he tried was even darker and dingier, and the alley that led to it was equally gloomy. Amid awnings, balconies, and piles of refuse, very little of the light from the overcast sky was reaching the narrow alley's cobblestones. He was nearly to the tavern door when a strange shape in the shadows made him do a doubletake.

Was that... a wing?

A screech made him look up. Four forms, like no creatures he had ever seen, glided through the sky over him. With dull thuds, he heard them landing on the roof of the building to his right. He scanned the alley with more urgency now.

Looking into the shadows, he spotted even more of them. How many, he wasn't sure. But he could hear the ones on the roof above crawling down toward him. The far end of the alley, just before the door to the tavern he'd been headed toward, was a dead end. Behind him, he heard a hiss.

Smoke squirmed out of his hands. "Wait—" he started, but it was too late. She dashed into the shadows.

That was probably the right idea—get the hell out of here. He spun, looking back to the part of the alley he'd come down.

It was too late. A new handful of winged creatures was landing as he turned. How many of them were there? That was the hiss he'd heard. Sparks of silver caught his eye, three points each near where a head might be. Inhuman.

He gritted his teeth. This was the part where he was supposed to draw his sword and cut them down with a combination of magic and vigorous swordplay. And he could do none of that.

Well. Not none. He had some limited options. If he'd brought a practice blade, he'd have had even more. The energy skills were the most natural to him, even without a sword to focus. Of course he kept his charms in his pocket at all times, as only made sense, so he gathered his energy at his core, one palm face-up, parallel to the earth, as he slid his other palm over top, facing down. Energy snapped between skin and skin, ready.

But who—or what—was he facing? What *were* these things? In all his years, he'd never known alleys to be particularly dangerous in the middle of the day. Nor had he seen anything like these things. What was the best way to fight them, even?

Looking up, he realized any time he'd had for strategy was long past. Several of the strange creatures were scaling the side of the wall down toward him, upside-down, their three-eyed heads all trained on him. As he raised his head to stare, the lowest one lunged, rust-red wings spreading, blocking out the blue sky.

He gasped at the sheer strangeness of it, but his instincts kicked in. A sparking, contorting ball of energy flung of its own volition toward the closest creature, zapping it in the head.

It screeched as it veered to the side, colliding with the wall of the building behind him.

The others on the wall leapt. He glanced left, right—those creatures were creeping closer.

They were going to surround him. He hurried to back up against the wall opposite, pressing his shoulder blades against the stone as he flung three, four, five more balls of light and energy at his attackers.

This was ironic, really. Literally, all he'd done today was try to help people. And where did it get him? Unearthly creatures trying to kill him in an alley.

Energy blasts got him a long way, but there were still too many of them. As he hit one creature to his right, its skin sizzling and smoking where the ball of power had hit it, another to his left got too close.

He smothered a scream into gritted teeth as the claws from one that got too close raked down his left biceps. Focus—keep your focus—he formed the largest bubble he could manage and swung it to the left, hoping to knock them all down like pins in a children's game.

No such luck. One in the group on the right did collapse into a smoking mess, and another from the group on the left was frantically attending to its wing, leading to it spinning in circles, but the central group was untouched—and undeterred.

Goddesses above, when he got home—if he got home—he sure hoped Sutamae was going to be there waiting for him. Were these creatures after him—or her—or just decided this was the time and place to ruin someone's day?

In front of him and on the right, his attackers had recovered. He tried for a circle of fire near his feet, a barrier to hold them back long enough for him to get ahead of them again. Thankfully, it did buy him something in the way of surprise—but it didn't last long. Fire had never been his favorite sphere of magic; that had been animals and humans, especially healing.

Which did him very little good now.

The other problem with a circle of fire in the dirt was that the creatures had wings. Two didn't hesitate to take to the sky, the wing flaps extinguishing even more of the weak flames, and lunged at his head.

One he caught with a ball of energy he'd readied; the other got through, wrapping itself around his upper half and sinking its claws deep into his back.

He staggered forward, trying to dislodge the creature, but others piled on. The force and weight of them sent him staggering back into the wall again. Claws pricked at his calves, his thighs, groping for his neck.

He groped back, tearing at wing and limb—they felt like cooked chickens, tough skin stretched taut across bones. Somewhere, another creature howled, and another—not from his handiwork.

Had someone else stumbled upon this horror show?

More claws found the back of his right arm and tore.

Enough. All rational thought and strategy fled him as pure instinct took over. Crackling energy gathered along his skin, like a coating of lightning, dancing back and forth until it gathered enough momentum to explode.

The magic blasted out from him, sizzling creatures screaming, but it was no victory. Looking down, he realized he had too many bloody wounds to count. Most of them weren't deep, but his back, and the arm... Both arms, really...

A blade flashing caught his eye, and he froze. Someone *had* joined him. A woman. A Bladed Woman? Her soft curls of hair and dress were black, her eyes flashing a sparkling blue. Her sword radiated fiery power, and her technique was utterly deadly, severing a limb, skewering a torso, in a way that made him catch his breath.

As she'd drawn some of their attention, he hurried to direct some energy to heal the wounds in his back and the right arm, the deepest wounds. He would reach the limits of his power soon, and there were still too many creatures, so he didn't even try to fully heal them. Just enough so that he didn't bleed out.

All the while he stared wide-eyed at her. He didn't know any female swordmages that looked like *her*. He definitely would have remembered. And he hadn't heard the door to the tavern swing open. "Where did *you* come from?" he blurted.

"Your dreams," she snapped. Her lunge caught a creature in the side, just under the wing, and from the gurgling lack of a scream, he was fairly certain she'd killed it.

"I'd remember someone like *you*. In dreams or real life. Yet you wear Obsidian colors." He threw small blasts of flames in the faces of those refocusing on him, remembering he was injured. And perhaps their primary mark?

The flames didn't stop them, nor did the water he splashed at them. If only he could find a spell that would make them turn and run. Another charge of energy built between his palms. By the Dark Dragon, he could do so much more if he had a sword.

"Is this really the time for a discussion?" Her blade was a whirl, slashing through the creatures. The flaming steel found purchase, dismembering an arm, then wedging deep into a creature's side.

Grel cringed at the screams she evoked, mixtures of rage and pain and fury. "What'd they expect?" he snapped, flinging another ball of energy at her latest victim. "A welcome-home party? A sacrifice?"

"I don't think... this is... their home," said the woman, through gritted teeth. One of them had seized her blade with its bare hands and was trying to wrench it away from her.

"Agreed." He wanted to help, but another was lunging at him. He summoned more crackling lightning between his hands, flinging it at the silvered points of light. On one hand, thank the Twins she was here. A sword could puncture a lung in a way an energy ball could not. On the other hand? They needed to end this, and she was doing far more than her fair share.

So he reached deeper. A new ball of energy between his hands grew, wobbling and almost uncontainable, and then he hurled it at the pair coming closest to him.

A wide swath of energy that felt like the broad side of a battering ram slammed them into the far building, cracking the stones and mortar. Their bodies fell to the cobblestones, limp, wings bending at awkward angles.

Only three were left. One, the largest of them, let out a scream of fury at its fallen comrades. Then it turned its silvered trio of eyes toward him.

Grel gathered more power, frantically, trying to hold on, trying not to flinch.

It lunged, wings guiding it through the air like arrow fletching.

He raised the ball of power higher, waiting as long as he could to release it, to give him a better chance to hit his mark, and—

"No." The woman stepped in front of him, facing the creature. Her voice was calm. But fire erupted around her like a tornado of flame, growing in power, multiplying.

The lunging creature tried to change course, but it was too late, and the spinning fire engulfed him. Sweat broke out on Grel's skin, the heat just shy of too close, nearly burning.

It enveloped nearly the entire alley—everything but him.

And then, abruptly, it stopped.

She was slumped in front of him, and instinctively, he released the energy he'd worked so hard to gather, just in time to catch her. His eyes caught on the burned, charred forms around them. Every creature had fallen, although he could still see weak jerks of movement in the carnage.

"No, I'm fine." She waved him off.

Reluctantly, he released her, backing away. "Who are—who—" he started.

"I'm nobody special," she muttered.

"Well, Nobody Special, you sure can sling that blade. Come with me and let me see to those wounds at my—"

"No." She cut him off, already jogging toward the mouth of the alley. "I can't."

"Wait, why? I—"

He didn't get to finish. She didn't get to run. An inhuman voice in the shadows hissed, then rose, a language Grel didn't understand, but something that every bone in his body told him was evil, was a curse.

A last dying blast of power shot from the charred bodies, hitting her. Her body flew, slamming into the stones ahead of him. He had a terrible feeling that that was more than just a blow. There was dark magic at work.

With one last laugh, the wreckage of the bodies finally went still.

He sprinted toward her. "Hey, hey—" He turned her over.

She didn't respond. Her dark hair was splayed across the cobblestones. Aside from a cut on her cheek, it looked like nothing was wrong. But he was fairly certain. Something was very wrong.

Grel gathered his strange savior, his unexpected guardian, in his arms and ran.

The inn looked like just the sort of place a large party might stop in for refreshment. Daridian would have usually avoided such places, but today he headed in, mask tucked in his pack, as though he were an ordinary traveler.

Because if he wanted to find his sister, he needed something to go on. Someplace to start. Some members of the Obsidian elite had her, somewhere to the north, but beyond that, he was gazing at a vast wilderness to have to explore.

The place was busy. A group of women sat laughing and drinking boisterously by the fire. He slid into a dark corner, and the serving boy approached.

"Can I get you an ale?" asked the kid.

"No, just water."

The boy gave him a dubious look. "Not ale?"

"I don't drink," he murmured. "Something wrong with the water?"

The boy shrugged.

"Cider then." He'd eat what was in his pack for now.

Nodding, the kid started to turn away.

"Hey—you see any large, wealthy groups moving through here?"

The boy raised an eyebrow, then leaned a little closer. "You lookin' for a mark, eh? I know the feeling."

Dar hesitated. He had no intention of stealing anything other than the damn sword, but would it help him here? How else would he explain his motives? But he hated to lie, even over something so trivial. "No. Not at the moment anyway. I'm looking for someone."

Brows knitted, the boy thought for a moment. And took a long time doing it. An impossibly long time, in fact.

Dar sighed, drew a silver from his pouch, and slid it across the table.

"There was a party two days back," the boy said quickly, snatching the coin.

"Two days?" That fit the timeline. "Who was with them?"

"Two women, five men. The women didn't look too happy about being there. I stayed away, to tell you the truth."

"Obsidians?" He had to remember to think in the strange system of the clans here. Sha'lien had been taken by power-hungry Obsidians, but she'd been dressed in the garb of the Pearl Clan before that, as they were the clan into which she would wed. Would she still? This broke so many treaties and agreements, hard to say for sure how it would pan out.

The boy shrugged. "So they seemed. All wore black. But some of the clans wear dark cloaks to travel, so it's hard to say."

"I'm looking for a Pearl," he said. And then he remembered his other target. "Oh, and a young man. Nyalin son of Linali, I think?"

The boy's eyes went wide as saucers. "He's *here*? In these parts?"

"Oh, no—I don't know. That's why I'm looking." That was quite the reaction. What did the boy know that he didn't? He shouldn't reveal his naïveté to this one, lest the boy realize he was an outsider. "I've heard he's traveling outside of the city. I have a message from his family, that's all."

Eyebrows flying higher, the kid snapped upright. "Let me get that cider for you, sir!" And he took off at a run.

Daridian shook his head. By the Great Spear, he hated this place.

No, that wasn't fair. The boy was polite, and a silver hadn't been much. At least to him. But he was royalty. Perhaps he was being too generous.

He hated not knowing the lay of the land, too, the full situation. The history. How would he ever find Sha'lien with one hand tied behind his back?

Sighing, he scanned the inn, but it seemed filled with tired farmers, laborers, and craftsmen. The women by the fire were gossiping and giggling. No one seemed up to much of anything but their ordinary lives.

He'd just have to figure out a way. And keep asking questions.

The boy returned with his cider. "Anything else I can get for you, sir? I can get you our finest smoked fish or a selection of salted meats from the back stores. It's not on the menu as we don't offer that to every patron, but I think we can make an exception for someone such as yourself."

Frowning, Dar took a long draught, the sweetness of the cider filling his senses. Setting the mug down, the musty, dank scent of the tavern flooded back in, and he tried not to wince. But perhaps there was one thing the tavern might have that he'd miss with long days on the road, and not knowing when they would end. "No, no food for now. But do you have a bath?"

"As a matter of fact, we do, sir! Not like in the city, but..."

"I wouldn't expect that in a crossroads inn. It's all right, son."

The boy smiled, a little too brightly. "Can I pull a bath for you then, sir?"

"How much?" He'd prefer coppers, but he'd pay gold at this point. A bath could be hard to find in the days ahead.

"For you, sir—consider it complimentary."

He opened his mouth to object—he was no one special—but the boy was already gone.

Who was this Nyalin moLinali, and how could he thank the man for his apparently free bath?

When Nyalin opened his eyes, he was no longer in his mother's house. He was on the side of the volcano. As had happened on his previous visits to the afterworld, his walk with Batu had moved him in the real world too.

He sprang to his feet, maybe too quickly, but Stragg was known to erupt from time to time. It'd be just his luck to discover the old guy was about to blow.

Fortunately, no smoke billowed as he glanced over his shoulder at the peak, and the ground was still. He carefully picked his way through the uneven black rock, the smoke and steam periodically billowing overhead which encouraged him to move a little faster. It was amazing to see how desolate it was, save a few trees stubbornly clinging to life at the edges, but then at a certain point far down the mountain, the lava slowed, and the forests and grasses returned.

He sighed. It was great that he wasn't going to have to run from a lava flow, but it was going to be a long walk home.

Well, to his mother's childhood house. He didn't really have a home right now, did he? Or perhaps his home was wherever Lara was. That thought sent a jolt through him. How long had he been gone? Had it been only one day? The sun had sunk low, about to set.

Memories flashed through him now, but not all entirely his own. Some were from the afterworld, those of spirits, of Batu's. Somehow, he knew it'd been more than a few hours. Maybe more than a day that he'd been meditating here. Or, there. Wherever.

Before he started down the mountainside, he narrowed his eyes at the spot where the vortex had appeared so clearly in the afterworld. No such distinction stood out on the horizon now, although he did think he could see a group of buildings breaking up out of the forest.

Batu had seemed to suggest that, with his instruction, Nyalin would have more control. That he wouldn't get stuck again. That he had a greater store of internal energy now. That was part of what had taken so long. But Nyalin wasn't quite ready to test his skills in that regard. Not without at least finding Lara first, letting her know he was okay.

Making sure *she* was okay.

With one final glare toward his target on the horizon, he started down the side of the mountain.

He didn't get far, though, before Nerutoa found him. *I see you have returned*, she observed. *Need a ride?*

He smiled. "I sure do."

*I trust you have learned much in the afterworld.* She bent her wing to lower her shoulder for him to more easily climb up her shining, black obsidian-encrusted scales.

*Indeed, I did. I met someone very interesting.* He scaled Nerutoa's side cautiously, as the jagged scales seemed far more likely to cut him than Yeska's smoother bone scales.

*Yes?*

*Yes, he said I should ask you about the forge.* Nowhere looked comfortable, so he chose the spot that seemed to present the least likelihood of injury.

The dragon chuffed, a gesture he couldn't read. Satisfaction? Annoyance? *Very well. It is quite near your mother's home. We shall go.*

He gasped as she leapt into the sky without warning. Clutching as tightly as he could, he shook his head, trying to make sense of it all. The things he'd learned almost seemed unreal. His mother was supposedly alive. And he was supposed to free her and topple the whole foundation on which magic was built while he was at it?

He was no sword smith, no blacksmith. His fingers weren't calloused by the hammer; they were black from the ink of the pen.

Although... less so today than they used to be.

But now, back in his real world and his real body and his real life, the afterworld seemed like a hallucination, even though he knew it wasn't. But who was he to make his own sword? Who was he to free prisoners? Or upend the entire social hierarchy? Could his mother really be alive? Could so many mages be doing something they had no idea was evil, for their entire lives?

*Imprisoned in each sword is a soul that can't move on...*

He shook his head again, then thought of the bored practice sword he'd used in Cerivil's tests. How it had seemed to have opinions, like it had longed to do more. Lara had commented on the sword's personality too.

By the Twins.

Wincing, he pressed his face against the smooth bone of the spike he was clutching. Knowing what he knew now, he'd have to do something—whether he'd made a promise to Batu or not. But the idea of it—it was overwhelming. He'd barely been able to receive teaching from the mages a season ago. He'd had no magic of his own until just a few hours—or days?—before this. How was he supposed to tackle something this big?

Well. Fortunately, he had something else he had to do first. Just go up against a necromancer who'd probably been trying to kill him his whole life and who his father thought had killed his mother.

What could go wrong with that?

This forge better be a magical forge, or he was going to be in trouble. Because he was going to need help. And a lot of it.

*Dark Dragon, can we stop at the house first? I want to make sure Lara knows I'm here, and I'm safe. And maybe she'll want to see this forge too.*

*Of course.*

But when he reached his mother's house, the setting sun casting it in a golden glow, Lara wasn't there.

-

Daridian had just settled down into the warm tub when he heard footsteps on the tiles. Someone else had entered. And she was... humming.

He sat still for a long moment. Maybe it was an attendant. Fetching a cloth or warming the water.

The steps to the other tub behind him creaked. The humming continued, closer now, as the woman slipped into the water.

Well, that was unusual. He was not used to public shared baths anywhere in Annikyre, but he'd heard of them. Weren't they usually segregated? Perhaps in a town this small, there wasn't enough demand to make it feasible.

Water dripped somewhere, and the coals hissed quietly where they warmed the steamy air around them. But the peaceful silence felt charged now, tense, though he couldn't say why. He needed to say something, anything, to dispel this tension.

"Long travels?" he asked. Maybe she'd seen Sha'lien. Or Sutamae.

"Mmm hmm." It was less of an answer than the continuation of the humming. He wouldn't get much information out of her at this rate.

"Don't they usually keep these to just men or women?" he said easily, keeping eyes on the ceiling.

A puff of soft laughter. "Sometimes, in the country they're mixed. Sometimes, they just don't care."

That *voice*. He caught himself before he jolted upright. But he glanced over his shoulder, keeping as still as he could and hoping the water wouldn't betray his movement.

Long black hair hung out of the side of the tub. Steam haloed her head, billowing up toward the ceiling. Nothing that would identify her was visible, but the fire that ran through him told him everything he needed to know.

It was the girl. Sutamae. And here he was, unmasked.

"I guess we'll just have to avert our eyes," she murmured, voice smooth. Relaxed.

"Mmm hmm." He dared not say more.

She sighed. The water lapped and quivered as she twisted into a different position.

He slumped back down into the water, wanting to sink under the surface. If he spoke again, would she recognize his voice? Damn his accent. Had he already given himself away? He should have taken his language lessons more seriously. But if he couldn't nail the precise accent of this empire, perhaps he could imitate a different one... Mushin? No, that'd be dangerous, and he was no bearish creature; he didn't have the mouth to do it justice. Could he manage something else?

Or perhaps he should simply get out of there as quickly as possible.

On the other hand, though. If she didn't recognize him, now was a chance to ask her questions. Or someone might join her, and he could listen in. Who knew what he might find out?

Although, if she really didn't recognize him, that meant he'd made much less of an impression on her than she'd made on him.

He sat still, wrestling with indecision, his relaxation gone and his shoulders bunched. He was still sitting and weighing his options when she made the decision for him.

"Do you believe in fate?" she asked.

He started to turn, then stopped himself, remembering the locale. "I..." He didn't really believe in fate. At least, he hadn't thought so.

But his fingers wandered to his lips, wet and warm from the water. He could still feel the Spark of her lips against his. Elder Maihei had spoken about her fated lover once, that she'd felt the Spark too. He'd dismissed it as the fancy of a person who longed for her dead mate, a way of romanticizing and reliving the past. But he'd seen the way her eyes had shone when she talked about it, and now that he'd felt it...

"Yes." He swallowed. "Yes, I do."

She said nothing. Murmurs rose in the inn, lowered again.

"Do you?" he said into the silence. He could fake an empire accent in short bursts, perhaps.

"No."

Where were her thoughts going with a question like that? He waited a moment, hoping his silence would invite her to continue. It paid off.

"I believe we make our own fates."

He smiled. "Perhaps it is both."

"Is that an option? I thought it certainly must be one or the other." The water swished idly in her tub, and he imagined her drawing circles across the surface. Imagined her drawing those same circles across his skin...

He cleared his throat—and his wandering thoughts. "Fate reaches out its hand. It is up to us whether we take what it offers."

Her sigh was long and deep, and a touch sad.

"What? What is it?"

A sharp swish through the water, a kick, a splash. "What if fate slaps you?"

He thought for a moment. "Then slap it back."

Her laugh was long and slow and husky, languid like a cat stretching in the sun.

He wanted to know more, needed to, really. He groped for words to draw her out, but nothing came. Even more, he needed to hear another one of those laughs.

"Why do you wonder about fate?" he asked. Simple and direct might be best, when negotiating with the feline variety.

She hesitated before answering. "A friend has been talking about it."

"A friend?"

"A man who says he wants me for his own. Of course, he's barely known me a week."

Something clutched in his chest. She certainly had felt the Spark between them—how could anyone miss it?— but she couldn't know how he felt. Indeed, he hadn't admitted he thought of her as his own, until she'd spoken these words. But everyone knew about the Spark, didn't they? Everyone knew what it meant. She couldn't be thinking of giving herself to another *now*. They belonged together.

Except... he'd left. He'd told her there was no chance of his return. He shook his head at his foolishness. He had no claim here. She *must* be talking about someone else.

The thought made his blood burn.

"I know it's silly," she said, misinterpreting his silence. "That's exactly what I thought too. Nobody knows their own fate. Although, perhaps you're right. Perhaps I should reach out my hand."

"What happened to slapping?" he said, too quickly.

She chuckled now. Loudly enough that some of the street traffic quieted, as if hearing her and wondering. "Well, since he's paying for my room and board, as his guest, slapping doesn't seem very polite."

The large group that had arrived. She was traveling with them. Curse his luck.

"As long as he doesn't require payment for those amenities that you're not willing to give. Then slapping is very appropriate."

To his utter disbelief, she chuckled again. By the Spear, she really did seem to think he was funny. Him of all people.

"Don't worry. I can handle myself just fine," she replied.

"I don't doubt it."

He'd let his guard down, and something about his response was too quick, too meaningful. Perhaps it was because it mirrored the things they'd said in the streets, but he heard a splash as she turned sharply in the water.

He sensed her scrutiny and could feel her eyes staring at the back of his head. He didn't move.

Looked like this bath was over. As soon as he could be sure he could get out of here without her seeing his face, he'd be gone.

Which might be an impossible challenge at this point, but he had to try.

They both jumped when the door opened and a handful of the women from earlier bustled in, by the variety of voices. Cooing and giggling, they piled into the two other tubs, but still didn't fit.

Water splashed across the tiles as one of them said to her, "Do you mind a little company in there?"

"I—uh—well, yes, as a matter of fact—"

This distraction was probably the best chance he was going to get. He rose, quickly wrapped his towel around himself, and padded out.

"Hey—wait—" she started to call after him, but he pretended not to hear.

More conversation would only risk her discovering too much about his mission anyway. His father would probably say a bath like that was a luxury that he didn't deserve if he hadn't found his sister. It was due time to stop dallying and move on.

And if the end of his bath allowed her to keep her tub to herself, all the better.

Lara caught her breath, the wind blowing through her hair. From above, the city was dotted with tiny points of light where fires or lamps or braziers burned in hearths and on streets. At night, the view from Yeska's back was totally different from what she'd seen during the day. She didn't know the city from the sky the way she did walking its streets. The aerial daytime view was fascinating, but at night? It was glorious.

Yeska flew slowly, gliding down to keep the sound of her great wings as quiet as possible.

*Do you sense him?*

*Yes. I will find somewhere to land.*

While Yeska circled, dipped, and circled again, Lara swallowed, gripping tightly to the spike in front of her. The night air was cold. Finding her father was paramount, but gliding over the city, its sheer size was almost overwhelming.

How could she possibly find her father in a city this size? Even just the Bone District alone felt intimidating, but if Andius had collaborated with Obsidians, he could have made deals with other clans too. That meant Andius could be keeping her father captive just about anywhere.

Still, Yeska seemed to narrow in on the Bone District, from what little Lara could recognize from the air in the dark. There were very few landmarks that stood out from the others, but a thin sliver of moon cast a little light on the emperor's palace, and she could just make out some lights by the docks and a strange glittering that she was fairly certain was the water. From the angle, they should be in her home district.

Finally, Yeska landed on the large, flat roof of a building just outside the walls of the Bone mansion. She could see her father's workshop. It was dark. *He is... close.*

*That was quite the silent landing. I hardly heard it.* She contemplated climbing down but, instead, decided to start by just listening. At the moment, the city felt sleepy, muffled.

*I can be subtle if I want to be.*

*Is he in his workshop?* That *would* be a likely place for her father to hide if he'd simply wanted to seclude himself from everyone, as Andius had implied. That didn't make sense, though. He would never refuse an audience with the emperor.

*It's strange. I can't pinpoint the location as precisely as usual. Something is interfering, I think.*

*Well, if Andius is behind this disappearance—*

*If?*

Lara shook her head. *—then he likely took the best precautions he could to keep Da hidden.*

*Sound spells perhaps. It is too quiet here.*

She frowned. Huh. Yeska was right. Perhaps she'd been alone in the wild ghost lands too long, gotten too used to the silence. She'd grown up here—it was never this quiet.

Stretching out her senses, she tried to feel for the magic around her, sniffed at the air for the citrusy scent of Andius's magic.

*I'm going to look around.*

*Wait. What if they see you?*

*It's a risk I'm going to have to take.*

*At least find a scarf or something.*

The night *was* cold, so it wouldn't have been unreasonable. Dragonhide was warm enough that she didn't freeze, but most flights were still fairly cold, and once she slid down...

*The transformation spells. Maybe I could at least make myself look a little different.*

*Excellent. That will make them more likely to ignore you than seize you at once.*

With a deep breath, she steadied herself, gathering her magic, spinning it through the charm Emperor Pavan had given them, and into the spell—and her face.

She shuddered when it was done. *I'll never get used to that.*

*Never say never, Daughter.*

Slipping down Yeska's side, she strode around the rooftop. The streets around were empty. How late was it? Or was there some magic at work—or more mundane reasons why no one was out? She didn't expect the night streets to be busy, but no one?

She chose the darkest side street and dropped down the single level to the cobblestones. Scanning around her, she eased to the nearest window and leaned slightly around the edge, looking inside.

*Do you think this is the place?*

*I can't say for certain. He is... nearby. Strange.*

Inside this window was mostly dark. The same was true for the next. She rounded the corner, but none of the windows revealed much. The building seemed unused, empty now. The eerie silence persisted.

She'd need to check each of the surrounding buildings. There was a cafe, closed right now but still smelling of roasted yak and pork and baking bread in the air. That place seemed truly quiet. The rest of the places appeared to be large homes, which she couldn't truly search simply by peering in a bunch of windows. Sneaking into dozens of houses alone didn't sound like a good idea. She focused on the back alleys, the back doors, sometimes peering through the tiny windows of underground levels and basements.

*I'm going in.* She had to check inside the Bone mansion's compound, inside the walls of the gardens.

She could sense Yeska's apprehension, but the dragon didn't try to stop her.

Would doing this have been better with allies? Yes. But she couldn't ask this of Pyaris, Nyalin had vanished into literal thin air and might never come back, and the only other two allies she had—besides Yeska—were the ones she needed to find.

The familiar tall trees, plants, and benches inside made her heart wrench. Huh. She hadn't realized what it would be like to come back here, after so long, after no real goodbye, with such an uncertain future.

So many memories of these trees, these limbs and branches. She could almost see Myandrin sitting on the bench, reading to her.

She blinked. Wait. Had she seen it? For a moment, she almost thought she'd seen a faint outline, like a figure etched in light, the same way the light glowed from Nyalin's eyes when his mother's powers started to overtake him. No, *his* powers. His powers, now. For better or worse.

But the bench was empty. Myandrin was long gone, and for all she knew, Nyalin was too. Her throat felt tight, so she swallowed hard, tried not to think about it, tried to forget.

Just for the moment. Right now, her father needed her. And maybe Faytou did too.

There was a guard near her father's workshop, as usual, but he paid the quiet woman walking past no mind. There was a fire burning in the hearth, and several lanterns lit, as if someone kept it ready should her father reappear at a moment's notice. But it was clear, no one was inside.

Did the average people really believe he was sick, tired... mourning his beloved daughter's betrayal? Were they actually buying it? Did they even know something was wrong? It wasn't like her father had held regular daily parades or met with members of the clan on a daily basis, although his students certainly knew he wasn't teaching his classes as usual. How long would it take for people to realize something was really amiss?

The mansion. She couldn't stomach the thought of trying to sneak in there tonight. To be an intruder in her own home. But she found it hard to believe he'd be there. If the emperor with his much more sophisticated transformations had gotten inside and found nothing, she needed to look elsewhere.

A few other buildings were dark. That left the warehouse. Then she'd go look for Pyaris and, maybe, if there was a little light of sunrise before she left, she'd see if she could recognize the street where Andius had held her and Nyalin captive. She hadn't seen it going in, as they'd knocked her unconscious, but when they'd fled... she thought maybe she could remember.

The warehouse was for storing grain, not working, so it had few windows, and most were high up. Fortunately, barrels had been stacked up outside—empty or full, she wasn't sure—and she was able to climb up three or four and peer inside.

She caught her breath. Inside, near the center of the warehouse, stood Andius. Everything around him was bathed in bright white light, like a star was being born on the rickety wooden table in front of him.

It was no star, though. It was magic. Magic drenched everything around the table, except the form that lay there. Pale and unmoving.

It was Faytou.

Her fingernails dug into her palms. What by the Twins was Andius doing to him?

*Chapter 9*

# Waking Up

Lara watched as beads of sweat appeared on Andius's forehead, anger and intense effort contorting his usually placid features. She had to think this was a more natural expression for him.

She had to stop whatever this was. Free Faytou. Somehow. She could see at least ten armed people, some of them positioned at each of the entrances and others clustered near Andius. All eyes were trained on Andius. And there could be even more of them that she couldn't see from this angle.

She leaned slightly further left, to see if there were more around that side of the building.

And the barrels toppled, rolling end over end, and taking her with them.

Her head was still spinning, back and knee and bottom aching from the fall when what she was hearing broke through the pain.

"What was that?" someone inside said.

"Everyone. Search the grounds." That voice. She'd know it anywhere—Andius.

Her thoughts raced as she struggled to her feet, pain shooting through her right shoulder. If they found her—even if they didn't see through her transformation disguise—they might still drag her inside as some commoner snooping around.

She glanced around. Other than barrels, there was a row of lazy, leafy plants to one side, then a wall. Not much room to hide amid those leaves, not when one's pale crossover caught the moonlight better than say an Obsidian's would. Yet another advantage Obsidians had on her clan, damn them.

Wracking her brain, she flattened herself against the wall. She could hear them coming closer, footsteps and hushed voices on both sides.

How could she get out of here unseen? Who would they be likely to ignore? A child? No, they'd be even harsher with a child. Emperor Pavan? While that seemed rich, she wasn't sure she could pull off his appearance perfectly, some of the details were foggy in her memory.

Maybe someone she knew better, had seen every day of her life. Maybe she could scare the piss out of them as Myandrin! Or simply appear as her father! Although, if they'd made her father disappear, they'd just do the same thing again if they found him wandering outside the warehouse. No, she needed—

She caught her breath as the idea hit her.

Andius.

As quickly as she could thread the spell through the charm, she was shifting her features to look like Andius, growing a little taller. Fortunately, their clothes would be nearly the same, thank the Twins for crossovers, because she had only managed some of the physical features of the spell, not the clothing illusion yet.

And not the voice. She swallowed hard. A deep flaw in her plan, but it was the only plan she had right now.

Hurrying around the corner as fast as she could walk without running, she immediately collided with someone's chest.

"Sir! I thought you went the other way."

She gave him her best Andius scowl.

"My apologies, my apologies, sir. So sorry."

"Did you see anyone?" asked the other man.

She shook her head sharply.

"Should we return then? If you've checked back there?"

She grunted, making her voice as deep as she could. Both men's brows furrowed. Twin's dreams, that was too low, wasn't it? She jerked a thumb over her shoulder, tried a more moderate grunt that she hoped said, "Get going." And then she started walking around them. Andius had better things to do, obviously.

It worked. The man kept going.

Behind her, she heard a voice say, "But, sir, you were just back there."

"What?" Andius again. "Explain."

"I just ran straight into you over by those barrels and—"

"You did not, you dolt. Don't be ridiculous."

She walked quickly and turned the corner around the front of the warehouse, heading toward the door.

"But—"

"You were mistaken."

"I—"

"Silence, or you'll find the consequence of disobeying me."

The voices started to become unintelligible as she moved too far away. Interesting that Andius was not quite so sugar-coated with his inner circle. It didn't seem wise, in her estimation. But *he* was the one who'd won the most power by winning people over. She'd only managed to steal things.

But stealing seemed to be working, so it was time to try it again.

Keeping up her best confident, brisk, I'm-too-busy-to-stop stride, she turned on a heel and entered the warehouse, heading straight for Faytou.

"Did you find anything, sir?" someone asked.

She gave him a curt head-shake and did her best to look extremely pissed off. Then she picked up Faytou, as though this was a perfectly normal thing to do, threw him over her shoulder, and turned back toward the door.

Her arms ached from the effort, but when Faytou whimpered quietly behind her shoulder, it was worth it.

"Sir? Where are you going, sir?"

She grunted, low again.

"Should we come with you?"

She couldn't slow down for a head shake to be clear, so she risked a few words, trying her best to impersonate him. "No. Stay here."

"Sir?"

She didn't stop to listen—or respond. She was at the wide doorway now, and she kept going.

She only made it about fifty paces before shouts went up behind her.

"I—what?" And a moment later, "Where is he?"

"Intruder!"

"Imposter!"

Heavy as Faytou was, she started to run.

*Change of plans, Yeska.*

*Ah, yes. Indeed.* The dragon's voice sounded odd.

*Is there something I should know?*

*I am not alone. Some, uh, people found me. I sought to fly closer and when they noticed the wings—* Lara sensed the new location where Yeska perched. She caught a glimpse of a small clearing in the gardens, where men and women were gathering around her, murmuring with hands covering their mouths, staring.

*I'm coming. I brought a friend.*

The guards' footsteps still pounded behind her on the path. She was *not* strong enough to carry Faytou much farther than this. In fact, she was surprised she'd gotten this far. Every muscle in her shoulders, torso, and thighs was bitterly complaining.

As she neared, she caught sight of the crowd surrounding the dragon.

*Yeska—I need help. I can't—* She was panting hard now, slowing down. *Can they help somehow?*

Yeska only hesitated for a moment, before suddenly her voice echoed in Lara's mind. *Part ways. Bring my daughter to me.*

Somehow, the crowd seemed to know what she meant, more than what the words said. They rushed forward, opening a path toward the dragon while also running toward Lara—and toward the people chasing her.

She dropped her transformation, sliding back into herself and nearly dropping Faytou in the process. Near her, two men noticed and caught Faytou, taking her charge from her and following along behind.

*Come, Daughter. Protect us, true members of the Bone Clan.*

A chill went through her at the power in Yeska's words. But there wasn't time to reflect on it, to see if it had affected the others too. There was only time to take Faytou from the men who'd taken him from her, climb onto Yeska's back, and get Faytou's unconscious form securely in front of her.

Yeska leapt into the air, the dark night sky welcoming them, shouts ringing out below.

*Scatter my friends*, Yeska added. *Do not let them find you.*

Still panting, Lara blinked down at the form slumped in front of her. Well, she hadn't made it to Pyaris, and no sign at all of her father.

But this was something. Nyalin would be so happy to see him.

If Faytou ever woke up. If Andius hadn't hurt him too badly. And if Nyalin ever came back.

It was a lot of ifs. She swallowed hard and stared down at the dark city below her, trying to decide how soon she'd need to come back.

---

It had been too long since Andius had contacted his... friend in the Obsidian Clan. He had never been able to decide definitely what to call her. Mentor? Patron? Debt collector? He shook his head as he sat down in front of the mirror and began the special spell she'd instructed him to use to make contact.

He'd carefully cleared his home of all who weren't unquestionably loyal. Only a few of his followers knew of this connection of his. Until his leadership was secure, he would continue to keep it a secret. But he didn't see why he should need to. High-level connection with such a powerful clan could only bring up the status of his own clan. That was precisely what was wrong with some of the Bone Clan leadership. Too many mistakes. Too many moral squabbles. Not enough getting the job done. Under Lara's leadership, it would just be more of the same.

Which was precisely why he would wrench the clan from her cold, dead hands.

"I'm going to need more money," he said as soon as Unira's face appeared. He had no time for games, for all of the effort to win people over. He didn't think Unira was much of a fan of such a style anyway, but where had all his efforts at charisma gotten him? It certainly hadn't finished the job of installing him as clan leader. It was time for some new tactics.

"Well, well, Andius. You are getting better at getting to the point."

"Thank you."

"Have you secured your leadership position in the clan yet?"

"I'm working on it."

"That's what you said last time. Why should I give you more money if you haven't done what I asked?"

"Because I am very close. I have Clan Leader Cerivil under my control. His daughter has run off into the hills and fled. No one has heard from her. It will only be a matter of time until I pressure the council into listening to me."

"Some here have said that I should stop payments altogether. Some have even said that perhaps this plan has failed."

Andius's lips pressed into a thin line. He wouldn't tell her about his own fears that it might be true, about Lara's cursed rescue of Faytou, of the mutterings he occasionally overheard. None of that mattered. He would show all of them in the end, Unira included. He was *not* a failure. "I have done everything you asked. I've done more than that. The clan *will* be mine."

"Anyone can say that. Few can achieve it. If you're so sure, kill the clan leader you've imprisoned then. Why haven't you done that already? Why are you keeping him alive? A ransom?"

"Do you kill all who have wronged you that you capture?" He knew for a fact she didn't. "I believe you harness their power as your own."

Unira narrowed her eyes. "You do have high aspirations."

"If we are to be allies, I should think that you would support me. Power that I gain will be power that is at your disposal." Maybe he was going to need at least a *little* persuasion to get through this. Inwardly, he groaned. He was tired of it all.

"Fair point."

"Help me learn the spell."

"What spell?"

"The one you use to tap your victims for their power." She knew very well what spell, but he let it slide. He'd been trying to master it for days now. Clearly, he was missing something. He needed help and there was literally no one else he could ask.

But if he could master the spell... his power could be limitless.

"I would need to be with you to teach you such a thing. I'm not in the city. You are."

"I could bring the Bone Clan leader to you." He cleared his throat. Was he being too forward? "At your estate."

"How are you keeping them from finding him? The dragon should be able to find him."

"A combination of sedatives and spells. He gave up the clanblade, so the link is weaker. Please, I can finish this. But I need just a little more help."

She pursed her lips, seeming to think it over for a moment. Something about the expression made him nervous. "All right," she said slowly. "Bring him to my estate. Quickly."

"As you command."

Mask on again, Daridian followed the caravan at a distance. His hunch that traveling Obsidians would have stopped at the little inn had proven correct, but even so, he'd gotten lucky to find this group of them passing through at the exact same time as he was.

According to the friendly boy, they came from a large silk estate to the north. Those were some of the wealthiest Obsidians in these parts, aside from those who owned mines, but most of those apparently lived in the city.

The boy had even offered him the purchase of a horse, and he'd been sorely tempted. But that would deplete his gold severely, even though the boy had offered him an excellent price. It would also limit his movement. And his ability to hide. And horses needed care and food—he couldn't stand to run an animal to death, even for his sister.

He'd gambled that a caravan of that size would be slow-moving. He might even be faster than they were, and he could keep concealed in the trees more easily without a horse.

As he came to the fork in the road, however, he had to admit that he'd lost the gamble on speed. They might be a large group, but they weren't as slow as he'd hoped.

Fool. He'd been a fool. What if he lost them here? What if he lost *her* among them here? Not to mention any guesses he had as to where he might look for his sister.

He surveyed the area. Luck was on his side. Rain the day before had muddied the road. Horse and deer prints. Many of them. Wheels of wagons. Only fools counted on luck, though. His father was right about him again.

The caravan would certainly reach their destination before he could catch up. The same luck might not hold by the time he reached the next fork, in which case, he could lose them entirely.

If he wanted to avoid that fate, he'd have to hurry. He started into a jog as he hurried on. They'd need time to set up camp for that many people. He could continue to travel and gain ground, and nod off against a tree if needed.

May the Great Spear speed his steps—and help him catch up to them before his strength gave out.

Yeska landed softly in the clearing outside Nyalin's mother's home in the Obsidian wilds, Lara on her back. The house looked unchanged, quiet. Lara bit her lip, not sure what she'd been hoping to see. She checked on her passenger. Faytou was still asleep.

*He's still alive, right?* She could check his pulse—again—but it wasn't always easy, and maybe all the prodding would disturb his rest and delay his recovery.

*Yes. He'll be fine. Eventually.*

*How long?*

*I can't say for sure.*

She'd slid down Yeska's side, contemplating how to get Faytou down in a way that wasn't ridiculous or injurious. But as her feet hit the earth, she heard the heavy door swing open.

She spun. There he was. Flesh and blood—alive in the doorway.

"Nyalin!" She ran to him, throwing her arms around him. "You're back!"

"It took quite a bit of walking and meditating and bargaining with a spirit—"

"A spirit? Bargaining? You?"

He laughed. "Yeah... It's a long story."

"Get explaining, young man."

"I will, but—is there someone else on Yeska? Are they all right?"

She beamed at him. "Yeska assures me he *will* be. He's a bit incapacitated at the moment, though." They jogged forward together.

"Faytou!" Nyalin exclaimed.

"Yes. I rescued him. Mostly accidentally, but I used the emperor's transformation charm and disguised myself as Andius."

"No. You didn't."

"Yes."

"How could you stand it?"

"Well, *I* didn't have to look at him... Me." She grinned back. "And then I just walked in and took him! They figured the trick out quickly, but well..." She gestured at their friend. "I got away anyway."

"Impressive!" He reached out and squeezed her hand, making her heart race faster.

"Come on, help me get him down. He's sleeping off whatever Andius was doing to him, but, hopefully, he'll be all right soon. Yeska says she's sure he's okay." Lara couldn't guess how the dragon could know for sure, but she decided she was going to have to believe her.

Once they had Faytou inside and resting in the bedroom, they sat together on the large, padded couch, and Nyalin explained all that had happened to him in the afterworld. It was hard to believe. If she hadn't known Nyalin so well, she'd have never believed it, especially the promises the strange spirit wolf had required of him.

"I was so worried," she whispered, bending her head to rest against his. But then she stood, a restless worry making her feel not quite able to relax.

"So was I. Everything that's worked in the past wasn't working. I wasn't sure I'd ever make it back."

She paced back and forth. "I'm sorry I didn't wait for you, I just—"

"Don't worry about it. It wasn't like waiting here was going to help me get back."

"I didn't know what to do."

"Neither did I. I think we're just going to have to make this up as we go along."

"Is it over now? Do you think you could get trapped in the afterworld again?"

"Honestly, I don't know." He spread his hands. "I definitely learned some things from Batu about how to move back and forth between the worlds, but I don't know... I just feel like there are no guarantees anymore."

"Maybe after some time passes..." She ran a hand through her hair. "We couldn't find Da. Yeska could sense him, but not precisely."

He rose and came closer to her, resting his hands gently on her shoulders. "We'll find him. We can go back after Faytou's awake and we're more rested. Or maybe even before then."

Normally, Yeska would have put in a snarky comment about why she was left out of the list, but like Faytou, she was asleep.

"I don't know what I'd have done if you didn't come back," she whispered.

"You'd have found your father, kicked Andius's ass, become clan leader like you deserved, and Myandrin and I would have admired your excellent work from afar."

She bit her lip at the pain of that idea.

"And you wouldn't have had to worry about the pesky baggage of being in love with a half ghost or an emperor's son."

"I'm not worried about any of that."

"Hmm. I am."

"I have enough to worry about."

"Forgive me if I want to be with you. My so-called father has already made enough poor choices on my behalf. I'm not sure I want to get you caught up in them."

"Too late." She narrowed her eyes at him. "You never had a chance."

"Lara, really—we must think this through. Would you want to be an empress?"

"As if all the clans would accept me. I can't even get my *own* clan to accept me."

"You will. And I think we could convince them. But do we want to? What if Pavan—"

"Let's cross that bridge—or burn it—when we come to it."

"But—"

There was a groan from the bedroom. She was loathe to leave Nyalin's side, especially with the way the conversation had grown tense, but he gave her a sympathetic look. He was already turning to head back to check on their friend. "We'll talk more—later."

"Faytou, are you all right?" she asked as they entered the bedroom. Some of the light was returning to his gray eyes, but his black hair was still quite disheveled, his skin still pale.

"By the Twins, Lara, Nyalin! I'm so relieved to see you."

"I can't believe—wow. You sure had me. I thought you were Andius!"

"I've been working on my transformation spells. How are you feeling?"

"I saw—Cerivil. He has Cerivil."

Her face darkened. "We know. But first, you—are you okay?"

"Oh, me? I could eat a wagonful of yak kebabs right about now, but, otherwise, I feel fine. As you might have guessed, Andius didn't serve us any fancy meals."

"I'm glad to hear you're all right," said Nyalin. "Now Cerivil? Is he all right?"

"Yeah, more or less. I only saw him once when we first arrived."

"Where did they have him?" Nyalin asked. "Was he injured?"

"Not when I last saw him."

Lara bit her lip, then looked to Nyalin. "We've got to get back there."

"Maybe we should go now?" Nyalin looked from Lara to Faytou and back again.

"If you're going to try, I'd go soon," Faytou said. "Andius could move him."

Lara winced. "Probably *will* move him, right?"

Faytou's expression was pained too. "How long has it been?"

"Only a few hours," she replied. "So I guess there's a chance he's still there.'

"Let's go, Lara." Nyalin rose. "Now, before it's too late."

"I'll go too—" Faytou started, struggling to sit up and lurch from the bed. But almost immediately, his legs gave out.

They both caught him, but then Lara stumbled too.

"First, let's get you some food," said Nyalin. "Both of you. I'm on it."

Lara helped him lie back down, then sank into a nearby seat. When was the last time she'd slept? For a moment, her head spun. When it had steadied, she focused on Faytou, who was watching her with concern. "Can you tell me anything more about what you saw, where they're keeping him? Any obvious ways to get him out?"

"The rooms are in the basement. He only had me up there in the open because he's trying some kind of crazy spell. I didn't like the feel of it—almost like I was suffocating. Or maybe I was falling asleep—except I didn't want to sleep, but no matter how much I fought it, I couldn't get free. He was having trouble. He'd tried about a dozen times. This time, though, I thought it might actually work."

Nyalin returned with some apples. "Anything else you can tell us, Faytou? Lara, are you all right?"

She immediately began devouring the apple. She hadn't realized how hungry she was—or how tired.

Faytou frowned as he accepted the fruit. "I... Hmm. I wish I knew what that spell was all about."

As they continued to talk, Lara's head began to swim even more. She rested it on the back of the chair, and before she knew it, her eyelids were drooping.

"All right. Lara needs rest," she heard Nyalin say. "We'll try to—"

She sat up quickly. "Hey— What do you mean I need rest? I can go now!"

"Rest. Don't you think you'll need all your resources if we confront Andius?" Nyalin asked.

*And wouldn't it be easier to sneak around as it gets closer to dark anyway?* Yeska put in.

"But what if they move him?"

Nyalin's eyes were sympathetic. "We'll go as soon as we can. But we don't need us *both* falling off a dragon."

Faytou raised his eyebrows but didn't ask.

She sighed. "I guess you're right." The dragon probably needed a rest too. "But not for too long."

"The faster you rest and get better," Nyalin reassured her, "the faster we can find Cerivil."

---

As bone tired as she'd been upon arrival at the estate, Sutamae expected to sleep like the dead. She usually did, anyway. But her sleep was fitful, dreams flitting through her mind, snatches of a nightmare, snippets of fears and fantasies. But one of the dreams was different from the rest.

A silver-blue eye opened in her mind. Catching her breath, she blinked, tried to look away, but nothing would let her.

*Daughter.*

She shuddered. Her mother wasn't here. That wasn't her mother's voice. This was—something else.

*Daughter, you are in danger.*

In the dream, and perhaps in her sleep, too, Su bit her lip. She already knew that was true, didn't she? It was what had made her nerves jangle with every bump of the carriage.

And when, in truth, had she not been in danger?

*There are those who would hurt you here. Who* have *hurt you here.*

*Who are you?* She demanded, heart pounding now.

*I am Orogoth, daughter of Torosoth.*

Su frowned. *Those don't sound like human names.*

*I am not human. Do you not recognize me?*

Slowly the eye grew smaller, the body of its owner becoming easier to see. After a moment or two, she could see the smooth, shining, almost iridescent body of the small white dragon. She caught her breath. *You came to me. In the solarium.*

*Yes. I am glad you remember me.*

*Why are you so small?*

The dragon seemed to chuff in her mind. *I am newly hatched. Only a few months old.*

If Torosoth was the great Pearl Dragon, the one bonded with their clan leader, then this would be her daughter. But why was this Pearl dragon talking to her?

*I am one of three. Our lands have been blessed with not one in a new generation of dragons, but three of us.*

Su raised her eyebrows. *Is that auspicious?*

*No. Quite the opposite.*

*What does this have to do with me? And will you someday become the great dragon then for your clan?*

Chuffing again. *No. I am the third born.*

*Me too,* she said.

*I know.*

*How do you know me?*

*You helped the one that carries my sword.*

*The masked man.*

*Yes. He had carried it away from those who would steal it, when you met him, but now he draws closer again to those who covet it.*

*The sword he carried... He was carrying a clanblade? But he said he wasn't even from the empire.*

*He is not, but he serves us all the same. The clan crafted it as a real clanblade, but as a trick. Their enemies sought to steal their clanblade. We used my scales to make a decoy, although a real blade. We call it the Blade of the Moon. Though it is not the one linked to my mother, it still must not fall into the wrong hands.*

*But I'm not a—not a—I'm an Obsidian.*

*Desperate times call for desperate measures.*

*Why are you telling me this?*

*Because he needs your help. I need your help. He grows closer to you. And you grow closer to she who would steal it.*

Her heart seemed to thump against her rib cage. *What do you need me to do?*

*If you see the sword, take it for yourself. And be honest with him about doing so.*

She hesitated, swallowing hard. She wanted a sword more than anything else, but now that this dragon was offering, it seemed too good to be true. *Stealing swords has gotten me into a little trouble at times, are you sure that's the right thing to do?*

*Oh, I know.* The chuff this time seemed almost like a laugh. *I know what you do. We're not so different you and I, Sutamae. I've seen your dreams.*

A chill went through her. There were things in her nightmares she never spoke of to anyone. Ever. *Why are you in my dreams?*

*Because we sense in you a great power. Power we will need to defend our land in the coming darkness.*

She froze, trying to think. Wasn't that what she'd always wanted to hear? Was this creature just manipulating her, telling her she was special? How could she even know who to believe anymore?

*Dragons are not like humans. We do not lie.*

*How can I know that in itself is not a lie?*

*Intelligent, but I can rely on facts. I will show you—awaken you. Reach out for the life you deserve, daughter.*

*What do you—*

A tingle in her chest. She reached to cover her heart with her hand, but it'd grown warmer, now a ball of fire. *This is your power. Awaken, Sutamae. Your power will be needed. The darkness grows.* The fire faded now, leaving her feeling abuzz, alight, and yet physically no different.

*What by the Twins was that?*

*Your magic.*

She nearly choked. *You've got to be joking. You're just trying to tell me what I want to hear so I'll help.*

*Decide for yourself. I have extended my hand. I have breathed my fire into you and burned away the darkness. You must step forth, into the light. No one can make that decision for you. Now—let me show you just one more thing.*

*Okay.*

She could see through the dragon's eyes now. They were zipping over the tops of trees, moonlight-kissed evergreens and an empty road below them. A short distance away, the estate where she now slept loomed under the starry sky. The dragon stopped near the woods' edge.

*There. By the wall.*

Su's eyebrows raised. There by the outer wall around the estate, a form was crouched. The person crept along the stones, seeming to feel for weaknesses or markings, or she had no idea what, until he—or she—finally stopped, scanning the surrounding area. As the figure turned toward her, she could make out a gray oval mask.

*Him. He's here?*

*He's close.*

*Why?*

*They've kidnapped his sister.*

Her mouth fell open. That was why he had to leave? To save his sister? Well, she couldn't begrudge him that.

Just then, a patrol of guards rounded the outer corner of the wall. "Hey! You there!"

In barely a moment, he'd vanished into the shadows.

Sutamae stared at the empty wall, the guards running toward that spot but clearly at a loss for where he'd gone. Every time she found that man, he vanished almost before she could blink.

*I'd help him do almost anything,* she told the dragon, and they both knew it was true. *I shouldn't. I don't really know him. But...*

*But sometimes you just know a person; you can see into them. Like I see into you. And you see into him.*

*You see into me?*

*Take the sword, if you have the chance.*

She woke in a cold sweat.

The sky was tinged lavender. Morning approached. By the Twins. Had any of that been real?

How frustrating was it that once she'd finally found a worthy match, once she'd finally tried to do the thing society said she ought to do, her heart would be off chasing some masked fool who wouldn't even tell her his name, let alone how to see him again. Could he really be here? Had her imagination cooked all that up? Oh, yes, not only do you have magic, but the man you fancy isn't so far away! Maybe he'll find you!

Of course that was nonsense. Her masked man had no way of knowing she'd be here, and if he looked for her, he'd look in the city, and she wouldn't be there. Because she was off with Idak.

Idak. Somehow, after the dream and in the cold stillness of morning, the fact that she'd accompanied him here seemed unreal. Ridiculous, even. But... his words still rang true. Whatever he was hiding, Idak had been straight with her, frank in his words. There was something real there, something worth pursuing.

Although... Grel had mentioned kidnappings too. Now the dragon had. Could that be what had so tainted Idak's reputation? Maybe the thing he hadn't been so keen to share?

What if her masked man's sister had been swept off her feet and brought along and then not allowed to leave? What if the difference between Sutamae's journey so far and the others was that she hadn't yet asked if she was allowed to leave?

No, no. She was letting herself get carried away with silly made-up dreams that weren't even real. The dragon was just a sign of how deeply she wished she could be important to someone. The masked man haunting her was just another sign that she... that she... Well, that she found him fascinating.

Who wouldn't be intrigued by a mysterious and completely unavailable man? A man who was also clearly kind? That didn't make it anything realistic. Nothing more than a dream. A flight of fancy. That was all.

She forced herself out of bed. It was even more challenging than she expected. She was still tired from the journey, and the sheets were *silk*. This should not have surprised her, as silk was how Idak's family had made its fortunes, but it still seemed shockingly luxurious and impractical.

They'd arrived late in the evening the day before, well after dinner, and had all immediately retired to rooms and sleep. She'd been glad not to have to deal with people after the days in the carriage, even if they hadn't pushed excessively hard and had stopped early at that small country inn to shorten the time on the road per day.

Su had expected a leisurely morning of unpacking her things and no particular commitments, but after her morning ablutions, she'd dressed quickly and found herself pacing around her room like a caged animal. A pent-up, restless energy from the dream clung to her, impossible to shake.

She didn't even bother to unpack. How long would she really be staying? It was hard to say. Something about unpacking made her stomach twist with nerves, like some animal part of her wanted to be ready to flee.

A knock sounded on the door, loud and abrupt.

Still pacing, she jumped and clutched a hand to her chest, then started toward the door to open it, but it opened without waiting for permission or acknowledgment to reveal Idak, green eyes sparkling.

"I see you're ready to face the day—and my mother."

She folded her arms. That door move was presumptuous to say the least. Had he hoped to catch her sleeping? The sun was barely up. Still, she *could* ignore it. Run to him, throw herself at him, flirt. If she wanted him to believe her smitten, that would be the move now. But no. No more pretending. No more lies. Instead, she let her annoyance show and pressed her lips into a thin line. "Good morning to you as well."

"Good morning."

"What's this about your mother? Before even breakfast?"

"Did you sleep well?" He came in, closing the door and leaning his back against it.

"Do come in." She narrowed her eyes. Certainly, those were questions he had to answer eventually, in a few minutes, in fact. Why dodge them? "The bed is delightful. My dreams were..." Her stomach twisted. Wild? Bizarre? None of his business? "My dreams were complicated."

He raised his eyebrows. "Were they? Do tell."

"Oh, I don't think so. You already owe me two answers to two questions."

One side of his mouth crooked up. "My mother's word is law around here. And her 'request' is that you join her for breakfast."

"Just me? You won't join us?"

"Just you."

"I, uh..." She searched for an excuse. "I only just woke up."

He smiled. "I know. But it's not really optional. And I promise, the tea she brews is exquisite. Absolutely worth enduring her company to have it."

She quirked an eyebrow. Not really optional. Would staying also turn out not to be optional? What had she gotten herself into? She took a deep breath. "Well. If there will be tea."

Laughing softly, he took her arm and led her out into the hall.

*Chapter 10*

# Misses

Even after a nap, Lara was still nodding off as Yeska landed again on the flat warehouse roof. She and Nyalin slid to the ground.

"How's my disguise?" she said through a yawn.

"Very good. You look exceedingly common. No trace at all of your usual beautiful self."

"Thanks. I think."

"How's mine?" His transformation was less dramatic, his hair and skin tone still the same, but the features of the face were enough to make him difficult to recognize.

"It's exceedingly adequate. Let's go."

They crept through the darkness, crouching as they peeked around corners, tiptoeing over the cobblestones. Everything was quiet.

*Cerivil's presence has changed. Not like before,* Yeska warned suddenly. *More distant.*

Lara's heart leapt. What if Andius had grown impatient and given up his plot and was trying to kill her father right now? If he succeeded, who would know the difference, now that the clan leader was already missing? How would anyone ever know what might have happened?

The worries quickened her steps, diminished her caution. Nyalin held up a hand in warning, but she saw it too late as she reached for the side door of the warehouse and wrenched it open. A loud groan of metal against metal from the hinges rang out in the darkness.

Wincing, she hurried inside. But what she saw made her heart drop into her stomach.

"This place looks deserted," Nyalin whispered.

The table she'd found Faytou on was gone, as were all the armed folks, any signs of life at all really. "They moved him." She gritted her teeth. "They already moved him."

"Let's look closer. But it does seem so. Maybe they left some clues as to where they went. Come on."

Every room they searched on the ground floor was empty. She steeled herself as they headed into the basement. Would it be empty? Or would they find her father—dead?

Once the basement door had closed, she lit a small bubble of light to follow them. Nyalin made his own as their search branched off to various rooms.

Several rooms had clearly been used as cells, with heavy padlocks on the door and chains that had been magical constraints hanging from the walls. Each cell was mostly empty, save a table, chair, and straw palette, but in one, Lara peered down at the wood of the table and caught her breath.

Designs had been carved into the wood. Of course—her father never could keep his hands still, especially around wood that was available for carving. She pressed a fist over her mouth, trying to force back the emotions. "Nyalin, look at this."

"Do you think he did this?" His eyes were wide, scanning the patterns.

"Yes." Flowers. It was an odd choice, maybe a bit uplifting, but she'd never known her father to be partial to such a feminine pattern. Still, she tried to burn the pattern into her memory. What if there was some clue here they were missing? "How can we remember this? I don't know, maybe there's a message here, or a warning, but I'm not seeing anything."

"Hold on." Nyalin hurried into another room, returning with a rough paper that looked like it might have been a wrapper for some sort of food. He laid it out across the table, then found a piece of colored wax in his pocket.

"Did you bring that intentionally?"

"What? This? Oh, no. I just never want to be without some way to make a note." He smiled briefly as he rubbed the wax over the paper, leaving a white outline of the indentations and darkness where the table hadn't been carved. It created a near-replica of the carvings.

"That's brilliant, I—"

She cut off the words as the door they'd entered through above screeched again. They met each other's eyes, concerned.

Someone else was here.

Nyalin quickly rolled up the paper and stuffed it in his pack. They extinguished the lights and listened. Footsteps were too hard to hear through the thick floor, so they made their way back to the staircase to hear better.

Several long minutes offered no further sound.

*Yeska, is someone still here?* Lara asked.

*Yes. Three someones.*

*Can you sense any magic about them?*

*No. Not Andius either. But not friendly.*

*Maybe you can create a distraction.*

*Distraction? That I can do.*

For a moment, Lara could see through Yeska's eyes, the way the ground lurched as she heaved up into the air. Her wings mightily shoved the air down, pushing her body up and up, then landing heavily on the roof—directly above Lara, though several stories up.

"What was that?" someone whispered.

Then Yeska let out her roar.

Three sets of footsteps rushed toward the gate to see what the commotion was about.

"Now," Lara hissed. "Run!"

It didn't feel good to run, especially without finding something to save her father to show for it. But she didn't want to kill any member of her clan if she didn't have to. Even if they supported Andius. They probably didn't know the whole story.

Shouts rose up, whether at her or the dragon, she wasn't sure.

Yeska landed on the ground outside the warehouse with a heavy crash, then circled around toward them, as close as she could get. The guards first screamed, then shouted as they raced after her.

*What are they expecting to do if they catch you?*

*I don't think they are thinking that far ahead.*

It didn't matter. Lara and Nyalin had quite a bit of practice getting on Yeska's back now. In a flash, they'd climbed halfway up, and Yeska was already in the air as they finished the climb.

Arrows whistled into the sky but missed their targets.

Just like they'd missed Cerivil. By a few hours? A few minutes? Had Andius relocated him right away? She should have realized he would. But what else could she have done? She had to rescue Faytou, and she'd been basically alone. Aside from having Yeska level the place with her wings or that strange fire... And they couldn't have known if that would have hurt her father, so that hadn't really been an option.

But now, they had no idea where to look, Yeska's sense of him was weakening, and all they had to show for the trip was a tracing of some flowers. A place her father's fingers had touched probably hours if not a few days before...

So close. And yet worlds apart.

She shook her head, crushed her eyes shut, and tried not to cry too loudly. She didn't want to be comforted right now. She just wanted this awful experience to end.

Andius—this was all his doing.

The next time she went back into the city, she wouldn't be running away. In fact... maybe it was too soon to leave just yet. Hastily she wiped away a hot tear with the back of her hand.

"Yeska—maybe we should check on Pyaris. While we're here. I think maybe we are going to need some help."

"Good idea," yelled Nyalin over the wind. "What about Grel?"

She shrugged. "If you think he'd come."

"I'm sure of it."

---

"Sutamae," Unira said quietly as Idak released the girl into the breakfast room.

Her son slipped away, sliding the door closed dutifully. The girl kept her gaze locked with Idak's until the very last moment, then turned, her fine porcelain features concerned.

Unira tried again. "Thank you for coming."

"Good morning." The girl scanned the place. Unira had to admire the suspicion in her eyes. From what she had heard of Elix's daughter, she expected this to potentially be a very fruitful encounter—one way or another.

Morning sunlight streamed in, dancing across the artfully arranged dark-grey tea pots and bowls heaped with rice and round golden apples on the table. The pattern of slate-blue blossoms created a lovely display, although she didn't expect they'd eat much.

"I am Unira, Idak's mother."

"He speaks well of you."

"Does he?"

"Not extensively, but yes. I wondered what you hoped to discuss with me today, but he wouldn't tell."

Her lips twisted, too pleased at that show of loyalty and obedience.

"Well, as I am the matriarch here, I seek to greet everyone who visits the estate. I shouldn't think it would do to ignore such a highly esteemed guest as yourself."

The girl laughed. Actually laughed.

Unira hated to admit that she liked her already.

She gracefully folded herself into a seat across from her host at the low breakfast table. "Highly esteemed. Me. Are you sure you have the right person?"

"Oh, don't be coy with me. I can see that neither of us is a woman to be trifled with."

Her hand had been reaching for a teacup, but it froze in midair. "Is that so?"

"Am I wrong?"

She finished reaching for the cup. "No... I suppose not. But most don't speak so plainly."

"True."

"If we're speaking plainly, is this really about greeting me?"

Unira smiled. "Hardly. I want to know if you're a fit mate for my son."

Again, audaciously, the girl outright laughed. "I don't think I'm a fit mate for anyone. My reputation is... not great. If others are to be asked, I'm a wild, temperamental, vile, evil harlot."

"I am not asking them."

"Are you asking me?"

"No. I decide these things for myself."

"Oh."

"Tea?"

"Yes, please."

She poured the tea for the two of them, pretending not to watch her prey out of the corner of her eye. "You and I are not so different, you know."

"Oh?" Her tone was skeptical.

"I was once a highly eligible match. You claim you don't see yourself as such. Sincerely?"

"Well, not particularly. You should know—"

"I know enough about you," Unira said, cutting her off. "Of your exploits and aggravations of your father. Of a bit of a wild streak. Is your intent to make yourself unmarriageable?"

"No. I doubt it would work anyway."

"What is your intent then?"

"That's personal. But it has nothing to do with other people. I don't care what others think of me."

Unira found herself smiling. "From most people, I wouldn't believe that, but I'm tempted to think you are telling the truth."

The girl's eyebrows quirked up slightly at that. Interesting. Unira had planned to go down the route of pointing out just how hard it was to find a good match. It'd been a disaster for Unira, and Sutamae had nowhere to go but down. But she sensed the girl didn't care much about any of that. Refreshing.

"I have heard from my son that you... don't always point out the truth of these exploits of yours. The thefts of swords."

Sutamae pursed her lips. "I let people think what they want. If they'd ask me, I'd tell them."

"This is a difficult world for women," Unira said slowly. "And you have chosen a bold path. I like that. I believe Idak deserves a bold path as well, and I think a bold wife would be less likely to hold him back. Not that anyone could easily hold him back, but... still."

The girl took a nibble of a pastry, keeping her eyes downturned.

"We live in a world where a woman's truth is so often inconvenient. It's an art to keep them all doing what you want them to, without them realizing you're pulling the strings."

Her lips twisted. "That's *definitely* not an art I've mastered."

"Oh, you've apprenticed yourself in it quite well, though, don't you think? You have them all thinking... whatever they wish... but it hasn't stopped your evening adventures, has it?"

"True, it hasn't." Her eyes remained cool, her gaze on the food, but Unira could sense the change in her in the way she sat, the tilt of her head. She was getting somewhere.

"For women like us, mastering the art of... sculpting and guiding those around... is critical, if you ask me."

"Women like us?" Her tone spoke volumes—that to her, they were not similar. "Bold women?"

"Yes." Unira couldn't help but smile, though, because the truth was on her side for this one. "But I was referring to women with magic."

The girl's dark gaze snapped up to meet hers, the naked glimmer of hope impossible even for someone as guarded as she was to conceal. "I... I don't have—"

"They haven't checked," she pretended to guess. "Have they?" No need to point out that the ban on teaching Sutamae was entirely *her* doing, forcing Elix into the agreement. Not that she believed he'd found that piece of the deal painful. Her intuition was that he preferred Sutamae as far out of the line of danger and notoriety as possible.

And how well had that worked so far? What a fool. Fathers can be blind, but now that Unira saw the girl before her, this was trying to hide a star under a blanket.

"Correct," she murmured, her head ducking again. "No one will check."

"I will," Unira said quietly.

Sutamae's eyes widened with hope for a moment before the girl thought to shutter her expression. She quickly reached for a bowl of rice. "I wouldn't dare to impose such a burden."

"Well, it would be quite the sacrifice for me. But I don't see why the men should get to have all the fun." Truthfully, Unira already knew the girl had magic in spades, but it had been slumbering, which had helped her verify so far that Elix had kept up his end of the deal. She wasn't, in fact, planning to do a simple check, but a more costly awakening ritual that would bind Sutamae's magic to her own, forever. It was all she could do to keep from grinning at the idea.

"Neither do I. It hardly seems fair. If we have magic, why shouldn't we assist in defending the empire? And there are so many other uses for magic."

"Indeed. And I should think training in the magical arts ought to make you all the more valuable as a wife. Not that it worked that way for me—quite the opposite. Although, I still did my best."

"Unfortunately, most don't seem to see it that way. Maybe if Linali had lived, she could have encouraged them to think differently of us."

"But alas." Her voice was cold as ice. Unira's hand tightened around her teacup, knuckles going white. For a moment, the room seemed tinged with red. By Seluvae, how did that woman manage to come up—every—single—time! "Alas. Linali is dead."

"Did I say something wrong? I absolutely agree magical training should be a valuable commodity in a partner of any gender."

She tried to shake off the rage. "Never mind, dear. Let's just say that... the past is complicated, and injustice makes me quite angry."

"Me too." Her guard was almost fully down. Perfect.

"So... Shall I check for your magic? An effort it might be, but that's a sacrifice I'm willing to make."

"I..." She gazed off into the distance, although what she was thinking about or considering, Unira couldn't guess. "Now?"

"No reason to wait. How can you stand not knowing? We simply sit as though meditating. Unless of course, your magic is asleep, then it may take some work to fully awaken, but I should still be able to sense it there."

"Yes. Yes, please."

"Of course," she said smoothly. Privately, Elix had to know. It was a simple inspection, most of the time; she was lying about how much it would cost her. Which meant he probably knew how much potential he was wasting. That only made her smile more. That he'd played his cards so poorly, that she'd both kept him from training his daughter *and* would be able to endear herself to the girl with that fact? It was too delicious. "Close your eyes and try to relax."

Unira closed her own eyes too and reached out with the magic.

But what she found only reignited her rage. The girl's magic, which had been perfectly asleep the night before when she'd arrived, had already been awakened.

"Your gift is quite powerful. Congratulations."

"I—I feel a little... dizzy."

"Perfectly normal. Feel free to lie down."

She rose and came to the girl's side as she collapsed. Her black hair splayed out across the dark wood floor.

Maybe she should just kill the girl now. What a waste. She was useless to Unira's magic now. How dare someone interfere? Who could it have been? Idak?

Her fingernails dug into her palms. Idak always went too far when she didn't want him to, and not far enough when she needed him. What if he had bound Sutamae's magic to *himself*? To grow more powerful than his mother and finally tip the scales?

Killing them *both* would simplify things. She could tell Zama she'd made her choice. It would be just like Idak to do as he liked while he was in the city. Although... it was not particularly like Idak to seek power. That was more Unira's style. Could the girl somehow have figured out how to awaken her magic herself?

Her eyes caught on the black ribbon around the girl's throat. She went still. Idak had given that to her, his slight enchantment of protection hovering around it.

Her mouth quirked up at the corner. Her son knew her well. Who else could Idak have been concerned about, in this girl's case, other than his own mother?

And he was right to worry—there were other uses for this girl. And for him. Unira marshaled her calm, sucking in a deep breath. The choker had done its job of making her pause, of letting her rage ease just slightly enough to remember that this girl could unseat Elix and his whelp from the clan leader's throne.

If they played things just right.

Maybe intertwining their magics hadn't worked—perhaps she'd try one more time, just to be sure—but she could still intertwine their goals, their purposes. Maybe even be open about it, with this one, who clearly was willing to start trouble in the right circumstance.

Unira folded herself to a seat next to the girl and waited for her to recover. It shouldn't be long, and she was good at biding her time.

*

Daridian crept along the ramshackle wood wall, moving toward the tent area at the edge of the estate. He'd been trying to find his sister for two days, and he'd covered most of the outer buildings. He'd found bakeries, storehouses, armories, barracks, silk-production facilities, and more. He'd even seen other people being held prisoner in make-shift cells. But no sister.

Reaching the tent area, he scanned around for patrols. They couldn't be far off, so he hurried forward, looking for an open flap to peek inside first tent. These tents were rectangular structures, like one might see in an army encampment near a battlefield. The paths connecting them appeared to be only moderately worn, so maybe this was all recently constructed? Sha'lien hadn't been kidnapped all that long ago, so maybe this was the logical place for her to be.

Footsteps reached his ears—behind him. He quickened his pace.

No, there was another pair ahead. Men coming closer. He caught his breath.

Two patrols had Daridian pinned. Out of desperation, he ducked inside the nearest open tent flap and crouched down behind a crate. Hoping he hadn't walked into an even worse situation and looking for a better place to hide, he glanced around the inside of the tent..

No such luck. More than a dozen pairs of eyes turned on him. He froze, preparing to run, bracing for the outcry.

But none came.

He looked closer. There were only a few cots lined up to one side, clearly not enough for each of them to have their own, and some of them seemed *heavily* soiled.

They were looking at him with more curiosity than alarm. Their clothes were disheveled and filthy. Then his eyes caught on the chain links hanging across a woman's brown linen skirt. Then another's, then another's.

All these people. They were all *shackled.*

He glanced from face to face until he saw a young man holding a bundle. His eyes were hard, intense, and boring into his own.

"Did you sneak in here?" the young man asked.

"I... yes," he said softly. "There was a patrol outside. These people have kidnapped my sister. I came to rescue her. Is this a prison? Have you seen a woman named Sha'lien?"

"No one by that name," said one woman.

"We're not prisoners," said a second. "We're slaves."

The young man holding the bundle in his arms cut in. "If you can sneak in, can you sneak out?"

"Well, I should certainly hope so."

"Then sneak the baby out," said another woman, pointing at the bundle. The man holding it shifted the blanket slightly to reveal a soft, sleeping infant's face.

His eyes widened. "Where is the child's mother? A baby like that is too young to be separated from—"

"She's dead," said the man, looking like he tasted ash.

His stomach turned. "Ah, I see. The father?"

"Me. Please, sir. Take the baby."

"I..." He started to say no, but there was far too much pain etched in their grim expressions.

Was he really going to do this? Curse his luck. He was a fool.

Another older man folded his arms, which was difficult considering the irons on his wrists, but it *did* make him look more powerful. "If you won't help, then I'll raise my voice and the guards will—"

He held up a hand. "No need to threaten. Just let me think for a moment." If Sha'lien died while he was off helping yet another stranger, he wouldn't forgive himself. And yet, she wouldn't have wanted him to ignore these people either.

"It is an hour till nightfall. I can't take your child alone. I can take you both when—"

"They make us serve dinner. We'll be called away by then."

He frowned. "How late does it go?"

"Sometimes, until morning."

Stifling a groan, he shook his head. "Fine. Get your things. We'll go now."

It would mean using his magic to some degree, and he'd rather not have to use any. He wanted to save it all for when he found Sha'lien.

But he'd do what he had to do.

"Hurry," he whispered. "But what about the rest of you?"

"We can't all possibly escape without notice. The baby has to be our priority for now."

"I understand. There is a village not far from here. Once we get the baby safely away, maybe you could—"

"We will do what we can if the opportunity arises."

The father returned with a small pack.

"Ready?"

The young man nodded.

Looking at the infant, he asked, "How will the child fair without milk?"

"The villages in the area should have women who can help him. None of us here are able."

"Ah, I see."

Shaking his head at himself, Daridian sharpened his senses, raised his guard, and peered outside the tent flap. He would get this young man and baby, all these folks free, and Sha'lien too.

Who did these Obsidians think they were?

Sutamae's eyes drifted closed, almost against her will, as her body hit the hardwood.

The world seemed to shift around her. Any support seemed to give way. But even with all the spinning, it was hard to ignore the sensation she'd first felt last night in her dream. Magic.

Now, though, her whole body burned. If this was magic, how did she control it? Colors swirled through her mind as her nerves ached.

Then she sensed it. A subtle nudge. Almost like someone was feeding the fire, stoking it.

Yes, someone was poking at her, stirring the pool of fire into a maelstrom. At first, the touch was gentle, but it grew more aggressive, soon crashing up against her violently. She wanted to recoil, pull away from them, or push them away, but it was like reaching for something that wasn't there.

A distinct smell burst through her senses suddenly. The smell of smoke. Or more specifically, the *thought* of the smell of smoke. The bruising in her mind did not lessen. The smell grew suddenly stronger. Whatever was probing her was working its way around her, and soon she would be trapped inside a net of the tendrils of smoke.

And yet there was another scent—also hot, but in a different way. Was it... mint?

Trapped. The psychic snare was tightening, and she'd soon be unable to escape. She had to do something. Desperately, instinctively, she thought of the sword, the way she'd learned to defend herself so long ago. The price for that knowledge had been too high, but she might as well use it. In her mind, she envisioned the sword cutting at the ropes of magic swirling closer, ever tightening.

Then silence. The assault stopped. The smoke was gone. There was only an image of herself, in her mind's eye, holding a sword under the moon.

Her hands tightened and her breath caught as she noticed the blade—the pearl-handled one that the masked man had carried. The one the dragon had mentioned in the dream. Was it truly hers to take?

Or was her obsession with this unavailable young man reaching new and strange depths of pathetic desperation?

In her mind, she sheathed the sword, closed her eyes. Gathered her strength.

When she opened her eyes again, she was in the real world. The fire in her limbs remained, but was more tolerable now. The energy that the dragon had stoked briefly trembled inside her, as if eager for more, like a sword itching to be drawn.

Unira knelt beside her, looking as serene as a mountain capped with snow.

"All this time... They could have checked. And they never did. They never knew. I could have lived my whole life never knowing?" she said as she struggled to sit up. Of course, she'd hoped the Bladed Women would have helped her learn the truth, but her parents... Why hadn't they checked? Why hadn't they wanted to know?

But maybe she was equally to blame. After all, she'd never asked to be checked. She'd always assumed that, if she had, her father would have refused her in all his scathing glory. That was *so* much more likely than if she had asked and he'd surprised her by agreeing. Avoiding asking left her with a shred of hope, an illusion of possibility.

Even with the quest from the Bladed Women, she'd put off asking her father. She could see it more clearly now. On one hand, this would make the quest easier. She knew for sure her magic existed. She had every right to demand a sword from her father, and he had far less justification to deny her.

On the other hand, this would alter the quest, make it easier because it was no longer a leap of faith. Would the Bladed Women care? And the rage she felt toward her father bubbling up—that wouldn't make it easier to do what needed to be done, to ask for a sword. To demand one.

"All this time," she murmured, still in shock.

"Sometimes, it is those we love who disappoint us most dearly," Unira replied, voice quiet.

"How can I even explain to them... What will I do?"

"How does one confront injustice? Does it ever pay off?"

She looked away. "True. It would be very unlike my father to apologize."

Unira snorted. "Indeed."

"But I'll need to confront him about it."

"Why? Let him play his little games. You're old enough to find your own team to play on."

When Su looked to her, Unira's eyes were twinkling with amusement. "But... if I want to use my magic, I'll need to be taught. If they'll let me. They didn't let Nyalin, so..."

"There are other ways, you know?"

Su arched an eyebrow. "Necromancy?"

"An under-respected art for under-respected people like us. But I have classical training... as well as a little other spice added here and there. I could teach you."

In spite of herself, her mouth dropped open. "You would do that?"

"Of course. As we said, why should the men get to have all the fun? Besides, I told you. Injustice makes me quite angry. I'd much prefer to rectify the situation to a far fairer one. So rarely can I do that. But in this case, with fools such as these..."

She winced at the words, but it was true. It *was* foolish of her father to think she'd go her whole life content to do whatever he said and ignore her magic. It was worse than that too... Unkind didn't seem strong enough of a word. "How cruel of them to simply... ignore me," she murmured, mostly to herself.

"You and I can make them pay, Sutamae."

She raised her eyebrows. "Excuse me?"

"They should pay a price for their mistreatment of you. Don't you think?"

Perhaps they should. But her parents weren't the only ones who had mistreated her throughout her life. "Justice is rarely awarded to the deserving in this world."

"Indeed. Shouldn't we pursue it when we can?"

She bit her lip, then straightened. "We should. All right. I'm listening."

Daridian taxed the magic of the mask to its extreme, finding narrow windows of three or four seconds where each patrol left gaps. Fortunately, the young man followed his directions precisely.

They were nearing the gate. As one merchant cart rolled past, he managed to snag a trio of apples as it took a corner too tightly. Another man might have broken a wrist, but the mask could slow down time, could make his senses so acute, he grabbed them with relative ease.

He peered around the corner. Behind him, the man started to rock the child as she began to fuss quietly.

The sentries at the side gate were not as lackadaisical and relaxed as he might have hoped. The earlier shift had been happy to doze, but it looked like two new people had taken over.

He scanned the area. The stone wall that circled the estate had a small wooden sentry house for the sentries to sit in and look intimidating. Nearby, there were two buildings—a stable of horses and what looked like an area for an armory. The armory's double doors stood wide open, and inside, he could just make out a helmet sitting cattywampus on a stand, looking like was nearly about to topple.

He glanced back over his shoulder. The child's fussing was growing louder. The man refused to meet his eyes. It wasn't as if he could blame the father; there wasn't anything he could do about it. His mask might be powerful, but calming a crying child? That was all too often purely a miracle.

He scanned the scene again, then considered his options... Run for it? Engage the sentries? The apples? Yes, a distraction—maybe that would do the trick.

Well. Let the Great Spear guide his arm.

He fired one apple at the lopsided helmet near the armory door and then the other two toward the stalls in the stable as best he could. One after another he threw them, hoping the sound would resemble someone running through the area. The helmet tumbled loudly to the ground, clanging. Horses whinnied.

Hopefully, at least one of the beasts got a snack out of this.

Both sentries went running, one to each building. Smiling gently, he ushered the man forward while they had the chance.

They were nearly clear, a full hundred paces outside the wall, when the child's whimpers grew into wails. Footsteps pounding the hard dirt told him the sentries had returned. They ignored the shouts and walked faster.

Just before they reached them, the arrows cut into his consciousness as they careened through the air straight toward their backs. Daridian dove, pushing the young man behind a tree for cover. He almost made it clear himself, but one projectile grazed the side of his calf.

Now swearing and bleeding a little, he pulled the man along and broke into a run.

The sentries didn't seem eager to pursue—or maybe they didn't have orders to. Or perhaps it was the dead tree branches Daridian managed to knock in their path. He could sense the weak ones high in the air, and a heavy kick to the trunk sometimes rewarded him with a few more obstacles guarding his escape.

They went about a mile before they stopped to rest. The running had calmed the baby, it seemed, but Daridian knew it wouldn't last.

"You'll get her to a wet nurse?" he asked the young man, still panting from the exertion.

"I will. Thank you. Seluvae's blessings upon you, many thousands of them, kind stranger."

"It is no great matter." He took his lockpicks to the shackles, regretting he hadn't thought of doing it back in the tent. Or for more of them. But there hadn't seemed to be any time for such things, in the press to escape with the baby. The disgusting iron fell to the dirt. "I hope you remain free and never encounter this evil again."

"I wish you the same. And strength to you, sir. No amount of thanks could ever be enough." He bowed, and Daridian bowed in return.

They parted ways there. As the young man hiked off, Daridian sat down on a rock to think. Thank the Spear. How had he pulled that off?

Panting, he wiped his forehead. This had been too much. Too much. Should he wait yet another night, for his power to rejuvenate, before he returned to his search?

There was no way of knowing the urgency of Sha'lien's situation. Was she in imminent danger? Slow torture?

Already dead?

Perhaps another night wouldn't matter, especially if he didn't actually have the energy to succeed in freeing her. Or even finding her.

On the other hand, if their situations were reversed, he wouldn't want to spend any more nights than necessary as a prisoner.

Sighing, he stood and checked his gear. There was no time like the present. If he failed tonight, he wouldn't regret helping the man and the child.

Then again, maybe the Spear had guided his hand a little. Perhaps running into those slaves hadn't just been a coincidence. He picked up the shackles from the ground. Yes.

If he hurried back, this might be the perfect way to sneak inside. His weapons and his mask would be an issue, but in the slaves, he would have allies. And an excuse. And a disguise.

He needed a way to find those in charge, because his searches of the general premises hadn't revealed his sister yet. If he could reach the dinner they were speaking of, maybe someone would mention Sha'lien or a woman being taken captive recently. Maybe he'd get a clue of where to look.

Maybe he could just slit all their throats for terrorizing his sweet, naive sister and then laughing over wine and roast duck.

He wasn't sure what he'd do. He hadn't decided yet. He had options.

First, he had to get inside.

*Chapter 11*

# VIGIL

IN THE END, NYALIN SHOULDN'T HAVE BEEN so sure of Grel's participation. Not that his stepbrother wouldn't have *wanted* to come, but when he'd snuck into Grel's rooms surreptitiously in the dawn light, they were empty. Grel had already headed off to his work about the city.

While the world was falling apart, it was easy to forget that other people had obligations. But in truth, Grel had plenty. Nyalin shook his head at his thoughtlessness.

He left a note on his desk and paused for a moment to pat Smoke the cat on the head before climbing back to the roof where Yeska waited.

Lara had retrieved her friend Pyaris in only a matter of minutes, the smiling necromancer waving to him as she'd climbed up onto the roof and onto Yeska's back.

Together, the three of them had flown back to Stragg's Beard, to his mother's childhood home, to rejoin Faytou.

After some introductions and a brief tour—and a few hugs—they all settled outside by the tall flowers and even taller trees to think about what to do next.

Nyalin started by giving Pyaris and Faytou a recap of everything he'd learned so far, even the wild things he'd experienced in the afterworld. He only left out a few things, like the emperor being his father, but even leaving that out, it seemed ridiculous. He smiled sheepishly at Lara, hoping by the goddesses above she'd back him up. "Bet you never thought you'd end up *here* when you agreed to help me show those Obsidians what liars they were."

She snorted with laughter. Those days when she'd agreed to help him find his magic and learn how to use it seemed so naïve and innocent compared to today. "Things seemed so simple then. As if our problems could be fixed with just some quick lessons and a lot of elbow grease."

"And now..."

"And now, we need to decide if we should look again for my father, search for your mother instead, or simply confront Andius. Or some other option we haven't thought of yet."

"Only that?" Pyaris smiled crookedly. "I don't see why you need me for such a simple choice."

Lara flushed. "Don't tease me."

"Sorry, I was just trying to bring some lightness to the situation."

Faytou raised his hand. "Does anybody else see any irony to the necromancer bringing lightness here?"

Pyaris elbowed him. Hard.

Nyalin snorted. "I think Pyaris is a ray of sunshine. I don't know what you're talking about."

"Sorry." Pyaris's crooked smile widened. "So did you come to any conclusions? Surely, you must have been contemplating this the whole way back here."

Lara bit her lip. "Not really. Well. Maybe I did, but I don't like them."

Pyaris folded her arms. "Spill it, my friend."

Nyalin nodded. He had to admit his thoughts were so mixed up from hunting for Cerivil and constantly worrying about unwittingly slipping into the afterworld, he hadn't really been able to weigh their options in great depth. He hadn't slipped back again yet, but he'd felt a strange tug at times. Some of them seemed to be related to certain locations, like he felt the odd feeling when he neared the spirit doorway. He had a feeling if he let down his guard, even for just a moment, he might blink and open his eyes on a different plane all together.

Lara shifted uncomfortably back and forth. "We looked for Da. Several times. We have no clues or leads. He could be anywhere. Literally anywhere. I don't think it makes sense to blindly go looking again, without some idea of where to look. I'm open to thoughts about it."

"Short of raiding Andius's home," Faytou said, "I think it'd be hard to guess where he could be. And raiding Andius's home could be an option, but it'd be a very hostile one. It would... set a certain tone. He might respond in some other way by force."

"Agreed. Also, we know what the emperor told us about my father and our suspicions of Andius. He's the one saying the clan leader will see no one. But we have no *proof* that Andius has done something nefarious. He could claim that Da went on a trip and left him with an order not to tell."

"Nobody would believe that," Faytou waved a hand.

"Maybe they wouldn't, but I'm not one hundred percent sure. So I don't think confronting Andius directly about my father would help. I think I could contact the council. I don't think I'll do it the emperor's way, though, making demands."

"Again, that's not what he did forming up the empire," Nyalin pointed out. "And that was *with* the Mushin breathing down their necks."

Pyaris nodded. "You catch more flies with honey than with vinegar, true."

Faytou leaned back on his hands. "Somehow, I think Andius prefers vinegar. Or any kind of acid really."

Lara snickered again. "I think I know what I need to do. Ultimately, it comes down to me and Andius. I need to think of some way to settle this, directly with him."

"Preferably by beating him to a magical pulp, please," Faytou muttered.

"Your preference is noted. But... I also think that we should look for Nyalin's mother first."

His eyebrows raised. "Are you sure? She's been supposedly dead for how many years. Da is probably more urgent."

"True, but we didn't have any clues to her location—or her aliveness—until yesterday. Since we don't have any idea where Da might be or even if he's alive, I think we have to turn our attention to Linali. And besides, Emperor Pavan must be looking for my father, too, right?"

"Hmm, I would assume he still is, but how easy can it be to stay hidden from the emperor? Come to think of it, don't you think it's odd we haven't heard from him?"

"A little." Lara nodded. "Maybe he doesn't know we're out here. I'd assumed he had some mysterious way of finding us. He knew where Yeska's home was, but we've left it now. We never mentioned to him that we were planning to come here, right?"

"Yes. Deliberately. I got the sense he didn't want me to come. Not sure why. Just like he didn't want Elix to give me the sword."

"I got that sense too. So I'm glad you didn't mention it. Coming here was a good idea. And I think we should use what we've learned to look for your mother."

"We could... split up." He gestured at Faytou and Pyaris. "Two of us go to each location?"

She shook her head. "We don't know what we're facing. If Unira was powerful enough to somehow trap Linali in a way that even the emperor couldn't find her, what kind of person are we dealing with?"

"Good point. Also, according to the emperor, the woman's been trying to kill me my whole life. So there's that."

"Yeah, that doesn't scream solo mission to me."

He chuckled. "All right. You've convinced me."

"So when do we go?" asked Faytou. "And what do we know about the place?"

"Hardly anything. Only that a number of people are being kept prisoner there so Unira can leech off their magic."

Pyaris made a disgusted face. "It's necromancers like that that give the rest of us a bad name."

"Maybe we can go closer and just observe the place first," Lara suggested. "See if we can find out where prisoners might be held?"

"Hey, wait. I think I saw something inside that could help us. Be right back." Faytou took off running.

They all exchanged looks.

"I do know the estate makes silk. At least I think so—" Nyalin started. Was this a bad idea to act without talking to Grel? With his close relationship with Jylan, he had to know something about these people. But it would take time to track him down. Nyalin was starting to realize he knew precious little about this Unira or any of her plans. Why was a woman he'd never met so damn dead set on making his life hard or killing him? But then again, if she really had his mother captive, what else did he need to know?

He had to try.

Faytou came racing back. "A spy glass, look! We could use this to observe them."

Pyaris's eyes lit up, and she reached for it. "This is a lovely piece. Perhaps we start with observing them, from the hills. We really know nothing about this place—or the people."

"Except that they're exceptionally evil," Lara put in.

"Yes. Except for that."

"Are you all sure about this?" Nyalin asked. "It's really kind of you to help me. But this isn't your fight. It isn't your mother. It's a bunch of Obsidians, not even on Bone Clan land. Are you sure?"

"It became our fight when you joined our clan, Nyalin," said Faytou. "And doubly so when you stood up and fought for it against Andius."

"Yeah, but I didn't win."

"But it wasn't a fair fight, and that doesn't change the fact that we're gonna be by your side for this."

"Yeah. Whether you like it or not!" Lara grinned.

"I think we're going to need some rest before then," he said. "We've been up all night."

"Me too," said Pyaris. "You two woke me up early."

"I don't need any more rest, but I can look for some more supplies to pack. Maybe I'll even find another spy glass!"

"Good idea, Faytou," said Lara. "When night comes, we'll go looking for Linali."

Nyalin shook his head. "We're becoming nearly nocturnal, aren't we?"

"Just don't turn into a bat like the emperor and stay that way."

"I promise I won't." On impulse, he kissed her on the cheek, and they all went inside.

"Excellent, Sutamae. Good to see you. You're not too tired from this morning's activities? I'm excited to continue our conversation from earlier." Unira's voice was overly sweet as Su made her way toward her place at the long, foreboding dinner table.

"A nap has refreshed me," Su replied. Though as she took in the other people in the room, she and Unira clearly wouldn't be talking about the plans and possibilities they'd discussed earlier, in her opinion. She'd expected a small dinner with Idak alone, or him and his family, but this was much more than that. Her nap had lasted a bit longer than she had intended, but she supposed her sleep the night before had been fitful with the strange dream of the dragon, and waking up early.

"What sorts of topics did you discuss together, Mother?" Idak was asking as she entered.

"Oh, a little of this and a little of that."

Su slid into the seat to which she was directed. The dining room was surprisingly dark, and the long, elegant table was made of wood stained nearly black. A large hearth burned with a roaring fire at one end, and torches dotted the walls, but the rest of the walls and floor were similarly dark.

At the head of the table sat Unira. Behind her, glass doors opened onto a patio, revealing hills and beyond them mountains. They were mostly dark now, kissed by a touch of moonlight, but not too far in the distance was a faint orange smoldering in the night sky—the peak of Mount Stragg, where lava flirted with invading the land below.

She'd never paid much attention to the volcano before; in the city it seemed like a distant shape on the skyline. They were only two days' carriage ride north, but it seemed so much closer.

Before anyone could strike up any other tense conversations, Unira rose to circle the table, speaking with each of the guests. A number of seats were still empty.

"Sorry about the nap today," she murmured to Idak. "I was exhausted after... well, you know."

"I know—Mother told me. Exciting." His green eyes twinkled. "Will you take her up on her offer to teach you?"

"Most likely," she replied, although she wasn't as sure as she let herself sound. She might end up with no other options, so she didn't want to say no. But some part of her, in her heart, still wanted to become one of the Bladed Women.

Would they still accept her though... She didn't feel like she'd exactly failed her quest. But it was hard to imagine doing it now, and the context had certainly changed. They'd been trying to teach her about honesty.

Had she learned? She didn't think so. Not yet. Maybe they would give her another quest...

The first course was wheeled out on a small cart covered in blood-red silk. Su did a double take when she realized the servant pushing the cart had shackles around his wrists. A faint clinking told her chains hung to connect the two.

"Why are your servants *shackled*?" she whispered to Idak.

He shrugged one shoulder, his eyes taking on that rare defensive, closed look. "Good help is hard to find, I suppose? I don't manage the staff here; my mother does."

"Doesn't that bother you, though? You live here."

He eyed the cart for a moment as if it had truly never occurred to him to question such a thing. "I don't know. We're all bound, aren't we? Do you have a choice not to be a clan leader's daughter? Do I get a choice not to be my mother's son?"

She narrowed her eyes at him. "There's always a choice."

"I believe you were the one who lectured me about how there's only so much we can do to better—or worsen—our reputations. Don't you see? We've all been assigned our stations; there's little we can do to change that. This isn't a bad life for someone born in the hay."

How could she articulate to him the distastefulness of that? She couldn't manage anything other than a sour expression.

"I've seen many dark things in these hills, Sutamae," he continued. "Shackles aren't the worst of them. I think choice is an illusion they like us to believe. If we ever made the other choice, the wrong choice—do you think they'd actually let us? Or would we find we have no choice at all?"

She bit her lip, thinking of her thoughts that morning. Did she actually have a choice to leave and go home, or were she and the masked man's sister in the same predicament already? "If I allowed myself think my choices didn't matter, then I would simply sit at home until my father marries me off to someone probably older and wealthier than you."

He snorted. "Sutamae. *None* of the clan families are wealthier than we are, except perhaps your own."

"Perhaps?" She pursed her lips. "That's not the point."

He smiled as he popped a cherry into his mouth. "I understand."

She wasn't sure he did, but a second course arrived, with a similarly shackled woman attending the cart. Su watched the other guests, none of whom she'd been introduced to, but no one seemed to bat an eyelash at the chained hand placing a plate before them. One old man on the other side of the table even grabbed onto the iron links briefly to make some sort of quiet request in her ear. The slave nodded in response.

Sutamae swallowed hard. First the strangeness of this morning, now this. It was a good thing she hadn't agreed to marry Idak without this visit, but would it have the effect he intended?

At breakfast, Unira had made a passionate case for an alliance—a pact for the two of them to both make Elix pay for all the people he'd cast aside and underestimated in his life. Of course, she'd been reeling at the realization that he could have groomed her to be a mage just like Grel. But at the same time, she was also thinking of Grel. And Nyalin too. Why was her father letting the sword smiths get away with torturing Grel? Why would he let his only daughter languish when she could be a powerful warrior for the clan?

And Nyalin. He'd given up looking for his gift. But the Bone Clan girl had proven her father wrong. Nyalin's magic had been evident during the Contests. Lara's father hadn't pushed *her* aside, but she was still expected to marry on demand—gag. At least Lara had power, training, a certain measure of peer respect.

Unira had railed at the injustice of it all, and Su had heartily agreed. She hadn't gone into specifics of what exactly the alliance meant, or would entail—but Su assumed it first and foremost had to do with marrying Idak and consolidating power.

Watching a slave place a bowl of dumplings before her, though, as others in chains wheeled in more carts filled with small bowls of soup, it was hard to believe Unira truly cared about injustice. Was it only the upper classes who deserved justice? The wealthy? Women with magic like the two of them?

And of course, with Unira's words, it had become clear her goals were not simply an alliance in marriage. Marrying Idak was sincerely her best option in many ways. And yet... as Unira had so delicately pointed out, the pairing would put Idak in closer competition to Grel. Grel losing his birthright would hurt Elix a bit—but it would hurt *Grel* far more.

Funny it hadn't occurred to Unira that Su would care about that.

And when Su considered Jylan's long courtship with Grel, all of it put together made her wonder how sincere any of it was. Idak... She found it hard to believe he could fake some of his comments. Most of them. He seemed truly attempting to be honest.

But that didn't mean he wasn't a pawn in a much larger, possibly sinister game.

"Excuse us for being fashionably late," said a man in the doorway. As more guests filed in, her eye caught on none other than Hendo among them. Instantly, she dropped her eyes to her plate. Her whole body felt like it'd turned to ice.

Years ago, when she'd been young and naive, she'd taken a risk and asked one of the renowned sword masters in their clan to teach her how to fight. He had agreed—in a way. He had forced her to fight him off, again and again. One day, she *had* beaten him. He still had the scar by his eye that she'd given him. And after that, she'd never gone back.

But her own scars, her own pain, remained.

"What is it?" Idak whispered.

Too late she realized the vice grip she had on Idak's hand. She let go abruptly. "Nothing. It's nothing."

She risked a glance up at the bastard. Hendo hadn't noticed her yet. He sank into a seat at the far end of the table. Maybe he wouldn't notice her.

"You're shaking. It's not nothing."

"Some choices we make..." she whispered. "Sometimes, they haunt us."

“Ah, Sutamae, have you met our guests?” Unira said casually as she slipped back into her seat. Thankfully, she hadn’t spoken loudly enough for the newcomers to hear, but there was a strange sadistic tone to the words. “You seem to recognize someone.”

“I thought perhaps I did,” she lied, “but I was mistaken.”

Idak found her hand and squeezed it in his again. She had to admit it *was* reassuring.

“Should I introduce you?”

Su looked back to Idak’s mother and paused. There was something in her expression, in the gleam in her eye, some sort of curl of her lip. And, somehow, Sutamae was *sure* that she knew—what had happened, what Su had risked, how Hendo had taken advantage of her trust that the world was safe and people were good. She’d learned the sword from him, and something worse.

The world was not safe. Some people were not good. Some people could not be trusted. And in this moment, whatever Unira might say, Sutamae was sure that Unira was one of the bad ones.

“Did you invite him here intentionally?” Su whispered.

“What is going on?” Idak demanded.

The quirk in the corner of Unira’s mouth only deepened. “It is fascinating how well we understand each other. You and I are quite alike.”

“No. We’re not.”

“Don’t people like him remind you of how cruel this world is? I, for one, have had enough of it. If only we could start over, or if someone *else* were in charge, perhaps there would be so much less cruelty in the world.”

“What are you two going on about?” Idak grumbled.

Su blinked. Had Unira really invited someone to a dinner just to make a point? To make her angry? No, not angry. To remind her of the trauma. The terror. She’d thought this would be motivating somehow? Su had trouble imagining it.

“This system is wretched,” Unira continued. “We could make a better one. You and I.”

“What about me?” Idak had been repeatedly looking back and forth between them, increasingly alarmed.

“The three of us, I mean.”

Su forced herself to stand. “I think I need some air.”

“I’ll go with you.” Idak rose too and followed her several steps toward the wide patio and the view of Mount Stragg.

"Sutamae, wait. I didn't intend to upset you." Unira held up a hand.

She stopped, turning back.

When Unira spoke, her voice was so low, Su was sure no one but the two of them could hear. "I brought him to you as an offering. A sort of... payment in advance, for the alliance I propose."

"What do you mean?"

"If you want him dead, I will see it arranged. If you'd like to do it yourself, I will give you that opportunity."

She was shaking harder now, her eyes widened. "I... I think you've misjudged me."

"Oh, I don't think so." Unira gave her a small smile.

Maybe she was right. It was a tempting offer. "I think I need some air."

"Go on ahead. Take your time. But he won't be my guest forever."

Su rushed away, out into the night air.

Grel had been staring at the woman for at least an hour.

Ordinarily, his honor—and his sense—would have prevented such ridiculous prolonged ogling. But he could have *sworn* she kept disappearing.

How was that possible? She couldn't always be reappearing just before he looked back... could she?

After an hour's vigil, he'd learned nothing more, and the mystery was going to have to wait, because there was a knock at the open door. He waved the visitor in. "Hello, there, Dalas."

"Good evening, sir." The baker's smile was wide as he entered, carrying a wooden tray of assorted goodies. "Just thought I'd bring by a bit more mead and oats for the lady."

"That's very kind of you. She hasn't woken much, but I'm sure we'll get her a few more sips before we—I—head to sleep." He'd meant he'd offer her sustenance with the assistance of Uli—okay, it was mostly Uli, while he watched and worried—but suddenly wondered if that was clear to Dalas.

For a moment, out of his peripheral vision, he could have sworn he saw a flash, or the bed linens sink as though the body inside had disappeared, but when his head snapped back, nothing about her seemed to have changed. Was he going crazy?

"So this is the woman who appeared from nowhere, eh?" asked Dalas.

"Indeed." Grel glanced back to the baker. The man had set down the tray and was just standing there, perhaps waiting to see if Grel needed anything else. Suddenly, the idea of being alone again and wondering at his own sanity sounded terrible. He still regretted missing Nyalin that morning. It sounded like he might be off on a daring adventure, and here was Grel, staring at a bedpost. Other than his efforts related to this woman and locating her family, he'd spent much of the time alone, keeping watch. He gestured at the chairs. "Please, take a seat. It's been a long day. I could use the company of someone I can chat with for a bit, if you have the time."

"That's kind of you. I wouldn't mind a bit of chit chat either. And to rest my tired feet before I head home for the night."

He glanced back to the woman. "This is my fiery savior, appearing from nowhere. I just wish I could wake her up to thank her..." Both of their wounds were already healed, and yet still she slept.

"Surely, someone must be looking for her?" asked Dalas.

"I sent letters to every prominent Obsidian family, and I had posters hung on two dozen streets." That was where he'd been when he missed Nyalin, attending to having the letters sent and overseeing the posters. Okay, perhaps he had hung a few himself.

"I saw one. Indeed, they were fairly hard to miss. You are... diligent."

Grel frowned. There was an odd tone to Dalas's voice, almost as if he thought Grel's efforts were... misguided? "I'm just doing my best to find her family, her friends. Someone has to be looking? Right?" Dalas had a way of allowing him to let his guard down, of not judging him harshly the way his father would. And the two of them had known each other for so many years. Plus, Dalas was one of few other people in this house who had been kind to Nyalin, and that had always served as a mark of good judgment in Grel's book. As such, he didn't want to disappoint him. Was there some mistake he'd made, something he missed?

"I just wonder..." Dalas hesitated, then began again. "We don't know much about her. What if she was hiding from something, or someone? On the run, let's say?"

He winced. "Then I've publicized her existence and location all over the district."

Dalas nodded. "Well, I suppose at least it's not the whole city."

"Um... Maybe it was? At least one poster made it to each district."

"Oh." Dalas laughed quietly. "Ah, I see."

"I didn't think about that. She just seems... This isn't someone who lives on the street, you know? She has a home somewhere."

"How can you tell?"

"For one, even after a battle, she's too clean. And for another, her cross-over is plain, but it's also not torn nor repeatedly mended. So it can't be that old, not if she lived the rough and tumble life."

"You know a lot about the common people, Grel. It's commendable."

"I'm not sure my father thinks so. But thank you."

"You are clearly very passionate about helping people too."

Grel snorted. "Sometimes, too passionate." Hence the posters and letters, and he hadn't even mentioned the few boys he'd sent off to ask around—after both Su and this woman, with sketches of them both.

"We have quite the deficit of passion for helping others these days, so I don't think you should fret. What were your attackers like? Rumors are spreading, and I don't know what to believe."

He sighed and leaned back, thinking. How could he even describe them? "I've never seen anything like them. And more than a dozen—how did they come out of nowhere? How did *she* come out of nowhere, for that matter?" Smoke had vanished at the same time and hadn't returned to the estate. It had been hard not to include a drawing of the cat in his search for Su and this woman's identity, but it didn't seem appropriate to put a pet on par with people. Besides, Smoke had a way of disappearing for a time, then returning. Maybe she was searching the Bone district to see if Nyalin had returned. He shook his head. Dalas had asked him what they looked like. he'd hardly said anything on the matter. "I, um... Hmm. They had silver eyes—three of them! And wings. Skin was like leather, rust-colored, taut. Screechers. Their noises were hideous."

Dalas shuddered and looked truly disturbed. "And that was all they did? Scream and howl?"

"And try to kill me. Claws all over the place. Fortunately, we're both healed now, thank the Twins for the magic. But that's why I don't understand why she won't wake up..." He was off on a tangent again. "Wait... No, they didn't just scream and howl. I thought of them as more like animals, but, at the last moment, one uttered something more like words. It almost felt like a curse. The words seemed to slam her into the wall, and then it perished."

Dalas had gone completely white.

"Terrifying stuff, eh?"

"Indeed," he managed. "You're lucky to be alive."

"I wouldn't be, if it weren't for her. That's why I have to help her. Why I need to find her family, her friends. Something to help me wake her up."

The two of them sat in silence for a moment.

"Any news of your stepbrother?" Dalas asked, almost a whisper.

"Yes, actually. Apparently, he stopped by here just this morning, but I missed him. He left a note saying he was looking for help, but that he knew I was busy. That he'd check in again soon."

"Help? With what?"

"Some trip he was going on. Said it was actually up in the Obsidian wilds. Can you imagine? You know, up by Stragg's Beard?"

Dalas choked. "The—the wilds? Why would anyone want to go there?"

"No idea." Grel shrugged. "Something about ghosts something-something, a lady harnessing them for her own power, something, I don't know. You want to read it? I know you always cared about him and looked out for him."

After a moment's hesitation, Dalas said, "Well, I mean, if you wouldn't mind."

Grel fetched the note from his desk and handed it to Dalas. "Hard to believe how things have panned out for him, isn't it? Who knows what he'll do next? My father might not believe it, but he'll do great things. I'm sure of it."

Dalas's eyes tracked back and forth on the note, then he handed it back to him. "Hard to believe. Indeed. What could he be doing up there?"

Grel shrugged and settled back in his chair. His dark-haired savior continued to sleep.

"Any news for you, Grel? Of your sword, at all?" Dalas asked, voice very quiet.

"No," he murmured back. After his wounds had healed, he'd ranted and raged about it—when only his father was around. He'd lost his temper a bit with him, because what else could he do? No other approach to convince the sword smiths had any impact or effect.

Of course, losing his temper with Elix had been like losing his temper with a brick wall. But for once, Elix had agreed—without even any reluctance—that something needed to be done. That Grel should have had a sword to defend himself. He'd never seen his father look so old, as he had in that moment.

"Can I get you something from the kitchens before I turn in?" asked Dalas, rising.

His words brought Grel back into the present. "I might need some mead for myself... So I'm not tempted to steal hers."

"Already thought of it."

Grel raised his eyebrows. He hadn't noticed the two glasses on the tray Dalas had brought. Had he been staring at his injured savior this whole time?

By the Twins, he hoped Dalas didn't think something strange was going on.

Well, something strange *was* going on. But nothing untoward or inappropriate.

"Thank you," he managed awkwardly. "You didn't need to do any of this."

"Ah, but I did." Dalas gave him a smile and a small bow, and then he turned to go.

~

"What was that all about?" Idak demanded as soon as they were outside.

Su waved him off with one hand, the other covering her face. Why had he come? He should just leave her alone. "I can't explain. I just can't."

He pulled her with him to the side of the patio, under some vines. She spun away from him, folding her arms across her chest. He stepped gently closer, so that his chest pressed against her back, and ran his hands up and down her arms. Was he trying to comfort her? That was sweet, even if the arm-rubbing was only making her feel more anxious.

"What if we play another round of our guessing game? I'll make a guess, and you just have to agree—or disagree."

"I'm not in the mood, Idak," she snapped.

"I want to know what is going on with you and my mother—what happened in there. Don't you think I have a right to know?"

"No."

"Oh, come on. Just try it."

She only gritted her teeth, pressing her eyes closed. "Leave me alone, Idak."

"First guess. You've met that man before."

She gritted her teeth for a moment and squirmed at his touch. His fingers tightened a little, not letting her run away. Finally, she nodded.

"See? That wasn't so hard, was it? Next guess. You don't just wish for a sword; you've tried to get one before."

Biting her lip, she nodded. Damn him for pressing her this way, for not leaving her be. But it was a tad bit addictive, this feeling of being seen. Of being understood, by someone.

"Next one. The Bladed Women will give you one."

"Yes. And also no."

"Fascinating, truly fascinating. All right then, another. You've tried some other way. Perhaps before you found the Bladed Women."

"Yes." The word surprised her. It escaped of its own volition, soaked in sorrow; it flew like a sparrow fleeing its gilded cage, spiting her every desire to hide the truth.

"And it had to do with him," he said softly.

"Yes." It was barely a whisper.

"He hurt you, didn't he." His hands had tightened on her shoulders. What would he do if he knew the truth? The truth no one knew. And yet, Unira knew. Somehow Unira had found out. How had an enemy been the only one to find out her darkest secret?

"Sutamae. Don't break the rules of our game now. Did he hurt you?"

Her voice was rough as a serrated blade when she spoke, and just as dangerous. "Yes."

"I'm going to murder him."

"Don't you dare."

"No promises."

"It sounds like your mother might not approve. Not yet, anyway. It's my choice if he lives or dies, isn't it?" She bit her lip. Unira's offer twisted her insides. What did Su even want? Justice? Revenge? If Hendo's murder was so just, why did the thought turn her stomach? She'd fantasized about finally cutting Hendo down at times, but could she truly want that?

Curse Unira for the offer. Either way, now, Sutamae would choose. Hendo's life was in her hands, and there was no way to abstain or walk away. It was a black and white, yes or no question. But could she really choose to kill him?

Could she really choose the alternative—to spare someone who had caused so much suffering?

Idak didn't respond right away to her comment about his mother not approving. While she was weighing her options, what was he thinking about? She found it hard to believe he'd go against his mother's wishes. But he certainly hadn't said anything of the sort. In fact, unlike her and Grel's frequent quips about torturing their father, Idak had said very little—if anything—that would make her think he'd ever question Unira's authority.

"Come. Let's walk—let's get that fresh air you wanted. Moonlight." He ushered her toward a set of stairs she hadn't noticed that led off the patio and away from the dining room, from Unira and her special guest.

"They say it's good for the skin," she murmured weakly.

They walked for a while in silence.

"I don't think you should go back in there," he said.

"I agree."

"The night sure is beautiful on these hills, don't you think? You should see the forests in the springtime."

It was all she could do to muster a comment that might sound like she cared about such banality. "I'm sure it is."

"Do you want to head into the woods? It's dark, but I know the trails—"

"It's been too hard a day, I think. Tomorrow?"

His expression fell, but he seemed to understand.

"I'm feeling much better now. I think I'll head back to my rooms. Just exhausted."

"Do you want company?" His tone was more cautious this time, less free. Had she said something to make him guarded? But what could she do? Memories of Hendo did *not* make her want any kind of company at the moment. She just wanted to curl up in a ball in the darkness.

"I think I need to be alone just now," she said, instead of saying all that.

"I shall go back to the dinner. Send for me if you need me."

"I will."

He left her at the base of the stairs into the wing of the estate where she was staying. His step was brisk as she watched him go. Because he was worried what his mother would think? What others would think? Was he required to go back there? Was he planning to go and poison Hendo's plum pudding? Just how under his mother's thumb was he? Was there any way to know?

She stood for a long while, watching him in the moonlight. He didn't look back, and she was glad of it.

He certainly had a way of seeing into the heart of her, but perhaps this trip had been even more rash than she'd realized. His mother was wildly murderous and vengeful, and that was confusing on its own, but even without that—would she really be content to live out her days in this country estate, so far from the city? Could she perhaps ignore all that boring estate management—leaving it to continue under the control of his dear mother? Instead, taking walks in the wilderness for hours with him? Because that was what he wanted; she was sure of it. A companion for this peaceful country estate, who could perchance tolerate a scheming matriarch in the picture.

That wasn't an unreasonable thing for Idak to want. But what did *she* want?

Although, it also seemed he wanted someone who could tolerate or even appreciate slaves in chains serving the soup.

And whatever the two of them wanted, it didn't change the fact that his mother clearly *was* a murderous, vengeful psychopath. Surely, she had her reasons, but Su wasn't sure the reasons really mattered to Unira. They were more like... excuses. Excuses to set things on fire. Excuses to delight in tearing someone down—her father Elix, Hendo, Grel—who else would end up on that list? The emperor?

Her stomach roiled again, growing even more anxious with each thought.

The growing darkness made her uneasy. She turned to start up the stairs when she caught the strange glimpse again, out the corner of her eye, the flash of glowing white. She froze.

That couldn't be real, could it? She must be hallucinating.

But she wasn't dreaming now. She crept slowly back down the stairs, peering through the archway. There it was again, perched on the roof. It seemed to be looking at her.

It looked just like the little white dragon from her dream. If it had been a dream.

*This way.* The words were clear and sharp in her head. *This way.* It flitted around the corner of the building.

She looked wide-eyed in both directions. Idak was long gone. No one else was in sight. She swallowed hard.

*Come, Daughter.* The same voice as in her dream. Had it all been real? One way to find out—get closer the creature. She crept silently on cat-like feet through the darkness, following.

*Chapter 12*

# Descent

"This way," whispered the scrawny girl.

Daridian limped after her, turning the corner of the building. Most windows were darkened in the estate as the small group hurried between buildings, from shadow to shadow. A handful of the slaves who were strong enough to travel had come along, hoping to retake their freedom in the process.

After seeing the young man and his child safely away from the estate, he'd returned to the tent as quickly as he could to help the others. It hadn't taken long for them to form a plan.

Originally, he'd hoped to simply sneak into the estate with them, take part in their duties, pretend to be one of them, so that he could get closer to the powerful people who might know where Sha'lien was. But he hadn't been able to find a way to conceal a sword or the mask in their pathetically worn and tattered garments. After telling them more about his true goals, his search for his sister, one girl had spoken up.

"Have you been in the catacombs?" she'd asked. "There are strange things down there. They have tunnels full of rows and rows of people—asleep."

His brow furrowed. "Asleep?"

"Yeah. One of them I knew from our village. They took the lot of us in chains here, but then they dragged him off. They're like... encased in glass or light or something. Hard to explain. But they look just the same—but asleep. What if they have your sister there?"

He didn't like the sound of any of that. But it was something concrete, where his sister might be.

As he'd scoured outbuildings of this estate over the last two days, he'd checked a number of cells in his search, and not a one had held his sister, even though many—most, if he was honest—were occupied. What were these people doing, with so many locked up and in chains? Unless they had her wining and dining with those that had kidnapped her, which certainly was possible, he was at a loss.

And now he was to believe there were people magically asleep underground?

It seemed ridiculous. And yet, he believed it.

His leg pained him the whole way forward, but he kept up with the girl. Thin as she was, she had a toughness about her, and a short cap of hair such that he'd almost mistaken her for a boy. The others managed to keep pace as well. He'd used his tools to unlock their chains, but they still wore them. The plan was to get to the mouth of the catacombs, then sneak out the back merchant gate and remove the chains only once they were free. Daridian would part with them at some point when their escape seemed assured, and he'd head down into the catacombs to see what he could find.

His leg didn't like the plan, but he didn't see any better options.

"Almost there." Turning the corner, the girl jumped and staggered back, swearing.

He rushed forward, hand on the hilt of his blade. And stopped short.

Just around the corner—it was *her*. The girl from the city. Sutamae. And at her feet sat a glowing creature, with two wings, its scales shimmering like the jewel in the clanblade he carried. He caught his breath.

"Is that a dragon?" whispered the girl.

"Yes, I think so," replied Sutamae.

"What's it doing here?" the girl demanded.

"I'd like to know that as well."

"What are *you* doing here?" Daridian asked. He knew she was at the estate, but what were the chances that he'd run into her of all people? "Do you make a habit of haunting the streets at night?"

"No, but I'm not afraid of a little darkness." She narrowed her eyes. "I could ask the same of you, though, masked man. Except I already know."

A chill went through him. "You do?"

"The dragon told me in a dream. You're looking for your sister who—"

They all stopped short. Heavy footsteps were approaching from up the path behind Sutamae. The dragon launched itself into the sky so fast, Daridian almost didn't see it move.

"This way!" he whispered. They all darted to the side, into the shadows, like he'd instructed. Everyone huddled there, even Sutamae, and he did his best to wrap his magic around them. As much as his magic could enhance his own perception, it could dim the perception of others—encourage them to look away, look for something more interesting, nothing to see here in this very boring shadowy corner.

After a minute or two, when the patrol had passed and turned a corner, they slowly eased out of the deepest shadow.

"We're going to the catacombs," the girl said boldly. "Have you seen them?"

Sutamae frowned. "No, why would I—"

"There are people locked down there. Asleep. In long rows, white like glowing tombs."

Su's eyes went wide. "Where? Can you show me? I'll come with you."

"It's just up there, but it's probably guarded. If you're one of them, maybe you can sweettalk your way in." The girl tilted her head, inquisitively.

A half-smile lit up Su's face. "Now what would make you think I can do that?"

"Oh, I, um, just, I thought, maybe—"

"Oh, I can. I just didn't know I let it on so clearly. Show me the way. I'll see if I can distract the guards for you so you can get in." She caught his eye. "You suspect she's down there?"

He swallowed. Why did it feel like his heart was in his throat. "It's a possibility. I've scoured this place and not found her."

"Okay, point me to the place and let me approach first."

The girl and Sutamae conferred for a few minutes, then she marched off toward the entrance to the catacombs. He brought the group up slowly behind her, sticking to the edges, trying to go unnoticed.

"Who's there?" A gruff voice came from where he thought the entrance was supposed to be.

"Good evening," was Sutamae's smooth reply. "How are you doing on this fine night? Beautiful night for a stroll, don't you think?"

"I suppose," the guard admitted begrudgingly. "What are you doing down there? This part of the estate is all business, no place for... for..."

"For guests of Idak and his mother?" she replied sweetly.

Daridian gritted his teeth. She belonged with *him*, not this fool Obsidian. It was a stupid, unrealistic thought that was impossible to act on. He had a mission, and, clearly, she was interested in someone else—and had taken him at his word.

But he still hated every second of it.

The guard cleared his throat. "Pardon me, but really—the dinner is in the main house, in the dining room just off the terrace. You shouldn't be here."

"I had to leave. I needed some air. Thank you for your concern, but I left with Idak's blessing."

"But, ma'am—"

"You wouldn't want me to have to tell him that you didn't respect his wishes, would you? Besides. I dropped the diamond and ruby necklace he gave me over there, near the wood piles."

A jeweled necklace? As a gift? That sounded... aggressive. Ostentatious. He hated this man, whoever he was, even more now.

"So what do you want *us* to do about that?"

"Well, obviously, I demand you help me look for it."

The guards seemed stunned into silence for a moment.

"As he would expect, I'm sure. Surely, your help locating his very expensive gift would be appreciated—and even rewarded. Or shall I go get *him* to help me look, and tell him you weren't willing?"

"No, ma'am, no. Where was it you dropped it again?" Two guards started forward.

"You two, as well. Chop, chop. All hands on deck, as they say. Over here."

She marched them skillfully toward a pile of firewood and old barrels that was at least somewhat out of the line of sight from the entrance. Who knew how long she could keep them occupied, but this was their only chance.

Daridian and his small group hurried through the darkness toward the entrance, his magic working overtime to mask their footsteps. He slid the last few feet down the steep dirt slope to the door.

His girl guide was just ahead of him. She grabbed the handle, but stopped short of yanking on a large iron door. "Curse it, there's a lock."

He could only hope the guards wouldn't hear their whispers or his tools clicking in the awkward silence. Sutamae valiantly kept up a string of noisy complaints, ordering them to overturn everything in the vicinity, but how long could she really last?

She'd used her guest status here to get them this chance. Was that the ultimate irony or karmic justice? His sweaty fingers fumbled and nearly dropped the tools, his mind flooded with thoughts about the man who was giving her fancy jewels and inviting her here. He must have some sort of intention.

He'd determined she must have some relationship with these people when he'd caught up with her at the inn, based on all the things she'd said there. But jewels, dinners, invitations? It was all he could do not to groan as he started again on the lock.

"It's got to be here somewhere!" she was saying, louder, an increasing desperation in her voice.

The lock finally gave up the fight. When he wriggled it off the latch hook, the door swung wildly inward, iron crashing against stone.

Loudly. Very loudly.

"What was that?" started one of the guards.

"Hurry, get in there! Get in and run!" He ushered each of them inside. Better that they hide in there and have to look for their freedom in a few hours than they all get caught immediately.

"Hey, what are you—" The rest of the guards Sutamae had been doing her best to distract now turned to the noise at the entrance and rushed over to face the intruders.

Steel rang as Daridian drew his sword, and the guards did in turn. He rounded on them, already slashing at the closest one. Perhaps the one with the best hearing would be the first to die.

Sutamae rushed past the startled guards, sliding to a stop at his side. "I have to help. How can I—"

"Got a weapon in that dress?" he asked through clenched teeth, heaving away the heavy weight of a guard, whose sword locked against his own sword's crossguard. The guard stumbled back, and Daridian advanced up the slope.

"Not tonight. I didn't think I'd need it."

He hesitated. The Pearl Clan's clanblade was tucked inside his crossover, but there were three guards, four? Maybe he could take them. He could handle this on his own, right? Because could he really risk handing someone allied with his enemies, those that sought the clanblade, the very thing they hunted? Spark or no Spark, beautiful or not beautiful—he didn't know her well enough to trust her.

"Help me by helping them," he growled, gesturing behind him with his head. "It's pitch black in there. Find a torch? Lamp? Something?"

She nodded and rushed through the doorway.

He was mildly shocked she'd listened. But there was no time to ponder that as a sword was already swinging toward his knee.

He swung his blade to block the strike, willing the power of the mask into his actions, bringing his senses to life. He could feel all four of his adversaries, their distance, their slight muscle movements forecasting their intent. He could have sworn he could count the beads of sweat on their brows.

He ducked under the next sloppy attack from the one closest to him, going down on one knee. Then he hacked into the guard's calf while he was down there.

Howling, that man fell, still trying to stab at him while also reaching for his wound. Daridian leapt up, away, all but forgetting about his own injured leg.

Three left. That was still a lot, but if he could get a little more space....

Still too close to the first attacker, he rolled into a tumble, but the uphill grade meant he didn't make it far.

His senses warned him. Three blades slashed down at his back. He rolled again, unnaturally fast, and brought up his sword to catch two of them, catching the third just barely with the heel of his boot.

Three pairs of scowling eyes glowered down at him. They'd been faster, more aggressive than he'd expected. Like a dog going belly up, he was exposed. They had him now.

"Hey, now, is that anyway to treat my friend?" Sutamae's voice was silky smooth, suggestive.

All three of them glared at the doorway. Daridian almost looked too; it was hard to resist. But he caught himself just in time and kicked the attacker he'd blocked with his boot in the nuts.

And rolled. And slashed and rolled and blocked.

He hated being on the defensive like this. He should have just fought from the doorway—or ducked inside and tried to stab them through the crack in the door. At least the iron would have been a shield, some sort of cover, *something*. That kind of error could cost him his life—and Sha'lien's.

He finally got in a few tiny stabs to the thigh of one, and the foot of another, buying him just enough time to stagger to his feet. A body touched the side of his—her. Sutamae.

"What are you doing? Get clear."

"I'm helping you. And following orders."

"*Whose* orders?"

She reached for the clanblade under his crossover.

Had *they* ordered her to take it? His thoughts after their first meeting flashed through his mind. She was either a vulnerability—or a carefully planned deception. Was it the latter?

He slid away, twisting to stop her, but she'd gotten her grip on the hilt just right. The blade slid from its sheath as he was forced to parry the guard who he'd kicked in the nuts and had finally recovered.

By the Spear, if he survived these fool guards, would he live just long enough to see her turn over the clanblade he'd so carefully stolen back to his enemies? They might share a Spark, but it wasn't like she owed him loyalty, she was not of Annikyre. She didn't even know him. But somehow, after the kiss and the night they'd shared—it still felt like betrayal.

"Sutamae—don't give it—to them," he begged, panting.

She frowned at him as if he was begging her not to grow a second head. "Stop," she ordered the guards, pointing the blade straight at them. The white jewel in the handle shimmered in the moonlight. It seemed brighter, unnaturally bright. Was that the mask's magic, or did the sword truly seem to love being in her hand?

By the Spear, he had it bad for this girl. Idiot. Swords couldn't have opinions.

"We don't answer to you," one guard bit out, breathlessly.

"Then you give me no choice."

She sprang into action. He only let his shock delay him for a blink before he joined her, pushing them back side by side.

A flash of bright white, like a falling piece of the moon, startled them all and gave Su an opportunity to stab one in the thigh. It was the tiny dragon, the one that had arrived with her!

The one whose scales seemed to match the sword... He frowned, trying to make sense of it all. He did not understand this empire at all.

The two of them plus the dragon's harassment were plenty of a match for the remaining guards. Abruptly, just as he thought they might actually come out victorious, two turned and ran.

"They're taking off," Sutamae said, sounding concerned, as the remaining two fled as well.

"Let them run." He waved a hand. "Enough blood will be shed without us insisting on shedding theirs, right here, right now."

"But they'll return with more help."

"I agree. Let us go quickly then."

She followed him as he ran toward the iron door, down into the catacombs. "Do you really think there are sleeping people down here?"

"I thought the dragon told you all my inner thoughts and feelings." He sure hoped it hadn't, but perhaps teasing her would be one way to find out.

"It told me you were looking for your sister. Is she really down *here*? In the catacombs?"

"We're going to find out. I thought I told you to help them find light?"

"I looked, but only the one of them remained, and she insisted I should be helping you, not her."

Inside, it was true. Most of the slaves had scattered or gone further in, but the girl who'd led them here remained. There was no way to bolt the door from the inside. They were going to have to hurry.

"Do you think these tunnels might be large enough to hide inside?" he asked the girl. "There are probably more pursuers coming."

"I have no idea. I never got far. They just sent me on short errands, and then I had to return."

"Well, let's go. Show us what you saw."

The girl looked nervous, as if she wondered if she'd imagined it or if they would still be there. But they didn't have far to go through the dirt-packed tunnel to find two alcoves that looked like they'd been designed to hold bodies—graves or caskets or maybe some other sort of preserved remains.

But where the bodies *should* have been, two human forms slept, their features still pink and lifelike. Each of them was encased in some sort of container, almost like glass, with the faintest glow of magic. Was it real glass or some magic at work?

"See?" she whispered. "Sleeping. They're not dead. If you look at their chests, they are breathing. There're many more of them. This way."

They hurried down the corridor and came to a wide room with four stone pillars supporting the ceiling, where a mural of snow-capped mountains was painted. The area looked like it had once contained family heirlooms, remembrances of the dead, but armor stands stood naked, and armoires gaped open, empty and dusty. Six separate tunnels branched off from this main room.

And they could see the softly glowing tubes lining each one.

"There have to be dozens of people down here," Sutamae breathed. "What by Seluvae's stars does she do with them?"

"I need to find my sister, but—" he started.

A heavy slam, like a door opening, sounded above them in the tunnels.

"But I think first and foremost, we need to find somewhere to hide."

"This tunnel looks oldest," said Sutamae. "That one looks like it might have some empty spots still. Newer?"

"Let's go." The three of them dashed down the newer tunnel. If Sha'lien was imprisoned in this strange place, then the newer area was where she'd be. And maybe empty graves meant hiding spots they could use?

Or maybe they'd be trapped when they hit a dead end.

Swallowing, he brought up the rear, as Sutamae ushered them down the tunnel into the dark, eerie glow. The hilt of the clanblade she still carried glowed faintly, caressing the folds of her dress with something like moonlight.

The rock Nyalin was sitting on was not the least comfortable seat he'd had during this time in the wilderness, nor was it the most. But it *was* a very good spot to observe the small town below him. Of course, it wasn't a town. It was a single family's estate. But it was also a massive silk farm. There were buildings that appeared to contain large looms and other equipment, plus dozens of other buildings. His knee bounced as he scanned over it all.

Nyalin wasn't sure how many buildings were part of Elix's family's wealth, or if they even maintained any facilities inside or outside of the city beyond the Obsidian mansion. But he had to think this would be more than any one person would reasonably control in the city. Why were there so many?

The trip here had been quick. After night had started to fall, they had followed his senses of the afterworld and closed in on the estate gradually. Yeska had carried them as close as she could while remaining out of sight. They'd chosen the highest hill in the range—almost a mountain—so she could land on the other side, and then they hiked in the dark to this spot near the summit, guided by the dimmest light spells they could manage.

They'd nestled among some craggy boulders and scraggy pine trees and gotten to work, taking turns seeing what they could see, in spite of the darkness. And fortunately, what they could see was a lot.

There was a lot going on in this little estate-town tonight. Patrols, music, some sort of dinner happening in a larger probably main building. And the buildings where weaving happened seemed to run both day and night, powered by what looked to be magical lanterns.

He hadn't tried to slip back into the afterworld intentionally since his meeting with Batu, but he was dreading that he'd have to do it soon. Especially here. There'd been a few accidental slips he had been glad no one had noticed, so his control on it still wasn't fully complete. And that made him nervous. As much as he'd learned there, the chance that he might not make it back nagged at him.

"I don't see anything new," grumbled Lara. "Here you go. Your turn." She handed one of the two spy glasses they'd found to Faytou.

"Maybe we shouldn't have come," grumbled Nyalin.

"No, no," replied Lara. "It'll just take some time."

"You're in." Pyaris held hers out to him, and he accepted it with a smile. "The spirits here... I can't see them, but I can feel them. Can you?" Her eyes were half-lidded, cautious. That he'd judge her? That maybe he couldn't sense them like she could? He probably couldn't, exactly.

But the place made his skin twitch. Like a graveyard. "They're... angry I think," he murmured.

She gave him a curt nod. "Whatever they're doing down there, it's not right."

They'd been watching the silk farm and attached estate for about an hour now. They'd seen guards change, and patrols made regular routes. Lara had sketched some of the activity patterns out in the dirt.

"Hey, look!" Faytou pointed. "There are some people fighting down there."

Nyalin lifted the spy glass and leaned closer. He caught his breath. "It's dark, but—is that Sutamae? What would she be doing here? And why is she fighting?"

"Let me see." Lara held out her hand for Faytou's spy glass. "I think it is! Wow—that's—that's quite a fight. I didn't know she could handle a sword like that."

"Look, the guards are fleeing." He frowned. Su and the man with her weren't pursuing the guards. That meant the guards would return—with reinforcements.

"Where is she going?" said Lara.

"Down. Inside or maybe... underground?" he replied.

"That's where we should go then." Lara nodded resolutely, handing the spy glass back to Faytou.

"How do we get in there, though?" Pyaris asked. "This place is heavily guarded. We've been watching for hours, and I haven't seen one gap in the guard patrols," she pointed out. "What could be so important in there?"

"Yeah, I don't see any Mushin in these hills," said Faytou. "And they're far from other clans. What the hell are they so worried about?"

Nyalin swallowed. "Or what are they hiding?"

"Could we go through the afterworld?" Lara asked.

"What? What do you mean?" Faytou asked.

"One time, your brother kidnapped us—"

"Wait—wait—wait—what?"

"A story for another time. When Nyalin uses... his mother's powers, he can move from one place to another in one plane, and when he returns to this one, he's moved here too. Right before the Contests, Andius had us locked in a cell underground. He helped me escape your brother by both of us crossing over.

Nyalin grimaced. "That was easier in the city. Here... the energy is twisted. Dangerous. You should have seen what it looked like from..." He hesitated.

"From the afterworld. Most of that plane is peaceful, but not here."

"I know there's risk, but I don't see any other stealthy options. Our only other alternative might be just bang down the door with blasts of fire. But we don't even know where your mother would be."

"Or for a fact that she's even here. I appreciate you all taking me at my word, that a spirit from another realm told me she would be, but that's not exactly hard evidence."

"Okay, but it does make sense," Lara pointed out. "Didn't the emperor say they never recovered Linali's remains? Maybe that's because she's not dead. And if her allies don't know where she is... who would the logical culprit be who would have captured her?"

He nodded. "Good point. Trying to go through the afterworld might still be worth a try but... I don't know what to expect—"

"I believe in you," Lara cut in.

"So do I." Faytou grinned.

"I, for one, believe in the power of spirits to be terrifying," said Pyaris, raising a hand. "But... I'm also finding the idea of seeing their plane sort of impossible to resist, even if it kills us."

Nyalin snorted. "I also haven't tried to go there with someone else since the lock came off. Nor have I tried with *four* of us. What if not all of us can make the leap? What if I can't get us back?" His leg was bouncing with nerves. The time when Andius had kidnapped them, he'd held Lara close. Would all four of them have to cuddle?

"Maybe we try with just one of us, then you could come back for the others?" Lara suggested. "There *has* to be a way to get inside."

"There you go again," said Pyaris, smiling. "Not necessarily. Not without getting caught, anyway."

"Hmm." Nyalin watched the spot where Sutamae had disappeared. She hadn't reemerged, but the guards who had fled had just returned with a dozen more men. "If we go just one or two of us, then the person who went first would be left alone for who knows how long." Nyalin shook his head. "I think if we're going to try it, we should try it together."

"What if we do a test?" Pyaris asked. "All of us, for just a few paces first? See what it's like?"

"Yes, that's a good idea." And then if they were all terrified out of their minds, he thought, they could give up and try to think of another plan.

"Let's try it now." Lara stood up.

The other three looked at each other, clearly worried. But she was right.

What were they waiting for? And now, Sutamae might be in trouble.

He took a deep breath. The tug of the vortex felt so close now. Could it pull them in? What would that even mean? He'd have to make sure they got inside, but not too close.

"All right. Everyone stand squarely, facing the wall of the estate. Now let's hold hands. Once we're in the afterworld, we'll try taking four steps forward. When we return, we *should* be four steps closer. If this works, we'll have to walk down the mountain to get there. So check out the terrain, see if it looks doable. Grab hands."

He took Lara's hand, and she took Pyaris's, who took Faytou's. They all looked back to him.

He hesitated a moment. By Dala, how could he prepare them? "And, um, it's not always like this. Sometimes, it's peaceful. So, um... hold on."

Then he closed his eyes and dove.

With the flicker of power from Lara's hand touching his, it was hard to let himself fall. In fact, it was more like he had to swim against the current. But it was also so much easier than it would have been so many other places. Was it the vortex or was there something about certain parts of the earth? Was it easier here?

It didn't matter; he had no way to know for sure. But when he opened his eyes, the vortex he'd seen with Batu loomed in front of him, bigger than anything he'd ever seen.

Beside him, three people caught their breath.

Snapping his head to look at them—there they were!

"You did it!" said Faytou.

"It worked!" breathed Lara, her eyes transfixed on the vortex. "What in Dala's dreams is that?"

"Nothing from Dala's dreams," Nyalin replied. "It's not right. I believe if we can free enough of those she has imprisoned, we'll destroy it. That's the goal, anyway."

"Sounds like a good goal." Pyaris was nodding, eyes wide.

"Okay, don't look at it. We have to get under that to get the job done. Watch your step."

Faytou was first to tear his eyes from the vortex, but soon, they were all focused on the ground.

"Okay, now four steps."

They each took their steps forward—one, two, three, four.

"I think we could make it beyond the wall," Lara said. Her voice was raised, because even with just four steps, the sound of the whirling vortex had gotten louder. "The path forward looks pretty even from here."

"I agree," called Faytou.

"Let's go back," said Pyaris. "To make sure we can."

"Agreed. All right, hang on."

This time, it took him a little longer, and the world tilted for a moment before he found himself solidly back on the nighttime mountainside.

"Yes!" Lara's cheer was quiet, but full of triumph. "We did it."

"We did." Pyaris stepped back, putting one hand to her forehead. "That was amazing. Incredible. And awful all at the same time."

Nyalin scanned the estate in the darkness below them. Somewhere down there, he might find his mother. And his stepsister. Was he really ready for what he might find?

How could he be?

He steeled himself, set his jaw. "All right. Get whatever you need. And let's do that again."

Lara nodded, tightening the belt of her crossover. "Farther this time."

---

As they raced down the tunnel, Daridian peered into row after row after row of sleeping faces, but none of them was Sha'lien. Great Spear, he was *never* going to find her. His stomach sank with every new unfamiliar face.

Eventually, they reached an area where their tunnel widened, and not all of the family artifacts had been removed from this little alcove. A stand of dusty old swords remained, as well as a pair of dusty chests and some scrolls in cases that looked like they'd seen better days.

"Other than those, I haven't seen anywhere to hide," he said, pointing at the chests.

"Wait, look here." Sutamae opened a large armoire he hadn't noticed behind him. It had been cleaned of everything, except the dust. She looked at him, raising an eyebrow.

"I'm going to keep going," said the chained girl, "and see if I can find the others."

"Okay," he said. Should he go with her, or try to hide here? Footsteps further up the tunnels hurried his decision. "We'll stay here, and, hopefully, we can catch a few by surprise, stop them from pursuing you. See if maybe there's a back way out?"

"Got it!" The girl took off, running now.

The two of them climbed into the armoire, which required a bit of careful arranging to keep their swords drawn and not cutting either of them. The clanblade gave off a dim light, reminiscent of moonlight. They continued to listen, and the sound of movements echoed in the tunnels, but it was hard to tell direction or distance.

"Did any of them look like your sister?" she whispered.

He shook his head, then realized she wouldn't be able to see him in the darkness. "No."

"What if she's not down here?"

"Then I don't know what I'm going to do." He tried not to sound dejected, but it was hard. He'd checked almost everywhere on the estate. "It's possible I've taken the wrong lead. What if she's somewhere else? Was this entire trip a waste of time?"

"I don't know much about what's going on," Su said gently, "but we haven't looked at all of them. Don't despair just yet. I'm sorry I phrased it that way."

"That's all right. I was thinking the same thing."

They sat in silence for a moment.

"Did they find your necklace?" he asked.

"My necklace?"

"The one you had the guards looking for."

She laughed lightly. "Oh, there's no necklace."

"Oh." He was glad she couldn't see his chagrinned expression. To think, he'd been gritting his teeth and bitter over a fictional necklace—one that she'd concocted the story of to help *him*. "But you are a guest here?"

She sighed. "Indeed, I am."

He hesitated. He wanted to ask about what she'd said in the baths at the inn, about a man who wanted her as his own. But she didn't know that he had been the man in the other tub that day, and it seemed strange to point it out now.

"If you are worried your trip has been a mistake," she said abruptly, "you have company. I'm sure mine has been."

"How so?" He tried not to hold his breath.

"Well, people aren't... always what they seem, I guess. I never really find people I can talk to, just, you know—truly be myself with. And then I run into two of them in one week. You, however, marched off into the hills, *supposedly* never to be seen again."

"Such was my regrettable intent. Fate seems to have other plans, I think."

"Someone told me fate reaches out its hand, and it's up to us to decide if we want to take it or not. I've never been one to hesitate to go after what I want. But now... I wonder if maybe I accepted fate's offering too quickly."

"Except here you are. In a dusty closet, inside a catacomb. How could that *possibly* be fate going wrong?"

She smothered a chuckle, and so did he. He hoped none of them were close, because the armoire was probably shaking.

"Perhaps you're right. What is to become of this trip is not yet clear, is it?"

"That could be said for both of us. But I do hope I find my sister."

They grew quiet again, listening to the footsteps. Were those guards? The slaves they were trying to help? Totally unrelated? It seemed like it'd been a long time.

He relaxed against the wood, tilting his head back to look up. "Where did you learn to fight like that?"

"Oh, here and there." She shifted uneasily.

"Your father?"

"No. Not any of *those* moves." She hesitated for a long moment. He sensed she was working up to something, so he waited. "I, uh, I asked a sword master instructor to teach me, when I was younger. He did, but he, um, he—abused me too. That was the price of his lessons."

He froze, horrified. "Sutamae. I'm so sorry."

"Yeah, well, not as sorry as I was for asking."

"May the Great Spear find and pierce his heart."

"You're really not from around here, are you?"

He straightened. "Where I am from, that is a powerful curse."

"Well. May the Twins hear you. Or the Great Spear. Or whatever."

A sad silence settled now, almost unbearable, and he found himself shifting and fidgeting at the tension in their tiny space.

Apparently, she couldn't bear it, either, as she brought up something else. "How is it that you fight so well in such a mask?"

"Oh, that's a long story. For another day."

"I told you my darkest secret. C'mon. You can't tell me that?"

"It is a... sort of magic. One I am not practiced at describing. Where I come from, everyone already knows."

"Will you tell me where you come from?"

"Another day. If we survive this."

A pause. He sensed his words had hurt her. "So you'll see me another day?"

"It appears I can't avoid you." He hoped his smile came through in his words.

"What does *that* mean?"

"You keep turning up."

"I didn't ask to be here, precisely. I followed the dragon."

"Ah, but why did you listen to her? You could have refused."

"Refuse a dragon? Isn't that bad luck? Besides, that wouldn't be very nice. And it seemed like the right thing to do."

Did she truly care about the right thing to do? Those who had captured his sister hadn't. He eyed her for a long time. A vulnerability, or a deception? He wanted so badly to trust her. He wanted so badly for his whole life to be different so he could be with her, and not have to hurry back to Annikyre once he'd found Sha'lien. How had he gone from hating this place to not wanting to leave? But it was the intensity of this feeling that worried him.

Vulnerability—or deception? She hadn't offered to return the clanblade yet. But they were also still in danger.

"I would like to trust you, Sutamae naElix moVanae. But I don't trust easily, especially not when my sister's life could be on the line."

"That sounds wise," she murmured. But was there another, deeper note of hurt to her voice?

"Sutamae," he whispered, reaching out a hand to touch hers.

"Call me Su, I told you," she chided.

His hand found the back of hers, the zap of power arcing between them making them both jump for a moment. But he kept going.

"What is that?" she whispered. "Why does that keep happening?"

"Your people... they do not have stories of the Spark?" His voice too was soft.

"We have... old tales. Of soul matches and... fate."

He tightened his fingers around hers, and she tightened back. "I am sorry I cannot offer my full trust, all my secrets. But I have a sister to lose, and as I understand it, you do not?"

"You're right," she replied.

"But let this be an acknowledgment of something between us—something more than trust, more than respect, a link we can't deny or destroy."

Her breath seemed to catch. "Can't you at least tell me something? Your name?"

He bit his lip, then lifted his mask to his forehead, though she could barely see him in the dim light. But he slid his hand up her wrist, along her delicate forearm and elbow, across the feminine curves of muscle at her shoulder, against her delicate neck to her chin. "My name is Daridian. Will you kiss me again, Sutamae? Before the guards come, or we go looking for my sister again?"

"We'll find her," she assured him. And when her lips found his, he almost believed her.

*Chapter 13*

# The Catacombs

This close to the vortex, Nyalin could hardly breathe. Over him, the massive thing swirled like a tornado that never touched ground, made of mud or some other horrible black-brown liquid. He could feel a subtle tug, a sense that if he let go entirely, it would be happy to suck him in. It pulsed like some kind of breathing, beating thing—like it was alive.

"And *that's* got to be the most horrifying spell I've ever seen," Pyaris shouted over the rushing wind, or maybe the awful noise was just a sound the vortex made, the sound of the energy imbalance sucking power from this plane into the other one, rather than the result of the movement of physical objects through space. Not all those rules seemed to apply here.

"Spell?" Lara called back. She slowed for a moment, her shoulder coming to touch Pyaris's as they stared up with wide eyes. All of them were still holding hands, with Nyalin in the lead, as each step took them more directly under the vortex. "That thing is a spell?"

"Yes. Awful, right? It's a necromantic spell. Only it's growing of its own volition, I think. A monstrosity. Spirits enslaved to consume other spirits, or at least forcibly relocate them!"

"Well, we're going to put a stop to it," Nyalin replied, trying to sound certain.

"Are we almost there?" asked Lara.

"I think so! Just a little further." The ground had started to slope downward. The landscape was too different to be sure exactly where Su had gone out of sight, but in this plane, there was a mouth of a tunnel at about the same location.

This had to be the place. Just before him, a sea of tiny, weak stars stretched out, a sea nearly the size of the entire estate. Maybe even bigger. He could see a shimmer for each soul imprisoned here.

Souls they were going to free. But they were definitely crossing back over before they could do that. The stars flickered weakly at times, like candle flames about to go out. He squinted at them, wondering if one being a little brighter or dimmer could indicate his mother. Nothing stood out as significant to him.

Just as they were about to step inside the tunnel, Nyalin leading while they still all held hands, an awful sound split the air, somewhere between a deathly wail and iron grating against stone.

Something rushed at them from within.

"Spirit guardian!" Faytou gasped.

Nyalin ducked as he staggered to the side, tightening his grip on Lara's hand. Lara yelped, and behind her, Faytou ducked so quickly that, for a moment, Nyalin thought whatever it was had knocked him down.

But Pyaris didn't flinch. She stood straight, shoulders back, unafraid. Her lips moved but made no sound. Her grip on her companions' hands remained tight.

The spirit—he realized that's what it was, now—whirled around them, its grating wailing taking on a tone of frustration and rage.

Pyaris's voice reached his ears, first a harsh whisper, then rising to a shout. She repeated the same rhyme, over and over, much to the agitation of the spirit. "By stone and sun, your work is done. Let the path be clear. No malice, no fear. Spirit, flee. Now you are free."

She didn't even look at the thing, just stared into the middle distance, as if all her mind were trained on something else. A spell? It hadn't really occurred to him he could cast spells here. The same ones as he could on any other plane? Were all planes the same, or did they have different magic rules? If the spirit got any closer to her, he'd try to help. But for the moment, he just watched, afraid he might disrupt her if he started throwing fire and water at her head.

On her fourth time repeating the words, she slowly closed her eyes and raised both hands into the air, bringing Faytou's and Lara's hands with her. A flash of purple seemed to explode out from their clasped hands, enveloping them all.

Bitterly, the spirit guardian fled.

"Phew," he murmured. No one could possibly have heard him over the vortex's roar. One tough knock from that thing, and they might have lost someone—or ended up back in the other world in a possibly very bad location.

Not that he really knew where he was taking them.

Underground was the most dangerous possible location, so as soon as they got through the mouth of the tunnel, and no other wailing spirits assaulted them, he decided to make the jump.

"Are you ready? Say your prayers to Dala for me," Nyalin said.

"Oh, I've been doing that the *entire* way," Faytou put in. "I've also asked to someday taste yak kebabs again and to return at least long enough to make my brother pay."

Nyalin gave him a nervous smile. "I owe you at least a dozen yak kebabs for all your help here."

"Repay me by putting my brother in his place. That's all I need."

"Is that all?" They both shook their heads, then Nyalin steeled himself to begin. "Okay. Here we go."

Lara squeezed his hand. "You can do this."

He shut his eyes and reached for home, his stomach turning and twisting. Every moment here in the afterworld hurt, this close to the vortex, or maybe it was the sustained effort of bringing all four of them this far for this long. He hadn't really thought of it as a spell that might drain his own energy, but now that oversight seemed entirely foolish.

In fact, could he run out of enough to get back? Could they be stuck here? His head spun at the thought. Or maybe from the exertion?

Gritting his teeth, he reached. For a moment, the world tilted again, the flicker and twist of reality—and then the air around them went quiet and colder.

"We're back!" Lara's excited whisper was almost a hiss.

Faytou clapped his shoulder. "And we're *in*. Now let's find your Ma."

He breathed a sigh of relief. While he couldn't imagine ever calling the great and legendary Linali that, he nodded. "Let's go."

They charged down the tunnels, stopping short when they reached the first imprisoned pair.

Pyaris's lip curled in disgust, and Faytou's eyes were wide. "Is this... How many are like this?" he asked.

"Dozens," Nyalin said quickly. "A whole, whole lot."

"Should we free everyone we find? How do we even start?" Lara asked, looking around the sides and bottom of where the figures lay, as if she'd find a lever or a rope to pull to release them.

"These are actively maintained spells, right?" asked Nyalin.

Pyaris nodded.

"Then if we start disrupting them, whoever cast them—probably Unira—will know, right? And she'll come looking?"

"I would think so, yes. It'd certainly be a safe assumption," Pyaris replied.

"Then we should find your mother and free her first," Lara said quickly. "With Linali on our side, we'll have a way better chance at handling anyone who comes our way."

All of them were nodding as they moved further into the tunnel.

Of course, if his mother had been strong enough to defeat Unira, then how did she end up down here in the first place? He shook his head but didn't voice his reservations to the others. No need to discourage them.

Quickly they came to a large open room. Six tunnels extended out from it, stretching far down into the earth. Every one of them lined with these poor prisoners. Nyalin caught his breath.

"Dozens is right," muttered Faytou. "Or maybe that's not even close to the real number."

"How are we *ever* going to find her?" Lara was turning in circles, looking and trying to get a grip on where to start.

"And where is Sutamae, if she ran down here?" he added. "And... do you hear that?"

"Footsteps," said Faytou. "Two groups of them, I think—more than one woman. Maybe five or six people in each group?" He pointed down two of the tunnels.

"I have no idea how you can hear that, but I'm just going to say, let's take a *different* one. And start looking."

They all nodded.

"And let's keep as quiet as possible."

"This one looks older than the others," Lara pointed out. "Maybe we start here? If Linali has been imprisoned, it has to have been for a very long time. Nyalin's whole life."

That made his gut churn again. He couldn't shake the feeling they were missing something. But if they could just find her...

Six prisoners in, they heard a sharp woman's cry. A loud crashing, almost like rocks falling. They exchanged glances.

Some part of him knew that was Su's voice. Had the guards found her down here? Should they go back and help? But they didn't really know where Su was any more than they knew where his mother was.

"What do we do?" whispered Lara.

"We keep looking," suggested Faytou. "We can help your sister even better, Nyalin, if we have more firepower on our side—and less on theirs."

He hesitated, looking back in the direction they'd come. What was it that they were missing? What was Su even *doing* here at this place? Was she in league with this Unira? If she was, would he track her down only for them all to get captured? And yet, Su had seemed to be fighting the guards, hadn't she? He didn't know who to trust.

Ultimately, Faytou was right. More power would make it that much easier to find Su to help her—if it was help she needed after all.

"All right," he said. "Let's keep looking."

Su broke away from Daridian, her lips hot and likely a little swollen. "Someone's coming."

They sat still, listening. Yes, her ears hadn't deceived her. Footsteps, heavy with the weight of boots, were coming up the tunnel.

"Didn't we search this one already?" one guard was saying.

"No, you idiot. Look, have you seen that sword rack or those two chests before?"

"I have no idea. It all looks the same!"

"Well, *I* know we haven't been down here. Search those chests!"

"For what? Your pet hamster? I was supposed to go home an hour ago."

"Quit grumbling. Get searching."

The sound of one set of footsteps slowly came closer. Through the crack in the door, they could see guards moving about, opening the chests. Was it only one coming closer, or more than one?

They were surrounded.

"Well, get on with it. Check that thing!" one of the guards called.

A hand reached toward the door.

Daridian caught the handle from the inside, holding it shut, then looked at her. "Remember me when fate holds out her hand, all right?" he whispered.

"Wait—wait—"

And then he shoved the door out, smacking the guard in the head, and leapt forward.

She saw a glimpse of his face, his smile, before he slid the mask back down. Between the shock and her attempt to memorize every line of his face, she sat frozen for a second, unmoving.

The sound of steel ringing against steel brought her into motion.

More than a dozen guards were taking swings at Daridian, but there were so many in the fairly narrow tunnel that they were getting in each other's way. Still, it wasn't a good matchup. They needed something else. A diversion.

Scampering out of the armoire, she slammed the doors shut and rounded to the back of it, Daridian's sword with its white jewel still in hand, she leaned into it as best she could and heaved.

It worked—the heavy wooden furniture toppled, knocking one man aside and catching another beneath its weight. Standing behind it, she stabbed at another, then smirked at him when he slashed back and she easily backed out of reach while the fallen armoire blocked his path.

One jumped onto the armoire—much to the disapproval of the man still crushed by the thing—and she met steel with steel. Keeping him from leaping down next to her with wide swings and quick parries, she waited for her opening. He wasn't a bad swordsman, but, eventually, a curse from the man he was currently crushing under the armoire stole his attention for a mere moment.

Su used that moment to pierce deep into his thigh.

The attack and the swearing of his comrade sent her attacker toppling backward, nearly on top of Daridian, who luckily dodged just in time. Noticing what she'd done to the armoire, he sidestepped closer, until he was by her side.

A group of them crowded on the other side of the armoire while two more rounded the corners of it, trying to get to them. As the group leaned close, Daridian kicked into the armoire hard, slamming it into their legs and pushing them briefly back. He managed to skewer one, who fell unmoving. Another took off running for the mouth of the tunnel.

"Not again," he groaned.

Meanwhile, Su had been ruthlessly puncturing her opponent like a tailor's pin cushion, leaving the woman panting and slumped against the wall. Another attacker took her place quickly enough.

Behind her, she heard a cry. From Daridian.

Even though she knew better, she turned, just halfway, just enough to see if he was okay or—

He was not okay. His opponent had cut deep into the upper part of his sword arm, but he was still able to swing his blade. Blood was already drenching his shirt. He seemed to be clutching his side with his other arm.

Her opponent didn't fail to take advantage of her distraction. His blade struck her forearm, weakening her grip on the sword.

The blade and its beautiful jewel clattered to the ground.

She met her attacker's gaze, eyes wide. The man had a look of smug satisfaction, as if he thought he had her beat. Perhaps that *should* have been enough to cow her, but as the man had clearly let his guard down, she lunged, tackling him to the ground.

The man tried to get his hands wrapped around her throat, but her hands were quicker, finding the dagger at his belt and plunging it into his gut. She staggered to her feet, putting her boot over his wrist until he released his sword, then she kicked it beyond his reach. He rolled onto his side, trying to crawl away from her, toward the others.

Her sword—Daridian's sword, the sword the dragon had bid her to wield. She whirled. Where had it gone? The guards, about half of the group remaining, were all focused around Daridian, ignoring the fallen blade.

One of the guards noticed as she leapt for the sword, and lunged away from Daridian toward her. But the masked man was preternaturally fast, somehow managing to complete a flourish by stabbing his weapon into her assailant's now open side. The man crumbled.

"How does he move like that?" one of the remaining guards growled.

He was right; Daridian's speed was uncanny. No time to consider it now, though. She reached the sword and wrapped her fingers around the hilt.

For a brief moment, as when she'd first seized the sword from his cross-over to help, the sensation of being somewhere else—someone else—over-whelmed her. Moon-kissed wings pushed her higher and higher, gliding through the night, the sensation of cold air caressing her scales... What had the dragon called it in the dream? The Blade of the Moon?

She shook herself. She couldn't be somewhere else—one more distrac-tion, and one or both of them could be dead.

Daridian seemed to have had a burst of energy, his slashes still unnat-urally fast, so all of the guards' attention focused on him. Capitalizing on that, she pounced, striking the nearest guard from behind and inflicting a massive slash across his back.

The guards screamed and whirled on her, rage boiling in his eyes.

Suddenly, over the clashes of swords, she heard more footsteps from farther up the tunnel. Fast, light ones.

"Hey!" It was the enslaved girl that Daridian had befriended. She'd returned.

"What?" Daridian grunted.

"We found a back way, a way out!" called the girl.

"A little busy," grumbled Daridian.

"Just cut and run for it! The gate is locked. We can't get it open."

"Go! They need your help." Su slammed a shoulder against his nearest attacker, quite to that man's surprise. "We can't all go, they'll catch everyone. Go—I'll hold them back."

He shoved the one he'd locked swords with. "I can't do that. I can't leave you to die here."

"They won't kill me." Addressing their attackers, she said, "Will you, you fools? My father is the clan leader! Do you want to face him for what you've done?"

That did slow their swords for a moment.

"That's right! I'm Sutamae naElix moVanae, and you'll kill me at your own peril!"

"M-maybe we better take them alive?" The guards exchanged glances.

"What if she's lying?"

"She looks like the type though. Look at that crossover, and a woman with a sword like that?"

Another shifted nervously, risking a glance at his comrades. "If we kill her, and she's who she says she is, they'll have our heads."

"See?" She said to Daridian, forcing a grin. "I'll be all right. Go!"

He hesitated. "The blade. Su, it mustn't fall into their hands."

Their eyes locked for a long moment. Instinctively, she didn't want to let the sword ever leave her sight. But he'd proven trustworthy so far. What would Unira do with such a sword in her possession?

"Get me one from that rack!" she told him. Quickly, he dashed backward, away from the fighting, and grabbed one from the rack. She tossed the beautiful sword to him, hilt up and then caught the dusty, old one. It would definitely not serve her as well, but she didn't expect to win this fight. Just to persevere long enough for him to flee. "Go on, go!"

"I'll come back for you!"

"Not if you're dead, you won't!" Already, the absence of the sword felt like an ache, an empty hole. Strange magic was at work here... "Bring the blade with you, though, if you do. I'm rather fond of it."

"I won't forget this." He fled, looking back over his shoulder one more time, then vanished into the darkness of the tunnels.

She turned to face the remaining five or so, gritting her teeth. She wouldn't last long, but if the slaves *and* Daridian got free? She'd count that as worth it.

*

Nyalin reached two more prisoners with Lara at his side. Crouching down to look at the first, it was a man. Nyalin shook his head.

As they stood and leaned over the next prisoner, Lara raised an eyebrow. "So, Nyalin, do you know what she even looks like? I mean, she supposedly died when you were born, so..." This prisoner was a woman, about the right age, with brownish hair.

"I've seen, um, drawings. This isn't my mother." He wasn't sure how he could be sure, but he was.

"Oh, goddesses above. What if she looks different?"

"What if she's aged?" put in Faytou. "Here come check this one."

Nyalin shrugged as he strode to Faytou's side. "No, hair's too light. I guess you should look for someone who looks like me. But her skin was lighter. *Is* lighter. Black hair." Now that he thought of it, his olive skin clearly came from his father. He sighed. Goddesses, that man. How would he ever make peace with him?

Thirty-six, thirty-eight, forty. So many.

Lara must have been thinking the same thing. "How did they carve out these catacombs for so many? Was this family truly that large?"

Nyalin shrugged. "I'm not sure. Maybe it held the bodies of honored or even average members of the household too?"

"About that... What happened to the bodies that used to rest here?" Pyaris pointed out. "We are *surrounded* by desecration."

Faytou shuddered. "Maybe that's why the spirits seem so angry."

"*One* of the reasons," Pyaris mumbled. "I can't wait to set every last one of these people free."

Lara put her arm around her friend's shoulder and squeezed. "Same here. Look, the tunnel doesn't continue much farther." She pointed up ahead of them. A small ancestorial shrine, laden with gold trinkets, sat in a dim outcropping, capping off the tunnel's end. Why were those trinkets still there, when so much else looked like it had been rifled through, looted, and pillaged? Maybe it'd been a long time since anyone was down here.

He stifled a groan at the thought of picking a new tunnel and starting again. And maybe even again after that... Six whole tunnels to search—one almost down, did they really have five more to go?

Forty-two, forty-four, forty-six. Sigh.

As he approached the next pair, a few feet short of the prisoners, he stopped cold in his tracks.

There it was—that face he'd expected, that he'd seen in drawings and books but never in real life. Never in a hug or a kind gesture or sitting by his side. Finally, after so many strangers. There she was.

"Dala's dreams," he whispered. He motioned the others over. "This is it. I mean—it's her."

"Help me shatter this foul spell," Pyaris ordered. She held out her hands to each of them. "Hold my hands."

Lara clasped hands with Pyaris without a moment's hesitation, closing her eyes. Nyalin took Pyaris's other hand, but he peered into the spell chamber instead. How could they know what would happen? They probably didn't, but that wasn't stopping them. What if something went wrong?

What if the chamber was warded or boobytrapped somehow so that if they broke it, it'd explode in their faces, or cast the same spell on them? He turned, intending to say something to that effect, but it was too late.

The illusory glass seemed to shatter, then disappear into midair. The woman's eyes flickered open.

They were all silent for a moment, holding their breath. None of them moved.

"Seluvae's stars," the woman whispered, eyes on the ceiling above her. Her voice sounded like a corpse forcing air through dry lungs.

Nyalin tried to force himself to breathe. Was this really happening? Was his mother *really* alive? Had he just done something that was going to make this Unira very angry? He swallowed. Let her be angry. He was angrier—over all she'd taken from him. Frightening others into keeping the truth from him.

"Water," said Lara, reaching for her waterskin and offering it.

The woman took it gratefully, struggling to sit. Her arm and hand shook as she tried to slowly to take a sip.

"Let me help you." Lara steadied the skin, guiding it carefully to her lips.

"Am I dead? You all don't look like spirits."

"We don't think so," Lara said gently. "It appears you've been trapped inside some kind of spell-based prison."

She glanced around, as if seeing beyond the group for the first time. "Ah, a stasis chamber. I see. How—how long has it been?" Her eyes came to rest on Nyalin. If she suspected, or sensed something, she seemed hesitant to say it. She finally managed to take a long drink.

"We don't know how long exactly," he said timidly.

Faytou had no such shyness. "Are you really Linali, the legendary mage of the wars with the Mushin? From the days of Unification?"

Finally, a small smile curved the corners of her lips, although they were painfully chapped. "I don't know about legendary or unified anything, but yes. I am known as Linali."

"Then this is your son," said Lara softly, indicating Nyalin. "Nyalin moLinali."

She went still as their eyes met, as she looked him from head to toe. "That long, then?" Her expression creased with pain and remorse. "I missed so much."

He nodded, all sorts of pain and darkness welling up in him. "Yes. That long."

"You don't wear Obsidian colors."

"It's a long story. We're all friends to you, though."

"Oh, I know."

He frowned. How could she be so sure she could trust them?

She beckoned him closer, and he leaned in. "You have his nose, you know." She winked.

More noise, crashing and yelling, echoed from the other tunnels. They all turned to listen. If there was a way to tell the direction it came from, Nyalin couldn't sense it.

"Are you able to get up? Walk?" Lara asked. "We should get you out of here."

"I'm afraid I'm not in much shape for a long journey." She gently eased herself to her feet, like a much older woman. What age was she, really? The age when he'd been born and she'd been imprisoned, or eighteen years older?

She stood for barely a breath before wavering, Lara and Nyalin just catching her in time. "It's the stasis sickness. It will take a bit of time before I regain my strength."

His stomach fell. Dammit.

They'd *thought* finding his mother—the legendary Linali—would mean finding reinforcements. His and Faytou's eyes met, as if they were processing the same realization.

But *of course*. He felt stupid for not having guessed it would be like this. Who could lie completely still in stasis for eighteen years without feeling like hell afterward? She was lucky she was alive!

And he was too. Wasn't he?

In truth, this woman was a stranger. Years and years had been stolen from them, and that was tragic, but if he was supposed to feel some surge of love because they shared the same blood, well, it wasn't happening yet.

Instead, he just felt—shocked. Was this really happening? First, his father was the emperor—and Dalas, too, no less—but now his long-dead mother hadn't been dead after all? If these were lies, what else should he not believe? Was the sky really red? Would the flowers still bloom in the spring? What was happening?

"Let's start by getting out of these catacombs undetected," said Lara. Her eyes caught his, drew him in.

The comment brought him back down to the ground. Yes, she was right. They just needed to take this one step at a time.

He didn't need to question every single thing he'd ever been told *right now*. That could wait till later.

"I'll go on ahead," offered Pyaris. "Faytou? Want to come? We'll watch for patrols coming."

"Let's go."

So with his mother limping between them, one of each of her arms around Lara and Nyalin, they made slow, excruciating progress toward where they'd entered the catacombs.

None of them spoke. Maybe they didn't need to. Maybe they were too tired. Nyalin found himself wondering if his mother had known that he would end up as Elix's ward, or if it only happened after her mistaken death and ultimate imprisonment. Would she approve of Pavan's choice? Be furious?

He tried to shut the thoughts away. Later. Later he would ask questions like these. For now, he just needed to go one step at a time.

And get out of this tunnel before Unira came looking for them. Since they were going at a snail's pace, he was starting to realize that might be easier said than done.

Over his mother's head, Lara caught his eye. He could tell from her expression she was thinking the same thing. By now, Unira probably knew someone was down here. That her prize prisoner was free.

And if that was the case... they were in trouble.

Unira leaned back in front of the fire, gazing at those of her guests who still remained. Even though it had been three or four hours since Sutamae had fled, Idak returning a short while later, the girl hadn't yet returned.

Perhaps she had miscalculated, offering her that pig of a supposed "teacher." Certainly seeing him must have been startling. If Unira had been in the girl's shoes, she would have leapt at that chance of revenge. She wouldn't have hesitated. So perhaps the girl was right, perhaps they weren't as alike as she'd thought.

Because Sutamae had blanched. She'd clearly been caught by surprise. Maybe she'd need a day or two to come to terms with the idea. Maybe she never would. Either way, the man was dead to Unira. She'd give the girl a week to come to a decision.

In her observations of Elix and his gaggle over the years, she'd kept very close tabs on them all, which was how she'd learned about the girl approaching a teacher. If Hendo had been teaching her magic, that would have violated Unira and Elix's deal, but the girl hadn't asked for that, just lessons in swordsmanship. Unira had kept a spy on them all the while, though, as she'd suspected Sutamae's desire to know how to use a sword for battle would naturally lead to a desire to use a sword for magic. Perhaps if Hendo hadn't been more worthless than pond scum on the bottom of a boot, it might have.

Now, she just needed to decide the means of his death—slow and painful or quick and merciful? She was leaning toward the former.

Idak had settled into the chair opposite her, and he, too, watched the guests. But he had seemed ill at ease since Sutamae had fled. He didn't sit still for long, and he'd downed more ale while she watched than he usually did. Not that he looked affected. He seemed to know his limits for such things.

Suddenly, the doors to the dining hall slammed open, and a small group of guards staggered in, dragging in a beleaguered-looking Sutamae, one clutching an arm on either side.

"What is the meaning of this?" Idak shot to his feet.

Unira rose to her feet more slowly, but her eyebrows had beat her to standing. "Indeed. What is going on here?"

"She's a traitor—lady, sir! Interlopers were trying to break in—and she fought alongside them. A warrior in a mask."

"A spy for Annikyre," someone whispered.

"Traitor..." another whispered.

"I'm neither traitor nor spy! I swear!" Sutamae tried to shake herself free of her captors, to stand up, but their grips held tight.. "The guards attacked me too. I picked up a blade to defend myself and—"

"She was inside the catacombs!" cried one of those holding her.

The room went silent. Unira's blood ran suddenly cold. Idak's mouth had dropped open, and he was still as a statue.

She walked forward, slowly, her shoes tapping against the polished floor. It was the only sound, echoing ominously, as if the whole room didn't dare to even breathe.

"Were you in the catacombs?" she asked slowly, sweetly. She needed to keep her control, to hold back the tidal wave of rage that was building. She could release it soon, but not just yet.

"Yes, but I—"

"Lock her in her quarters," Unira snapped, voice shaking. "In *shackles*. We'll discuss the proper punishment for what she's done in the morning."

"Mother—" Idak started.

"Silence." His eyes widened, but he closed his mouth. The rest of the room had erupted in murmurs, so she clapped her hands. "Enough. *No one* enters the catacombs without my permission." She scanned over each of them, as if daring them to. "No one."

Then she raised her hand and a bolt of energy shot out, hitting Sutamae in the chest.

The girl cried out, then slumped in the guards' arms. She wasn't unconscious, not yet.

"That's just a taste," she said softly, "of the agony that awaits those who defy me. You could have been by my side. But if there's one thing I hate, it's a liar, and we all know you're an excellent one."

The girl struggled to raise her head, and when their eyes met, Unira smiled. She could see just the right pain there. She'd struck the nerve she intended. The biggest lie was that Unira cared about lies. But this was just one of the many punishments she'd dole out for this betrayal. Physical pain could heal, but damage to the mind could be everlasting.

She turned away and glided back to her comfortable seat as they dragged Sutamae away.

But she'd barely sat down before she felt it. Like a crack in her power, a fissure in the foundation of the building, as powerful in her mind as if an earthquake had shaken the whole estate.

She shot to her feet again, then staggered. Where the hell was Zama when she needed him? His portal plan better pay off, or she was banishing him back to his pathetic plane in a heartbeat. "Idak—Idak—"

Idak rushed toward her, alarmed. "What is it?"

Her voice was a harsh, strained whisper between clenched teeth. "You must send the patrols. More of them—everyone we can spare."

"Send them where, Mother?"

"Into the catacombs. Someone is down there."

"What? How do you know?"

"Because they've cracked one of the chambers—freed someone—"

He caught his breath.

"I felt the power leaving me."

"I—uh—"

"Move!" she ordered. "If they did it once, they'll do it again—go!"

As he rushed out, she staggered back into her chair, panting, the world spinning, feeling the eyes of her guests on her. She summoned one of the servants, the few she had that weren't slaves. "This party is over. Please escort everyone out."

Nodding, the woman scurried off.

Her fingers dug into the leather padding on the arms of the chair, and she gritted her teeth, willing the world to steady. Whoever had dared to strike at her heart, whoever had made her appear weak in front of all these fools—they were going to pay.

They were going to pay dearly.

*Chapter 14*

# Rebellion

The guards threw Su to the floor of her room with gusto.

A cry escaped her despite her best efforts to muffle it. Cold iron scraped her wrists as they shackled her, but she was too weak to fight them, too staggered by Unira's attack. What had she even done? Su had never even seen a spell like that.

Sutamae felt like a snake had crawled inside her chest and was wrapping itself around her heart, tighter and tighter with every minute. She tried to crawl, but she couldn't make it to the bed.

The world tilted, splotches of yellow flickering before her eyes, before everything finally went black.

She wasn't sure how long she'd been unconscious, but she woke when she heard her door open, then close again. The sound was soft, almost like someone was trying to sneak in undetected.

Someone was walking toward her, but she couldn't open her eyes. Couldn't move, even. Was the spell still in effect?

Would it kill her?

Fingers ran gently up and down her arm, then hands gripped her, lifting her into strong arms. She would have resisted, but her body only barely responded this time. When the arms released her, she was now on the bed, not the floor.

She struggled to move again but managed only a finger, then a toe.

Then suddenly, a sharp, unfamiliar smell hit her nose, and she jerked back. She opened her eyes and tried to sit up, backing away from the powerful scent.

Before her sat Idak, on the edge of her bed, screwing on the lid of a jar.

"What are you doing here?" she managed.

"What were *you* doing down there?" He tilted his head.

She groped for an answer, but how could she explain? Would he even believe her about a tiny white dragon? Or following a man she hardly knew into tunnels she hadn't realized were off limits? Not that knowing that would have stopped her. But she didn't know Daridian—or this dragon—even as well as she knew Idak, which was hardly at all. How could she possibly make it make sense to him? That sometimes you have to follow your gut about who is a good person? If she wasn't the sort to follow her gut and act without fully understanding, she'd have never accepted his invitation *here*, either.

Her silence did her no favors. His expression clouded darker. "Was this all a trick? A ploy? Did you *use* me, Sutamae?"

"No, of course not."

He set the jar on a nearby side table and folded his arms. "Be honest."

"For once, I have been nothing *but* honest with you!" Her body seemed to be regaining some movement, so she pushed herself up to sitting—or she tried. She failed, but she was propped a little against the pillow now. "After walking a ways, I started back and saw some people in trouble, so I tried to help them."

"Help them. Really. Random people, fighting guards of this estate."

"Yes. I know it's wildly forward-thinking of me, but I don't think guards should just murder any old person, and I think slavery is bad. Imagine that!"

"Sutamae—"

"Can you let me go, Idak? Who knows what she'll do to me in the morning."

He hesitated. "I wish I could, but—"

"Am I wrong? What do you think she'll do? Send me home in a carriage to my father with a sternly worded missive?"

He stared at her for a long time, before sharply shaking his head. The movements were jerky, almost painful. "No. You're not wrong."

"Then let me go."

"No. You shouldn't have been down in the catacombs."

"Do *you* know what's down there, Idak?"

It was a long time before he answered. "I do."

"It's not dead people."

"I know that—"

She finally got herself up to sitting this time. "I never took you for the kind of person who would overlook injustice. There is evil *all around you*. Don't you see it?"

"It's more complicated than—"

"Why do you deserve to walk around here, with all this wealth, while those people, those *mages*, sleep to serve you?" Suddenly, she realized he was shaking. What did that mean?

He stood and backed a few steps away, toward the door. When he spoke, his words were tight. "I told you my reputation was beyond repair, Sutamae."

She caught her breath. "I..."

"You didn't believe me."

"I thought we had that in common. I thought that meant we didn't care what others thought. I didn't think it meant you would *enslave* people. I could never marry someone like—" The words escaped her mouth without her thinking. She bit the inside of her cheek. She'd cut off the thought, but too late.

He flinched, but he didn't seem surprised. "I did suspect my mother would scare you off. I didn't realize I might also. Perhaps I'm more like her than I like to admit."

"No," she said quickly. "You're nothing like her."

"You don't know me, Sutamae."

"I think you're wrong."

"You don't know how much I helped her. You don't know how much she pressured me to do. You're my son, Idak, you must, Idak, just this once, Idak, how could you refuse me after all I've done for you, Idak—"

Suddenly, his eyes flicked over her shoulder. She turned and saw a familiar mask and dark cloak flash past, just outside the window. It was *him*. Daridian!

Her heartbeat raced faster. Would Idak try to catch him? What was Daridian doing here? Metal clinked against the windowpane.

"You..." She turned back to Idak and their eyes met, as if they both knew in that moment what they'd seen. "I... You're not like her, Idak. You are clever and genuine and intelligent—but apparently, you've decided using your brain when it comes to your mother's demands is optional."

He opened his mouth, but faltered, sighing as he closed it again.

"You can change, if you want to. This isn't right."

He took a deep, slow breath. "As always, your words are sharp as arrows, Sutamae naElix moVanae. I've heard you loud and clear. Why do I deserve any of this? Why indeed." He hesitated, as if he wanted to say more, as if more was bubbling up inside him, but he couldn't quite understand any of it, let alone form the words.

The clinking at the window made them both twitch. His eyes flicked to the window again, then back to her.

Was he... was he pretending not to hear it?

He raised his chin. "Thank you for this experience, Sutamae. It has been... most illuminating. May I see you again when you've returned to the city?"

She frowned. What was he talking about? "I... *if* I make it back, I'll consider it. And if you change your ways."

"Fair. A deal then. All right, I shall take my leave. Good night, again. And don't say my overlooking things never amounted to anything. I think it may be one of my core skills." He turned and strode toward the door.

"That's not true," she said softly. "Deep down, I think you are a good person. Who has maybe made some mistakes."

"How horrific does a mistake need to be, to be irredeemable?" He stopped but spoke without turning back.

"I don't know..." She thought of her own torture in her past. She had not forgiven Hendo, and she didn't intend to. She didn't regret not taking Unira up on her offer... though she still wished Hendo every bad thing in life. She wanted some sort of justice. But was death justice? Nothing could give her back the trust or innocence she'd lost.

She swallowed before she spoke. "Some crimes are not easily forgiven. Others are. Perhaps it depends on the magnitude of one's regret. Or how much they do to remedy what they've done."

He was still a moment longer. Then, without another word, he walked out, closing the door behind him.

She stared at the closed door then heard that clinking at the window again.

Quickly, she wiggled her fingers and toes, circled her wrists and ankles, making the chains clink. Those were going to be a problem. Whatever spell Unira had hit her with no longer seemed to be wrapped around her heart. Was that the effect of sleep, or had Idak helped her? Either way, all her movement seemed restored, although she felt weak and shaky from it all.

She scrambled to look around the room for anything she should take. Technically, her things were still here. She grabbed a cloak and tied it around her shoulders, then looked out the window.

Seluvae's tears. The sky was no longer black, but a deep purple. She couldn't see it yet, but the sun was beginning to rise.

The clinking suddenly stopped, and behind her, the window swung open. She whirled, then hurried to the window.

Silently, Daridian nodded and curled his fingers, gesturing for her to climb out.

She looked down. They were exposed. Two stories up. But a ledge did stretch along the length of the building, leading toward a vine-covered trellis at the end where they could climb down. She swallowed. She wasn't getting out through the door—or with Idak—so she might as well try. The chains, though... She held up one wrist.

To her surprise, he withdrew two tiny tools from his belt, then rotated the cuff until he found the lock. She held the cuff still for him while he slid the tools inside, turning and twisting, and then *click*. The first cuff fell free. She barely kept it from falling and crashing loudly to the floor.

He made short work of the other cuff, then eased back, leaving her room. Tossing the chains on the bed, she took a deep breath and swallowed, staring out at the garden below them. About half of it was shrubbery, flowers, and a few ornamental trees. She supposed if she didn't fall straight into a stone sculpture or pathway, she might survive a fall. She had a feeling Unira did not particularly plan for her to survive, at least not unharmed, so it was worth a shot.

Holding tight to the window casing, she eased herself out onto the ledge and followed him, doing her best not to make a sound.

"Won't they see us?" she whispered.

"My magic will do its best to guide their eyes away. This is one of the powers of the mask." They passed one window, then another, easing along the building. "There are vines we can climb down at the far corner," he added.

"If we make it that far." Looking down, she saw guards standing sentry at an entry *right* below her. She swallowed again.

"Don't look down. Look up or at your destination."

"All right." Step by step, she eased over closer to him, until suddenly she felt something under her foot crack.

A shard of the ledge broke off and fell. Even though she knew she shouldn't, she automatically looked down.

For a moment, she and the guard locked eyes, staring at each other in shock. Then she couldn't help herself. She winked.

He took off, shouting.

She turned and looked at Daridian, who was shaking his head. "Well, I said the mask would *do its best*. I didn't say you could hit him with a rock."

"I believe I barely grazed a bush, but point taken."

Laughing a little, they kept moving. He glanced over his shoulder. "We're in for company. After the vines, we run for the gate."

"Got it." Reaching for the next window casing, she gritted her teeth. By Seluvae, let the night hide them a little, even if dawn was approaching. Let them get free of this place. But then something occurred to her. "Wait—did you find your sister?"

"Not yet. But the slaves made it past the walls. They've fled into the forest. So at least they've been freed."

"Well, then we can't leave. Not without your sister."

He looked at her in surprise, not that she could see much of his expression beneath the mask. "We should get you out. And the sword. It's been too close to them, for too long. Then I can return."

She couldn't argue about the sword, exactly. But how dare he act like she was a fragile vase, needing to be insulated from danger? "No, we should go back in and find her. Two of us can search more quickly than one, right?"

"I—" He glanced over his shoulder. "Let's just try not to get killed first?"

"All right," she grumbled. But she was not giving up his search just yet. She didn't want to be the one getting in the way of his mission. She wanted to be helping. Was there anything more she could do, any other way to help? A ridiculous thought to be having while climbing along a high ledge, but something did occur to her...

She visualized the little sparkling white dragon that had guided her so far, the one who had encouraged her to take up the sword. Not just a sword, but a clanblade—the Blade of the Moon. Could she speak to this dragon the way her father and the other clan leaders supposedly could? What was her name again? Orogoth? Such a heavy name for such a spritely creature.

She tried to focus her thoughts, as she continued to follow Daridian's lead along the ledge. *Hey, little dragon, isn't there something you can do? A little help here?*

*As you wish, Daughter. My sister will soon be needing help anyway.*

*Your sister...?* Su was still frowning when she heard the roar and saw the wings soar up into the sky. The spiny pale creature burst into flight. Pale, acrid flames had enveloped one of the exits from the estate.

Another, smaller roar echoed off the roof of the building behind them. Shining like the moon, her dragon was raking a path in the roof tiles with her claws—drawing attention.

No, not her dragon. She couldn't be hers, could she?

*Dragons belong to no one,* she heard in her head. *It is you who belong to me, Daughter.*

She snorted, hoping Daridian wouldn't notice.

"Hurry," Daridian reminded her, and she quickened her pace. "These distractions won't last forever."

They were almost to the vines when she saw it—a thick black fog enveloping the ground around the base of the building. And growing, spreading outward. Its tendrils seem to reach up toward her, almost as though it was reaching out for her.

She pointed. "What is that?"

"I have no idea," he answered. "But I think we're going into it."

The bolt that Unira had hit her with had been black too. Jumping into a whole cloud of darkness seemed like an *immensely* terrible idea. But what was the alternative? Stay right there, clinging to the wall, like a terrified insect?

Daridian indicated the vines, how to grab and which to climb down on, and started quickly down. She scanned the estate behind her as she found the best grip she could. One gate was burning. The black fog now covered nearly half the roads and open areas. Behind her, roof tiles were flying. Shouts rang up in all directions.

Chaos was breaking loose around her. Which might just mean she could get away and survive this. *If* the fog didn't dissolve her alive or something even more gruesome.

She shifted her weight onto the vines and steeled herself to descend.

Pyaris and Faytou were hunkered down near the mouth of the tunnel when they arrived. Lara held tight to Nyalin's mother's arm as she opened the iron door to peer out. "Purple," she murmured. "It's almost dawn. We'll lose the dark soon."

"Lara, can you call Yeska?" asked Nyalin. "My mother's in no shape to fight. Maybe she can get her out of here?"

*Yeska, can you—*

*Coming! I've been getting so bored over here. About time I had something important to do.*

*Well, we just need you to fly Linali to safety.*

*Disappointing, but I will do it.*

*Flying away may not be as exciting, but at least no one is trying to kill you.*

*Are you absolutely* positive *I can't incinerate the whole place? Then no one would be trying to kill you either, save a few stray embers.*

*I'm sure. Some of these people just work here. Probably most of them. They're innocents.*

*What about the ones trying to kill you?*

*Maybe not those ones.*

*Can I at least incinerate* them? *Or bite them briefly?*

*Yeska!*

She shook her head in a gesture that probably made sense to no one. "She's on her way."

"You speak with the Bone Dragon?" Linali asked softly, tilting her head.

"Yeah, it's, uh, a long story."

"Is that Cerivil's Dagger I see?"

Lara lifted her chin. "Technically, it's mine now."

"And how did *you* come to have it, dear?"

The question came out sweetly enough, but Lara felt herself tense. She opened her mouth but hesitated. "None of your business" didn't seem like a very trustworthy response in this moment. And even if this woman was a stranger to Nyalin now, she might not be in the future... She might eventually hold a great deal of sway over him.

In which case, blurting out "I stole it" didn't seem like a very good choice either.

Nyalin cleared his throat. "Cerivil stepped down for his son, Myandrin, to take his place, but he was tragically killed."

"I thought that was an accident," Faytou put in.

Lara shook her head, closing her mouth and looking down at the floor. Would it be better to mentally tune out and slide into Yeska's mind for a bit, to feel the wind going over her wings and scales? Hmm, no. Then she wouldn't know what had been said—and what hadn't.

Shaking her head, Pyaris put a gentle hand on Lara's shoulder and squeezed. The small gesture was surprisingly comforting. "Lara is Cerivil's daughter," Pyaris added, "so due to her brother's death, she is now in line to be married to a real jerk."

"Don't you hate it when that happens?" Linali rolled her eyes.

Nyalin cleared his throat. "So she, um, took the matter into her own hands. And by matter, I mean—the Dagger."

Linali frowned. "Took it? Took the Dagger?"

"Yep."

"You mean—do you mean she stole it?"

Lara winced. She'd sort of hoped Nyalin would find a way to gloss over that part.

But when Linali's head snapped around to hers, her eyes were wide with amused laughter. "Bravo, girl. I should have recognized the rebel streak in you. I have it myself. But also, you look so much like your mother. And all of her spice, too, clearly."

She blushed. "You—you knew her? Yeska is almost here, by the way."

"Not well. But I do remember she loved a good green apple."

Lara frowned. "A—a what?"

"We need something for cover," Nyalin muttered. "Or they'll be skewering us with arrows as we run toward Yeska."

"What about fog?" Lara asked. "Faytou, you can cast that, too, can't you?"

Linali leaned a little closer, lowering her voice conspiratorially. "I don't know if you've tried it, but did you know you can make it any color you want?"

"What?"

"The fog. It'll be whatever color you visualize. Try it!"

Lara leaned toward the narrow opening again. Was the sky incrementally lighter? Slightly paler? "Black," she said. "Let's make it black."

Pyaris let out a delighted laugh. "I love it. Let's flood the place with even more darkness."

Reaching into her pocket, Lara gripped one of her charms. She needed them less and less these days, but she wanted to get this one right. She let her eyes drift closed, concentrating, visualizing a black cloud filling each street and corner, deep enough to hide their movements.

Each of them grew quiet, focusing on the spell.

"Is it working?" Faytou murmured. "Is it really black?"

"Sure is," Nyalin answered. "Because now, I can't see a single thing out in the street."

*Landing.*

"She's here. Run! Go!" Lara, Nyalin, and Linali burst through the iron door, rushing up the hill. The power of Yeska's wings had blown back some of the fog, but, otherwise, it seemed to be everywhere she could see.

"We'll stay here and keep building up the fog for now," Faytou shouted even as they ran. Shouts from the nearby sentries rang out. A bell started to ring.

She and Nyalin were nearly dragging Linali with them, but there was no time for anything more gentle. Linali, for her part, seemed unperturbed by this, and easily started to climb up Yeska's side, using the jagged scales as handholds until she reached the dragon's back and could settle between two spikes.

"My, Yeska! You haven't aged a day.... What has it been, two decades?

That long?"

If they continued to chat, Yeska didn't share her thoughts, but Linali did seem to be muttering—to the dragon and herself—as she climbed on and lay stomach down on Yeska's back in one of the few spots large enough to accommodate the posture. Her arms spread out wide in a large ineffectual hug.

*I'll be back as quickly as I can.*

Lara nodded, mostly to herself as she and Nyalin hurried back into the cover of what fog remained near them. Fresh darkness rapidly enveloped the area around Yeska.

Before the dragon leapt into the sky, a dozen arrows bounced off her scales. Why had these been so pathetic while the poisoned one shot by the creatures back in Yeska's cavern had sunk through? Was it the poison? Or had the otherworldly arrows been partly magical?

There was no time to consider it now. Another volley of arrows flew, and this time, she realized their aim had sharpened—not on the dragon but on Linali.

*Go... Go! They're shooting at Linali!*

Yeska sneered back in the archers' direction. White flames roared forth, enveloping both the small wooden buildings and the sentries themselves in the strange acrid flames. Screams rang out.

But Yeska was already heaving her great wings into the sky.

*Sorry. I couldn't resist.*

*I can't blame you.*

Yeska soared up, higher. The bells were still ringing, and she could hear a gong sounding among them now. "*What* is that alarm?" She spun around, trying to see where it was coming from, and if there was some danger other than the dragon, who was now flying rapidly away.

Nyalin grabbed her arm. "Hey—look up there. Isn't that...?"

She looked where he was pointing. Two figures were repelling down the side of the largest building, one in a black crossover with a long black skirt, hardly equipped for the task at hand. "Sutamae!"

"Who is that helping her?" he wondered.

"I have no idea..."

"The other guards, they see her." He pointed.

"We have to help her," Lara said, "More of this fog. Lots of it." As her eyes narrowed at the people descending, the puffs of white fog started to form, swirling up and around, trying to block the view. Right, that was the wrong color—she needed to visualize.

She imagined darkness wrapping them in a protective hug.

"Let's get Pyaris and Faytou," Nyalin said. "Then let's try to reach her. Maybe we can get out of here together better as a group than how we came in?"

"But the vortex," she started. "Do we need to cross back over to destroy it?"

"I don't know. But if so, I think we may need to make a second trip. If we get Linali and Su out of here, I'd call that a victory, wouldn't you?"

She nodded. Partial gains secured were better than shooting for too much and losing everything. Knowing this was why she'd chosen not to keep looking for her father—risking capture—instead getting Faytou out while she could. "Let's go."

Who was he to deserve this?

Jaw clenched, Idak marched from Sutamae's rooms down to the kitchens. He should be checking if the guards he'd sent to the catacombs had found anything. He should be leading them himself, ferreting out any trespassers.

Here he was—in the kitchens, instead. Laughing bitterly to himself, he jerked open the expensive liquor cabinet and grabbed the finest cherry brandy they had.

Who indeed. Who was he, indeed.

He grabbed a tray, then the most ostentatious glass he could find. He poured a healthy portion of the brandy, probably twice what the glass was properly supposed to contain.

Then, from his pocket, he took the vial he'd retrieved from his rooms before he had headed back to the dinner. Not the concoction he'd used to wake Sutamae—that had been a fairly innocent but rare herb combined with his own neutralizing spells. She might have rejected him, but she was still his guest, and he wouldn't have her cast askance and immobilized on the floor.

No, this vial was even rarer and more special than that. He poured in more than the few drops he needed.

Better certain than sorry.

Smiling bitterly, he snapped his fingers, sharply summoning one of the servants over.

He smiled. "Take this to Sword Master Hendo. Tell him it's a special gift from me, as his former student, for joining us this fine evening. Take care not to sample it... it's a... rare but bitter vintage. A favorite of the master's but not commonly very appealing. I wouldn't recommend it."

Eyes a bit wide, the servant nodded and complied.

He watched the man carry the tray off and up the stairs. He didn't know what his mother's plans for Hendo were, especially now if her offer to Sutamae was off the table.

He didn't especially care. The man needed to die.

To think that while he was a boy, the teacher who had taught him diligently, who had treated him with respect and probably overmuch deference, had simultaneously been laying his lecherous hands on a young girl... a girl ultimately hardly different from himself... It turned his stomach.

Maybe some mistakes could be forgiven, but he had no desire to forgive this one. Perhaps this justice could be part of his redemption for all he had done—if any redemption was even possible.

And he owed Sutamae this much for bringing her here.

After the servant was gone, he took the stairs toward his mother's rooms. The hour was late, but he had a feeling she wouldn't be sleeping yet. There was something strange in the air, something wild and terrifying.

Who was he to deserve any of this? What did he even have to offer a woman like Sutamae?

When it came down to it, he spent his days reading and walking morosely in the woods—and avoiding his mother's demands by being either busy or entirely absent.

On the days he hadn't successfully avoided her, that's when he'd probably done the most notable, horrible things. Things his mother would consider their achievements.

But if that was the case, if he should be proud, then why did their village raids still haunt his dreams at night? He'd burned homes, captured innocents, separated families...

Why did he deserve to sit and enjoy the fruits of others' suffering?

He could pretend he hadn't noticed, and he was grateful Sutamae had seemed to believe him. But he had noticed. He had noticed a long time ago, but chose to mentally escape, burying his nose in his books. How else can a child respond to a mother like his?

But what choice had he had? The world he knew insisted *this* was the way the world worked. He'd tried to avoid it, avert his eyes, forget what was happening.

But his world had a crack in it now. Light was shining through and illuminating the hideousness.

And as though Sutamae had poured moonlight on it all, he found himself now unable to look away.

His mother wasn't in her rooms, so he checked the dining room where he'd last seen her. What if she hadn't recovered from the attack on her powers? What if she were ill because of it?

But he found her not ill, but not well either. She was standing out on the terrace, fire in her eyes as she gazed across the dark estate, wind ruffling her hair.

He stood beside her in silence, scanning the buildings in the predawn light. There was just starting to be enough light to make out slight outlines of the buildings.

He cleared his throat. "I sent two dozen men to the catacombs. I'm sure they'll eliminate anyone who opposes you."

"They're all dead," she whispered.

"What?" he frowned. "How can you know?"

"I felt their spirits rise, ready to do my bidding."

He frowned. "More necromancy... Can't you just let them rest?"

"Oh, you don't approve?"

"Of course I approve. But I was just talking to those men. To think they are dead..." He swallowed. He'd lost men before. But everything about this night was strange and raw. Something about it stuck in his craw. What had they died for? For their families? For his mother's power? For his own?

"Death comes to us all eventually." She waved her hand carelessly in the air. "Worrying about it won't stop anything. Mourning the dead is pointless. Harness their power—or someone else will."

He winced. "Is it too late to get you a sword, Mother? To do things the proper way? You have the training. If you have the sword smiths under your control, have them make you one while you're keeping them from giving one to Grel." He had no idea where the thought had come from, but it didn't seem like a bad idea. Why not?

But when her narrowed eyes pinned him to the stone wall behind him, he swallowed. He'd miscalculated somewhere in there.

"You're just like them. All of you think you're so superior."

"Who?" He frowned.

"Every swordmage—Elix, Pavan—"

"The emperor, you mean." He didn't like the way this was going. Panic was rising in his throat. Shifting uncomfortably, he continued to scan the estate for threats. His eye caught on something.

"Pavan of all people should know better. He should know better. All of you should know better. But you think the swords are so pure, and my magic is foul?"

"I never said foul. I thought you could have more power if you could openly carry a sword. Mother, what are those Bone Clan people doing here?" He pointed and squinted, trying to see them clearly, but black fog was flooding around them, obscuring everything.

"What does it matter? Who cares?"

"I care. Elix would care. Inner-clan conflict could destroy the entire empire, weaken us to the Mushin, and—"

"And I don't care."

His voice was barely audible as he finally looked at her, finally stopped overlooking just how much hate burned in those eyes. "What have you done?"

"I've never done *anything* that wasn't to make a better life for you!" she snapped. Nothing about the words rang true.

"What does the Bone Clan have to do with that?"

"You could have been great if you had stepped up. You could have had this world in the palm of your hand!"

"What is going on?" Should he be concerned she seemed to be talking in the past tense? He took a step back, away from her. "I don't want *this* world. You never asked what I wanted. You only care about what *you've* wanted."

"How dare you, after everything I've sacrificed—"

A bell started clanging near the north gate. The sound of the alarm. So... Sutamae's friend at the window hadn't gotten her very far, had he? That gave him a sort of smug satisfaction, even though he hoped she would get away. He'd been glad there'd been a way that didn't require him to directly intervene. Not that intervening was really an option. It'd certainly have meant his death.

A harried armed man dashed onto the terrace. "The girl has escaped! We're searching for her, but—"

"Don't talk to me, find her!" His mother whirled on him. "You! You did this. You helped her!"

He took a step back. "Seluvae's stars, Mother! I did no such thing."

"I don't believe you."

"I would never defy you like that."

"You would. I know."

"I didn't."

"Men will do anything for a beautiful face."

"Well, I didn't."

"Please." She grabbed his scabbard from where he'd left it leaning against a baluster. A careless mistake, he could see now, but he was *supposed* to be safe here. He had dozens of armed men at his command. He shouldn't need to always be armed, but—the magnitude of the mistake was churning in his gut as she drew the blade from its scabbard.

"What are you doing?" he whispered.

Her eyes ran along the blade. "A simple piece of metal, and yet so much changes when it comes into your hands. The whole world shifts—for a strip of sharpened, polished metal."

"What's going on? Stop that, and give it to me."

"It's more than that, of course. It's the spell the smiths use to make the swords. Did you know they use necromancy too? Just like me."

He faltered. "Wha-what?"

"These swords are just more enslaved spirits. They just don't tell you, so you swordmages don't have to worry your pretty little heads about it."

The panic was nearly overflowing now. His breath was fast, his heart racing. "So?"

"So you shouldn't have helped her." She took the other end of the sword in her hand, barely avoiding the sharp edge, and raised it in the air.

"Mother, stop! I've only done everything you ever asked!"

But she didn't seem to hear him.

With a flash of deep green, she snapped the sword in two. Time seemed to slow down, even freeze.

The shards of his precious sword fell, clattered, blood from where they'd managed to slice into her palm in self-defense dribbling around them. Memories of pride at earning his sword flashed past, shattered in their own right.

Pain stabbed into his soul. He collapsed to the ground, curling up into a ball. His limbs spasmed, they wouldn't respond. Was this how Sutamae had felt? It gave him a little, strange pride that he didn't understand.

"It's over now," she whispered. "Go back to being the child you once were. Useless to me. Neither you, nor Nyalin, nor Pavan—none of you is a match for me."

Pain wracking his body, he could do nothing but watch as she spread her arms wide, tiny drops of blood splattering the floor before his eyes.

Black spirits, ephemeral like the fog, seemed to emerge from nothing, lifting her into the air.

"Mother!" he tried to call.

But she was gone.

He tried to crawl, tried to reach out toward the shattered remnants of his sword, his magic—his life, in fact. He'd have no power, no magic now. No future.

Who was he to deserve all this? Indeed.

## *Chapter 15*
# The Vortex

Lara's thighs burned as she raced toward where they'd seen Sutamae descend into the fog.

"Sutamae?" Nyalin called. "Are you there? It's me!"

"What if we can't find her?" asked Pyaris. "Should we head back to those catacombs?"

"Or get the heck out of here and come back another day?" asked Faytou. "Look at all this madness. This is our chance."

Suddenly, a sword cut through the fog in front of them. They skidded to a stop, Nyalin drawing his mother's blade.

Lara's hand found the Dagger at her belt. "Who's there? This can end peacefully—if you choose it. No one needs to die today."

The sword lowered slightly. A form in a black cloak and crossover emerged from the fog, an intimidating gray mask covering the facial features. Lara caught her breath. The mask was beautiful, its white lines curving in intricate patterns, but terrifying too.

"I have no desire to die. Let us pass, and we shall let you pass," said a man's voice.

"We?" asked Nyalin.

"Nyalin!" Out of the fog another form emerged, lunging at Nyalin. Instinctively, Lara drew the Dagger, rounding on their attacker—but the interloper was too busy wrapping her arms around Nyalin in an ardent, if somewhat terrifying, hug.

It took him a second, but he hugged her back. "Sutamae!"

Lara blew out a breath and sheathed her blade.

"You two know each other?" the masked man said slowly.

"This is my stepbrother I told you about," Sutamae explained.

"Ah, yes. Nyalin moLinati." The man didn't sheathe his blade, but he lowered it to his side. Probably wise.

"Lina*li*," Sutamae corrected. "Look, you found him after all! Didn't expect that, did you?"

"You may feel jovial that you've escaped, but may I remind you we are far from surviving this?"

Su shook her head. "Nyalin, what are you doing here?"

"Long story," he said. "But we saw you on the side of the building and thought we should help."

"We made the black fog," Lara said, a little too proudly. But it still was pretty impressive, in her opinion.

"Your crossovers are not black," the masked man pointed out.

"We're Bone Clan," Faytou said.

"Are you with the others here?"

She frowned. "Others? We're the only Bone Clan here."

The masked man shook his head. "No. I saw another wearing your colors. He was in a cell."

"Where?" Lara demanded.

"In the tall building in the corner over there—by the north wall, near the forest. There were others with him, guarding him, also in your colors."

They all exchanged glances. She bit her lip. "Could it be? Could this be why we couldn't find Da? Because he wasn't even *in* the city in the first place?"

"You didn't know there were others here?" the masked man asked.

"There's no reason any members of my clan should be kept in some Obsidian's cell," said Lara firmly. "Andius has to be behind this. We need to find him. I—"

Nyalin grabbed her arm. "Look!"

All of them raised their eyes to the sky. She caught her breath.

Rising up into the air was a female figure, dark robes billowing in the wind. Wisps of inky black seemed to flow around her, as if they carried her, buoyed her up, taking her to roughly where the vortex had been in the afterworld. In fact, the dark forms swirled, almost like they were made of the same energy...

"Abomination," Pyaris was muttering behind her. "Disgrace."

But Nyalin had pointed at something else. An eagle screeched high above, its form a silhouette of black against the purple sky. It glided smoothly down toward the main building from which Su had emerged. They watched as it landed on a building's roof—and transformed.

"The emperor," Lara breathed. "He's here?"

The spirits whirling around the woman above spun faster all of a sudden, and then a beam of energy crackled out from her, heading toward the building, black and deep red. Smoke billowed where the energy beam had split open the roof, most of which was now missing.

But through the smoke, the emperor was still there.

"He dodged it!" shouted Faytou.

Drawing his sword, Shadow Wing, Pavan pointed it into the sky. Straight at the floating woman.

"He's challenging her," Nyalin whispered. "I have to help him."

Lara was looking north, toward the tall building the masked man had mentioned. "I have to check that building to see if Da is there," she said. "While we still have the remaining shreds of the dark and the fog to hide us."

"And we need to look for someone in the catacombs," Su said. "His sister"—she nodded toward the masked man—"we think she's down there."

"Releasing more people from the catacombs will weaken Unira—I'm pretty sure that's her"—he pointed toward the sky—"so that'd be good," Nyalin said.

"Oh, that's her," said Sutamae. "I don't recommend the acquaintance."

"If you find this sister of yours," Pyaris said, "do you know how to free her? Is either of you a necromancer?"

They glanced at each other, then shook their heads.

"I'll go with them," Pyaris said. "And we'll free every goddess-blessed person we can."

"I'll go with Lara," said Faytou, "and deal with my brother."

Nyalin nodded crisply. "And I'll go help the emperor."

Lara's eyes locked with Nyalin's. She reached for his hand and squeezed it. "Are you sure splitting up is a good idea? Let him fight his own battle. Come with Faytou and me—or help the others weaken Unira."

He threw his arms around her and pressed her tightly against his chest, murmuring in her ear. "I thought I had no parents for eighteen years, Lara. Flawed as he might be, I have to help him. If she overpowered my mother once, years ago, what are his chances on his own?"

She pulled back, struggling not to tear up. "Okay. I understand."

"I have to try. Give Andius hell for me."

"I will. But only if you promise to come back to me," she shot back.

"I promise. I might come back as a ghost, but I'll do it."

"Nyalin!" She pecked a quick kiss to his lips before backing away.

He squeezed her hand one more time.

"If you want to escape this place by the easiest route, the south gate looks to be completely destroyed by the dragon, and the east one has been the easiest for me to sneak through," offered the masked man.

"If we need to find each other after all this, let's try to meet at the south gate—if we can," said Lara. "Or just beyond it in the woods. Or if you have to, just run, and I'll see you in the Salt City. Luck to all of you!"

"And strength as well," Su quipped back, echoing the traditional greeting.

And they took off running.

The description the masked man had given her was excellent, because they spotted the building easily, rising above the fog near the walls. They narrowly avoided two different patrols, judging by the volume of the shouting and swearing.

But the two of them froze when they saw him. Andius, on horseback, was out front, trying to calm a beast terrified by the black mist surrounding it. And yet, he seemed to be making gradual progress away from the building and toward the north gate. Lara took special care to build fresh fog higher around him.

Even though she'd had the warning, it was still shocking to spot him here, amid all the black crossovers and all the wealth. She knelt on one knee, and Faytou followed, so the fog would keep them thoroughly hidden.

She held a finger up to her lips for quiet, then reached into her pocket for the charms. But—this deserved something special. She had no fire charms, but she wondered...

Closing her eyes and centering her energy, she spun the spell carefully in her mind, building it up until she thrust it full force at Andius—and incidentally the horse.

A massive fiery ball of energy hurtled his way. The horse screamed in terror, rearing, and she heard more than saw Andius hit the ground.

"Going somewhere, Andius?" she called out. She hurled three pulses of water this time. That would likely put out the flames, but they hit with brutal force.

The shushes to calm the horse stopped. Silence stretched for a long moment. The horse knickered uneasily. Cedar mixed with other magical scents from the fog saturated the air around her.

"Be right back," Faytou whispered. He eased away from her into the darkness.

"Where are you going?" she replied, but got no response.

"Well, well, is that my little thief who needs to be taught a few lessons?"

Clearly he knew she was there, but she could not see him, nor could he see her. For now.

"I am not yours, Andius," Lara called out. "I never will be. I think I've made that abundantly clear."

"Have you come to receive your beatings to put you in the proper place? Your punishment awaits. Face me openly, like a civilized opponent."

She gritted her teeth. Gradually, he worked to remove the fog, his magic creating a cold wind that blew the fog away from the area around him, slowly clearing a larger and larger area. She could see him now, and he would find her eventually—or maybe he'd find Faytou, if he was sneaking closer.

"Where are you going?" she asked. She saw him trying to settle his horse, again easing it toward the gate. It wasn't like Andius to run from conflict—from her or anyone. "Are you running away?"

"The emperor is here," Andius said slowly. "I do not have any desire to make an enemy of him."

"Oh, but you are his enemy, if you're here. And you know it."

"Yes, but *he* doesn't." Andius's smile was cold. "Are you going to continue to hide? Little coward. Face me!"

"Your enemies have found you, Andius." The cleared area was growing larger. If she wanted to keep her advantage, she had to act now. "Enough talking."

Lara bombarded him with five more fiery blasts, carefully directing them from different angles so they wouldn't reveal where she knelt.

With clearer vision now, Andius dove to the side, spun, and ducked. Only one managed to hit him, but he swore when it did. It might be petty, but she wasn't putting it out with water this time. Let him burn.

"Drop this relentless, annoying tactic," he growled, patting at the flames. "Clear this fog and face *me*. Is this darkness *your* doing? You always were underhanded, sneaky—breaking honor and tradition."

The clear air was almost to her now, so she scurried back further, casting blasts of shadow and earth.

In frustration, Andius peppered the fog around him randomly with small spurts of energy. But to her luck, all of them missed. She smiled crookedly. Maybe her clan's luck was on her side for once. They'd come close enough, though, that the lemon smell of his magic caught her nose.

The next blasts she aimed to set his boots on fire, then tore through his cloak. But his efforts to clear the area were paying off, the circle getting wider and driving her back away from the building.

And potentially away from her father.

Time to handle this more directly. She ought to control when she appeared, rather than letting him expose her. She strode forward, stepping out of the fog, with the clanblade in hand. "If following tradition creates leaders of *your* quality, then I'll happily break tradition again. Or your bones."

He laughed, the expression taking on a disturbing, almost manic tinge. "You want to settle this? Fine. Certainly. Let us duel. Let us settle this once and for all! Blades only, like in the Contests."

"No. We're not in the Contests. This is real life."

"Have it your way then." He stifled another laugh.

"Why are you laughing?"

"Only because as we fight, your father bleeds to his death inside his cell."

Her blood turned to ice. "You're lying. You're bluffing."

"Maybe I am, but maybe I am not." Grinning wider, he drew his sword and swung it left and right, as if warming up for a fight. The area around them was all but clear now. Where was Faytou?

"If that's true, then why didn't you tell me before now?"

"Because I wanted to see your face when I told you."

She faltered, trying to figure out how to respond.

"He's bleeding out, you know."

She started toward the building, shooing him toward his horse. "Fine. Run away then. Go, get on your horse, hide away from the emperor, and let me save my father."

"Oh, let him die. It's easier for everyone."

At the last moment, as she came closest to him while still keeping her eyes on the archway into the building, she lunged at him with the Dagger. He parried but just barely. "How could that possibly be, you disgusting tick of a human being?" She lunged again, aiming for his arm.

He danced back away from her—in the direction of his horse, she noted. "This is why you're not cut out for politics, and I am. Think about it—whichever of us wins, it will cement our rule. And it will finally settle the leadership situation, bringing peace back to our clan."

"You're a monster." She considered going after him, but she eased toward the door of the building instead, keeping her eyes on him all the while.

"Everyone is." He grinned again. "I'm just a practical one who is clear on my goals."

"Go on and flee if you want to, you miserable wart." Walking backward, she picked up speed toward the building. If she got far enough away, would he drop this and run?

"So you concede to me? Give up your claim to our clan, and I'll let you chase after your precious Cerivil."

She held up the clanblade in her hand, looking at it then back to him. "I thought you were smarter than this, Andius. I couldn't give up my claim, even if I wanted to."

"Then fight." Surprising her, he hurled a blast of energy directly at her face.

On instinct, she raised the blade, cutting at the ball of light. To her surprise, it worked, the pieces of energy shearing on either side of her. One sizzled, melting stone on the outer wall, the other setting a barrel ablaze.

She narrowed her eyes, preparing another attack. "My father's *life* is more important than *you*. You want to run from Pavan? Run while you can."

"A truce it is then." He continued to back toward the horse, reaching for the reins. But something about the words rang false.

Energy slams had never been her strong suit, but fire wasn't defeating him. On the other hand, she had powerful shadow charms in her pocket, but she'd never been quite as deft with that sphere of magic...

She cast her best version of the shadow spell, slicing her arms through the air as part of the visualization, imagining tossing Andius like a rag doll into the stones.

The power of the magic collided with Andius, jerking the horse's head when he tried not to release the reins and making Lara wince. Ultimately, he lost his grip, slamming against the outer strong wall of the estate.

This was her chance. Maybe he was at least stunned. Running backward, trying to keep her eyes on him while still moving toward her father, she headed for the archway into the building. The fog was completely clear now, at least in the area around them. Maybe she could make it inside and out of his sight before he recovered—

Her heel caught on an uneven cobblestone, and she fell backward. At the same time, Andius attacked, his fire magic coursing through the air toward her. She tried to roll out of the way, but she wasn't fast enough.

Pain exploded in her lower back. The force of the impact of his spell sent her rolling a few more times, busting her head and face and elbows off the cobblestones.

When she finally stopped rolling, she lay still. How did her arms even work? Everything—everything—was just on fire.

Smirking, Andius staggered to his feet, then moved closer. "A word to the wise. Don't let your enemies get in your head." He stumbled forward until he was standing over her, admiring his conquest. She glowered up at him. "They might cause you to make a terrible mistake—"

A soft whistle caught her ear, then a *thunk*. His smirk faded as abruptly as his words. His eyes went wide, white. For a moment, she thought he'd fall on her, but footsteps dashed forward, and someone pushed him to the side.

Andius's body collapsed face first in the dirt beside her, eyes still open, unseeing.

Faytou reached down his hand. "Are you all right?"

"No. Are you? I don't think I can get up."

"I'm not all right either. But I couldn't let him kill you. Oh, by the Twins—let me heal you."

"No, save it for Da—Cerivil—he's inside—"

"Do you know which way? I have to heal you, Lara—there could be more of his goons inside, and I can't shoot them all in the back."

She winced as he worked his spells, at each second passing without finding her father.

"I—I'm good enough. C'mon. Look, we can follow Andius's footprints. There's blood on his boot. I think it was there all along, not from the fight."

Helping her to her feet, they cautiously made their way inside.

Andius's footprints weren't the only ones, making it hard to follow them. There were many making their way through the sand, apparently. At each turn, they followed the blood in the sand, but they found no one else.

"They all ran, I think, when Andius did," Lara murmured. "This place is empty."

"Wouldn't you?" Faytou replied. "Who wants to make an enemy of the emperor? Not me."

"Look!" Lara pointed as they turned a corner and found a row of cells. They raced toward a cell where a door stood fully open, a man inside. Had they stabbed him and run for it? Not even locked him in? That was a bad sign, if they weren't worried he would flee or give chase.

And, indeed, the form lay still, unmoving.

She dashed the rest of the way, skidding to a stop at the pathetic cot they had him in. "Da! Da, I'm here!" He was pale and thinner, and deep wounds on his chest and neck were covering the cot in blood.

His eyelids flickered but didn't open. "Lara? Lara, is that you? I can't—I can't see anything—I can't think straight—he's been drugging me—Andius did this—find him—"

"I already did," she said gently. "We're here now. It's me. We'll heal you."

And she poured the power of the dragon into his wounds, breathing deep and hoping, under all of Dala's light and Seluvae's stars, that they weren't too late.

Nyalin raced along the stones, keeping his eyes on the sky while trying not to run into anything in the thick fog. But he needed to reach Pavan if he wanted to help him, didn't he? His father had transformed back into avian form to glide down from the roof to a terrace.

He found stairs leading in that direction—up. He took them two at a time and found himself on the wide terrace with his father. The roof above them where his father had first landed was still smoking—or was that from some fresh attack of Unira's that he'd not noticed while sprinting over here?

"Nyalin! There you are. It took me *forever* to find you. First I went to Stragg's Beard, and—it doesn't matter. What are you doing here, of all places?"

"Long story." How had Pavan known to look at Stragg's Beard, and what had made him start looking *now*? He supposed it didn't matter. But it seemed his suspicions about the lock were correct. Maybe Pavan no longer sensed his exact location without the lock to track.

Pavan's eyes flicked toward Unira without moving his head, then back to Nyalin. "Would your presence here have anything to do with... uh, that?"

"Indeed, it would. Let's just say... I promised a ghost I'd deal with something."

Above them, Unira laughed wickedly. When he turned to look up, he saw she had nearly reached the vortex—did proximity increase her power? But then she seemed to float back down a bit. Was she going to throw another attack at his father? As she neared, he could see her face more clearly. And her malicious smile.

"Pavan, fancy seeing you here, and—" She faltered, going silent for a second. When she spoke again, her voice had drained of mirth, all amusement replaced with rage.

"And Nyalin moLinali. I was *told* you were dead."

He raised his eyebrows. Well, that wasn't exactly untrue, he'd been a *little* bit dead several times but... He doubted he could capture the nuance by shouting at a woman swathed in ghosts floating in the sky.

"You were told wrong," he called instead.

Her hands clenched into fists. "You evade me again."

Pavan brushed a speck of dirt off his shoulder. "Don't you think it's time to quit this project of yours? Clearly, you'll never kill him."

"I'm nothing if not persistent. You should know that."

"It's not always a virtue. It's been two decades, Unira. Move on."

"Hm, I don't think so."

He could feel the air change, like thunder before a storm. The hairs on his arms stood on end. He danced back, drawing his mother's blade.

At the sight of it, Unira's eyes went wild. Only then did he catch sight of the writhing power gathering in her hands, her arms spread wide. Orange as a poppy, energy gathered lightning-fast, faster than he'd ever seen.

And when she brought her hands together, she unloaded all of it on him.

Bracing himself did little. The sword seemed to cut a chunk out of the power she threw, but all too much of it went around the sword—and onto him.

*Into* him.

The world around him disappeared.

He looked up. The vortex loomed above him. He'd crossed over. Or she'd made him cross over. He could see the spirits inside it now, swirling like inside a whirlpool in a swamp. Were they reaching to get out?

Were they reaching for him?

As he tried to get his bearings, he could see the tiny stars of the souls underground in the catacombs. Their lights burned so bright he could see them even through the dirt and rocks at his feet. As he watched, one of the lights winked out. Pyaris and the others doing their work?

Above him, the vortex shook, the moaning, whining sound of the wind amplifying for a moment. He was so close now, he could almost hear a wailing amid the sensation of rushing air. He glanced around him. He had to get back, had to do something to help Pavan.

To help himself, help all of them.

His eye caught on Mount Stragg in the distance. Was Batu there, watching him? Wondering if he would succeed?

The spirits moaned again. He remembered the spirit guardian Pyaris had deflected when they'd entered the catacombs. Had Unira put it there, or had it been older than that?

It didn't matter—but it did mean he could fight these spirits with spells. Maybe the whole damn vortex with them...

The attack Unira had slammed into him had filled him with so much power that he was forced to cross over, just like he had been so many days go when Andius first attacked him, and he'd first visited the afterworld. That time, he'd returned after a moment or two—and to excruciating pain.

But the lock on his magic was gone now. If he was ever going to get control, this would be a good time to learn.

If the attacks filled him with magic that transported him here, maybe if he expended the magic by casting spells, he'd more easily get back home.

Taking a deep breath, he raised his hands toward the vortex. Did it move in response? Did it flinch, or was he imagining things?

It moved like water, so maybe he could freeze it, then shatter it somehow. He closed his eyes and tried to focus—this time not on a charm, not on a sword, just on himself and the idea of ice.

Pain was what made him realize his plan to expend the excess energy and get back to his father had worked all too quickly and that he'd returned—to utter agony. Had he managed to freeze the vortex? He wasn't sure.

He was collapsed against a wall, Pavan rushing to his side. Every piece of his body screamed in agony. Looking down, he realized his crossover was scorched, but almost like he'd been hit by acid more than fire.

The vortex—was it spinning more slowly now? Like it'd been cooled, chilled? It definitely wasn't frozen.

Unira threw a sphere of pulsing red light directly at him. Pavan hurled a silvery bolt as he leaned to the side, trying to shield Nyalin.

The bolt collided with the sphere in the air between them, exploding in a shower of sparks and embers.

"Let her hit me!" he cried.

Pavan glanced over his shoulder at his son. "Are you mad? She'll kill you with another hit or two like that."

"But it's the only way I can use her magic against her, to defeat her. Remove her power once and for all."

"We'll defeat her by fighting her, not giving in!" Pavan shouted. But there was sweat on his brow. The silver spears he threw—were they also some sort of ice magic?—were flying one after another, but Unira wasn't slowing down her bombardment.

"She's got the power of dozens of those enslaved. Maybe hundreds. We're no match for her unless we break her link to that—"

"I'm *not* letting her kill you to do it!"

"I need her power to fuel me!" He gritted his teeth, struggling to his feet. His skin felt like it was melting, or maybe evaporating. "We'll never match her power."

Around her, Unira had gathered another dozen balls of energy. They grew in size, and she reached for one after the other, throwing them as quickly as an archer plucking arrows from a quiver.

"Linali could have!" Pavan snapped.

"How?" he demanded. Never mind that if she'd been captured, that couldn't be completely true.

"You broke the lock—how many spirits are you connected to? Dozens?"

He stared at Pavan, his mind racing. Inside him, he'd always known the connection was there. Like the doorway to the spirit world back as his mother's home—was it so different from the vortex above him?

Yet his connection *was* different—because he hadn't sought it out for power. It was just a part of him. The connection that Unira had forged—it wasn't the same. She had forced the spirits into her service. And Pyaris did something different, didn't she? She asked for their help...

But he didn't know how to talk to them, here and now like Pyaris did. He needed one more hit, one more charge of power to figure this out.

Just as she was about to throw, he lunged to the side. Both of them noticed.

Pavan dove, trying to protect him. But he didn't dive quite far enough, as Nyalin scrambled further away.

Unira did not disappoint. The energy slammed into his chest. He was going to pay for that in pain when he got back.

*If* he got back and he survived that hit.

But he opened his eyes in the afterworld. And now, he knew what he needed to do.

He could expend his energy, and he'd make progress, and maybe he'd eventually break the vortex down. But what he really needed was even *more* resources than Unira.

And he could get them.

"Batu—spirits of the afterworld!" he shouted around him, away from the swirling eye of the storm. "Aid me in defeating this monster! Come to my side, so that I may destroy it!"

Before he could blink, a pale form had materialized beside him. Then another, then another.

He fought off the rising panic as a whole throng of spirits began to crowd around him, reaching for him, reaching for each other.

But as their ghostly hands laid on his shoulders, his neck, he felt the magic flow like the waterfalls at Yeska's cavern, clean—and powerful.

He raised his hands again toward the vortex. His whole body chilled as freezing energy flooded the vortex, its spinning slowing to a crawl.

More spirits joined him. The very ground below him blistered with crystals of ice, the air of the afterworld chilling colder and colder.

Then, the spinning stopped.

Dropping his arms, he stared at the thing. The moaning wind had grown quiet. The mud-black disk hovered in the air above him, as if waiting for something.

Squatting down, he picked up a frost-kissed rock about the size of his fist. Imbuing it with all the energy he had, all the longing he had for the justice these spirits deserved, his fingers squeezed tighter and tighter.

And then he threw.

Power chased the projectile, creating a tail like a comet in the heavens, the blue-white energy soaring through the greenish sky.

The spirits around him vanished. Above him, the rock that had seemed small in his hand smashed into the now-still vortex.

With a sharp crack, the disk split in a dozen pieces, shards splitting in all directions before starting their curve toward the earth.

Toward him.

Swallowing, bracing himself for the pain, he reached for his home plane again.

The first thing he heard was the screaming. It took him more than a minute to realize it wasn't his own.

The pain that overtook his senses blinded him, and something seemed to have crawled inside his chest and was squirming its way toward his heart. But as he wrenched his eyes open, he realized two things.

First, it was a woman's scream of horror, over and over and over again. Second, Pavan lay on the ground before him, motionless.

Nyalin was still on the terrace, but he'd collapsed against a large glass window behind him. Everything around him seemed to be either charred or on fire. The darkness squirming inside him turned his stomach, but he gritted his teeth against the pain and crawled toward Pavan.

"Don't you... dare sacrifice yourself... for me..." he grunted at his father. "That was *my* plan."

"Get out of here, Nyalin." Pavan's voice was faint, but even the sound made Nyalin's heart leap. "There's no defeating her."

"No, you were right. I got the other spirits to help me—she's vastly weakened now—" He reached Pavan's side, rolling his father toward him.

A slithering, crackling ball of black and purple energy smashed into the paving stones just in front of Pavan. He could have sworn he saw the brief flash of a huge serpent trying to reach him, wreathed in forks of lightning.

"I think she would beg to differ," Pavan coughed.

Nyalin knew it was true, and that if he'd lost what she had, he'd be running from this fight. But when he glanced around him and found Unira, the look in her eyes chilled him to the core. Whatever she was doing, he didn't think she was going to run.

The pavers were also spattered with blood, so he hurried to inspect Pavan as the emperor continued to try to deflect a new battery of crackling attacks. There—his side was wounded.

"I'll heal you—" he started.

"No—save your energy to survive this fight," his father commanded him. "Run."

"No," he snapped. He turned toward his enemy. "Unira! This has gone on long enough. I never did anything to you. Let us go!"

"Oh, I agree. It's long past time I ended you."

"You won't succeed—I've destroyed your link to the afterworld. Those souls are no longer yours."

A moment of realization washed across her face. "You—*that* was what you were doing when you disappeared—you filthy, conniving—"

"You're defeated. Give up." Nyalin struggled to stand. "Don't make me kill you."

"Kill me if you like. But you will still lose."

Nyalin frowned. "What are you talking about?"

"While you're here, worried about me, my allies are unleashing hell on your little city. So talk all you want. Kill me all you want. There will be nothing but chaos and ash when you return!"

His eyes met Pavan's. Was the city truly in danger while they were here fighting? Something in his gut told him there was truth in what she'd said.

Unira seized just that moment to release another bombardment, and this time, she got through.

Three of the crackling, slithering attacks hit Pavan—none of them aimed at Nyalin this time at all—and he screamed, clutching at his chest. The blood flowed faster out across the stones.

It was too much—too much damage, Nyalin knew.

He rounded on Unira, raising his mother's sword. He'd channeled his own magic. He'd channeled Lara's and Yeska's magic. He'd channeled the other spirits in the afterworld.

But if he was truly connected to them, he could do it here as well.

*Spirits,* he murmured in his mind, *Hear me. Aid me.*

Unira raised her arm, fist hot with power. Nyalin closed his eyes. The energy bloomed out of him, like the sun rising over the horizon, bathing everything around him in burning white hot power.

The intensity of it was so strong, he too screamed—but he shoved the power flowing through him as the conduit toward Unira.

Toward the woman who had likely killed his father.

Everything went white—he couldn't see the pavers, Pavan, the pre-dawn sky, the buildings—any of it. The whole world had been swallowed by pure energy, exploding out from him.

And then just as abruptly, it faded.

He staggered back, blinking. The sky was empty. There was no Unira floating, no black wisps of ghosts. The black fog in the streets was all but gone. At the edge of the horizon, the sun was indeed beginning to rise, orange kissing the peaks of the hills.

On the stones, his father lay, unmoving.

He rushed to his side. Curiously, the pain inside him was gone. Had his blast of magic healed him as much as it had thrown Unira from the sky? Where had she gone? The thought nagged at him, a warning, but he had to check the emperor first.

"Pavan!" He hurried around the other side, trying to see his face.

"You did it, Nyalin." His smile was weak. "You defeated her... Something none of us could do."

"I... Are you going to be all right?"

Pavan minutely shook his head.

"I'll heal you." He immediately started searching for the wound.

"I'm not like you, my son," he said gently. "Sometimes, when we humans are too close to death, there is no wrenching us back."

"Father..." he whispered. "My mother—she's alive. Unira had her imprisoned here. I found her."

His eyes lit up, widened. "What wonderful news, that I shall not leave you alone."

"No, come on—you can't die. Don't do this." Nyalin closed his eyes and began funneling energy blindly at whatever wounds he could find.

"Tell her... Tell her I love her," Pavan was saying. "And that I'll see her on the other side. Perhaps there we can finally be together."

None of the magic seemed to be doing anything. Was it a curse? "I'll tell her," he said, still searching for whatever wound or magic was killing him. "But Emperor—Pavan—wait—"

"Don't give up, Nyalin. Defend my city from whatever she's done, will you?"

There—the hot, evil snake curling around Pavan's heart, his stomach, his leg. Three of them—how would he break the curses fast enough? Or at all—Lara had far more practice at that.

"I believe in you, Nyalin. The city will be safe in your hands. And those of your friends."

Nyalin tore at the evil spectral creatures, tried to rip them out with his mind. It was all ineffective. None of them budged, only tightened as he watched, squeezing the life force out of his father.

Hot tears flooded his eyes, interfered. "Father—don't. Don't go. Did you leave a succession plan, something I should do, who should follow you—"

"The empire is not on your shoulders alone, Nyalin, nor was it on mine." He coughed. "The empire is everyone, all of us."

"But what does that mean? What should I do?"

"What you do is your choice. Your life is your life. Find a way to sustain the empire, if you choose. Or turn your back. Walk your own path. I will not judge from the afterworld."

The snake spells had tightened into tiny balls, almost no space left for souls or organs inside.

Nyalin grabbed Pavan's hand, squeezed. "But you united everyone—how will we possibly fill your shoes—"

"You'll find a way. You might even—find a better way." For the first time, he winced, as if the pain was finally becoming unbearable.

"I wish we'd had more time together," Nyalin bit out.

"Me too. But I am glad to see the marvel you've become. Don't mourn me, son. You of all of us know, death is just the next step on the path."

His eyes closed.

And Nyalin screamed into the morning sunrise.

*Chapter 16*

# Ruins

With Cerivil's arm around her, Lara eased her way through the doors to the council meeting. As soon as they stepped inside together, the room filled with gasps.

Then it went silent.

Their walk to the dais, where the council sat at a long table, seemed to take forever, passing row after row of seated observers. Council and clan members alike stared at her, eyes wide. She swallowed, glancing over her shoulder. Nyalin stood guard at the door and watched as they made their way forward, his mother's sword at his side. It'd taken days to heal the worst wounds he'd gotten in the battle with Unira, and it would take many more before he was fully healed, but for now, from the look of him, none of them would guess the true extent of what he'd endured.

A few paces short of the council table, she stopped. All of the old men's and women's eyes were on Cerivil, their expressions filled with emotion and concern.

She cleared her throat. "I've found my father. I had to go all the way to the Obsidian hinterlands to do it. He'd been kidnapped. He is safe now, but he had been imprisoned and drugged for quite some time."

"Who did this?" one of the council members demanded. "You say this was the Obsidians?"

"No." Cerivil struggled to speak. "I was taken by Andius naLevin moShra."

A roar of voices rose up around them.

"As proof," Lara shouted over the tumult, "I have brought you his sword."

The council members looked at each other in alarm. The council member in the center stood. "Let me see that." Stepping forward, he took the sword and examined it, gray eyes glinting. "It is, indeed, Andius's sword. He would not have parted with it willingly."

Another council member raised her gnarled finger in the air. "Further, Clan Leader Cerivil would not lie to us about this. He cares only for the clan. He has long sought to remain neutral as we have tried to sort our... situation. I move, we must reject Andius's bid for leadership."

Echoes of agreement rose up around the room.

Lara swallowed. Would it be helpful to point out he might be dead? And yet... his body had not been there when they returned from searching for a wagon to bring Cerivil home again. Then she'd seen the strange, blinding white-out and heard Nyalin's scream, and she'd had far too much to worry about to try to track down Andius.

She *definitely* was not going to mention the emperor was dead. None of them knew that yet, and she hoped it would take them all a long time to figure it out.

"It's long past time we had a new clan leader," Cerivil said, surprising her. "Though it breaks with tradition, I would like to suggest we consider my daughter, Lara, as an excellent candidate. Although I do seek to remain neutral, she has shown initiative through seizing the Dagger of Bone. She has many plans to further the wealth and prosperity of the clan. And perhaps most importantly, the Bone Dragon approves of her."

"Regaining the support of the dragon more directly may matter more than we know," said another council member, this one with a scar over his eye. "I have been receiving reports of Mushin tossing poisoned animals over the barriers, lobbing strange exploding projectiles at the border villages. We will need all the power we can get, if they choose to test our long-lasting peace."

The first council member who'd spoken narrowed his gray eyes. "What say you, Lara?"

She took a deep breath. Then she drew the Dagger of Bone, laying it across her palm.

"There was a time when all I wanted was to wander the world," she said slowly. "I dreamed of getting away from the city. Of expanding our trade and our horizons.

"But when I lost my brother, and then my Da too—I saw more of the world, a piece of it at least. I saw how much we could grow and how much we lack. I saw new enemies that claw at our tenuous peace and what little we have. I want us to have more. More resources, more coin, more time for each other, more safety for our families through greater strength." She paused. "I can't bring Myandrin back. But I fought hard and brought my father back, by Dala's great light.

"I began this journey to escape. I stole the clanblade, seeking freedom. But now I would choose service to my clan—if you would have me."

"She will make a good leader," Cerivil put in. "If you would have her, of course, honorable Council."

"This is highly irregular," said the gray-eyed council member. "The Contests should decide. But as things stand..."

The scarred man cleared his throat. "If we let the Contests rule all, Cerivil would still be in some Obsidian's cell! Perhaps it is time for another system."

The center councilor was silent for a moment, letting the weight of that sink in. "I concur. Let us all acknowledge she who wields the Dagger of Bone, beloved of the Bone Dragon, as Lara, Clan Leader of the Bone Clan. If you agree with me, stand and let us know your truth."

One by one, all of those present stood. Not just the council members, but every single clan member in the hall.

Lara bowed her head. "You honor me. I hope I can live to deserve it."

"You already do, my little fig pie," Cerivil murmured in her ear. "You already do."

Later, when Cerivil had been resettled in the clan leader's official rooms—there was time to rearrange such things later, much later, after he recovered—she found her way to Nyalin's room in the Bone Clan mansion, the one she'd taken him to when he'd first joined the clan.

When he opened the door, it seemed like a room from another lifetime. The room was entirely the same, untouched, even the tall stacks of books about to topple. He struggled to give her a smile, as he followed her eyes to the books. "Care for a poetry reading?"

She laughed lightly, remembering the days not so long ago when he read her poetry in this room. When he'd first stolen her heart. "May I come in?" she asked quietly.

"Of course."

He shut the door, and they settled together in silence, sitting side by side on the bed. The wounds he'd sustained in the fight with Unira had been horrifying, but they were mostly healed, although she could see a stubborn scar or two that refused to be totally erased.

"I'm sorry about... your father," she said gently.

He let out a long sigh. "I am too. I barely knew him, and now, he's gone."

"Everyone will figure it out soon." She didn't want to push him on this, but... as a clan leader, she needed to. And as his friend and a woman who loved him, she needed to know a few things. "Did he tell you if he left any succession plan?"

He shook his head. "He said he didn't."

"Did he want you to..." She didn't know how to phrase it.

He let out a snort of bitter laughter. "He, uh, wanted to leave it up to me. Of all the things he decided for me—he didn't decide that one. I guess since it was his job, he knew how hard it could be, knew it was a lot to ask. But I'm still a little surprised he didn't decide my future for me like he did everything else."

Some tension eased in her shoulders.

"He said the empire doesn't belong to him or me or anyone. It belongs to all of us, and if we want to keep it—and our hard-won peace—we'll have to find our own way."

"That sounds... difficult. Unlikely, even. We may be in for a rough ride."

"Unira seemed to suggest she had allies that would soon terrorize the city. I don't know if it was a bluff, but my gut said she wasn't lying."

"Even without external enemies, the empire could be but a memory, without Pavan holding it together. It wouldn't take much for all the clans to return to war and reduce these districts to nothing but ruins. Life back in the desert, like I always wanted." She sighed, then rested her head on his shoulder. "I hope it doesn't come to that. But without a central, charismatic leader... Have you thought about it at all?"

"About what?"

"About claiming your birthright? Announcing your heritage?"

"Oh. Oh, no. Not at all. I mean, he's dead."

"But Linali isn't. She could tell everyone the truth." Linali had stayed at her home in the Obsidian wilds, so for now, no one knew the truth. About any of it.

He was silent for a long moment. "Is that what you'd have me do?"

She straightened abruptly. "What? No! I just thought, after everything, your thoughts on the matter might have changed—"

"I don't want to be emperor, Lara," he said, running a hand over her hair.

"But we may *need* an emperor."

"Maybe Grel can do it," he offered.

"Not without a sword."

He flinched.

"Sorry."

"No, you're right," he said. "Maybe now, one of the sword smiths will make him a sword."

"But do we even want that? After what you've discovered? After what that spirit wolf told you?"

"Maybe I could make him one... Batu mentioned something about a forge."

Lara bit her lip. "That may take time that we don't have. Someone else may need to step in before then."

"Not me. I'm a simple scribe at heart."

She hesitated, then gently put her hand on his thigh. "Perhaps you could tolerate being a clan leader's official consort? Or husband even."

A slow smile spread across his face. "I take excellent notes."

She stifled a chuckle. "Perhaps I could employ you as a poet."

"Lara, please. I just copy the stuff. Appreciate it. Decorate it. Admire it. But I don't *write* it. Simple scribe, remember?"

"You are *anything* but simple, Nyalin naPavan moLinali."

His lips twisted at her addition to his name, but he didn't correct it. He leaned forward and brushed his lips gently across hers, lifting a hand to caress her cheek. "I don't know what is to come, Lara. But I'll happily face it at your side."

Stress melting away, she leaned into his kiss.

Daridian swallowed as he waved to his sister. Sha'lien waved from the deck of a ship bound for Annikyre. Her smile was small, wistful. She'd had dreams of a different life, he realized, and maybe she'd been just as desperate as he'd been. Desperate enough to walk into a no-win, foolish situation.

He hoped his father wouldn't treat her too poorly on her return, but he wasn't truly worried. It had always been *he* who'd been the brunt of his father's bad jokes and rage. Sha'lien could handle it, and she'd find something else, some other way to get away.

What would his father say when he didn't return with her?

He looked over at Sutamae standing by his side, the winds coming off the sea blowing through her hair, a soft, contented smile on her face. Sadly, something told him the expression wasn't very familiar to her. She too waved at Sha'lien.

Then his sister stepped away from the railing and retired belowdecks. He and Sutamae turned and strolled through the Pearl and Glass Districts, as if they didn't have black robes or a single care in the world.

"What did the Bladed Women say when you showed them the sword?" he asked.

"Varene raised an eyebrow and said she hadn't seen anyone go quite so far to avoid having to deal with Elix." She snickered.

"When are you going to tell your father that a Pearl dragon has taken you as a pet?"

"I thought just after I told him I've fallen for a spy from Annikyre. If I tell him both at once, he'll likely believe neither. But maybe I'll finally fulfill my quest to be honest with him."

He smiled. "I'm not a spy, you know. It was just a dangerous situation." Although his father was certainly *not* going to be pleased with his decision to let Sutamae keep the Pearl Clan sword. But his father didn't understand dragons, or clanblades, or any of the magic. And nothing he'd done in his life had pleased his father much, anyway, so did it matter?

It did, of course, matter. There would be repercussions. But for now, he didn't care. The sword hung unabashedly at Sutamae's hip, and he knew that was exactly where it belonged.

"Are you sure you're not a spy? With the percentage of time you spend wearing masks?"

"I'm not a spy, Sutamae. I'm a prince. All great warriors in Annikyre master the mask magic."

She faltered, sobering slightly. "A prince?"

He nodded.

"For a prince, you hang out in back alleys with questionable people a lot."

"Do I really?"

She leaned forward conspiratorially and whispered, "You're doing it right now."

"The only thing I find questionable about you, Su, is whether or not and how we can be together."

She shrugged one shoulder. "We're together right now."

"I meant for more than just a stroll."

"I'm not meant to be some foreign queen, Daridian, and I—"

He raised his palm to stop her. "I'm not going back. Possibly ever. Plus, I'm the youngest of many siblings."

"Oh. Well. I see. So you think you can just give me a sword with a pretty jewel in it, wear a mysterious mask, and win me over forever?"

"Maybe?" He smiled.

"You might just be right." Squeezing her hand in his, they crossed the line into the Obsidian District. "Come. Let's go say hello to my father. Then we can see what you think."

"How bad can he be?" He had heard stories, but now, he worried if any—or even half—of them were true.

She just laughed.

As they arrived at the large mansion he presumed was her home, a sharp screech split the air. They both turned in its direction.

"What was that?" she whispered.

"I think if we stay out here, we're going to find out. Let's get inside. And keep your blade close."

"Okay. This way."

—

The charred, twisted remains of the creature that had once been Unira no longer knew how to fly. But it did know how to crawl. It did remember a little, when it could put two thoughts together. Which at first, wasn't very often.

It remembered a few spells. It remembered it had once been powerful. It remembered breaking a sword in two and murdering an emperor in cold blood.

It knew it had greatness within it. It had known true power.

It was so weak now. But... it was not giving up.

Crawling could lead to climbing. Wagons could move, especially when it hitched them up to spirits and commanded them to drive.

The charred husk had somewhere to be. A date in the city.

In the time it took the wagon to make it to her home in the Salt City, the charred husk had remembered a little more. It had healed a little more. *It* was a *she*, and she'd had a name and a home, and she knew things.

She healed her face first. The other parts of her could be better hidden by clothing and wrapped, but for her first and primary purpose, and to claim even a shadow of her former greatness, she would need her face.

Spirits were conscripted to gather her the appropriate garments, and when her wagon rolled to a stop outside the back entry to her mansion in the city, no one who had known her before she was a charred, twisted husk would know any better what she hid beneath the cloth.

Her walk, though. That didn't help. She should have worked more on her legs, but the face had taken all the energy she had. She hobbled into the storage warehouse she had ordered cleared, its emergency grains completely liquidated to make room for Zama's little project.

It was time for the charred husk to see what her demon had wrought.

"Unira!" he called as she entered. "It's incredible! It's almost complete! We have only to finish the final components of the spell!"

Three stories tall, the wooden construction glowed purple, red, and silver, its center swirling with light.

She realized abruptly that she had barely made it in time, that even with just another few hours' delay, the project would have been complete, activated, and beyond her control.

"I told you not to activate the portal without me," she said through gritted teeth. A strange hissing accompanied her voice that she didn't think had been there before, but she had no patience or care to hide it just now.

"I didn't. I didn't. Of course, I didn't!" He held up his hands. "We still have to speak the spell three times. I waited."

He was lying. She was sure of it. Just like he had lied about Nyalin moLinali. Just like they had all lied to her.

Just like them, he was going to pay.

"Proceed, then," she ordered.

He spoke the spell, a strange demonic tongue, but one she had mastered before she summoned him—the best defense. She committed it to memory as well as a charred twisted husk could.

As Zama spoke the words a second time, she took a bottle from her garments and removed the cork.

"Zama?"

He faltered but didn't turn. "Yes, darling? We need to finish opening the portal, can it wait?"

She splashed the liquor from the bottle she'd found in the wagon over his back, then lit the liquid with a simple fire spell. She'd seen how the water demon liked the lick of the flames. "Zama, I banish you back from whence you came!"

"What? No—you can't—" He was patting desperately at the tiny flames, dousing them with spritzes of water, trying to smother it to no avail.

"Nyalin moLinali is alive," she snapped.

"What? No—we can try again—"

"He destroyed half my estate. Freed my slaves. Stole Linali from the catacombs. While you were *here,* starting this portal without me."

"I wouldn't—you can't do this—my portal!"

"I can. And I just did."

She threw a much larger swirling sphere of flame, now—at him, at the portal, at all of it.

Zama screamed, but more in anger and rage than in pain, as her banishment took hold. She wasn't truly *burning* him as much as sending him back across the planes. Not that she imagined that'd be a pleasant journey.

But he'd failed her. Just like Idak, just like the rest of them.

Now, she would take things—and these creatures—into her own hands. As the flames licked up the sides of the portal's frame, she laughed, gold and red dancing before her and reflecting in her eyes.

She pushed his smoldering form aside. He fell to the ground, silent. Perhaps the demon that had been her Zama was already gone. Standing where he'd stood, she raised her arms and did her best to repeat the words he'd said for a third time.

To activate the portal, but this time, under her control.

She said the words and waited.

She'd tried to choose a simple solution, to follow some sort of rules, to employ order, dominion. But that plan had always been doomed, hadn't it? Her last pathetic vestige of thinking they would ever accept her, accept anyone *like* her or *connected* to her, her pitiful wish that she could work within the system to change things.

But no. That plan had always been doomed. Maybe the idea of it wasn't even possible. The system had been flawed from the start.

And now she would burn it down and tear it apart—from its heart on out.

A monster lurched from the portal. Goo dripped from two sets of wings as it turned a horned head toward her, bearing two rows of teeth the size of her thumb, even though its standing height was only a little taller than her.

She raised her fire again, ready to defend herself. But she spoke the command words, the ones Zama had practiced when he'd thought she wasn't listening.

It looked to her with calm eyes. Waiting for her commands. Behind it, another similar being stepped through.

"Find the emperor's palace," she ordered. "Find the tree of the empire. Tear it to the ground! And anyone who would stand in your way!"

She snuffed out the flames creeping up the wooden frame. It would remain, a charred husk like her, feeding destruction into the heart of the city. Other flames reached the outside of the warehouse, and she let it begin to burn. It'd make it easier for the monsters to do their work.

They came faster and faster, and she gave her orders one by one, then a dozen by a dozen.

She would make this city just like her—charred, twisted, ruined.

Dead.

# Afterword

Thanks for reading *Blade of the Moon!* I hope you had a blast. I'm excited to dive into the chaos Unira will unleash on the city... Stay tuned.

Get updates on the next book by signing up for my newsletter at **www.rkthorne.com/getupdates**. You'll get news and goodies like free stories, extra scenes, maps, and character interviews.

# Share what you thought

On Instagram, share a pic of your book and tag **#rkthorne** and **#clanblades**!

I'm posting pictures of books, notebooks, games, and random flowers at **www.instagram.com/rk_thorne**.

# Also by R. K. Thorne

**The Enslaved Chronicles**

*Mage Slave*

*Mage Strike*

*Star Mage*

*"Takar at Night"*

**Legends of the Clanblades**

*Dagger of Bone*

*Blade of the Moon*

*Untitled Book #3 (Forthcoming)*

**The Audacity Saga**

*The Empress Capsule*

*Capital Games*

*Child of Wrath*

*Songbird Rising*

*Oath of Duty*

*Deserter (Free Prequel)*

Check **www.rkthorne.com/books**
for the most up-to-date listing.

# About the Author

R. K. Thorne writes romantic epic fantasy and space opera that bubble over with action, humor, and hope. A long-time gamer and dungeon master, she's fueled by her addiction to notebooks and yoga. Too much coffee, RPGs, and really good books all keep her awake.

*For more information:*

Web | rkthorne.com
Facebook | facebook.com/ThorneBooks
Instagram | instagram.com/rk_thorne
Pinterest | pinterest.com/rk_thorne

www.ingramcontent.com/pod-product-compliance
Lightning Source LLC
Chambersburg PA
CBHW030429310726
48979CB00009B/1687/J

* 9 7 8 1 9 5 0 9 9 3 1 0 9 *